Beneath the Devil Tree

Beneath the Devil Tree

A NOVEL RECOUNTING THE EVENTS OF MALABAR 1921

Anjana Varma

Vitasta

CALICUT
CHALIYAR
Kondotti
Manjeri
Pookkottu
Mambram
Tirurangadi
PONNANI

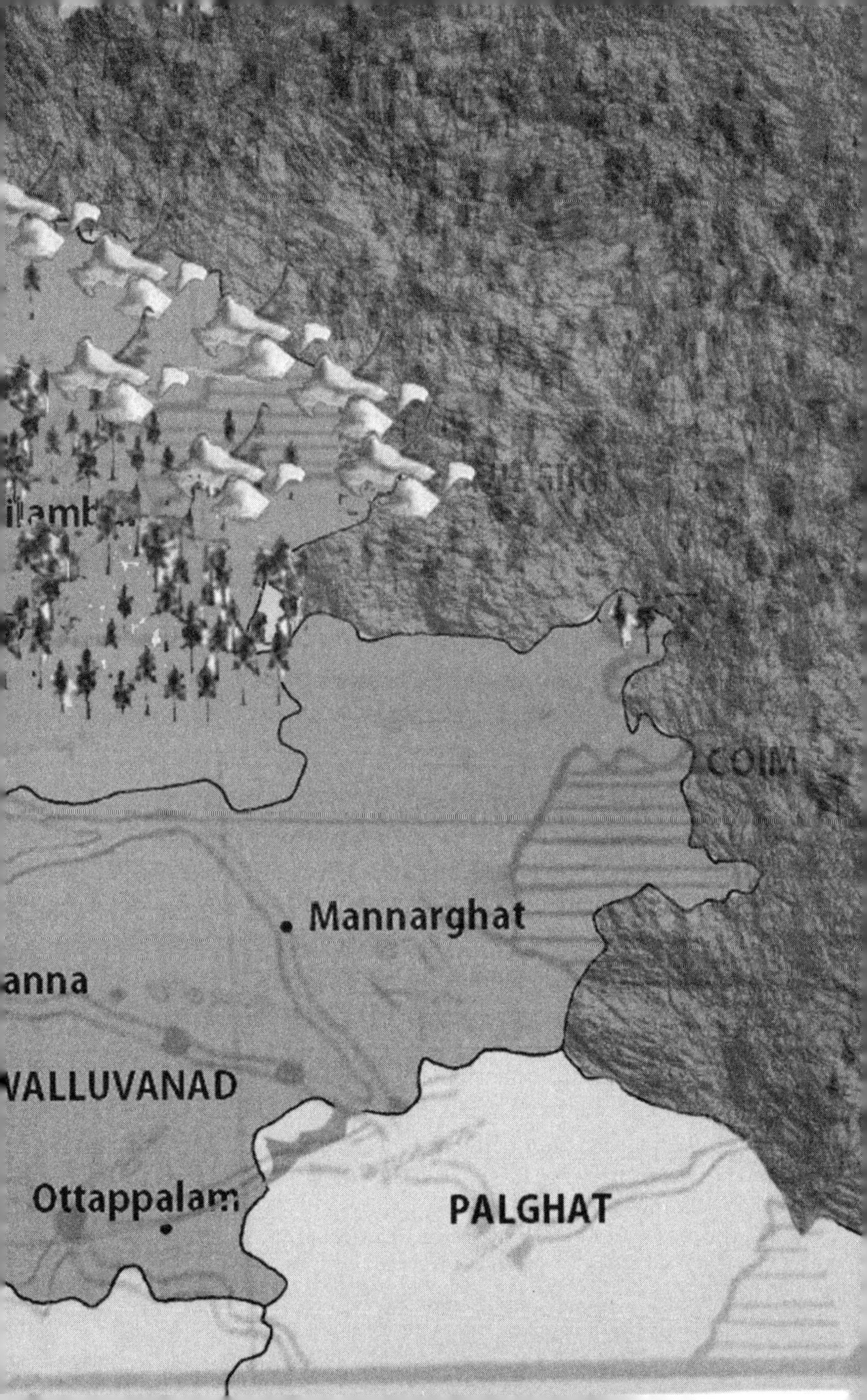

Mannarghat
anna
VALLUVANAD
Ottappalam
PALGHAT

Published by
Renu Kaul Verma
Vitasta Publishing Pvt Ltd
4348/4C, Ansari Road, Daryaganj
New Delhi - 110 002
info@vitastapublishing.com

ISBN: 978-81-19670-84-0

First Edition 2024
MRP ₹ 495

Edited by Soumitro Das
Typeset & Cover Design by Somesh Kumar Mishra
Printed by Vikas Computer and Printers, New Delhi

Contents

Madras

Dear Reader,

I have written quite a few books but never before fiction. This one just happened.

All the research was done. I had notebooks full of facts. I had travelled around Malabar for months, seen the damages, conducted scores of interviews and recorded my observations. My intention then had been to bring out a series of articles but I could never do better than Madhavan Nair's pieces in the Mathrubhumi. So my notes were shelved and remained so for decades to come.

Early this year, I had a recently published book sent to me by the author himself, a former student. The book had an impressive title and the subject was one after my own heart.

The writer had been a good student and was now a reputed historian and professor of history. His book would be studied by many *a keen scholar. I shuddered to think of what they would learn. It was then that I realised that the way people viewed the Outrage of '21, was far cry from the real thing.*

I spent a frustrating month going over the faded scribblings. I wanted the world to know the truth, but the paradigm shift had been deliberate, slow and clever. During the interim years much had been written on what happened in Malabar in 1921. If I organised my matter and wrote a few articles or even a book, it would be brushed aside as a narrow and biased work.

If you really want the truth to come to light, there is no better medium than fiction. That way, your readers can live in the world you create, make friends with the people, and delve deep into their minds. They can explore and uncover. Their understanding will be wider and richer. Use your imagination to restore order. Without having historical data jammed into their heads, they will know what happened in 1921.

Thus Beneath the Devil Tree came into being.

—The Outcaste

Prologue

In jail, we tend to reach within ourselves. I have done this often enough in the Dark Continent and I find myself doing this now when here in Yerwadah, I can do little else.

It is no wonder that the first stop in my inward sojourn is Chauri Chaura. Three civilians and twenty-two policemen have died. I have halted the Non-Cooperation. Nehru doesn't like it. Bhagat Singh protests vehemently. Yet, I have called it all off. I am now serving penance, by fasting. Fasting is my nature. It is how I atone for my crimes and those of others. Crimes for which I am directly and indirectly responsible.

My heart thumps painfully against my ribs. Am I unwell? No, it cannot be the lack of nourishment. My body, frail though it may be, is accustomed to the rigours of abstinence.

Am I ready for this?

The world hails me as a Great Soul. Everyone thinks the country's future is in my hands. My methods of truth and non-violence are feared by the British, lauded by the rest of the world. I myself am staunch. I will uphold these values till my last breath…

The wheel of my Charkha spins faster than I intend and among the whirling spokes I see the young man who visited me in jail the other day. There was nothing about him that gave me a clue about his identity. Not his attire for it was simple, neat but ordinary. Nor his accent which was absolutely neutral. The keen eyes and broad forehead stood out but told me nothing. Was it a shallow dimple on his lean left cheek that had flashed when he had looked at me straight in the eye and spoken with a reverent bow?

'Pray do not sweep Malabar under the carpet. The country cannot withstand another Himalayan miscalculation.'

Himalayan Miscalculation. My own phrase. It felt like an arrow that had found its mark.

The visitor had little else to say. He dropped the letter into my hands and left with a smart about turn. He did not look back.

I read the letter which was in reality a copy. It was written by the women of Malabar and addressed to Lady Reading. But in my eyes it was for me. Each word was an accusation hurled at me like a brickbat.

I had no idea who my visitor was. I was too muddled to care. Malabar. What is Chauri Chaura in comparison? I have been like the cat that sneaks into the kitchen and laps up the milk quickly with its eyes tightly shut, believing that no one else could see either and hence it was safe.

I have erred. And powerless to make amends. Chitragupta, in his fat book of accounts, has already entered in bold letters against my name: **Malabar 1921**.

A Grim Portent

Nilambur, Ernad
8 January

Mathu
Dhanu was drawing to a frosty close. In a week the month of Makaram would set in and the cold would begin gnawing into one's bones. Why, even the sturdy teak trees in the surrounding forests would soon be attacked by spasms of muscular cramps.

The Palachod was clothed in black silk. That was what they called the area under the Pala tree in front of the temple. The Pala was older than the temple. At the Palachod today, innumerable torches lit up the festival venue. This penultimate night of the Pattu fest and the darkness seemed bedecked in the brightest of jewels. The air smelt pleasantly of burning wicks, scented clothes and fresh elephant dung. Beats from the rolling drumsticks of Trithala Poduval and his band of Chenda artists were in a frenzy. The Lord's festival idol sat atop the broad back of the tallest tusker in the Kovilakam stables. He and all the others lined up symmetrically on either side, caparisoned in solid gold headdresses.

Mesmerised by the show, the crowd barely remembered to feel the cold. The women and children of the Kovilakam stood by the temple walls, clad in their best mundus with fine auric borders. Gold and precious gems glittered on their persons.

Vettekkara!

Prayerful whispers fluttered on the lips of the onlookers as the Hunter God approached.

Skirting the circumference of the festival grounds, in the shade of the Pala were the Paniyan tribes from the forests of Chungathara, Vazhikadav and Nadukani. Vettekkaran was believed to be the son born to Shiva and Parvathi when they masqueraded as hunters to test the devotion of Arjuna the Pandava Prince. As the Lord's dearest kin, the forest folk were honoured guests at the Nilambur Pattu festival. Every year they arrived at Nilambur in the last days of Dhanu and camped on the outer edges of the Palachod. The Kovilakam served them delectable meals from which they saved bits of rice to be taken back to their sylvan homes and eaten throughout the year to ward off illness…

Surrounded by the spiritually charged atmosphere of the Pattu, Mathu began to experience an inner peace much like what her great uncle had revelled in, as he rode through the forest years ago.

He made it a point never to miss this ride if he was in Nilambur. After lunch, instead of lying down for a siesta, he would have his favourite horse saddled and quickly gallop in the north easterly direction. It was always the same route he took and he could see that the grass had worn off in the parts where the horse had trodden each day for decades, to form a sort of pathway.

His destination was a house on the edge of the forest in Nambolakotta. He could see the tiled roof along the bend. The horse was so familiar with the routine that it knew exactly what was expected. The animal neighed softly and lifted a leg for him to step on as he descended. In his youth, he used to get off his mount in one single action, a leg swinging arc-like in a graceful, fluid motion. But he had celebrated his *shashtipoorthi* a couple of years ago. Princes of the Samoothiri, Kolathiri and the Valluvarkonathiri clans, Namboothiris and Nair chieftains from all over Malabar had been invited to the feast and the Kathakali performances that followed…

He made his way towards the house. The Hunter was already seated in the shady stone mandapam outside.

'Late again, Thampan?'

Not raising his eyes from the board he was setting up on the bamboo mat laid out in front of him, the Hunter chuckled as he carefully positioned the chessmen carved in golden teak and dark rosewood.

'I was beginning to think I would have to play with myself.'

Rather laboriously, great uncle flopped on to the

raised platform. The trip had taken its toll on him.

'Riding doesn't come as easily as it used to. I am no more a young man', he smiled at the Hunter, 'unlike you who are ageless'.

In his youth, no one outside the Kovilakam even knew great uncle's given name. To everyone else he was Bhakthan, the devout. For even as a child he had had a spiritual inclination. His brother Inni was Shakthan, the powerful, as he was the stronger decision maker, the better administrator.

Great uncle Bhakthan was no more than twenty years old when he had once lost his way in the woods and chanced upon this house. It was a wealthy kinsman of the Balusseri chieftain who managed his forest land, who resided there. He was known as the Vazhunnor. The simplicity of the Vazhunnor and his family, their humble home and kind manner belied their status and the fact that they owned acres and acres of lucrative forest land. The Vazhunnor at the time had been no older than Bhakthan himself and lived in the forest house with his mother and a mentally challenged sister. The Vazhunnor's mother had welcomed the lost youth into her home, served him ripe jackfruit and fresh forest honey and invited him to rest for a while before returning home to Nilambur. Bhakthan had stretched out on a bamboo mat in this very mandapam where he was joined by the Vazhunnor and a tribal lad. The three young men had hit it off and thus began a special friendship.

Vazhunnor had been dead for a few years. It was just

Bhakthan and the Hunter now. The surprising thing was that while Bhakthan's hair had turned white, his belly rotund and his joints rheumatic, The Hunter looked no different. He was still tall, his form slender and sinewy, his hair and beard as thick, dark and luxuriant as it was that long ago.

Soon the game was underway. The Hunter was enjoying himself. 'Aha! There you go Thampan', with an animated move, he flicked his opponent's knight away with his own. Vazhunnoramma chose that moment to come in with refreshments and Bhakthan welcomed the distraction. They paused the game to talk to her between sips of sweet honey. The old lady's daughter, poor retarded Unni watched them with her dull eyes from the house.

When Vazhunnoramma went back inside, great uncle addressed the Hunter on a serious note. 'I am beginning to feel my age, my friend. I am afraid my trips here will have to stop. And I can't bear to think of sitting tight in Nilambur without coming here to Nambolakotta. Without our games of chess. You do know I suppose that your place in my heart is far above that of my siblings, my nieces and nephews who will take family traditions forward, of my Ammu and the children, the lovely Sinnamalu, Sinnan, named after my dear brother and my precious little Sinnu, even that of my old mother. If I can't see you when I feel the urge, I don't see the point of living on this Earth.'

'Now, now, Thampan, pull yourself together,' said the Hunter, 'I have never seen you this way before'.

'I have never felt this way before,' Bhakthan's voice cracked and tears threatened to drip. 'Tell me my friend, will you come to Nilambur with me? Will you care for me in my old age and when I am gone will you protect my future generations? Will you shower on them the same love you have bestowed on me? Will you promise that hundreds of years from now, you will still be in Nilambur as the family's guardian and ward off all enemies, both external and internal? Will you promise, my friend?'

The Hunter remained silent for a moment but to great uncle Bhakthan, it seemed like a lifetime.

'The residents of this forest need me. I am afraid I cannot abandon them, Thampan.'

'They will not suffer. I will ensure that they are taken care of. You only have to tell me what needs to be done. But I implore you to come to Nilambur'.

Then slowly and thoughtfully, stroking his beard, the Hunter nodded. 'Alright. I will. When have I been able to refuse you something, Thampan.'

Bhakthan's joy knew no bounds.

'But on three conditions.'

'Anything. Anything, my friend. What are they?'.

'Let us not be hasty, Thampan. The first is no one but you will be able to see this physical form of mine.'

Bhakthan thought it over and understanding the implication, nodded.

'You know that Vazhunnoramma and Unni have no one but me. If I come away with you, they will be left all alone in this jungle with no one to take care of them and their vast properties. They could come to harm here. My second condition is that you take them with you to Nilambur, give them a home and your protection. As I will not manifest myself in this form while I am there, I will not be visibly involved. So they will be your responsibility and that of your successors after you if either of them lives that long. Do you agree?'

'I do.'

'Thampan, you know that the forest is my home and the forest folk my family. If I am to come to Nilambur, you will have to promise me that once a year my people will be invited to your Kovilakam and treated as the most honoured guests. They will stay there for seven days. Seven days of celebration, feasting and fun. That is condition number three'.

The Hunter looked at great uncle with a quizzical arch in his brows.

'I agree. I agree.'

'Remember Thampan, a promise is a promise. If you or someone in your family happens to dishonour any of these conditions, I shall withdraw. You may not even realise it, but my spirit shall no longer be around to safeguard you.'

'No. Never shall I go back on my word.'

'And your family? Your generations to come? Ten years from now? Fifty? Hundred? More?'

Bhakthan had decided. He would agree to anything. There was nothing he wanted more passionately than to bring his friend home to Nilambur.

'Very well. You may come tomorrow with a palanquin for Vazhunnoramma and Unni. I shall be in Nilambur to receive you.'

Thus, the old lady and her poor daughter were brought here and put up in a specially set up apartment in the mansion called Puthiya Kovilakam where many of the family's female members still lived and Vettekkaran, the Hunter took up permanent residence in the Kovilakam premises. Every year during the Pattu festival in the end of Dhanu, the forest folk arrived.

Mathu came out of her reverie as the procession advanced with Karayil Panikkar, the Oracle in the lead. A step behind him strode rows of Tirumulpads flourishing their gleaming swords. This year, the Kovilakam men bearing the sword in the sacred parade were a relatively young group. The oldest among them, whose mother had been Mathu's sister was barely sixty-five.

Drawing her magnificent upper cloth closer around her shoulders to protect her bare breasts from the biting cold, the Kovilakam matriarch surveyed the procession with a smile. Her eyes lovingly caressed one elephant after the other. She had grown up with these animals and knew them as well as she did her siblings. Sriraman, Lakshmanan, Bharathan and Shatrughnan, Bheeman, Arjunan, Nakulan and Sahadevan ... named after famous brothers in the Puranas. A fond chuckle rose in her throat. Her gaze closed in on the idol bearing Sriraman and his brother Lakshmanan on his immediate right. What dear little calves they had been.

One monsoon…when the Chaliyar had been in full spate…. It was a morning like any other at the Nilambur Kovilakam. Children doing their lessons in the *Ezhuthupalli*, women going about their regular Bhagawatham readings, the men finishing their worship at the Vettekkaran temple and conducting various businesses from their residences or the Kovilakam office. But today they were all eager to be at the Palachod.

There was plenty of chatter in the *oottupura* as usual when the young women were at breakfast. White men were the topic of discussion that day, the Matriarch remembered as if sixty-six years were but a day.

'I have heard they have hair of gold,' Mathu's elder sister exclaimed.

'Hair of gold? What foolishness, Uma Devi!'

'It is true,' Uma Devi insisted in her usual snooty tone. 'Gold such as this,' she held up the border of her mundu, 'Unnimmama's grandson, Appunni Menon told me. He sees many of them in Kozhikode. Arguments ensued as to whether Appunni Menon could be believed.

'I think the Thampatties better talk less and eat more', gently chided the Kovilamma in charge of the young ladies' meals. She heaped hot rice on their banana leaves and laded dollops of ghee on top.

It was then that she herself had burst in with the news.

Mathu had been just seven and the only little girl in the Kovilakam with the exception of a couple of babies and so she had been served breakfast with the nine young

Thampans who she also went to the *Ezhuthupalli* with. That day, she had delayed going for lessons to hang around with her older sisters and cousins

'Moideen Mapla is on his way with a baby elephant from Akkara.'

Aanachevi Mathu, or Mathu of the Elephant ears as she was fondly known, had latched on to bits of conversation among the uncles. Moideen Mapla, who managed some of the Kovilakam properties on the opposite bank of the river had sent word that a baby elephant had been washed up in last evening's torrential downpour. This was a common enough occurrence and many of the tuskers now gracing the Kovilakam stables were procured in this fashion. Forests were Kovilakam property and so was the wildlife. However the arrival of a new elephant, especially a calf never ceased to thrill them all.

As it happened, the heaving Chaliyar had washed up not one but three that time. Two bulls and a little cow. Three at a time! A rare phenomenon even in Nilambur. The Kovilakam men sauntered out to the Devil tree, their upper cloths flapping in the wind quite in contrast to their unflappable temperaments.

Completely ignoring the cow, each of them as he arrived, made a bee line for the little males. One Thampan stroked the head of a small animal where coarse hair grew in tufts. Another draped a trunk fondly on his forearm as he carefully weighed it. Someone squatted on the ground and meticulously counted their nails. The elderly quoted from the Matanga Leela. The women hovered in the periphery whispering to each other for they were no less knowledgeable in elephant lore but were raised not to barge into the forefront. Unable to contain herself, Mathu remembered jumping up and down in excitement, the necklace of palakka emeralds bouncing on her thin chest. Her cousins, the nine vanaras waited impatiently for the seniors to retreat so that could examine the animals to their hearts content.

The uncles were long gone. So were the *edathies*. Mathu's coevals, the nine vanaras had all passed on quite prematurely. It was just her and the elephants now.

By then the caparisoned elephants on the outer edges had withdrawn and their number had reduced to three. The procession was at the threshold of the temple. They made a grand entry into the holy premises, circumambulated the shrine to the accompaniment of Poduval's *melam*. The crescendo of the Panchari ensemble rose as it progressed from stage to stage in a pyramid formation. When the performance concluded, the parade dispersed and the elephants were lead away by their mahouts for a well-deserved rest, the *melam* still echoed in everyone's ears.

Now all eyes were on the Oracle.

Karayil Panikkar made his own circumambulation of the shrine in the company of a lone *chenda*, swaying and gyrating as he held his sword aloft. The sudden silence created when the *melam* ended was deafening in itself. The Earth reverberated with each of the Oracle's footsteps. He made his way up to the rostrum just outside the inner shrine where a gigantic drawing of Vettekkaran, the Hunter God, covered most of the floor. Green leaves, white rice, red vermillion and yellow turmeric, dried and powdered, had gone into the creation of this larger than life depiction.

The onlookers joined their palms together in prayer.

The Oracle circled the enormous picture, stepped right into it and began to erase it with his feet. By now the Lord's Divine spirit had taken complete possession of him. The Panikkars of Karayil were ordinary middle class men in their everyday lives but during such occasions, one of them would come down to the venue and turn into a special medium through whom the Lord spoke. Whether all this really happened each time was never questioned. For years someone from the family had come for the ceremony, performed his duties and gone away laden with gifts. Did great uncle Bhakthan's hunter friend, their very own Vettekkaran really manifest himself in this small, balding and non-descript person? It was the faith that mattered.

After the *kalam* was rubbed off, he would speak. He would present himself before the Senior Tirumulpad and say all the customary things. Everything has gone off perfectly, I am pleased…really pleased… all is well…the future is bright… these words were what they called the Oracle's *kalpana*, his portent.

Karayil Panikkar had worked up a state of frenzy by the time the *kalam* was expunged. He was sweating profusely even in the midnight chill of late Dhanu. He bowed deeply before the Valiya Tirumulpad and panted out his routine kalpana.

Everything has gone off well... I am pl... but...he muttered something unintelligible and broke down. Sobs rent his thin chest but his words became clearer as he lamented about a terrible state of things that awaited the Kovilakam and the land.

When he came out of his trance he remembered nothing so there was no point asking him to explain. Only Vettekkaran knew what he meant.

There were a lot of hushed whispers when everyone trooped home in the early hours of the morning after the rituals were finally complete. Knowing her Kovilakam relatives, Mathu knew that soon it would be dismissed with a shrug. Everyone would have brushed it aside in a few hours and would be back to cracking their favourite Gulikan jokes and enjoying the last day of the Pattu.

Mathu herself was no alarmist by nature. But in the innermost chamber of the Southern Naalukettu where she slept, stretching out on the bed that the maids had so meticulously made that evening, she kept replaying the *kalpana* in her mind. What the Oracle said had been grim indeed but there was something else that kept peeping into her memory and disappearing again. Try as she might she couldn't get hold of it. She closed her eyes. There wasn't much sleep to be had anyway. Soon it would be time to rise. It was always like this during Pattu. That was when it suddenly came to her and Mathu was not sure if she was asleep or awake. It was what the Oracle had muttered before collapsing. Inarticulate as he had been at the time, no one seemed to have heard that part of his maunder. Neither had she but somehow it must have penetrated her brain for she now remembered what he had said. Something about having to pay for an old woman's tears.

An old woman… Once upon a time there had been one here in this Kovilakam. An old woman who had done nothing but weep in that last year of her life. Her last breath had been a lament… 'Unni… Unni…'

In the years to come, the Kovilakam people would sweep her into the most remote corners of their minds and pretend Vazhunnoramma and her daughter had never existed.

Pookottur Abuzz

Pookottur, Ernad
12 January

Mammad

The people thronging into the usually sleepy hamlet of Pookottur that day had but a vague and nebulous idea about what to expect. Most of them were Maplas from nearby *amsams* like Athanikkal, Muthiraparamba, Pallipadi, Pullara, Aravankara, Myladi and Valluvambram. The word Khilafat had been tossed around for quite a few months now and they had an idea that this congregation would concern it.

Few Ernad Maplas could read or write. It was passion that led them and loyalty that grounded them. They trusted their leaders and went by what they propagated.

Mammad was in reality not such a leader, but those who had been impressed by the earnestness Soon

Mammad was a part of budding Khilafat activities in the region. He had been largely responsible for organising this event.

The surge of rebellion had begun rising in him a few months ago. Nothing seemed fair. It was time for a change but what kind of change? The Khilafat movement that had recently taken root in Malabar gave him an answer which his staunch and steadfast heart welcomed.

'My dear brothers of Ernad,' Kattilassery Mohammed Musaliar addressed the expectant crowd. 'For you to understand why we are gathered here today, I must tell you a story.' A buzz of anticipation swept through the crowd. Mammad listened hard though he had heard it all before.

Far far away there is a land called Turki ruled by the Islamic sovereign of the Ottoman Empire known as the Khalifa. The Khalifa is not just a king. He is a spiritual leader who upholds the Prophet's values all over the world. Brothers, you know how the recent war had rocked the world. In this war the Khalifa fought bravely on the side of Germany.

During the war, the Indian Muslims were in an awkward situation. You know that many of us are soldiers in the British army. In his heart each soldier was devoted to the Khilafat rule. But his job was to fight for the British against Germany and the Khalifa. The soldiers hesitated. But the British Sayippes persuaded them to fight on the promise that after Germany was defeated, the Khalifa would not be deprived. That our holy places in Turki would not be disturbed. But have you ever known the Sayippes to be men of word? The Viceroy was cheating us brothers. When the British and their allies won, what do you think they did? They wrested away the Khalifa's throne and he was reduced to a mere puppet who had to dance when they pulled the strings. The Allies tore Turki apart and divided the territory among themselves. Our holy places were razed to the ground.

We will not stand for this, fellowmen.

The Ernad Maplas knew not the Khalifa, had never before heard of Turki and the Allied forces was a term they could barely comprehend. But Islam was maligned.

Muslims all over India are rising. This realisation and the resulting upheaval is known as the Khilafat movement. Maulana Abul Kalam Azad was arrested and so was Maulana Ali Johar. So were Maulana Shaukat Ali and his brother who were here in Manjeri last year to campaign for this noble cause. The audience was further enraged. Islamic brethren arrested?

A susurrus of approval engulfed the crowd.

Bolo Taqbeer Allahu Akbar! The leaders on the dais cried.

Bolo Taqbeer Allahu Akbar! The crowd roared in unison.

Khilafati Raj Zindabad! The leaders initiated.

Khilafati Raj Zindabad! The listeners echoed.

Mammad observed the crowd keenly. The general response pleased him. Suspicious frown lines creased his forehead when he caught sight of a group of four. They squatted on the ground a few feet away from where he stood. They smirked and cackled and whispered to one another and cackled again. One of them, a beak nosed goon even made an obscene gesture and set the rest of them clucking again. He recognised the fellows. The Valluvambram Adhikari's uncouth aides. Mammad was aware that the man was anti-Khilafat. He would keep his eye on them.

As the next speaker took over, Mammad noticed the man who stood by himself, a little towards the outer edge of the mosque grounds, leaning casually against a tree. He seemed to be about Mammad's own age. Mammad could not understand what it was but he was sure it was not just the distance from the crowd that made him stand out. He was not a Mapla apparently but the Hindu presence in the crowd, though scanty was definitely there.

A Congress leader was now addressing the crowd. Someone called Shekharan Nair. The Indian National Congress under Mahatma Gandhi had extended full support to the Khilafatkar. A couple of months ago, Mammad had had no idea who Gandhi was but on his initiation into the Khilafat activities he had learnt a lot about the world. The leaders of the Congress and the Khilafat met in a place called Amritsar, the man was saying, and now a nationwide agitation had been launched. Congress and Khilafat loyalists all over the country are giving up government titles, resigning from government jobs. Students are boycotting classes. The movement was now so powerful in the country that the white men were forced to pay attention.

'The nation needs you, brothers!' It was a voice they all knew and loved. When Alijan Sahib stood up on the dais, heartbeats rose at the sight of a familiar figure in white shirt, red fur cap with a *rumal* wrapped around his neck. As he rose to his feet, the crowd was struck mute and in the resulting silence, those in the front rows could hear his squeaking slippers. 'We will fight together,' held forth Pookottur's own leader.

Alijan Sahib Zindabad!
Khilafati Raj Zindabad!
Bolo Taqbeer Allahu Akbar!

'A Khilafat Committee for the whole of Ernad will begin functioning in all the nearby amsams', announced Alijan Sahib. 'Office bearers will be elected. With your support, the committee shall work for our joint aims. Upholding Islamic honour. Waging war against the white men. Ending the oppression of callous jenmis'.

The Khilafat Movement was officially born in Ernad.

Pookottur, Ernad
14 January

Razia

Kunhaishumma was having a field day.

Her *patthiris* were as succulent as her gossip. So she was a welcome caller at all Mapla, Thiyya and even a few Nair households. She was Pookottur's biggest source of news as she carried her varieties of *patthiris* from *pora* to *pora* and shared juicy tidbits of information to go with the snacks.

Kunhaishumma had attended the yogam in the *pallithodi* two days ago. The whole of yesterday she had spent in teashops and the market place listening to people's responses to the massive event. Today, Razia saw her armed with her basket of snacks and bursting with information, hobbling around Pookottur, rattling on and on about the Khilafat meeting and its aftermaths.

'You couldn't drop a needle at the *pallithodi* that evening. It was so crowded,' Kunhaishumma's eyes widened expressively and her voice fell to a theatrical whisper.

'Alijan Sahib says we in Ernad are going to fight the Whites and the jenmis for what they are doing to the poor Maplas. Mighty guns came to mind as did the formidable image of the Sixth Tirumulpad of Nilambur who lived the palatial manor and went about with a permanent sneer on his lips.'

'Sure. Sure. Easily done,' someone commented sarcastically.

Razia who had hesitantly drawn closer shivered. The old lady suddenly pointed at her. 'Her Mapla is one of the main Khilafatkar in Pookottur.' Alarmed, Razia slid behind a rather stout woman to keep out of the limelight. 'They are saying he is second only to Alijan Sahib.'

Razia had been worried about Mammad for a while. His quarrels with the Tirumulpad. The fact that he was always out of the house these days. To top it all the Matriarch of the Nilambur Kovilakam had summoned him. Nothing to worry, he had assured her. She is kind and fair and loves me like a son. And now this Khilafat business and fighting the big shots.

Razia followed the *Patthiri* woman at a distance trying to learn more. The old woman reached the village square where Razia saw her husband sipping tea at the busy stall with his friend Basheer. She slipped into the shadows and made sure her *thattam* kept her face hidden. But she listened hard. She knew Mammad was not going to keep her updated on the happenings so this was her only chance.

The group of men lolling on the shop veranda noticed Kunhaishumma shuffle by with the basket on her hip.

'Here comes our Patthiri Umma.'

'We hear you are bursting to the seams today. Come sit and tell us your news.' Kunhaishumma was willing enough. She heaved the now nearly empty basket on to the verandah, sat down on her heels and settled down to her Khilafat accounts.

'Mammade, Basheere', she noticed the green eyed young man and his companion inside the tea stall. 'What a *pukil* it was at the *pallithodi* that day. Nothing so big has ever happened in Pookottur. Everyone wants to join in the Khilafat activities. The whole town is on its toes.' Neither Mammad nor Basheer said a word but Razia was an expert on her husband's body language. A hint of a suppressed smile, a chest that puffed out for a fraction indicated that he was listening to the Umma and was pleased.

'But you know what? I am sure the Adhikari of Valluvambram is against it.'

That caught everyone's attention. Mammad gave Basheer a look that said, 'didn't I tell you' and the other man responded with a barely noticeable nod of understanding.

'Oh-ho! One would expect that from him,' said one of the men on the veranda.

'What makes you say that, Umma?'

'That fellow who looks like a vulture was there. You know the one who hangs around with the Adhikari. With a few others they were whispering and smirking and wiggling their eyebrows. I saw the same men in the village today and I heard them talking. The Adhikari believes all this is rubbish and that it is foolish to try and defy the Sarkar. He is supposed to have asked, has Alijan Sahib lost his mind.'

'And that Mammad has always been a fool, I believe he also said.'

'And that Ahmed Adhikari has always been an arse scratcher,' said one of them quite boldly and Kunhaishumma tittered. 'He scratches the arses of anyone in authority. The sayippes, the police officers and specially the Tirumulpad.'

Mammad hitched up his lungi and tapped Basheer on the shoulder. He had apparently heard enough. Razia slipped away hastily.

The Sixth Tirumulpad

Pookottur, Ernad
15 January

Mithran

The shot struck Divakaran's cue ball and the red one at the same time. Mithran allowed himself a small smile and slipped his pipe between his lips. He opened the tin of Imperial tobacco on the side table and filled it.

'New one, Mithretta?'

'Huh?' Mithran carefully lit up and raised an eyebrow not quite understanding Divakaran's question.

'The pipe,' said his cousin. 'Never seen it in your collection before.'

Mithran nodded. 'Achile Savinelli. Italian design. Sourced from Corsican briar. A gift from Collector Thomas,' he explained between puffs.

Mithran enjoyed Divakaran's company. He was his second cousin. The grandson of Cheriya Ammamma, his little grandmother. Besides, he shared Mithran's passion for billiards and often dropped by to play.

Divakaran was good but a far cry from Mithran himself. He was yet to see someone who could beat him at the game. None of his cousins did. The Collector would never accept it but he was more of an enthusiast than a player. A pair of big shot *vakils* from Kozhikode, having heard so much about the extraordinary room and equipments had come all the way, begging him for a few lessons but Mithran had no patience to teach. Later, Mithran had learnt that the set up they were used to, was poor and amateurish.

For the first time since Pattu, Mithran felt relatively at peace. Concentrating on the balls helped him relax.

'Mithretta,' said Divakaran cautiously, 'I hope it is alright to ask...'

Mithran grunted with his eyes fixed on the table.

'What exactly happened during Pattu? None of my business maybe. Just curious. If you don't mind talking about it.'

Mithran walked around the table till he found the right position and bent over. It was not until he had completed the shot and straightened that he answered.

'No. not your business,' he said polishing the cue stick with the cloth on the side rack. 'But since you are curious...' his mouth twisted as he hmphed in a show of amusement.

Divakaran's shoulders rocked in silent laughter with his upper body practically sprawled over the green felt. 'Ammamma and the Seniors had you riled, did they?'

'I have been trying to think as little about your grandmother as possible since Pattu. And that is putting it mildly.' Mithran's mouth still remained in that scornful irregular curve.

Divakaran laughed again. 'She is as much your grandmother as mine. I've always felt you are dearer to her than I am.'

'Then she has a funny way of showing it.'

Mithran had put off going to Nilambur for the Pattu as much as he could and arrived at the last minute on the eve of the festival. He knew there would be questions. How he hated people interfering in his official matters! He was the prime authority regarding The Pookottur estates. When the then Valiya Tirumulpad had appointed him the manager of the Kovilakam's vast holdings in that area, Mithran believed he had earned the sole right to take important decisions concerning the estates. He knew every inch of the land entrusted to him. He was aware of exactly how much rent came in from where. Every para of grain was accounted for and not a single *paisa* did he make for himself other than his allowance from the Kovilakam. Yet certain steps he had recently taken met with active resistance from the public and his own staff. Mithran knew it had reached the ears of his elders.

His firm, even ruthless and often slightly discriminatory actions sometimes procured disapproval and hostility from outside but no one in the Kovilakam had ever faulted Mithran for not doing his job well. To think that they were going to begin now.... Mithran had been indignant. For a while he had even considered not going to Nilambur for the festival.

'Miss the Pattu? Really Mithretta!'

Mithran was the Sixth Tirumulpad of Nilambur. Meaning there were only five men his senior in the family. The last few years had seen the demise of several of the senior males and Mithran, just past thirty at the time, found himself hoisted up in the order quite suddenly.

None of his five older cousins would poke their noses in his business affairs given their typical laid back natures. Except for some playful, lackadaisical exchanges, they by and large let Pookottur alone. Even Cheriyettan, who was number two and clearly the cleverest and ablest of the lot. But there was Cheriya Ammamma. The younger sister of Mithran's grandmother, Uma Devi. The present Matriarch. She, Mithran had been sure, was the one to look out for.

'For the first four days of the Pattu, I managed to give her the slip. But the morning before the Karayil Panikkar's strange prediction...'

The riverside rituals had been in full swing by noon.

The oracles, blood oozing from the self-inflicted wounds on their foreheads bounded up the rocky path. The loud, resonant clangor of their anklets and the *eee-yyyo* hoots emerging from their throats filled the air. Mithran stood among the other men, waiting for the oracles to shower them with the customary grains of rice. He had felt relatively safe. The Kovilakam women usually remained in their mansions and did not come out for the rice shower ceremony. The oracles went to them. But as things would have it, that day, the Matriarch had raised several eye brows with her presence. Even the oracles hesitated before releasing the first fistful of rice. To Mithran's chagrin, Cheriya Ammamma had refused to budge from the vicinity and when the rites concluded, she needed no more than a summoning jerk of her chin towards the women's quarters to ensure that he presented himself there immediately after lunch.

The scene that followed had not been pleasant. Mithran was ushered into the massive reception porch, resplendent in carved teak and ivory furniture. Cheriya Ammamma perched on the straight-backed chair that was her customary choice for formal meetings. Surprisingly, the five Seniors were in attendance too, scattered around the room, reposed on the couch and the built in wooden benches, all looking awkward and somewhat embarrassed.

'Mithran *irikku.*'

He had politely refused a seat. He leaned against the rounded pillar with his arms folded in front of his chest and his head poised at a defiant angle.

The Matriarch glanced at the oldest of the Five.

'Er …,' the Senior Tirumulpad cleared his throat and looked at Cheriya Ammamma and when she fixed him with an urgent glare, continued, 'er… what exactly is the situation in Pookottur?'

'Which issue in particular does Ettan mean, I wonder?' His voice lowered a shade when he spoke to his oldest cousin.

'Er… the evictions for one,' such confrontations were certainly not the Senior Tirumulpad's cup of tea. It was obvious that Cheriya Ammamma had brow beaten him into it, Mithran had thought at the time and Divakaran echoed the opinion now.

'We are having problems with some kudiyans. They are refusing to pay their rents and generally instigating trouble. They are Maplas mostly. There are rumours that they are forming anti-government and anti-jenmi organisations. We are better off without them and I had them evicted.'

'Well, they are rumours no more, considering that massive yogam they had in the grounds of the mosque the other day.' That was another thing Divakaran was keen to know about. But later.

'What is it with Beeran Mapla's son, Mammad?' The Matriarch's question was sharp.

Mammad! The name that irked Mithran the most these days. He preferred not to go into the topic for he knew of Cheriya Ammamma's soft corner for the Kovilakam driver's son.

'And I hear the rents have been raised shockingly high.' Fortunately, the second in line changed the topic while Mithran was hesitating over the Matriarch's query.

'Times are changing. The days of extracting a mere one-third from the *kanakkars* are long gone. Cheriyetta, you know the Government has made it clear that we have the right to fix the rent on our own holdings. How profitable the Pookottur estates have been in the past year, is no secret here. Thanks to the rent hike.'

'But eighty percent!'

The Second Tirumulpad was beginning to nod in thoughtful agreement but froze on the Matriarch's indignant cry.

'If you take eight percent of the net produce from the *kanakkars*, they will naturally encroach on the *verumpattakkaran's* share. What are the poor men supposed to live on? Straw?'

'Cheriya Ammamme, you do not understand,' Mithran had explained with a conscious effort. 'If we want proper returns out of our estates we cannot afford to be so … so sentimental. We have to take a firm stand.' He had begun to feel rather frustrated..

'It would do well, Mithra, to remember that we are not merchants. Profits and returns are not our priority. We are a noble race and the welfare of the people cannot be compromised for our personal gain.'

'What is this about the Maplas and these societies you said they are forming?' The Senior Tirumulpad was mildly curious.

'Some kind of extremist group. They call it the Khilafat.'

'Well, I wouldn't call it extremist', said Cheriyettan. 'At least not on the national front. Though in Malabar… I am not sure.'

'Cheriyetta, there have been so many incidents of brutal murder. I function right in their midst. If this goes on… it's going to be worse than what we imagine.'

The Matriarch said nothing to that.

'Some of our staff and kudiyans are fraternising with this Khilafat lot. It is not just about the rent. I have my own ways of making sure they pay up.' Mithran had glanced around hoping the Five would agree. Particularly Cheriyettan. His views were held in high esteem even by the Matriarch.

'When you get back to Pookottur after the Pattu, ask Mammad to come and see me. I need to know what he thinks of the matter. He is an honest fellow. He will not lie to me. We will take up this issue again after that, Mithra.' Cheriya Ammamma's voice had been more subdued than usual but it was clear that she considered the matter far from closed. Mithran had been in a terrible state of mind for the rest of the Pattu. The anger still surged in his breast as he stood in line with his cousins in Vettekkaran's majestic cavalcade. He realised deep down that he shouldn't be entertaining these negative emotions while bearing his sword for the Lord. But Mithran wasn't feeling particularly righteous at the moment. He actually found satisfaction in the antipathetic thoughts. He had felt a renewed rush of fury when he remembered Mammad's disloyalty and arrogance. Tackling the fellow had not been a problem in itself. But to think that Cheriya Ammamma valued that man's opinion over his. That filthy, treacherous Mapla! The silent expletive awarded him a moment of petty pleasure. The humiliation of having been called in and questioned like a naughty child stung and rose up like a wave of heat reddening his ears. After all he had done for the Kovilakam coffers, it rankled to think that his efforts were so little appreciated. Even Poduval's breathtaking *melam* flooded out as Mithran reveled in these thoughts.

It disgusted him now to think that he had for a moment wondered if he should seek a night's solace at the bosom of a dusky forest damsel camping on the outskirts of the Palachod. The Paniyatthis were always ready to provide the Thampans with sensual gratification. They even considered it an honour. Such games usually revolted him and he had quickly put the thought out of his mind. Ever since his wife's premature death, Mithran's prime concern had been the Pookottur estates. But he knew that some of his cousins sought pleasure in the arms of these women. Others who didn't, amused themselves looking for familiar features among the naked Paniyan brats with runny noses.

'You shouldn't let it upset you, Mithretta. Ammamma means well,' Divakaran's casual attempt at soothing him brought him back to the moment.

'Oh absolutely,' he replied caustically and prepared to resume his game.

'She is of an entirely different generation. You can't expect her to think like we do.' Mithran shrugged and chose to lean low over the table and focused on the ivory balls.

Divakaran said, 'By the way, Sethu is demanding to be allowed to come here for a few days.'

'Sethu? She wants to come here?' Mithran's mouth twitched in a barely detectable smile.

Sethu was Divakaran's little sister and Mithran's favourite female cousin. She was the one person who brought out his soft side. The only one he couldn't say no to.

'She's been badgering Amma ever since Pattu. Amma wanted me to check with you before saying yes.'

'Oh she is welcome of course. But won't she be bored?'

'She says she wants to see the Billiards room. I know I have raved enough about it. And maybe she can sample your collection of books.'

'Books?' Mithran exclaimed in surprise. 'I didn't realise she read. I mean apart from *Bhagawatham* and *Narayaneeyam* and that sort of thing.'

'Nor had I. But she seems insatiable. Always buried in some book or paper.'

'Where does she get them?'

'It appears that the girl, Priyamvada has been surreptitiously supplying my sister with reading material for a couple of years. Her brothers Chandran and Vijayan have a fine library.' I discovered a lot of books and back issues of newspapers, magazines and even pamphlets in her possession. They are keeping it a secret. They think the elders won't approve.'

Mithran felt a niggling sense of awkwardness.

Apart from the altercation with the elders, there was

something else about this year's Pattu that perturbed him. That something now raised its head with a faint hiss.

Young Priyamvada was a regular visitor at the Kovilakam and great friends with Sethu. It was during the rice shower ceremony, a little before Cheriya Ammamma put in her appearance. At first he had been too preoccupied to dwell on it. Then it happened again and again. The girl's laughing eyes kept following him in the large crowds trying to put across some very personal messages. When that became obvious, he had glanced around to see if the coquettish looks were aimed at someone else. With a tiny smile and a flutter of her eyelids she had coolly confirmed that they were designed for him. When Divakaran mentioned her, it all came back and made him uncomfortable.

'Amma was asking if Sethu could come in a week or two. I'll escort her myself. She may bring along a companion. So you don't have to worry about entertaining her.'

Mithran grunted in reply and aimed his cue at the red.

A servant lad cleared his throat at the door.

'The Adhikari of Valluvambram is here.'

On the veranda below, waited a middle aged Mapla with a sickly sweet smile. The fellow had his uses and Mithran generally put up with his oily ways.

'Yes, Ahmed, what bring you here?'

'I was just wondering if the Tirumulpad was back from Nilambur.'

'Mm. Got back four days ago. What's it to you?'

'Then the Tirumulpad must have an inkling about what happened here two days ago.'

'If you are talking about that yogam at the mosque premises, yes. I heard.'

'Oh Tirumulpad, this Khilafat-Kulafat is not a good thing. We can't let it grow here.'

'You are against it?' Mithran's eyebrow quirked. 'All in the interest of your community, isn't it?'

'No. No. I think it is nonsense. We must stop it.'

'What business is it of mine?'

'You have to make it your business, Tirumulpad. Or it could prove costly. One of the first things on their agenda is to suppress the landlords.'

'Let them try, Adhikari. Let them try it with the Sixth Tirumulpad.'

The Adhikari was disappointed at not having succeeded in shocking Mithran. Then he pulled out his trump card quite carefully.

'The Khilafat committee met yesterday to elect office bearers. The Tirumulpad's rent Collector is the new secretary.' This time the waxy smile got on Mithran's nerves. Much to the Adhikari's satisfaction he leapt to his feet in a moment's fury. Checking himself in time Mithran refrained from expressing his anger in front of this man. Without further ado he went inside and summoned one of the servants to ask Mammad to present himself at the manor with immediate effect.

As soon as his rent collector set foot in the courtyard, he gave him his marching orders.

Mathu

When she was in a logical bent of mind, she told herself it was a natural consequence of the strange *kalpana* on top of her rather uncomfortable confrontation with Mithran the same morning, that her sub-conscious mind had acted that way, but reasoning did not change the fact that the dream had disturbed her. There was nothing nightmarish about it as such. Not Unnimmama, the devout but Innimmama, the powerful. It had been a common enough scene in her childhood when Innimmama came over to visit his mother. She had never seen him enter the *naalukettu* for that was purely the domain of women. Rarely did a male over the age of ten cross that threshold. Mathu had faint memories of feeling scared at the sound of his ivory handled walking stick tap impatiently on the floor.

There was no reason why this memory, when it came back in her sleep should upset her, even if it was Mithran's face she saw, transplanted on Innimmama's body as he strode up and down the portal. Dreams were often amorphous, Mathu knew.

A century and a half ago, the Nilambur Kovilakam was in danger of being wiped off the earth. It was certain no more children would be born here to continue the family line. It was a matter of grave concern and after serious consideration and discussions with experts, it was decided that three pre-pubescent girls be adopted from a family distantly related to them. The Kovilakam as Mathu saw it today had sprung from the loins of the one of these adoptees, the other two sadly remaining childless. The middle girl, Mathu's Muthasshi Amma, the Kovilakam Matriarch of her childhood days, had had two boys and a girl. Muthasshi Amma had believed that each of her children had a definite role to play. True enough the girl of course had been instrumental in carrying the matriarchal line forward. The elder boy, prayerful by nature had established the Vettekkaran shrine and ensured that the Lord's blessings protected the entire clan. The youngest, an assertive lad, had persevered to make them one of the richest and most powerful noble houses in the whole of Kerala whom even the Samoothiri feared to cross.

Mathu had only vague memories of Great Uncle Bhakthan, or Unnimmama as he was known to the family. His name conjured in Mathu's mind not the slightly overweight old man with swollen joints whom they saw in the Vettekkaran shrine if they went early enough, but of the slender athletic youngster with a serene face, who sat cross-legged in a stone mandapam in the middle of the forest with the Hunter Lord, a chess board between them. The fantasy was more vivid than the memory.

But his brother, she remembered well enough. The governor of all the Kovilakam estates, the decision maker in all family affairs, Innimmama, Shakthan to the rest of the world, was a distant but distinct figure in her childhood. Muthasshi Amma, his mother was the only woman who dared to speak to him. Even the men hovered respectfully in his presence. Everyone said that Innimmama had a soft corner for Mathu as they shared a birthday.

The villain of yet another story no one in the Kovilakam

ever told out loud. The story of Vazhunnoramma and Unni that Mathu had again pieced together from all the little hints and suggestions that she had heard in her seventy-six years.

Great uncle, Bhakthan having brought Vazhunnoramma and her daughter to the Kovilakam and entrusted them to his mother's care, had retired to a life wholly dedicated to Vettekkaran. The old lady had been put up in the innermost chamber off the southern naalukettu, the one Mathu herself used now. Even though in terms of her estates Vazhunnoramma was three times as rich as the Nilambur Kovilakam, she had always lived a simple life. The sheer size of the mansion intimidated the old lady and she preferred to spend most of her time indoors with her daughter. She was comfortable enough in the earlier days.

One night, as a child of no more than five, Mathu was put to bed in the *naalukettu* where rows of mattresses were laid out for the younger women whose consorts did not happen to be visiting at the time. She lay curled up between two aunts and went to sleep only to be woken up by the screeches from the inner rooms. She sat up with a jolt. 'Shh… go to sleep little Mathu,' said one of them comfortingly and pressed her back into the mattress. She lay down quietly with her eyes tightly shut and the aunts began to whisper together.

'They say, the half-witted girl is ill,' said one aunt, patting Mathu on the back to lull her into sleep.

'She is having one of those fits.'

'Yes. I believe they have been especially bad of late.'

'Wasn't the physician consulted? I do wish this would stop. It is difficult to sleep here at nights with all this noise. Why can't her mother keep her quiet?'

'Poor thing,' one aunt was kinder than the other. 'But I believe Innimmama was consulted and he said there is no need to send for a doctor. There is no point in prolonging such a worthless life.'

Young as she was Mathu was shocked. Were some lives more worthy than others?

It had been years later when she heard of her great uncle's only foray into the *naalukettu*. It had been during the pula days after his passing, they had been reminiscing about him when someone mentioned the day he had actually walked into the *naalukettu*, a sheaf of papers under his arm. Old Vazhunnoramma had been summoned from her chamber. She had been hesitant to leave her sick daughter and moreover, she had always been scared of the intimidating Shakthan. Apparently he had read out from the papers.

'What was in those papers?' Someone asked. It had been one of the uncles who answered. 'I have seen them in the room of records. They were the papers with Vazhunnoramma's thumb impression.'

'Oh! The documents signing over all her lands!'

There had been further speculation as to how the property was transferred to the name of Unni Thampan, head of the Nilambur Kovilakam.

Such discussions on Innimmama's actions were few

and far between. No one really knew what had transpired between him and old Vazhunnoramma in the *naalukettu* that day. Those who did were gone, like the great uncle himself and Muthasshi Amma.

But the gaps created by lack of proper facts, Mathu had filled with her imagination. It was a neat little job of treachery, as she saw it, the way he had deliberately misunderstood it when the old lady named 'Unni' as the sole beneficiary of all her estates and had them all transferred to Unni Thampan, the head of the family and thereby to the Kovilakam. Once the paperwork was in order, it was no coincidence that Vazhunnoramma and Unni were no more treated as valued kin.

In the days following Pattu, many a time did Mathu tell herself off for allowing an old family legend, part of which was a figment of her own imagination, to addle her brain.

Benazir Manzil

Pookottur, Ernad
22 January

Benu

Benazir Manzil was a large house hidden in a leafy haven created by cashew, guava and tamarind trees growing together. This was where the people of Pookottur and nearby *amsams* came for justice. Where several civil and criminal cases were resolved. Today, the court met for the hearing in the front yard. Alijan Sahib, the self-appointed judge sat on a wooded chair on the porch and down in the yard, the two disputing parties stood on either side. The petitioner looked expectant and the respondent fearful.

A few minutes before the hearing was to commence, callers dropped in on Alijan Sahib.

'By Allah it is an honour. Kutthirikkeen,' he ushered them in.

Interested as always, Benu had sought the chair by the window in the inner chamber that gave her a good view of the porch and the inquisition when the two men approached. The older of the two, she knew. He was one of Ernad's chief Congress leaders and had been here before. The other was a stranger whom apparently, Alijan did not recognise either.

'You look as if you have much to say, Naire,' Alijan addressed the Congressman. 'I hope you will not mind waiting a while. There is a little issue I must resolve. By the way, who's the new *changathi*?'

'He is an acquaintance of mine. Just back from Madras. Home on leave.'

'Janab!' The young man grinned amiably and flicked his broad forehead in acknowledgement. 'Just dropped by to see Shekharettan and deliver a few parcels and messages.'

'Naire, will you and your friend have some water while you wait?'

'Water? Have you no sherbet to offer us, Sahib?'

This man looked like a well born Hindu. And he did not mind consuming something made in a Muslim household. Comes from living and working in a city like Madras, thought Benu from her seat by the window. Alijan Sahib bellowed for some of the newly acquired Gulabi Sherbet and she had to leave her seat for a while to go into kitchen and have it sent out.

The disputing parties arrived shortly and the hearing began.

The visitors shuffled and dragged their chairs back when Alijan pulled his forward and began to address the people waiting in the front yard. The Congressman looked worried and uncomfortable but the man from Madras settled back to watch, the smile never leaving his face.

'There are certain ground rules you need to be aware of,' said Alijan Sahib coming straight to the point. 'Both the disputing parties will be expected to speak clearly and truthfully when asked a question. There will be no interruptions from either side. Abusive language should not be used at the hearing.' He looked at each one piercingly.

'The petitioner, Planthodiyil Hydrosutty, age forty two, occupation daily labourer. The respondent, Pachel Kungi Amma, age seventy nine, occupation none. The petition submitted to me by Hydrosutty two days ago states that the respondent, Kungi Amma stoned his goat to death the previous afternoon. Am I right, Hydrosutty?' The bare chested man clad in a checkered waistcloth and sporting a shaven head nodded. 'Yes, Sahibe.'

'No! No, I did not,' wailed the wizened old woman.

'Kungi Amme, you will be given a chance to explain. Please remember what I said about not interrupting and remain silent, I am not speaking to you. Hydrosutty, where was your goat when it was killed?'

'In her *purayidam*, Sahibe.'

'And what was your animal doing in the respondent's compound?'

'Our *purayidams* are adjoining, Sahibe. She lives on the patch of land north of mine. The goat accidentally wandered over.'

Alijan Sahib bobbed his fur capped head in rhythm to Hydrosutty's monotone. It appeared the man was well rehearsed.

'Kungi Amme,' he turned to the trembling respondent, 'you deny having done it?'

'I didn't do it, Sahibe. I did not see the goat. I did not even know it was in my *purayidam* that day.'

'Meaning you have seen it there on other days?'

'It always gets loose and eats our greens and *payar* creepers. I have quarreled many times with this man over this.'

'The old hag is getting back at me. She killed my goat intentionally,' raged Hydrosutty.

'I warn you, any offensive language will turn the case against you.'

The hot tempered Mapla bit his lips and hung his head.

'Were there any witnesses?'

'No, Sahibe,' said the petitioner. 'There was no one at home. I got back from work to find my goat dead. Its skull was broken. This is the stone that hit it.' He produced a small rock wrapped in a rag. 'See, Sahibe, there is dried blood on it.'

Alijan Sahib examined the rock in silence.

Hydrosutty had come well prepared, thought Benu as she watched the proceedings. Kungi Amma, it appeared, stood little chance. But Benu had faith in her husband.

He was clever at finding out the truth.

'Where exactly was the animal found?'

'Maybe it had just crossed over. It lay not far from the boundary. There are witnesses for that. Chathu and Kunjali were passing by when I discovered the dead goat. They heard me cry out and rushed over.'

'Are they here?'

Hydrosutty nodded towards the two men who waited a few feet away. When the witnesses had testified, Alijan asked Kungi Amma, 'Who else lives with you?'

'My poor son and his little boy.'

'You were asked to bring them. Where are they?'

'Pakkara!'

A nervous looking man clad in nothing but a soiled towel approached with a small boy clinging to his left hand. The right was just a stump.

'Is your name Pakkaran?'

The disabled fellow nodded meekly.

Alijan Sahib frowned at the man's deformed hand. 'Was he born this way?'

'No, no. He was a strong and handsome child, my Pakkaran. Born in my later years. He used to climb coconut trees for a living. Two years ago he slipped off one and hurt his hand. The Vaidyan treated him for a while but it only got worse. They had to cut it off.'

'The whole business of the goat has an improbable ring to it,' reflected Alijan. 'Hydrosutty, it could not have been this old woman who wielded this rock. She wouldn't have the strength…'

Hydrosutty made protesting noises which the Judge ignored. 'Pakkaran is disabled and the boy too small…'

Hydrosutty began to look disheartened and Kungi Amma hopeful.

'Now you will wait a distance away while I think the matter over.' He turned his attention to Pakkaran's little son. 'What's your name, boy?'

'Velu.'

'Velu, do you like guavas? You may go get some from those trees if you like.' With that the court was adjourned.

Alijan Sahib turned to his visitors and inquired after their health and families. Even as Benu listened to the men, her eyes wandered to the yard where the petitioner along with his witnesses stood way off discussing the possible outcome of the case in hushed tones. Kungi Amma sat on her haunches, visibly more relaxed. She produced a tobacco pouch from her waist and extracted some. The boy dragged his father to the grove and spotting some nice, golden fruit, set about procuring them.

While the hearing was going on, she noticed that the Congressman looked slightly distracted and impatient at having to wait. He fidgeted restlessly in his chair but the other man watched the proceedings keenly. The smile on his face was rather difficult to decipher. Some amount of fascination along with a teeny bit of sarcasm, Benazir had finally decided. She remembered that he was from a big city, maybe a lawyer, he looked well educated. And she wondered what he thought of her husband's inquisition. Benu herself was rather proud of the way he handled such cases.

The men chatted on general matters for a while and many a time, Nair looked on the verge of bringing up what he had come to talk about and decided against it.

'You were supposed to be thinking up a solution but you were talking to us all the time. I hope we have not been a hindrance,' said Nair. 'Oh! I can do many things at a time,' her husband chuckled.

Hydrosutty walked up hesitantly and Kungi Amma hauled up her bent figure to shuffle back on her bandy legs. Pakkaran hoisted his son up with his good hand and the boy, his arms laden with the golden fruit looked delighted. The two witnesses hung back. Alijan Sahib smiled at the child. 'You got some good ones, Velu. Pakkara, you have no difficulty carrying the child with your left hand? He must be heavy.'

'No, Sahibe. It is fortunate that it is my right hand I lost.' Alijan's kindness to his son seemed to have given the poor man some courage. 'I have always been left handed.'

'And you have a good aim too, Pakkara. How cleverly you brought those guavas down with your left hand.' Pakkaran looked pleased at the praise. 'So it must have been easy to fling that rock bang on the goat's head, eh?'

There was a minute's silence in response to the sudden and unexpected question. Hydrosutty's face broke out in a triumphant grin and Pakkaran began to blubber.

At this point a young woman appeared through the leafy pathway leading up to the house. When she saw that something was going on, she kept to the edges and made hastily for the back of the house.

Benazir saw the girl and rose. She went up to the doorway and beckoned her in.

'Razia, come in this way.'

The girl toyed with her *thattam*, embarrassed to walk in on something like this and even more so when she saw strangers on the veranda. 'Neighbourhood lass. Come to see the beewi,' Alijan explained to his visitors

'Pakkara,' he turned back to the frightened man. 'Why did you kill the goat?'

'I didn't mean any harm,' he answered between sobs. 'The payar creepers and the greens I grow help to fill our stomachs and sometimes bring in some money. After the mishap, I have not been able to feed my family. And the goat was always after my plants.

'Is that the goat's fault? It only did what was natural to it. Well, there will be no punishment for now, but another time I will not be so lenient.'

'But Sahibe, what about my compensation?' Hydrosutty was indignant. 'The goat gave a lot of milk. Pakkaran must buy me a new animal.'

'There is no need for him to do anything of the sort. Pakkaran's crime was against the animal not you. He shall atone for it by taking care of my bullocks for me. Kungi Amma's *purayidam* was just north of yours, you said so didn't you?' The Mapla nodded sulkily. 'Each individual is liable to fence the northern boundary of the plot he lives in. It was your responsibility to build a fence and that would have stopped the goat from wandering into another's compound. So technically, you are at fault. You shall waste no time in doing the needful.' Alijan Sahib gave his verdict.

'We will go inside in a minute,' Benu pulled Razia down beside her on her window side perch. 'I am curious to hear what the gentleman has to say,' she cocked her head in the Congressman's direction.

'Well Naire, I am all ears,' Alijan pulled his chair up to face his guest and pulled off the coloured *rumal* around his neck. The young man from Madras had stepped off the veranda with his hands locked together behind his back as he inspected the guava grove. He stopped at Velu's chosen tree.

Nair cleared his throat. 'Er… the Congress and the Khilafat have agreed to work together in Malabar. We… we must be honest with each other.'

'True. How true,' said Alijan.

'Sahib, as I said, the Congress and Khilafat have vowed to work together in Malabar for our common goals and help each other achieve their own noble ends. It is important that our ideals and approaches do not clash. If the leaders do not take care, the people will be confused.'

'Sahib,' he said in a stalling, hesitant tone. 'We have been worried that there is violence brewing. Madhavan Nair, Gopala Menon and a few of us had meeting the other day regarding this. The Khilafat movement has been exciting the people. I mean the common villagers who do not understand things in the actual sense. Innocent minds are often inflammable. When ignited they are likely to catch fire immediately. Many of us are worried that the people of Malabar are confused.

She had been debating with herself whether or not to mention her suspicions to her husband. To try and prevent it before the public started getting a whiff of it. Now this man had said it.

Alijan knotted the rumal around one wrist, unwound it and then wrapped it around the other.

'Here in Pookottur, the people regard you highly. You are the right person to guide public feelings in the appropriate direction. Please do stress the importance of peace and non-violence.'

'If the Congress and the Khilafat do not have a clear understanding, the message we convey to the general populace will be ambiguous.'

Alijan's jaw was set and the rumal back around his throat.

'The prime purpose of my visit, which Madhavan Nair and the others have assigned me to do is to request you to ensure that the people understand the need for peace and the importance of standing together, Alijan Sahib.' Having said it, Nair looked relieved. His companion, chose that moment to jog back from the orchard, tossing a big golden guava in the air and diving to catch it. He laughed as he perched on the veranda's stone ledge in one leap. 'Hope you don't mind, Janab,' he held up the fruit and cheerfully bit into it. Alijan smiled indulgently as if the man had been Velu's age.

Benazir could not make out this man. Was he smart and streetwise? Flippant and shallow? His companion was making serious and difficult conversation and he sat there enjoying a juicy treat like a child.

Alijan for his part seemed pleased with the lightening of the air.

'You over estimate my power over the public. A better man for the job has been identified, hasn't he? If Yakub Hasan cannot convince a populace inclining towards violence, who can? Do not worry Naire. He will talk to the public on the 16 of next month.'

The Congressman nodded slowly. Yakub Hasan's name seemed to have done the trick. He appeared satisfied for the moment.

It was then that Benu noticed Razia's pale face and worried eyes. She decided to quit eavesdropping and led the girl inside.

Off the spacious kitchen was a comfortable room for the ladies. They could sit around on the built-in wooden benches, chatting and sharing goodies.

Benu *Thatha* coaxed some gulabi sherbet on her. 'What is the matter my dear?'

Razia's black eyes glistened with unshed tears.

'It's him.'

'Mammad?'

'Mm.'

'What's with him? Thought he was the man of the hour? Secretary of the Ernad Khilafat committee and what not?'

'But he has been very depressed lately and doesn't tell me why.'

'Are you sure you are not imagining it?'

'He doesn't even speak to me properly. Comes home

late, has a bit of kanji and lies down. He turns the other way and pretends to be asleep when I get to bed.'

'Now, now, we can't have that can we?' Benazir asked mischievously.

'It is true, Benu *thatha*. He is upset about something. These Khilafat matters can be quite scary too. And now they are saying in the village that he is going to fight the White Sarkar.'

Benu *thatha* had vivid memories of the day she had first set eyes on Mammad. He had been a just a boy then. No more than six or seven. She had just been through the worst years of her life and had just begun anew here in Pookottur. Alijan Sahib had just opened a new timber mill and needed a cart driver to carry their load. In this context, they had happened to meet Beeran who drove one of the Nilambur Kovilakam carts. He had heard of the vacancy and brought along an acquaintance for the post. A little boy skipped beside him.

As newlyweds half a century ago, Alijan and Benu had settled down in a village in the neighbouring district of Valluvanad and there they had lived for several years and raised two strong and clever sons. Sons whose whereabouts were now unknown. After all these years, Benu, in her mind's eye often saw her boys walk towards her making their way through the gaps between rows of fruit trees. In her *kinaaves*. How glad she was of her ability to day dream. It was what helped her see through those terrible times, of the revolt of Mannarkad. Both Alijan and his sons had been involved, when it was clear that they would be arrested anytime, the boys with Alijan's brother had gone into hiding. And Alijan himself had disappeared with the promise that he would be back. Benu spent three years living with one well-wisher or the other, had it not been for her childhood habit of weaving pleasant *kinaaves*, her heart would have broken. She dreamt of Alijan coming back. And he did. They had moved to Pookottur and begun afresh and Benu had settled down with daydreams about her sons.

Beeran had walked in that day, accompanied by the man who hoped to get the job and a small, grave faced child . It had been on this very same land where they had a tiny house. Benazir Manzil was to be built only a few years down the line. The cashew and tamarind trees were but saplings, the guavas yet to be planted. Beeran and party had assembled in the very front yard that the hearing had proceeded today and Benu had been watching them from inside. The boy had looked endearing and she invited him in for a snack. His slight build and luminous green eyes set in a thin, serious face triggered something in her. At first she thought that it was because he reminded her of her own boys at that age. But the little face kept coming back to her even after the child had left.

She lovingly stroked the girl's cheek and tucked her *thattam* behind her ear. 'Don't fret. I'll have a word with him. He comes here almost every day. We'll soon find out what's upsetting him. Now finish your sherbet. I'll pack up some biryani for you to take home. Feed it to Mammad for dinner and mark my words, he will not turn to the wall tonight.'

Laughing at Razia's flush, Benu looked out of the window and saw the village gossip hobble up the steps of the back porch, her basket of refreshments balanced on her hip. 'Why, here's Kunhaishumma with her patthiris.'

The Patthiri Umma spread out her goodies and squatted on the floor.

'Four different varieties today. Just out of the pan. Thought I would bring them up here first before going to the village.'

Benazir smiled. The thick circlets of gold adorning her ears shone in the semi darkness of the ladies' room.

The sight of the Patthiri Umma unsettled Razia again. She got up to leave, nodding good bye to Benu thatha.

'Wait, my child. Don't forget the biryani'. She called for the housemaid to pack some of it up. 'Kunhaishumma, some of your best *patthiris* for Razia's young man, please.'

The old woman scooped up a generous heap on to the banana leaf that Benu thatha's maid held out. 'Yes, my patthiris ought to cheer him up a bit. Poor Mammad. What a shock he's had.' She gave Razia a sorrowful glancc. 'How will he take care of this girl now? Having lost his job and all. She is lucky to have you to console her, Benazir Beewi.'

With a gasp, Razia rushed out of the back door, leaving behind all the wrapped up delicacies.

Merry Maids

Pookottur, Ernad
22 January

Sethu
The cart trundled into the village of Pookottur.

At first a palanquin had been arranged for the young Thampatti's travel. But Sethu hadn't fancied being hauled all over Ernad by four men. And the party had left Nilambur in three carts. Sethu and her brother who was to be their chaperone for the trip, started off in the Kovilakam cart driven by Beeran Mapla. Her cousin, Priyamvada travelled in her own vehicle. Priya's family was enormously rich and she had a cart for her own personal use. Sethu belonged to Nilambur Kovilakam, the richest noble family in the whole of Malabar but she had never had a cart of her own. She was just one of the many junior members of a large matriarchal family. Priya on the other hand was the only girl in her extremely well off *tharawad* and thoroughly pampered by her uncles and brothers, not to mention her late father, the late Senior Tirumulpad. Sethu wished she could ride in the same cart as her cousin.

The carts soon left the Palachod and passed out of the Kovilakam's massive arched gateway.

The trip was Priya's brainchild. Such an idea would never have crossed her own mind. Much to Sethu's amusement, Priya had decided that she was in love with their cousin who was a widower and at least thirty five years old. For the past year, she had used every possible opportunity to pursue him but with no success so far. Mithrettan barely knew she existed. Priya had then announced to Sethu that she needed to interact on a more personal level with him and not just among crowds at Kovilakam functions. At Pattu two weeks ago, she had masterminded this stay and bullied Sethu into presenting it to the Elders as her own wish.

It appeared they had already reached the village of Pookottur. Sethu had been so engrossed in the sights and Priyamvada's chatter that the ride had seemed quite short. The cart rolled past a pathway flanked on either side by clusters of cashew and tamarind trees. They suddenly noticed a young Muslim woman about their own age come hurtling down that way. She was sobbing into her veil as she ran. Their cart stopped. Old Beeran, the driver climbed down and waylaid the girl.

'Razia! Eeyo? What are you doing here and what is the matter with you?'

'Bappa,' she exclaimed through her tears.

Bappa? Wasn't that what the Maplas called their fathers? Was this Beeran's daughter? He didn't have girls, Sethu remembered. His daughter-in-law then.

Sethu and Priya hung out of the cart, inquisitively taking in the scene. Sethu was familiar with the way Beeran spoke Malayalam and how different it sounded from the way they spoke it at the Kovilakam. But now when he spoke to one of his kind it seemed almost like a foreign tongue. By then the other cart had also caught up and Divakarettan leaned out to see what the holdup was about. Down the same pathway that the teary girl had come charging down, out ambled two gentlemen. They broke their conversation in surprise to take in the tableaux at the end of the byway. From their expressions it seemed as if they recognised the girl. Wide eyed, they stared at the plush carts, one of them with the Nilambur Kovilakam crest and the pair of young women nearly toppling over each other and out of the cart.

'Go home at once, Razia. I'll drop the Thampatti at the manor and come straight there.' Divakarettan shrugged and climbed back into his cart and the two strangers went their way.

The Pookottur Manor
26 January

The lessons had begun after considerable hounding. When the girls first asked to be allowed to try their hand at billiards, Mithrettan had paid no attention. But Sethu had kept after him so persistently that he had grunted and nodded his consent. But there was no way he was going to do the actual coaching. He had waved Divakaran into the Billiards hall with a twisted grin. And the girls began training.

'Sethu actually shows some promise,' said her brother to Mithran a couple of days later. 'My sister is really full of surprises these days. But Priyamvada keeps knocking the balls off the table. She is furious,' he laughed.

That afternoon Mithran decided to inspect Sethu's game.

The Billiards Hall at Pookottur Manor was Mithran's pride and joy. When the girls first saw it, they had been in raptures. Eleven feet and eight inches long, five feet and an inch wide, the table was built in rich teak from their own forests. Two massive elephant tusks had been used in the crafting of the balls and the ivory inlay on the edges of the table. The imported crystal chandeliers that hung from the ceiling had the girls in oohs and aahs.

He approved of the keen hand-eye coordination Sethu displayed. He liked the way she kept her head down and the cue stick nice and parallel to the table. Mithrettan didn't say much but he had grunted appreciatively. He also noticed Priya making a mess of things. Her small palms kept perspiring and her hand position was maladroit.

Mithrettan walked up to the cue rack and after a moment's thought, selected one. He went over to Divakarettan and tapped his shoulder. 'Have the girl use this one,' he picked up the cue Priya had been playing with. 'See, this is all wrong. Look at the wrap. It is too large for her hands. This one is more her size and has an Irish linen wrap. More absorption.'

That night in their room, Priya was grinning gleefully.

On their arrival at the manor, Sethu had asked to be roomed with her cousin. The Elders at the Kovilakam needn't know and Mithrettan couldn't care less. He generally left such matters to the household staff. So the girls enjoyed the rare treat of talking into the night.

'He noticed my hands,' Priya bubbled on as he held up her tiny palms and her rings on her fingers glittered in the darkness. Sethu found it quite comical. Priya received proposals from the richest *Namboothiris* and *Samoothiri* princes but she had eyes for no one but their middle aged cousin.

While her cousin rhapsodised over Mithrettan's skill at billiards, how observant he was and how much her game had improved with the new cue, Sethu lay back and leafed through the copy of *Ivanhoe* she found in Mithrettan's library. She hadn't read many English books and was struggling with this one. After reading *Indulekha* which Priya's brothers had lent her, she had fallen in love with novels but there weren't too many in Malayalam. She had been yearning to explore the new world of English books and to her delight, Mithrettan had so many. If she got a good start now, she could borrow a few when she went back home. She now had the novel open in front of her and a dictionary placed aside in readiness, but she couldn't concentrate.

'Go lie down on your own bed and give me some peace,' she gave her cousin a gentle shove. Priyamvada made a show of landing on her bed with an exaggerated bump and Sethu lengthened the wicks in the oil lamp. 'Go off into your dream world with Mithrettan strutting about wielding a cue stick. But make sure you do it in silence,' Sethu waggled an oil tipped finger at her cousin and went back to her book with renewed attentiveness.

'I wish you would fall in love with somebody too,' said Priya.

Well, Sethu for her part hadn't actually *met* anyone. She could hear the brittleness in her voice and was quite sure Priya would too. She felt her ears burn a little and was glad the lamplight was not bright enough for her companion to see them redden. In a Matriarchal and matrilineal society like the Kovilakams and Nair *tharawads* marriage did not mean what it did to the rest of the world. The women in her family were reasonably well educated. They were taught Sanskrit and Malayalam. Music and arts. They were trained to manage internal affairs efficiently. When a Thampatti attained puberty, the Elders wasted little time choosing a suitable consort from among the Namboothiri Brahmins of the most distinguished families in Malabar or even Kochi. The union brought about little changes in the Thampatties' day to day lives, except they were allotted a suite of their own in one of the manors meant for the women folk where their Namboothiris would come at night. The Consort Namboothiris of the Nilambur Kovilakam usually lived in their own *illams* and visited their wives when they were so inclined or when the Thampatties summoned them. The women in Sethu's family hardly bonded with their husbands or children with their fathers. The Kovilakam men for their part, were often closer to their own families consisting of their mothers, grandmothers, sisters and their children than they were to their own wives and offspring. The Namboothiris came and went as they pleased and some were politely asked not to visit anymore. Mithrettan's sister Umedatthi had sent three packing.

Sethu was her mother's only daughter and the Matriarch's favourite grandchild. When her monthly cycles began six monsoons ago, proposals had started trickling in. But neither Amma nor Ammamma approved of any of them. By the time Sethu was sixteen, several of her younger cousins were married and there were murmurs within the family about no one being good enough for the Matriarch's little Princess. For when less desirable proposals came Sethu's way, Ammamma conveniently elbowed them towards the other eligible girls. This suited Sethu just fine.

It was over two years ago, to be specific, soon after she had read *Indulekha*, that Sethu began to have a concept of the kind of husband she would like. First and foremost, she wanted a real marriage not just a relationship with a stranger. She wanted a man she could really talk to. To have meals with. She fantasised about touching her husband other than in the confines of the suite that would be allocated to them on the upper story of a Kovilakam mansion. A casual pat on the arm, a mischievous tug of the ear. She dreamt of sitting by his side on the wooden seat in the entrance portal. Of cuddling their children together. Deep inside, Sethu knew that all this was no more than a fantasy. Eventually she would succumb to norm and her marriage would be no different from those of her cousins.

Sethu's dream husband would be strong-willed and well educated. He would have seen something of the world. Not unlike Indulekha's Madhavan. He would have more profound interests than Kathakali temple festivals and sumptuous *sadyas*.

It was a little over three years ago that Sethu's reading habits began to diversify from the customary religious texts. When her uncles and brothers discarded old newspapers and periodicals, she would pounce on them and hide them wrapped in old cast off mundus at the bottom of her massive wooden chest. When she was sure there was no one around, she would smuggle some of them to a secluded spot and devour them. Sometimes she climbed the narrow staircase leading to the third floor of the manor, the folds of her clothes bulging with paper. The rooms on the topmost floor were mostly uninhabited and used largely to store unused furniture and extra brass and chinaware. She was rarely disturbed there. During her time of the month, Sethu was the happiest. When she was younger, she had hated the Dark Room but that had changed. Nobody entered the special room designated to house menstruating women, except to serve them food. Here she could read to her heart's content. Each month she prayed that no one else would be in the room with her. For months she told no one of this for she was worried the Elders would object if they knew. It was by accident that she let it slip to Priya and what a blessing that had been. Priya's father and both her brothers were fond of reading. They stocked books in their *tharawad* and well as the house just outside the Kovilakam premises where they stayed during their visits to Nilambur. Her cousin began supplying her with reading material from their collection. The first proper book she had read was the historical novel *Marthanda Varma* and then its sequel *Dharmaraja*. She read and reread till the scenes were imprinted in her mind. *Kundalatha* about the Kalinga princess. Back issues of the *Vidyavinodini* periodical that were over two decades old in which a story called *Kalyani* by an anonymous writer was serialised. And of course her favourite *Indulekha*. She had especially relished the delicious old legends rewritten by Kottarathil Sankunni in the literary magazine *Bhashaposhini*. Priyamvada's supply had been relentless and Sethu's appetite insatiable. Newspapers, magazines, journals, supplements, she simply inhaled whatever she could get her hands on.

For over a year now, whenever Sethu opened an issue of the *Kerala patrika* or *Sanchari* or one of the other popular weeklies or fortnightlies which she got a month late when Priya's brothers were done with them, she found herself breathlessly scanning the pages for the byline, one name in particular. *The Outcaste.* A range of light essays appeared in many of these publications under the pseudonym. *The Outcaste's* pieces always carried some new information, or some different perspective. Even when *the Outcaste* criticised, he never slandered. His style was so hilarious yet so subtle that she had chuckled in delight over them. She took to collecting his works. Sometimes Priya's brothers didn't want the old issues back and she saved the cuttings. When the papers had to be returned, she painstakingly copied them out word for word on whatever bit of paper she could find. When the Chettiar from Palakkad came in with his wares ranging from pots and pans to crisp new mundus, lengths of silks and velvet to wood and china curios her aunts and cousins swarmed around him in excitement, competing with each other's purchases. Sethu had surprised everyone, even the Chettiar, by choosing nothing but a couple of ledgers from those he had brought for the Kovilakam men to record accounts, some paper which was in fact quite expensive and a piece of blue velvet. She had sown the papers together bound them neatly and covered them with the blue velvet. It was in this notebook that she copied out every one of *The Outcaste's* works and this scrap book became her most prized possession.

Before Sethu herself realised it, the man of her dreams had an identity. That of *The Outcaste.*

Who was he in real life?

As she read his articles over and over again, she tried to understand more about the man behind the pseudonym. For one, she knew he was of Malabar origin – either Ernad or Valluvanad. Age? Somewhere around thirty, she supposed. His frequent mention of the Madras Presidency College made it obvious that this was his alma mater. From some of the events that he wrote about, he seemed to have studied there in the latter half of the past decade. He made constant references to English stories and poetry. That made him either a voracious reader or a student of English literature. And yes, in the whole of 1919 and a part of the following year, he had been abroad. He had done a whole series of articles called *Sheema Kurippukal* on life in England and interesting happenings…

Thus *The Outcaste* had taken shape as a complete human being in her mind, formed with the scraps she had put together and to fill in the blank spaces, she gave her imagination full reign.

Priya had sprung off her bed again and Sethu saw her tiny cousin looming over her now, making menacing faces.

'What am I missing here, Sethu Thampatti? Tell me. I demand that you tell me at once.' She clambered on to Sethu's bed and began tickling her sides.

Sethu gave a little involuntary shriek and wriggled out of her clutches. Resignedly, she put away *Ivanhoe* and the dictionary on her bedside table and sat up.

Sethu couldn't imagine sharing her fantasies with anyone. Even Priya. Priya would think her so ridiculous. She who advised her against her non-viable romantic pursuit of Mithrettan. Why, her cousin's dreams seemed more likely to be realised than hers!

'Tell. I say tell me now!' Priya wore a mock sinister expression as she reached for Sethu's sides threateningly.

Sethu sighed.

'You know of Chitralekha?'

'Who is she?'

'Chitralekha of the Puranas, you ass. The daughter of the Asura king Bana's prime minister.'

'Oh that Chitralekha? What are you trying to do? Change the topic by telling me Puranic tales?' She wiggled her fingers once more and aimed for Sethu's waist.

'I said, you can be my own Chitralekha if you like.'

Chitralekha was the closest friend of Usha, the Asura princess. Usha had once seen a stranger in her dreams and fallen madly in love with him. She woke up in a flutter and found herself sweating profusely. Her heart was beating so fast and hard that it hurt. Yet, she had a starry-eyed expression on her face. Usha could think of nothing else for days. She stopped eating. At night she stood at her window staring at the stars. Chitralekha was worried about her friend.

'Tell me, Sethu Thampatti… che! Tell me, Princess Usha, what's bothering you? Usha had at first been hesitant. Priya imagined Chitralekha tickling the princess's sides till she came out with the whole story.

'Do not worry, Princess,' said Chitralekha who was a very gifted artist, 'I will find your Dream Prince for you.'

She immediately began to sketch man after man.

She began with Indra, the King of the Gods. No, said Usha. Vayu, Varuna, Agni, the Ashwini twins… No, no, no, no-no. Usha negated all the gods one by one. Chitralekha then started on the Asuras. The Yakshas. The Gandharvas. The Nagas. Usha kept shaking her head, looking more and more disheartened as each one proved wrong. Chitralekha set about doing human faces. Sages with their wiry bodies and matted hair. Brahmanas, saintly yet poor. Usha barely glanced at them. The princely races. Gandharas, Kurus, Panchalas, Chedis, Mauryas, Maghadheyas, Kalakeyas… the list was endless but Usha's dream man was not among them. Chitralekha embarked on the Yadava clan. Krishna, dark skinned and ageless. Usha stared at the picture for a second and slowly shook her head. Encouraged, Chitralekha quickly did Pradyumna. There was a tiny spark in Usha's eyes as she looked hard at the handsome face of Krishna's son. Usha threw herself back on the bed, nearly in tears. Aniruddha, the son of Pradyumna. Determinedly, Chitralekha went another generation down. Usha had turned towards the wall. The artist had to drag her up and force her to look at the sketch. Suddenly, Usha blushed. Her lotus eyes glowed and she made patterns on the floor with her big toe. That night, Chitralekha kidnapped a sleeping Aniruddha and presented him to her friend.

So, Sethu Thampatti, there is a man in your dreams and you know not who he is. Priya grinned from ear to ear. Well, she was up to the challenge. The vision of herself flying through the night skies, holding up in one hand a bed, complete with a butter soft mattress, lacy canopy edged with strings of pearls and a sleeping prince in it took shape in Priya's mind and the project excited her.

The Flaming Forge

Pookottur, Ernad
6 February

Alijan Sahib

Nestled deep within the fruit trees in the vast premises of Benazir Manzil stood the smithy. It came to life late in the night as Pookottur slept. After ensuring that his Beewi was dead to the world, Alijan crept out of bed and made for the hidden unit. He pulled his shawl more snugly around his shoulders and took careful steps so that his slippers squeaked less.

As he drew nearer, the slow meticulous rhythm of heavy sledges could be felt. The thuds fell on few ears for no one but an inner circle of his men were actually aware of the smithy's presence. He knew from the Congressman Nair's words that there were suspicions but it was not easy to find or prove. The spineless Magistrate had slapped Ernad with the 144 and police were vigilant but the smithy had not been discovered. Alijan and his men made sure of that.

As he entered the workshop, the workers muttered a hushed Asalam Aleikum and went on with their work. There was a feverishness with which they chiseled and pounded. Setting up the shop hadn't been easy. The building itself, apart from being well camouflaged had to be properly ventilated because of the fumes and dust the smithing process generated. The equipment had not been easy to come by. The bulky anvils and the forges. The hammers, tongs, chisels, punches and drifts. Finding skilled blade smiths who would not wag their tongues. Alijan had managed it all.

The smithy was warm. Alijan cast aside his shawl and settled down on a small wooden stool to watch the swords, knives and daggers take form. He observed in silence, the metal being shaped on the hard tempered face of the anvil, curved and bent at the tapering horn. He gazed intently at the red hot forge where the metal was heated. The heat of the flaming forge meant many things to Alijan.

The hellfire of *Jahannam.*

Verily, Allah has cursed the disbelievers and prepared them for a blazing fire.

The raspy voice of the old Mullakhah who gave scripture lessons at the Yatim Khana still rang in his ears.

Sinners are the fuel of the fire at Jahannam.

To Alijan Sahib, the flaming forge was the hellfire to

which he would feed his enemies. The British, for they were sinners. For what they did in Turki. For the promise they broke. For the treaty signed in the porcelain factory in faraway Sevres. For rejecting the petition put forward by Shaukat and Mohammed in London. For laughing at them, calling them ridiculous…

For what they have been doing in Malabar for over a century.

Alijan Sahib had not always been Alijan Sahib. Sixty six years ago, he had been plain Alikutti, the yatim boy who had known no home but the orphanage, no family but Jawad ikka, Aimutti and the other abandoned boys.

That night, a few weeks after the Collector's assassination, the Yatim Khana had been raided. The police were frustrated, having been unsuccessful at capturing the three prisoners who had escaped from jail and later on proceeded to murder H V Connolly, the District Magistrate and Collector of Malabar. Leads had brought them to Alikutti's town. Alijan remembered quite clearly, the man called Abdul Kadar who had stayed at their orphanage for a few days and become very friendly with the boys. They had no idea who he was but he was kind and affable. Alikutti had admired his tall athletic form and gentle voice. Then he had disappeared without a word. Jawad ikka's eyes were wet that morning when they found him gone. No blood brother would have bonded deeper with Ali than Jawad ikka had. Alikutti had been too young to understand adult relationships but he had realised the depth of the young man's sorrow when Abdul Kadar left.

The boys did not know of Kadar's return till the night of the raid. Every corner of the building and grounds were being searched. Alijan remembered the two policemen poking around in the dormitory where Alikutti slept along with Jawad ikka, the dumb Aimu and some others. There were two rows of mats on which the boys were sitting up in fear. It was a long and narrow room with no furniture. There was no place where a suspected murderer could hide. Yet the constable left no stone unturned. 'That box,' said a constable pointing at the rusty trunk in the corner where the orphans stored their cheap little treasures. Carelessly, they had strewn little feathers, pebbles and other odds and ends the orphan boys valued so much. Aimu sobbed noiselessly and Alikutti felt his heart lurch up into his throat as they flung aside the lone anklet that had slipped off Benu's delicate ankles as she pranced about the rocky country side with her lamb. She hadn't realised it and he had picked it up intending to return it to her. Only he felt he didn't want to part with it. On one side of the trunk were the only really valuable objects in it. The stack of Jawad ikka's pictures. The older boy had magic in his fingers and he often entertained the orphanage inmates with his delightful sketches. One of the sponsors of the orphanage had heard of the young man's talent and sent him paper whenever possible. There were random landscapes and everyday scenes at the Yatim khana. Alikutti's favourite was a picture of them all sharing a huge plate of biryani at the *nikah* of an orphanage girl to an elderly Arab. The joy in their eyes and the warmth of friendship that pervaded in the atmosphere as they enjoyed the rare treat were all captured by that bit of charcoal Jawad had salvaged from the dying kitchen embers. While Alikutti was fighting the urge to give the constable's starched khaki backside a solid kick for the irreverent treatment of Jawad ikka's work, the man gasped and motioned his colleague over. In a trice one of them was back with the white officer who began examining the sketch that they handed over. The officer's yellow brow rose in mild surprise. Alikutti knew which picture interested them. Though Jawad had not shared this one with the younger boys, Ali had seen him one afternoon after Kadar had disappeared, retire to a quiet corner with his sheet of paper and his bit of charcoal. He had watched from a distance as Abdul Kadar's image took shape, sitting on the sandy banks of an unknown river, hugging his knees. The British officer stared knowingly at it and gently nodded his head. Slowly he turned to the boys squatting on their threadbare mats. He looked at them one by one till his eyes fixed on Jawad. He crooked his finger and beckoned him over. 'Did you do the sketch?' Getting no reply, he asked again, 'What's your name?'

Jawad simply tightened his jaw and pursed his lips.

Then he began giving instructions to his subordinates in their stiff short pants. He spoke in a foreigner's stilted and slow way, but it was Malayalam and Alikutti could understand words if not their actual meaning.

'Good work, my men. You were quick to recognise

the wanted. Now this young man here will lead you to him.'

The policemen stared at their superior, wondering how he had singled Jawad out and come to the conclusion.

'Don't you see? He is Kadar's pretty little Nancy boy!' He punctuated his sentence with a gesture which Alikutti knew was obscene. 'Use him to get the bastard out of hiding.'

With that they had dragged Jawad ikka away.

Sitting on the stool in the smithy, Alijan Sahib became his boyhood self. In his fear for Jawad ikka's safety, he had forgotten everything else. The minute the policemen were out of sight, he had shot out of the room as poor, retarded Aimu, sobs still shaking his little body, went about picking up the pictures the men had strewn around in disarray. He had to find Kadar. These men seemed to think he was here at the orphanage. He didn't care for what would happen to Kadar when they got him. If he, Ali could find him, they would set his beloved Jawad ikka free. He stormed into the room where Uppuppa, the toothless warden of the yatim khana was crouching in fear.

'Uppuppa,' Alikutti shook the old man ferociously. 'Don't you realise what's happening? If you know where Abdul Kadar is, tell me. Or they will kill Jawad ikka. If they do, I will kill you.' The old warden had broken down, frightened of even an eleven year old's threats.

'Allah! Why did I agree to this? If I had known that my poor boys would be in danger... I never would have...

when they said it was Holy War…that we were fighting the kafirs…' He kept muttering as he took Alikutti to a store room off the kitchen, dragged off a few sacks of grain and opened a trap door.

The scenes flashed in Alijan Sahib's memory like a series of sketches. The dark lamp lit cellar. Abdul Kadar had not been alone. He was talking in hushed tones to a policeman! No, on peering closely Alikutti recognised the big man who owned the teashop in the village. Why was he in police uniform? There was no time to reason.

'Where's Mujeeb?' The big man asked. Abdul Kadar answered that he had left. 'Take Rahim Haji to safety.' He indicated the weak old man lying on the floor.

'Rahim Haji? This was Benu's father? Was he a killer too?' The boy's eyes widened in surprise

Ali knew he couldn't waste another minute. He had burst into the cellar and blurted out everything to the astounded men.

'They'll kill my Ikka. You have to come out.'

Relieved that the tea shop man was here to take old Haji to safety and that the other man had escaped, Kadar decided to surrender.

The triumphant police party led Abdul Kadar away with his hands tied behind his back. In jubilation, the constables burst fireworks. As he walked away, the prisoner kept his soft eyes fixed on Jawad. When the party had crossed the courtyard, the young man, his face a deep red, crept up on the British officer who made up the rear, wrestled his pistol from behind and shot him in the back, again and again, all in no more than a minute. Even as the white man toppled over, Alikutti clearly saw the look in his older friend's eyes as he looked at his victim. A deep sympathy and kindness so contradictory to his action that the boy shivered. The words Jawad muttered as Ali swiftly dragged him back still rang in Alijan Sahib's ears. *Paavam, paavam*... Because the officer was right at the back of the marching group no one saw him fall and the noise from the fire crackers drowned out his cry. By the time they realised it Ali and Uppuppa had shoved Jawad to the back of the crowd and away from the limelight.

Abdul Kadar, they later reported had been court martialed and shot to death.

Jawad ikka was never the same again.

Not long after, they had left Malabar. Jawad was soon to be eighteen and boys older than that were not allowed to live in the Yatim Khana which was meant for children. Jawad's sponsor had funded his education. He had requested that Alikutti be allowed to travel with him. Years in the dry plains of North India. Both the boys had used to time the learn. Jawad, a scholar by nature had always found teachers to study with. After the massive uprising of the sepoys two years later there was a wave of awareness about the imperative need for proficiency in English and modern sciences if Indian Muslims were to maintain a degree of social and political clout. Jawad's scholarly pursuits took him to Moradabad, Ghazipur and Aligarh.

Alijan Sahib called to mind the boy who had accompanied Jawad ikka on his travels. Though he hadn't lacked intelligence, he'd had no desire for academic quests. He preferred to learn from life not from books. Jawad had tried to get him to study at the Mohammedan Anglo Oriental College but he chose to roam the markets, business units and small industries instead doing all the jobs that came his way. He mingled with all sorts of people acquired multiple skills and hoarded quite a bit of money. Jawad's hatred of the British had found its way to young Ali's heart.

The boy grew up. They returned to Malabar and Alikutti, a rich young man was known to the world as Alijan Sahib. Now on the threshold of a new life, with money in his purse and courage in his heart, somewhere within him nestled the cherished image of a young girl, her *thattam* flying in the breeze as she chased her pet lamb and deep in his pocket clinked a lone silver anklet.

He found Benu and made her his beewi. Jawadikka, tired of his travels had chosen to return to Malabar with Ali in whose home he knew love and respect.

This had been, thought Alijan Sahib, half a century ago. A lifetime of losses, gains and further losses. Losses that made way for greater gains.

They had set up a similar smithy in Valluvanad during the rebellion three decades ago. Having settled down there after his return to Malabar, Alijan and Benu had raised two good sons who at sixteen and eighteen were old enough to work for the cause. Their beloved Balyuppa was their mentor as he had been their father's. They forged daggers and swords in the smithy. The police were suspicious of them and kept a keen watch. One morning the smithy was found in ashes. Jawad was nowhere to be seen and the boys had vanished too. Alijan had only waited long enough to console his heartbroken wife and assure her he would be back before going away himself.

Even after thirty years, Benu still believed her sons and Jawad would be released from jail someday and return to them. She fed her daydreams with these hopes.

The men fed more fuel into the forge and the flames roared.

The Khilafat was god sent. All these years, the anti-British revolts had been localised. This time it was different. The temperature of the hearth itself was intensifying each minute and the sparks rising from it flying off in every direction. There were leaders like Ali Musaliar and Mohammed Musaliar of Kattilassery operating the bellows in Malabar while in the National Smithy it was the Ali Brothers who were in charge. To supply the additional air required to keep the fire kindled nationwide, there was Gandhi. Here in Ernad, staunch and trusting Congressmen aped his thoughts and actions. Dexterous smiths forged deadly weapons meant to bring an end to British rule in Malabar.

Alijan Sahib's thoughts went to young Mammad. He was one such smith at the Khilafat's forge. His commitment to the cause pleased him. He was not letting his personal problems come in the way of Khilafat.

Young, wholehearted Khilafatkar like Mammad were

not just the smiths working at the forge. They were the weapons too. They were the metal to be heated to the perfect temperature so that they became easy to shape. At this malleable state, Alijan knew they would be too hot to handle. One would have to be very cautious, he thought as he watched the smiths use tongs to transport the heated metal from the forge to the anvil. Alijan looked at the anvil itself. It was tempered to be hard and smooth. The edges were slightly rounded so that the iron was not gouged or marred.

Allah! He was getting a kink in his back. At his age sitting too long on a three legged stool was not too comfortable. Alijan rose and began pacing the length of the shop. This visit to the smithy was now a nightly ritual. His aging bones protested against the walk through the groves in the chilly darkness and sitting stiff for hours on the backless stool. He watched the blade smiths at work. He was not as young as they were but he knew his presence stoked the fires within them. Alijan Sahib was well aware that though he was not a native of Ernad, most of the Musalmans there looked up to him for guidance and motivation. He was their governor. For a moment he plunged into a fanciful reverie. The Sultan of Ernad. Maybe the whole of Malabar. The head of that kingdom they all envisaged. Some fiery Khilafatkar had proclaimed that they would seize control of the Kovilakam at Nilambur and make their headquarters in the lordly manors. Without realising it he smiled. The thought of Benu as the Sultan's Begum brought it on. In his mind, he could see her in the Kovilakam's inner rooms, singing songs in Arabi Malayalam and swinging her legs to and fro as she drifted off into *kinaave* after *kinaave*. Well, let it remain just that for now, Alijan Sahib laughed to himself. A *kinaave*. A dream that would lend purpose to the Khilafatkar. All in good time. And the time wasn't far away.

Ali Musaliar had been quite firm that non-violence would not be compromised.

It was disappointing but in the past three decades, Musaliar had been a trusted friend and guiding light. One of the very few people who knew the actual whereabouts of Alijan's sons. One of the very, very few who called him Alikutti. He did not wish to go against Musaliar's wishes. So he opted to hold himself back. He did not however stall preparations. One day, Musaliar would see things more pragmatically and give the nod and Alijan did not want to be ill equipped then.

Somehow, his mentor had got a wind of things. A few days ago Musaliar's aide Lavakutti had come down with a message requesting Alijan to pay him a call. It hadn't been just to inform him of the notice delivered personally by Amu Sahib the Deputy Superintendent of police issuing a ban on both Musaliar and himself along with that genial congressman, Madhavan Nair and some others, prohibiting them from speaking in public. Alijan had but smirked at the news. Fools! Did they think he needed a podium to get to the hearts of the people of Ernad? Did the British Sarkar really think that their 144 scared him?

Ali Musaliar had raised a knowing eyebrow and said softly, 'Not thinking of disobeying the notice, are you?'

'I wouldn't dream of it,' Alijan had replied. 'Not with your eagle eyes watching over me, Musaliare.'

Musaliar's eyes narrowed into slits. 'Then there are other little serpents crawling about in that wily brain of yours, Alikutti. One can never say when they will raise their nasty heads.' Alijan shrugged and looked innocent.

'And would one such reptile bear resemblance to a hidden smithy where vicious daggers are forged?' Ali Musaliar locked gazes with him. Alijan shrugged again attempting to make light of it. 'Would another be a godown deep in the jungles stock full of gunpowder?'

Ali Musaliar's eyes, yellow with age had acquired a steely sharpness. They were of nearly the same age but Alijan often felt like a child in his friend's presence.

'I am not denying it. I don't see the need to lie to you of all people. Not many know the White bastards as well as I do. What if there is an attack from their side? We don't want to be caught unawares, do we?'

Musaliar sighed. 'I still stand unswerving that Non-Violence should be the foundation on which the minar of Khilafat should be erected. It would do us good to remember that it is not bricks and stones we are using to build this tower, but human hearts. The fiery, passionate hearts of the people of Malabar. Allah has fashioned the Malabar Mapla's heart using a highly inflammable substance, Alikutti. Remember that.'

'Non-Violence,' Alijan muttered under his breath. 'That spineless, kafir's favourite shout.'

What Ali Musaliar feared so much was what he

himself secretly longed for. That the Khilafat Movement turn into a great roaring fire that would purge the land of the Sayippe's oppressive rule. Musaliar wanted it to be a mild and gentle breeze that he hoped would blow the whites away. Deep within Alijan wished to spread the heat of the fire far and wide.

Even as he gave Musaliar an unwilling word that he would not resort to bloodshed and brutality, Alijan felt a tiny twinge at the back of his mind. Not guilt. But something similar for he was not happy keeping things from the Musaliar. He thought of the plan to invite Yakub Hasan to address the people of Malabar. Or rather his real intention behind it. He knew too well that the top Congressmen and even some Khilafatkar like the Musaliar and his followers took some comfort from the fact. They truly believed that if Yakub Mia insisted on the need for self-control, the people would take it well, coming from a great national Khilafat leader. They would succeed in spreading the message of peace. Alijan had been capitalising on this intense need of theirs to achieve the opposite end. It was this deception that pricked his conscience now in the presence of Musaliar. The suggestion that Yakub Hasan would be the right man to control the mobs had been his. It was his influence and contacts, his friendship with Shaukat and Mohammed Ali that were used to get the important man here. The Congress leaders of Malabar, so worried that Gandhi's milk-and-water axiom of Non-Violence would be shattered in Malabar had swallowed the idea quite readily. And Yakub Hasan was to arrive on 16 February. Yogams had been arranged where he would address the crowds. The people were excited and the leaders hopeful.

But Alijan was not so deluded, so naïve. He knew the way the White Sarkar worked. They would not sit back while the Khilafat leader made his speeches. Collector Thomas was already in a frenzy. His desperate declaration of 144 was proof enough. He would, by hook or by crook try to put a stop to it. An arrest at the very least. The arrest of a renowned Islamic leader while in Malabar would be like stirring a hornet's nest. The people would burst out spitting and hissing. This was the immediate and widespread animosity that it would incite.

'You must be careful of every matchstick you strike in the vicinity,' Ali Musaliar was saying. 'Put aside your daggers and gunpowder, Alikutti and pray to Allah. When you calm down you will realise which the better weapon is.'

'Insha Allah. As the Lord wills,' Alijan Sahib had replied meekly.

The sparks from the forge crackled as they spewed out in semblance of a fine firework display.

'Allah! May the future of Malabar be cast at the forge of the Khilafat. May the Almighty agree with me that the fire needs to be stoked.'

The Matriarch's Musings

Nilambur, Ernad
10 February

Mathu
The Matriarch smiled at the familiar rumble and felt the comforting warmth of friendship wash over her. She leaned against the rounded pillar and sat with her legs outstretched on the stone seating ledge that ran all along the open side of the entrance porch. Eli swayed peacefully by the sturdy jackfruit tree outside, so close that from her position on the ledge, Mathu could reach out and stroke her massive side. The rumble was Eli's gentle response to the pat. It felt good when Eli's thick, dry skin prickled her own soft, wrinkled palm. It was this pleasure and the security of a seven-decade long friendship that induced the beam on the Kovilakam Matriarch's face.

This get together was a routine of sorts. Three or four afternoons a week, Billi, the mahout would walk Eli over to the Kovilakam and tether her legs loosely to the jackfruit tree that stood a few feet south of the entrance post. Allowing her moving space, so that she could stand by the Matriarch's seat. He would then maintain a polite distance, napping in peace under the trees till it was time to return. The two old ladies would then enjoy a quiet heart-to-heart.

Not more than a year or two ago, Mathu did not hesitate to slip down to Eli's stall in the stables whenever she desired to see her.

But now you have to come to me all the time. It is this rheumatism you know. I can barely make it to the temple twice a day.

The Matriarch knew that Eli comprehended whatever she said. It was with her elephant that she shared everything and had done for years. Eli never misconstrued the meaning of her words. Nor did she babble secrets like some of Mathu's sisters and cousins had been wont to. Talking to Eli was a way of organising her own thoughts and often finding solutions to difficult problems.

But it is not as if now is the time for laughter, Eli. In fact things are getting too serious for my liking. I can sense something in the air. A red hot rage that has been lying dormant for years, threatening to burst open like those fire-mountains we read about. Why do I think it is going to start spitting sparks soon? Why do

I feel the molten heat pouring itself all over and searing lives? Why am I unable to sleep at nights? Why do I hear Vazhunnoramma weeping when I go to bed in my chamber which had once been hers? Why do I actually feel the all-consuming anxiety she had suffered till her last breath. The misgivings about her unfortunate daughter's future.

Am I paranoid?

Eli flapped her enormous ears reminding the Matriarch of a time when she herself was known as Anachevi Mathu. She was thus tagged for the curious way in which she heard things and latched on to all kinds of information. Nobody now used the moniker to her face but the skill was far from dead.

Sometimes she picked up scraps from the servants. Not always reliable but their gossip usually gave a general picture. The washer woman came in each day at dawn and dusk without fail. The Pattambi Chettiar who traipsed about the country sides of North Kerala peddling his wares in rich homes. Their own managers like Govindan Nair and Kadar. Beeran the cart driver.

There are advantages to being the Matriarch don't you think, Eli? You can actually command the men in your family to come out with information. The men are my own grandsons or those of my sisters and cousins. I have fastened their loin cloths and smacked their bottoms. They can't ignore me. Though they do try to evade. Mithran is a case in point. Is that not so, Eli?

For instance the District Magistrate's visit. She

heard he was at the Pookottur Manor recently and in a proper state too. Mathu was quite eager to know what he had to say about the situation with the Maplas. She had sent word for Mithran but he had made excuses for not turning up. In the end she had got it out of her grandson Divakaran who had been there at the time. He had obediently given her a fairly thorough account of the essentially one-sided conversation in Mithran's Billiards Room where Magistrate Thomas had raved and ranted, clearly panic stricken by the impending visit of a Muslim figurehead and what he thought it would do to the already fired up Mapla population.

Khilafat. It was neither Malayalam nor Sanskrit. The only languages she really knew. But the word had become increasingly familiar of late. Even Mithran had mentioned it that day at Pattu. The Matriarch had known about the Khilafat for quite some time.

More than a year ago, she had chanced upon a brand new and quite unexpected source of news that changed her perspective entirely. Up until then she had obtained facts mostly by either eavesdropping, tactfully leading conversations in the direction she wanted, or on occasion asking point blank. But it all invariably came from the mouths of individuals. It was surprisingly her granddaughter, Sethu who opened these new doors for her.

If there was one room in the Kovilakam that the women hated, it was the small, dark one tucked into the corner of the western *nalukettu*, as far away from activity as possible. No one went in there if they could avoid it.

But every Kovilakam woman was bound to spend three days a month in there hardly ever stepping out. During your time of the month you were confined to that little dungeon with just a mat to sleep on. You were allowed to touch no one. Unless someone else was serving time in there, your only contact would be the maids who served your meals. Sethu had dreaded the room.

'Ammamme,' she had protested as a thirteen-year-old. 'Why can't I come out for a while? I just want some fresh air. And why can't someone sleep in there with me at night? It is so dark and creepy. Please, Ammamme,' her granddaughter had pleaded. 'I will not touch anyone. Satyam.' Mathu Thampatti could only shrug indulgently.

Just a year ago, the Matriarch recalled, she had woken in the middle of the night for a drink of water and remembering that Sethu was in the Dark Room alone and peered in at the door. To her surprise, a couple of lamps were lit in there, filling the room with a dull glow. The girl was sitting up on her mat and sheets of yellowish paper. She took care not to touch the girl or her belongings and listened to her read out bits from the paper. Soon they fell into a pattern the two of them. Whenever they could manage a bit of private time, Sethu would read to her.

Thinking about the Khilafat brought Gandhi to mind. It was around Onam, last year. Sethu had read to her about his visit to Malabar. He had come by train, conferred with leaders and addressed crowds. Gandhi. It was soon becoming a household name and the Matriarch was fascinated by him. She had seen grainy prints over the year and his tiny, wizened figure and bald head never failed to astound her. Looks apart, this was undoubtedly a powerful man with an unbending fixity of purpose hidden behind his mild demeanour. And that purpose was to free the country of the white man's rule.

I am sure the Sayippes sense it too, she had told her big confidante many times in the last few months. She brought it up again this afternoon. They are terribly afraid of this man. Looks like The Magistrate Sayippe is too.

When Gandhi visited Malabar last year, she had a vivid recollection of the reports of the day he, along with that man called Ali, had arrived in Kozhikode. A throng of people gathered at the train station and overflowed on to the streets, eager for a glimpse. The British had tried to shrug off this allurement as mere curiosity. 'Just a handful of fanatic Mapla lads and a smattering of brief less Vakils,' Hitchcock the Chief of Police was reported to have sneered. 'Were not the flowers and garlands the people carried to the station evidence of their admiration,' he was asked. 'Clearly not. They probably considered the two leaders a huge joke.' He went as far as calling Gandhi a semi-lunatic. Hitchcock's bravado did little to hide the tremor in his heart.

Who is this Gandhi, Eli? A joker? A lunatic? A resourceful little Chanakya who moulded the nation like soft clay? Or a fool who himself is moulded like soft clay into the forms that men like the Ali Brothers desired?

Even now as she sat comfortably on the broad stone

mantel, reassured by the company of her strong, silent friend, creases appeared on the Matriarch's brow. Why did Gandhi bring up these issues in Malabar? Would his philosophy of Non-Violence work here if the Maplas were agitated? Mathu feared bloodshed above everything else. The thought of widespread attacks, rapes, murders sent a shudder down her erect spine and for a moment her mind went back to the days following her eighth birthday.

The river flowed at a calm steady pace and the barge bobbed gently along in the mild breeze. Lush greenery laced the river banks and were reflected in the water, making it appear a dark leafy green. The air smelt fresh and open with a whiff of weeds and aqua life. It was typical of the river and surprisingly pleasant. Today, it cascaded over rocks and pebbles all the way from the Ilambalari hills, filling the ears of everyone in the barge with a delightful gurgle. Further down where its path was smoother, the sound would fall to a lulling hum. Just a month ago it had actually sounded like deafening rolls of thunder that could be heard for a mile away as it surged ferociously down the hills. Though the monsoon had died down, rafts still floated downstream carrying piles of logs from the forests to the mills of Kallayi where they would be sawn to size later to be shipped across the world.

When the barge had set sail from the Kovilakam's private jetty, the sun was barely out. A short way off, the Ananga Para rose out of the water, solid and black in the rosy morning light. It had a reputation of being immovable, braving the river's brutal thrashings for centuries. The fiercest floods had not succeeded in uprooting this rock and hence the name Ananga Para.

Mathu was a regular little fish and could race her nine male cousins to the rock and sometimes win. She and the boys, known as the vanaras for their monkey-like antics, would clamber over the slippery black surface and dive into the water. Roughhousing and frolicking would follow. Mathu knew she would not be allowed to bathe with the boys much longer. She was eight years old now. She had had her birthday just last week. Mathu's birthdays were always special for it was also Innimmama's birthday. Innimmama was her great uncle, one of the senior-most males in the Kovilakam and his birthdays were always a splendid affair and Mathu got a share in the glory as well. This was Innimmama's sixtieth and the festivities grander. Three nights of glorious Kathakali performances, brand new mundus for everyone, special pujas at the newly constructed Vettekkaran temple, not to mention a sumptuous *sadya*.

Every year in his birthday month Innimmama visited the Guruvayur temple for special prayers. Some of the family got to go as well. On account of her sharing his birthday, Mathu and Amma were fixtures in the travelling party. This year there were rumours that the trip might not happen. Mathu had listened in on the uncles' conversations. It would be too dangerous to travel. There was unrest all over following the Collector Sayippe's assassination. It was a terrible murder. Mathu listened wide eyed as they quoted news reports.

The doctor had arrived too late, they said, and all he could do was stare helplessly at the chunks of flesh, bits of bone and pools of blood that had been the District Collector. Mathu had been so terrified that she would have run away without hearing the rest had curiosity not got the better of fear. No less than twenty-seven wounds, he noticed later on examination. Seven of them on the head, three of which had penetrated the brain. The one that went right through the ear and the mastoid process of the temporal bone had been the cause for death. Arms nearly severed from their sockets. Wrists chopped off. Two stabs from a bayonet on one arm. Those on the back were many in number and very deep. The right knee joint was opened and the thigh bone cut straight through. One servant had lost an arm and another all five fingers on his left hand.

The police were searching for the killers. Maplas all over the district were running haywire. Stabbing people as and when they fancied. It was going to be Tipu's *Padayottam* all over again, said the uncles. And it would not be safe to venture out. Mathu feared that the Guruvayur trip was off but as it happened Innimmama was not about to call off his yearly ritual just because a band of Maplas had gone crazy. His arrogant optimism was typical and he waved away all doubts to go ahead with his plans.

Perched on the broad wooden seat in the barge, Mathu listened to the tee-hee-hees and chortles coming from the *Edathies*' corner of the boat. For once, she wished they would shut up. She wanted to enjoy the river's rumbling music and think. All that her sisters and cousins were interested in was which pathakkam went with which *kodakkadukkan*. Or whether there was a spot on someone else's mundu. Sometimes the younger male cousins joined them and there was a round of Gulikan cracks.

Jokes featuring Gulikan had been a part of Kovilakam life forever. The demi-god Gulikan, son of Shani, was believed to be the bearer of obstacles. Whenever someone had a bout of bad luck, they ragged him about being Gulikan's special pet.

Some of their jokes were so funny she laughed till she had stiches but today she was in no mood for them.

'Muthasshi Amme, will you tell the story of Tipu's *Padayottam*?' Mathu asked when they had gathered in the *nalukettu* for the story telling session one afternoon last week. The Matriarch said nothing for a while and merely frowned. Mathu was worried. Was she angry?

But Muthasshi Amma dropped her voice dramatically and launched into her account.

Tipu was a *dushtan*, a bad, bad man from a faraway land that lies miles north of our forests. He was as powerful as he was cruel. It was his ambition to convert everyone into Maplas like himself. Then he climbed the hills and crossed the dense jungles to reach Malabar and began his *padayottam*. It was the most terrible times our land has ever seen. Tipu and his men were barbarous and blood thirsty. He tried to force the people here to become Muslims. He destroyed thousands of temples. He had in his possession a potent gunpowder which he used to burn down the houses of God. The Mahapapi. Mutthasshi Amma's voice was a hoarse whisper.

Tipu had a mighty army. It was soon after my sisters and I were adopted into the Nilambur Kovilakam. I was no more than ten. I have heard eyewitnesses relate tales of their atrocities. A corps of thirty thousand barbarians marched through Malabar butchering everyone they came across. Tipu, on a big elephant wove his way through fields littered with massacred victims admiring his handiwork. Innocent men and women were hanged. Mothers were lynched with their children tied to their necks. Namboothiris and Nairs were tied to the legs of elephants and dragged around till their bodies were torn to bits. The lower castes were so scared that they willingly converted.

Mathu and the vanaras listened in horror.

'How can you make one a Mapla?' Someone asked. 'You are either a Mapla or not.'

'There are rituals,' answered the Matriarch. 'We are not sure. The maya of Rakshasas is known to none but the Rakshasas themselves. But there are certain things we hear. They force you to cover your heads, it seems. Men have to wear a cap and the women wrap a cloth round their heads, like Moideen and Kadar and their families do. That is the easy part. They make you eat the meat of a cow. Vettekkara!' Mutthasshi Amma invoked the Lord to forgive her for saying such sinful things.

Mathu felt the contents of her stomach churn and push up to her throat. She looked around and saw the boys look equally nauseated.

'You can't go to the temple anymore. Or chant the Bhagawatham.'

She lowered her voice and continued. 'And for the men… bits of their unmentionables are sliced off.' She rolled her eyes menacingly. The vanaras covered their crotches protectively.

Mathu could not believe her ears.

Countless temples were burnt down or defiled. Triprangot, Trichambaram, Tirunavaya, Tiruvannur, Tali, Parambitali, Tiruvanchikulam, Peruvanam…'

The old Matriarch recited the names of some of the temples Tipu had desecrated, in a singsong voice and her body rocked in rhythm to the chant. She told them what happened to most of the Hindu families in Malabar, how their own relative, Trichera Tirumulpad had been captured and converted. How two hundred Namboothiris were beheaded and their heads displayed in plain sight at the Palakkad fort. How many families fled Malabar and took refuge elsewhere. We ourselves went to Kochi where Shaktan Thampuran, the king, offered us temporary asylum. Then she wound up with the tale of Tipu's defeat at the hands of the King of Travancore.

Mathu and the vanaras had all had bad dreams that night but the boys had later dismissed it as another of Muthasshi Amma's yarns and may be in time Mathu would have done so too but for what she saw when the Guruvayur party reached Kozhikode.

It was nearly five in the evening when the barge covered the last few miles of the river that formed the boundary between Ernad and Kozhikode and reached the mouth of the Chaliyar not far from where it emptied itself into the sea. It was not far from the *tharawad* of Innimmama's wife where they would break their journey. They had to be there before the lamps were lit. Bullock carts and a *manjal* awaited them. Some of the men, stiff from sitting in the barge too long, decided to walk. The women would go by cart and the *manjal* was of course for Mutthasshi Amma. She beckoned for Mathu to get in with her. Four muscle bound men heaved the *manjal* on to their shoulders and began moving, making humphing noises as they walked. The carts maintained a slower pace so that the party could keep together.

The roads would not be very crowded until they entered the city. There were cashew trees lining either side. Mathu sat back on the cushioned seat, taking in the sights while Muthasshi Amma dozed. They had travelled thus for an hour when voices sounded at a distance. Innimmama ordered a halt and asked one of the drivers to take a look. The man scampered off and was back in a few minutes, his face drained of all colour.

'Maplas, Thampran. Hundreds of them. They are carrying burning torches. We can't go further. Nor can we turn back. They are coming in all directions,' he panted.

The carts were quickly rolled into a thick clump of trees and the *manjal* hauled in there. Mutthasshi Amma began a loud chant of Narayana-Narayana and had to be hushed. As the shouting got nearer and the burning torches came into view. There were hundreds of them dragging along some others who were obviously their victims. Mathu strained her ears to hear what they were saying. It was a slogan of sorts that had an indignant, enraged sound to it. As they approached closer to where the Kovilakam party was hidden, the chorus was clearer.

Benam benam mayyathe!

Naiyinte makkade mayyathe!

She recognised the Mapla accent and the words. We want death. Of the sons of the bitches. Though Mathu had never heard such words uttered, she understood well enough. Even as war cry rang out, they drove daggers into the bellies of their captives, spat on their faces, trod on their slashing bodies and went on.

Benam benam mayyathe…

The Guruvayur trip had not materialised after all and they were back in Nilambur in two days' time. She had rushed to the stables as soon as she could to tell Eli of it all. She had hugged the baby elephant's soft trunk, rubbed her cheek against the coarse skin and related the horrible experience.

The abhorrence of bloodshed was embedded deep inside her but as she grew older and more rational, the terror that that Maplas induced in her waned. How fair was it to fear someone just because he was a Mapla? Were all Maplas bad? No one in their right mind would say so. Her contact with the community was limited to a few employees of the Kovilakam. Loyal and steadfast were just a few adjectives she could use to describe them. A truer and more devoted man than old Beeran the cart driver couldn't be found among the many Hindu servants.

Admittedly most Maplas she knew were high-strung and emotional people. If they love you, they lick you to death and if they hate you they stab you to death was the common maxim. Murderers either way. That's how we brand them. Eh Eli? They are unlike us, yes. The food they eat is revolting, but that's just their choice. The clothes they wear. The God they worship. Why we have thirty-hree crore of our own, what harm can another do? Eventually it is the goodness of the heart that matters. To herself and to Eli, the Matriarch could not deny that there were quite a few Muslims with good hearts. She would not want those hearts to ache any more than Hindu hearts.

Slowly, the Matriarch rose from the stone bench and descended into the yard to stroke Eli's pillar like foreleg. 'Ammalu!' She called out to the maid. 'Bring me the jaggery.'

Both she and Eli could do with something sweet.

Friday Flashes

Pookottur, Ernad
18 February

Alijan Sahib
'Allahu Akbar Allah...'

At exactly 12 noon, the Mukri's voice rang out loud and clear, summoning the Pookottur Maplas to Salat aljum'ah. But that Friday everyone was at the mosque much before the sound of *banq*. Those who came first were already in the front rows awaiting the commencement of Khutbah. Many were just trickling into the dim interiors of the *palli* and the latest arrivals were at *vudu* by the water tank splashing themselves a little less punctiliously than usual. There was a general air of impatience. As if they couldn't wait for the prayers to be done with. Talking before *niskaram* was unheard of and so the Pookottur Maplas were bursting to the seam that day.

Not far from the doorway, Alijan Sahib perched on the stone ledge that ran all along the wraparound veranda. He leaned back against the rounded pillar and fingered his neck *rumal*.

'They are all bound to take home loads of blessings today,' he thought, smiling to himself.

He too was admittedly anxious for prayers to wind up that day so that he could see how Pookkottur had received the news. The curfew meant they couldn't discuss it in public places but the mosque was one spot the Collector's dirty paws could not reach, thought Alijan getting up from his perch and moving towards the *akapalli*. 144 or no 144, the Maplas would assemble at the *palli* on Fridays. The Sayippe's law had absolutely no control over what was being said or done there.

'In that way, we the followers of Islam are one up on the others,' reckoned Alijan. The first sermon was already underway and he was, though seated in the swaff as usual, paying very little attention.

Nearly forty-eight hours had passed since the dramatic arrest of Yakub Hasan and Madhavan Nair at Kozhikode. The news had reached Pookottur as well but it was all mostly hearsay. Scraps of information, some true, some wildly misinterpreted, were flying around. Today he would get wind of how the people were taking it all. How far his ploy of bringing Yakub Hasan down to Malabar to provoke an immediate popular reaction had worked remained to be seen. But he had the satisfaction of knowing that the foolish Collector had played right into his hands. Mr Thomas's fear that the Khilafat leader from Madirashi would instigate the Maplas into violence had all but driven him crazy and propelled him into the impulsive decision. Now, if things went by plan, the people would not sit still. The needless arrest of the important Khilafat man would make them indignant and all the more committed to the cause of the movement.

The bee hive had been prodded nice and firm. Now he would sit back for a while and appraise the intensity of the resulting buzz. That people may get stung in the process was of little relevance.

Sure enough, the *niskaram* rituals had barely concluded when a sudden bombination exploded in the mosque, causing the old laterite building to vibrate. People began talking all at once in animated whispers that grew louder and louder by the minute. A rare occurrence in the *akapalli*. The akapalli, the purappalli and the yard. All over the premises of the mosque, people were talking all at once.

Alijan let his eyes and ears wander in different directions.

One particularly well informed villager squatted on his haunches and stroked his scanty beard importantly. For once in his life he had the undivided attention of a group. One of his own cart drivers, Alijan observed with a small smile.

'Kunjikadare! Tell us what happened at Tirur that day!'

Kunhikadar cleared his throat.

'I had driven the cart down to Tirur with Alijan Sahib's load on…' he inclined his head as he thought back and counted out on his fingers. On Tuesday. There was a big crowd by the theevandi office. They said Yakub Hasan Sahib was to arrive soon. I went in myself as I was curious. I saw him alight. His beewi was there too. They say she is from Turki. Ma'n Nair, Gopala Menon and all those Congress people were there to receive him.

'Is it true they arrested him?' Someone asked in hushed tones.

'Arrested,' the clueless Moidu blinked. 'Whatever for?'

'I heard the arrest took place directly as he got off the *theevandi*,' another Mapla shared his half-baked knowledge.

'No. No,' Kunhikadar the driver said. 'It didn't happen at the *theevandi* office. I was there, I tell you. Ma'n Nair and the others welcomed him with garlands and they went away in a motor car. To Tanur for the big yogam, people were saying.'

'And the Tanur yogam was cancelled, can you believe it!'

In another huddle in the *palli's* front yard, Mammali was passing on the information not many were privy to. Mammali knew someone who worked in the house of a big Nair honcho in Manjeri and got it directly from him.

'My friend Kunjan said that his employer got a *kambi* on Tuesday evening,' he said. 'It seems the Collector

Sayippe had ordered that the yogam was not to be held. Thousands of people had already gathered, Kunjan said there were nearly twenty thousand there, to hear Yakub Hasan speak. They all had to return like the dog who went to the market place.' Mammali's mouth twisted in ire as he made the comparison.

'Allah! How disappointing,' his listeners pictured the let-down masses having to return without realising their dream of hearing Yakub Hasan speak.

'How did they react?' The small crowd around him enquired anxiously.

'Can't say. Not as strongly as they could have, I suppose. Kuttikrishna Menon mentioned to Kunjan that those Congress-kar Ma'n Nair and Gopala Menon somehow managed to pacify the crowd and send them home.'

'The spineless fools,' fumed one young Khilafat worker called Umar.

'True. I have always said that joining hands with the Congress-kar will only hinder the Khilafat cause.' Aboobacker was a purist of sorts. He believed that Khilafat activities should be confined to the followers of Islam and that the Independence struggle was a different matter altogether. The two should not be mixed.

'It is this Kandi, by Allah! Putting all this nonsense about peaceful resistance and such rubbish into people's heads. Don't understand how that is possible,' said the hot-headed Umar.

'Yes, Kandi. Bloody Kafir. So also these other

Congress-kar. Kafirs all of them.' His group of cronies agreed.

'You can't say they are all like that. Don't forget Shekharan Nair. He has always been on our side,' said Alikutti in all fairness.

'Quite right,' another middle-aged Mapla was quick to second. 'Shekharan Nair has been my *changathi* since my childhood days. I remember he used to get into trouble at home for wearing a *kalli mundu* and playing with us Mapla boys.'

'Oh yes. Shekharan Nair is different. Passed all those big vakil exams and after all that started practicing in Perinthalmanna. So many tenure evictions he has fought for us poor Mapla *pattakkars*,' said his neighbor and good friend.

'Well, he is Kafir all the same,' one of Umar's gang insisted.

'So are Ma'n Nair and the other fellows. I still feel strongly that they were wrong to stop the crowd at Tanur,' young Umar seethed.

Under a massive jack tree in the *palli's* backyard, Mammad formed a threesome with his closest friends, Alavikutti and Basheer. They were talking quietly by themselves, preferring to stay away from the buzzing crowds. Basheer had a lot of firsthand information about the Yakub Hasan affair. After all he had been Alijan's own handpicked representative at Kozhikode. A quiet serious man not unlike Mammad himself, Basheer had an inborn poise and always came off well in the company of high born and educated people. As Alijan's lieutenant, he had been in touch with the top Congress leaders in Kozhikode. Honest as he was the information he had brought to Pookottur with him was absolutely authentic.

'Yakub Hasan Sahib along with Madhavan Nair and Gopala Menon had long, serious discussions after the Tanur yogam was annulled,' Basheer told his companions. 'In general they talked about the orders passed by the Collector Sayippe and in specific about what was to be done regarding the yogams planned in Kozhikode. There were supposed to be two on Wednesday. One was at the Jubilee Town Hall for the Congress-Khilafat Committee members. Entry by tickets only. The other was to be a public affair on the beach.'

'Did the order say they were both to be cancelled,' asked Mammad.

'So it appears. The leaders had first assumed that it was only the beach yogam, but later they realised they were wrong. Town Hall meeting was not to be held either.'

'The leaders were in two minds. On the one hand the crowd needed to be pacified. For this the meeting had to go through. On the other, there was this crucial issue. If a national leader disobeyed the order and went on with the meeting, what message would that convey to the public?'

'Well, by majority opinion it was decided that Yakub Hasan Sahib would talk on the beach. What he had to say to the public should reach them. That was the very purpose of his visit. They sent off *kambis* to the newspaper offices and Khilafat committees drummed out the information in different parts of the taluk. I think it was a good decision,' said Basheer. The admiration was evident in his voice. 'The importance of a peaceful approach must be instilled in the minds of the people.'

'Why, yes. It must. By Allah, it must.' A soft chortle interrupted them. Alijan Sahib ambled into their midst. He tried to throw an arm around Basheer's shoulders but the young man was too tall for the posture to be comfortable and Alijan settled on encircling his waist affectionately.

'Ah Sahibe! Basheer was just telling us what happened that day at Kozhikode.'

'I have already given him a proper report, Mammade,' said Basheer. 'And by the way, Sahibe, I forgot to tell you, Lava kutti was there to represent Ali Musaliar.'

If Alijan Sahib winced a little at the mention of Ali Musaliar, he was quick to straighten his face before his three young companions noticed his discomfiture.

'I met him at the house where Yakub Hasan was staying. You know, we were there for the cancelled Jubilee Hall meeting. The change of venue was sudden. When they received the orders calling it off, it was quickly shifted to the residence and was to be held as a more private affair. All of us, the Congress-Khilafat workers were asked to gather there before noon. Lava kutti and I talked a bit. He was saying how much the Musaliar appreciated the work these leaders were doing to get the right message through. And to appease the people. The

Musaliar thinks Madhavan Nair is a gem of a man. It is sad some people view him as a mere Kafir and close their eyes to all the good work he is doing. And Ali Musaliar is never wrong. Is that not so, Sahibe?'

'Certainly,' agreed Alijan and hastily changed the subject. 'Go on, Basheere. Tell Mammad and Alavikutti about the arrest.' He sauntered off, leaving them to it.

'As I was saying, we were all there, waiting for the meeting to commence when Amu Sahib, the Deputy Superintendent and Inspector Kidavu swooped down. They had with them warrants for the arrest of Yakub Hasan, Madhavan Nair, Gopala Menon and Moideen Koya. Truly speaking, it sent us reeling. As if an earthquake had struck. But the leaders were brilliant. Especially Madhavan Nair. They repeatedly told the people gathered there not to react. No violence should ensue as a result of this arrest, they insisted. So just one or two people went with them to court. In fact many in the city didn't even know about the questioning.'

'And what happened at court?'

'The Magistrate was there. And the Police Chief, Hitchcock Sayippe. What I heard was that after reading out the charge, the Magistrate asked them if they were planning to disobey orders. Yakub Hasan answered that what he intended to do was to merely talk to the crowd and impress upon it the importance of Non-Violence. Give that assurance in writing, said Thomas. Our word is our assurance, replied Yakub Hasan and Madhavan Nair. A security sum was demanded. Their reply was a definite 'no'. They were given an hour to think it over. 'No,' they said again. Then came the arrest, I was told.'

'Kannur jail?'

Basheer nodded. 'That evening they were held in Kozhikode. A large crowd had assembled at the *theevandi* office the next day. But Thomas acted cunningly. He drove the prisoners to the small station of Elathur and boarded the train from there. You can imagine how furious everyone was.'

The Adhikari of Valluvambram was frowning, Alijan noticed.

And the frown reflected the path his thoughts were taking.

This Khilafat business was going too far. It was disrupting the comfortable life he had created for himself by remaining in the good books of those in power. He couldn't care less for this *pahayan*, Yakub Hasan everyone was harping about.

'Can't understand what all the fuss is about. Is there nothing else to talk about? All this Khilafat nonsense is so vexing,' he grumbled, picking the gap in his yellowing teeth with a twig.

'Just when we wanted to make plans for the Nercha,' said his beak nosed sidekick.

'Yes,' another member of the Adhikari's clique agreed. 'I especially wanted to get the troupe together to rehearse the *muttumviliyum*.'

'That reminds me, Ahmed kutti,' Alijan Sahib chose that moment to wander in and address the Adhikari. 'It has been suggested that all festivities be cancelled. This year, the Nercha will be a quiet affair with just the basic rituals.'

'What!'

'I am not sure I heard you right, Sahibe. What did you just say?'

'Mammad, Ahmed kutti seems to be having trouble understanding me. Would you explain about the Pullara Nercha,' Alijan called out in a mocking tone.

'As the arrest of Yakub Hasan Sahib is a big blow to the Khilafat cause, we are calling off celebrations this year. Meaning there will be no *muttumvilium* at Pullara.' Mammad's manner was equally sarcastic.

Mammad's presence always made the Adhikari see red. Being a man who constantly cosied, up to bigwigs, he would not have disagreed with Alijan Sahib to his face but this was Mammad and he didn't think twice.

'No *muttumviliyum*!' He all but squawked. Then he turned to his companions. 'No muttumviliyum,' he says. All three snickered.

'Listen,' Ahmed Adhikari turned to Mammad. 'Whatever you deranged lot may say, there will be no niggardliness in the festivities. I will see to it myself. It will be as grand as always.'

Had it not been for the arrest, the young kundans of Pookkottur and nearby amsams would certainly have been the hottest topic of discussion at the palli that Friday. Though the worshippers gathered at the Palakkal mosque, with the latest events buzzing in their ears, had not had the leisure to figure things out properly, many of them had observed strange goings on.

'By the way, did you hear?' One Mapla tried to grab the attention of the man standing next to him by jabbing his am with a knobby forefinger.

'That boy Sayyed has disappeared, it seems'.

'Who's Sayyed?'

The Mapla clicked his tongue. 'That Kunjimoideen's son. Kunjimoideen of Valiya Parambil.'

'Ah! Yes. I know Kunjimoideen. What do you mean his son has disappeared?'

Apparently Sayyed of Valiya Parambil was not the only kundan to vanish without a trace. Amidst all the Khilafat talk, more than twelve such cases were mentioned in passing at the palli that day.

Ali Mohammed's son Beerankutti had not been seen for a month.

A lad called Mustafa was missing.

Kochappu, Palikkal Pokkar's youngest.

Somebody's seventeen-year-old brother-in-law.

A pair of twins.

Several others in the Tuvvur-Karuvaramkund belt.

Unmistakably the masked fellows in black had appeared with money and goats at all these *kudis*.

But these disappearances merited but fleeting attention that Friday.

In The Pullamkode Valley

20 February

Kerala Estates, Pullamkode
Winifred

Her breath cast fluffy white ringlets as she panted after her husband. Bob, Barker and Bruno ran ahead, stopping to sniff at the bushes or lift a hind leg and let out a proprietary stream in the spot of their choice. Stanley Pat marched steadily, swinging his arms with gusto and brandishing his stout and polished walking stick. Winifred Eaton had spent her childhood all over the dry, dusty plains of North and Central India and the bracing air here in the valley had come as a pleasant surprise.

She enjoyed these morning walks with Stanley Pat and the dogs.

The rhythmic crack of the whip was punctuated with cries of Ayyo! Ayyo!

'Get on with it, Koya,' said Stanley Pat briskly without even slowing down at the sight of a man being flogged mercilessly. Koya the overseer swung his weapon with renewed force. 'The bastard is lazy,' Stanley Pat threw over his shoulder. 'We don't pay him good money to slack.'

'Really, Stanley Pat, must you do this?' Winifred cringed at the poor labourer's yowls of pain.

'Don't you worry your pretty head over it, love. I've told you; these fellows expect it. Acts as a fuel, it does. Helps them work better.'

This was the umpteenth time the topic had come up. When Winifred married Stanley Patrick Eaton and came to live in the Kerala Estates, it hadn't taken her long to realise how badly her husband treated his employees. She couldn't bear it but Stanley Pat simply brushed aside her protests.

Winifred found her husband a difficult man to fathom. Stanley Pat ran the estates with an iron hand. No slacker was spared. During the evenings, however, tired out after a hard day's work and mellowed by the drink at his elbow, he seemed no more than a fireside tabby. With his friends, like Colebrook and Brown for instance, he was rough and jolly in that typically boisterous fashion with much backslapping and trading of insults. Brave and fearless, thought Winifred affectionately, and a little bull headed too.

'You never got around to tell me about Mancherry', she said, thinking it best to change the subject. 'Why did

Mr Thomas wish to see you?'

Eaton had just returned from Mancherry last night where he had a meeting with Mr Thomas, the District Collector and Mr Hitchcock, the Police Superintendent, who happened to be in Ernad.

'To warn us. Something ugly looming over the whole of Malabar and he thinks Ernad is the hub of it all'.

'What was he talking about?'

'Some kind of unrest among the Moplahs. Mostly religious fanaticism, he thinks. They are turning strongly anti-British these days. Plain hotheadedness. But they are a dangerous lot. What with all these Khilafat issues to boot.'

She had been afraid of this. Winifred, as the daughter of a senior officer in the British Army, had been around a lot. She had met people and was aware of what was happening in the world. She had read about the situation in Turkey after the war. There was increasing support among Indian Moslems for the cause. They had this deep-rooted devotion for the Caliphate. During the war they had supported the British. Then Thrace and Anatolia were wrested from Turkey and distributed among European powers. Now in India Moslems renounced titles, resigned from government jobs and students boycotted classes. It was not an easy situation. To be frank, she hadn't expected it to extend to Malabar where most of the Moplahs were illiterate and poorly informed. And if it did… well, the Moplahs of Ernad were not like the Ali Brothers or Maulana Abul Kalam

Azad and the rest of the sophisticated lot.

Yes. Mr Thomas was right. They were a dangerous lot. And if provoked?

One of the dogs growled. He had seen something among the bushes.

'Barker, heel!' Stanley Pat called sharply.

There was a crackle of dry leaves as the tribal girl called Cheenkanni nearly jumped out of the bushes and out of her own skin. Winifred smiled at her. Ever since her arrival at the Kerala Estates, she had tried to befriend this pretty forest girl who did some cleaning jobs in the Bungalow. She learnt that the lass's name meant 'crocodile' and Winifred had been surprised. Who would give such a lovely girl such a name? There was nothing crocodile-like about her. Her skin was the colour of rich coffee with cream carefully stirred in and her eyes black and bright and shapely as a doe's. For some reason, Cheenkanni had resisted Winifred's friendly overtures and slipped away as fast as she could, a penitent expression always clouding her features. Some misguided fear the poor locals had for the whites, she supposed. Considering Stanley Pat's ways, not surprising either. 'Win, my love, why don't you finish your walk at leisure? I must hasten. There is something I need to do before breakfast,' suggested Stanley Pat and quickened his pace.

Winifred's mind alternated between two plans for the rest of the ramble. How to win Cheenkanni over and how to find out more about the real situation with the Moplahs.

Cheenkanni

The Sayippe's dogs scared Cheenkanni. It seemed to her that they knew how bad she was. They growled and barked and wasted no opportunity to pounce on her. One of them had even chased her around the Bungalow the other day, till she had been ready to drop. And she would have had the Madama not stopped the dog. If even the dogs knew what kind of a girl she was, people would too. What if the Madama finds out? Cheenkanni could not bear to look at her mistress's face. All the more so after what happened yesterday.

How her heart had thudded as she followed the overseer into the building at the bottom of the hill! She had never been in there before. It was always one of the bungalows she was summoned to. Even secluded spots behind bushes. She had no idea whose house this was. Her mother had done odd jobs at the Estate Bungalow when she was a child, just as she herself did now and Cheenkanni knew almost every foot of the Estate, but this house she had only seen from afar. It was not as big as the Bungalow where the family resided. But the compound walls were high and clusters of trees kept the building obstructed the view of passersby.

They entered by the side door of course. No tribal girl would be allowed in by the proper entrance. For that matter, she doubted if even the overseer went into the Sayippes' houses through the front. Once inside, Cheenkanni found herself shivering though it was a lot warmer in here than among the trees. They reached a doorway made of wood and glass, guarded by a man in a grand white, red and gold costume. His mustache hid most of his face but the suggestive look in his eyes and the snigger were evident. Koya, the overseer gave a silly little giggle before slinking in, leaving her outside the now wide open door. Her heart began to hammer painfully against her chest and her shiny brown skin flushed in anger, shame and self-disgust.

At the corner table of what was actually the club house dining hall, Stanley Pat Eaton leaned behind in his chair, his long legs stretched out in front as he slowly rolled the stem of the glass in his hand. His back was to the door.

Cheenkanni flinched and moved away from the door. She could hear the conversation going on within though she understood nothing of it.

Colebrook sat opposite Eaton and he grinned as the door opened.

'Well, well, Eaton, I reckon the spicy curry you ordered is just being served.'

Eaton took a sip of his drink without turning back.

'What say you, Colebrook? And you Brownie? Dish look appetising?'

'Delectable,' leered Brown, craning his neck for a proper view.

'I myself am all for sampling local flavours every now and then,' said Colebrook enthusiastically.

'Ha ha. As long as you don't burn your tongue on them. Nothing like our bland English fare, I warn you.'

'Then you'd better lay off, Brownie. Dyspeptic aren't you?'

'Indigestion or no indigestion, I am not passing up,' growled Brown. 'I must congratulate you, Eaton. You do come up with the choicest, most indigenous items on your menu.'

'And nice of you to invite us to dinner,' laughed Colebrook.

There were guffaws all round and Eaton put on a 'least-I-can-do' expression to go with an exaggerated shrug.

Cheenkanni clutched the end of her coarse cotton *chelai* and shifted from one foot to the other as the overseer walked towards the Sayippes' table. She hated herself more than ever when the other two Sayippes looked her over from head to foot, mocking and lascivious at the same time.

Eaton barked instructions at Koya in crisp business like tones as if he were giving him directions concerning the running the Estate. He nodded towards Cheenkanni and pointed his chin at he stairway. Nothing about the planter's manner suggested that the was arranging for his friends to have their turn with the tribal lass he himself sampled from time to time. Cheenkanni simply stared at the polished hardwood floors wishing they would open up and swallow her.

'Penne, come on,' Koya slipped out of the dining hall and attempted to grasp her elbow but Cheenkanni kept her arm out of his reach. 'All those tiger and elephant gods of yours must be really pleased with you. Or else how would you get so lucky? First it was just Eaton Sayippe. Now the others seem to want you as well. What they see in you, I fail to understand though,' the overseer wrinkled his nose. 'You are nothing but a smelly little chit, if you ask me. And they are so generous too. They are going to pay you a lot of money.'

Once they were upstairs, Koya held a door open and gestured for her to step in.

'So this is how you manage to buy all the medicine that sickly brat needs. Go inside,' he urged. 'I am to wait outside till the Sayippes are done with you,' he turned away tittering.

When he was gone, Cheenkanni backed into a corner and wrung her *chelai* ends harder. When the overseer mentioned Muthu, a small forest fire raged within her chest. Her poor little brother. The human being she cared for most in the world. When Muthu was born, no one believed he would survive more than a few days. She remembered the tiny blue baby who didn't even cry at birth. The *othachi* attending to her mother had smacked him on the bottom again and again till a faint mewl was heard and the baby lived. Several monsoons had come and gone. The boy was nearly ten years old now and he still spent every minute fighting death. She pictured him lying on the palmyra mat she had woven herself, by the hearth in the *alai* that they shared with several of their kinsmen. Usually boys his age slept around a small fire built outside the *alai* but Muthu was too sick to spend the night outdoors. Some of the elders in their clan had tried to get him shifted out with the other boys pointing out norms and traditions but Cheenkanni had tucked the ends of her *chelai* firmly around her waist, planted her hands on her hips and yelled till she was hoarse. Her black eyes flashed, her nose reddened and the elders backed down. Muthu, she remembered, had giggled uncontrollably and she was alarmed that it would set off a bout of coughs. He spent most of his time coughing as it is. Sometimes it was so bad that it seemed his skinny little chest would burst open. When he wasn't coughing, he would be gasping for breath. Cheenkanni hated leaving Muthu in the *alai* when she came to the Estate after their mother's death. But they needed the money. Eaton Sahib was generous if nothing else and it was even better after the Madama came.

The healer in their tribe was a greedy man. These days he was not satisfied with the wild fowl, rabbits and civet cats Cheenkanni and her father hunted for him. He had begun to demand cash each time he replenished Muthu's stock of potions.

Cheenkanni built an armour of hard iron around her heart, offered a silent prayer to the forest deities and took a deep breath as footsteps sounded on the wooden staircase.

Later in the evening she had scrubbed herself at the stream near her alai till she thought her skin would come off. This morning before setting out for her duties in the Bungalow, she had taken another bath smearing herself with a paste she prepared out of herbs and flowers she gathered in the woods and Muthu had teased her about being obsessed with her beauty care. Did she have a beau?

It was clear those dogs hadn't liked the scent of the herbs from the way they had growled. Now the Sayippe had left the Madama to continue with her walk alone and gone ahead. Cheenkanni knew what that meant. She would be expected to present herself at the outhouse before starting her work at the Bungalow. Nausea rose in her throat.

Winifred

Winifred sat back in her chair with a satisfied sigh. When Stanley Pat had come in for a hurried breakfast and rushed off to the office, she had immediately made for her writing desk. The desk was her favourite piece of furniture. Soon after she had arrived her in Pullamkode as a new bride, she had had it made from the choice Nilambur teak after a pattern she designed herself. Stanley Pat was so indulgent in such matters. He loved giving her whatever she wanted. Her gaze swung to the lovely little ornaments on the top of the desk. Five in all. Exquisitely carved wooden animals, all small enough to fit in the palm of her hand. A little elephant, holding its trunk up as if it were trumpeting, with curved tusks exposed underneath. Polished so dark that it looked almost black and the tusks a creamy white. There was a graceful deer, a small tiger ready to pounce and a pair of gorgeous peacocks with an intricately carved pattern of feathers in their tails which swooped downwards, one towards the right and the other the left. The two birds sat on either end of her desk. These beautiful pieces were a source of great pleasure to Winifred and a mystery as well for she had no clue where they came from.

21/2/21
Kerala Estates
Pullamkode
Nilambur Valley
Dear Jack Horner,
Surprise! Surprise! Surprise! And a thousand apologies. The expression of regret, of course is for the break in communication. A few discreet enquiries tell me that you have fled the heat waves of Madras and are back in your homestead deep in down in the verdurous abyss of southernmost India. Surprise one, two and three are because, my dear Jack, so is yours truly. In the same abyss I mean. Wondering why and how?
There is this trifle which I have neglected to inform you of. Your old friend Winifred Helen Cranwill is no more. No, don't start beating your chest just as yet, let me complete. And in her place stands Mrs Eaton of Kerala Estates, Pullamkode. And the consequence? I am practically living in your backyard give or take a few miles. Pullamkode is not really far from your little village is it?
The morning mist rising above the slopes

behind our Bungalow by itself makes living here worthwhile. There is green, green and nothing but green all around. When you once told me that the Hindoos believed your emerald land that emerged from the Arabian Sea one day when a powerful warrior-sage threw his plough into the waters, little did I expect so much beauty. This, Jack Horner, is truly the Country of the Gods. I suppose I have my husband to thank for the opportunity to live in this paradise.

And coming to my husband, I should be telling you a bit about him. A planter by profession and typical British male by nature. That should be it in a nutshell. But within the shell the nut is hard to crack. I am just back from a morning walk. I set off early with Bob, Barker, Bruno and Stanley Pat but ended up strolling on my own for a while towards the end and that gave me the space to think. By the way, if you are wondering which one of the four is my husband, it is the last and the rest have four legs and wagging tails.

Jack Horner, why do these planters think it is acceptable to beat the workers?

Stanley Pat thinks that lashes are good motivation. My otherwise pleasant morning ramble was quite spoilt by the sight of Koya, the overseer throng a poor skeletal fellow with a shaven head. Koya seemed to be having fun and Stanley Pat was actually egging him on. Did I walk down the aisle

with a callous, sadistic man?
No, no. this will not do. No good English lady wears her heart upon her sleeve. So we will just leave Stanley Pat be for now.
Tell me what you have been up to.
It was from dear Mrs Besant's letter to Mother (who is living with me at Kerala Estates for a few months while Daddy is in the Sunderbans) that I came to know of your return to your home state. And your job? Do you plan to return to it anytime soon? I hope your people are doing well. And your little talking bird of a sister you have told me so much about? How I wish I could meet her. Kerala Estates is quite jolly in terms of beauty but I do get lonely sometimes with not a kindred spirit in sight. I am afraid I will have to pause for a while and resume the letter another time, for there is something outside the window which demands my attention.

Winifred had known Jack Horner for a few years and if there was a friendship she enjoyed, it was with him. They had met in Madras where Daddy had been stationed. Their family had become close to Mrs B because both Daddy and Mother had unconventional views on religion and were friendly with Madam Blavatsky. Along with Mrs B, they were actively involved in the Theosophical Society in Adayar. Mrs B had several clever, young protégés whom she groomed into brilliant writers and orators committed to the National Cause and Winifred met many of them at meetings and classes. Some of them taught at Panchama schools with her. One of these young men, a pleasant South Indian about her own age accompanied Mrs B to the Cranwills' place for dinner one night. They had talked about school and politics. When the meal was served, Winifred found him frown suspiciously at a slice of pie and realising that he still unused to European food, teased,

'What are you contemplating? Putting in your thumb to pull out a plum?' She had laughed merrily at his puzzled expression. He had never heard the rhyme before and she had ended up telling him about Little Jack Horner and the moniker had stuck. During the middle years of the war, Winifred had been really close to Jack. Apart from school, they spent several hours a week helping Mrs B with her correspondence and typing of manuscripts. A month in Bombay in 1916 had cemented their bond further and warm, light hearted camaraderie had developed and continued till Daddy's transfer to the North and Mrs B's internment. Even then they had faithfully corresponded every week. Then Jack left for England and letters became few and far between and she had lost touch with him. It was when Mother read out Mrs B's letter where she mentioned that her old protégé was back in his home state Malabar that Winifred remembered they hadn't been in touch for nearly two years now. She realised she missed Jack Horner. As if on cue, their old friend Mr Ramaer, who lived in Calicut these days paid Mother a visit when he was in Ernad last week for a meeting with the Nilambur nobles and he had given her Jack's address.

She placed the little carved elephant on her unfinished letter to serve as a paper weight and rushed out of the house. She looked around for Cheenkanni. Where was the girl? From her window, Winifred had seen her hurry by, her small frame rocking and tears streaming down her face. She suddenly entered a small clearing among the bushes and dropping down on her knees, began to retch. God! What was wrong with her? Was she ill? Winifred was determined to find out. Come to think of it the girl had looked wan these days. She had heard the cook take her to task for not being quick enough in her jobs. If she was really feeling bad, Dr Walker will have to see her, Winifred decided. Whether the doctor would be keen on treating a sick tribal, remained to be seen. And Stanley Pat? I'll worry about their reactions later, she thought. Let's find the girl first. But Winifred combed the entire area, calling out to Cheenkanni but the girl was nowhere to be seen. Frustrated she had sighed and returned to her desk. Somewhat half-heartedly she had gone back to her letter.

> *Now on a more serious note, Jack Horner, you must tell me what is going on in the district. There is a lot being said about these matters concerning the Khilafat. Mr Thomas was in Mancherry last week and Stanley Pat and the other planters of the Valley were required to meet with him. He appeared anguished and pessimistic, Stanley Pat*

said and I believe he warned the planters that there might be some bad business and ask them to be on their guard. Riots and mob violence are on the cards, he said. The British and the upper caste Hindoos were in danger.

I have been scanning the papers but the English ones from Madras do not give an accurate picture, just the one the British authorities wish to project. I wish for an authentic report, my friend. So send me a nice long letter.

Now, she read the letter through, right down to the end where she had signed off with an artistic squiggle.

Your friend,
Winifred Helen Eaton.

The Woes And Joys Of A Storyteller

Pookottur, Ernad
28 February

Sethu
Would it feel the same, wondered Sethu as she tried to relive the story? Yes, Sethu had actually lived the story of Ittichiri. Reveled in her small childhood pleasures, experienced her fears. Dreamt with Ittichiri and cried with her. The searing pain that the girl felt as a part of her anatomy was being torn off, had truly been her own…

But would Ittichiri's story be the same when she rewrote it? Worry gnawed at Sethu even as her pencil flew across the sheet of paper. But she had to do it. Do it before Ittichiri died within her.

Frustrating though it was to have lost her manuscript just when she had completed the story and been rather pleased with the outcome, she could not afford to lag or

Ittichiri would be lost forever. She could not allow that to happen to her beloved character. Sethu had been sitting in her cousin's library at the Pookottur manor leafing through it and adding a few finishing touches when something had come up and she had to rush downstairs, quickly putting the papers away. She hadn't had the chance to go back there that day and the next morning she saw that they had simply vanished. Sethu searched the manor thoroughly but to no avail.

Sethu had discovered the joy of writing less than a year ago when just for fun she had spun in her mind the story of a girl much like her favourite heroine Indulekha, and written it down one afternoon when she had nothing else to do. Thinking back, she knew the story hadn't been particularly good. She had been so impressed by Chandu Menon's story and his characters that she patterned hers too close to them. But she had so enjoyed writing it. There had been several stories since and she knew that they were getting better and better. She still wrote about women but her characters were getting more original, more genuine each time and they seemed to assume three dimensional proportions as her stories progressed, always developing minds of their own. They began to decide the course the plot would take. As Sethu read more her awareness of the world improved and her stories became more relevant. And it was Ittichiri who gave her the most pleasure and satisfaction.

Ittichiri the star-crossed girl.

Ange illathe Ittichiri

Omana pen kidavu...

Sethu wrote and was pleased that the ballad came to her word perfect as she tried to recollect what she had written in the original.

Ittichiri of yonder house
A darling girl was she...

It did not occur to Ittichiri's family to educate her so she could barely read and write but she was clever and only had to hear something once to learnt it. Nobody paid much attention to little girls at her Illam and she spent a happy but uncared for childhood, splashing in the pond, playing carefree games and dancing kaikottikali numbers till one day at the age of ten.

Fluffy rice and chethi flowers
Rained on her bowed head
Rallying arpoo calls echoed
And dainty feet stained red...

The dainty feet stained red had taken the first steps into the inner chambers of hell.

Back breaking work, insults, accusations and thrashings made up Ittichiri's married life. On rare nights when the planets were in a position favourable for the conception of a son, there were the wild, unsuccessful advances of her husband. Anger at his own incompetence led to slaps.

Sethu was surprised at how the story came back to her as if she had actually learnt it by rote. In fact in a more refined way as if it had evolved within her. Sethu realised that she had always known the story deep inside.

Priyamvada

'Sethu Thampatti', she addressed her cousin whose head was bent over her pencil, her lips pursed in concentration. 'Why don't you give it a break and do your hands before the paste dries up? What's it anyway? New story?'

'No,' replied Sethu. 'Remember, I told you I seem to have misplaced the Ittichiri one you liked. By the way, all you want to do these days is to do yourself up.'

'Actually I wanted to talk to her,' Sethu took a deep breath and put aside her work. 'Remember we ran into her on the road the day we came here? She was crying and Kadar stopped the cart. Something about her touched me.' Seeing Priya raise her brows, she added, 'If you must know, I thought her story would be interesting. But looks like that story will have to wait. I have this one to redo.'

'Aha,' laughed Priya. 'So that's one mystery solved. Well then see that the new story doesn't dry up like her special blend of mailanchi.' She deliberately returned to topping her nails.

'Maybe you should too,' said Sethu slyly. 'The secret ingredients they use are said to have certain properties. The resulting stain brighter and redder and I believe has the power to melt the hardest male heart.

'Can't be much use to you then. You haven't identified your dream prince yet, have you?'

Something flashed in Sethu's eyes for a fraction of a

second and Priya noticed her ears redden. But she lost no time in donning the veil of normalcy and picked up her pencil again.

Her thoughts moving to Sethu's stories, Priya chuckled to herself. Ever since her cousin had begun writing, Priya had been her sole reader. She would write them and put them away in her chest wrapped in those silk and velvet bags she sewed herself and the next time Priya was in Nilambur, Sethu would sit her down and make her read everything over and over again and ask her hundreds of questions.

'Do you think the course the plot takes is too tedious? Will it bore the reader?'

'Which character do you like best?'

'Should I have used a different word here?'

She would go on thus till she had exhausted herself.

Putting aside the fact that she could pen juicy and newsy letters, Priya hadn't written anything original in her life but growing up with her book lover brothers, she had always read a lot. When she introduced Sethu Thampatti to the pleasures of reading hitherto unknown to Kovilakam girls, she hadn't realised she had actually been creating a monster. That she would become a writer had been nowhere in her imagination. And a really good one too! She had seen her cousin's evolution in astonishment. Now this Ittichiri story that she was rewriting… when Priya had first read it, something had clutched at her heart. Sethu had brought it to Pookottur with her as she had just a paragraph or two to go. When she was done, she had actually pressed it upon her one-woman readership. Priya had held her breath till the very end and found it hard not to cry. She couldn't remember ever having read something so touching, so full of life.

'Readers? Which readers?' Priya would quip and tap her chest. 'There is but the one.'

Mithran Thampan's cousin on his father's side, a Namboothiri called Damodaran was visiting with a friend and Priya had gone down to the kitchen to supervise lunch. She liked to play the woman of the manor and dream of a time when the role would in reality be hers. Of course she didn't make it too obvious by going out to the dining area. She just remained in the inner part making sure the servants did a good job.

The two Thampans Mithran and Divakaran and the two visitors, Damodaran and his companion were all seated at their leaves and the cook's young helper served them hot rice from the bamboo basket. Priya stood in the inner kitchen watching the men eat.

The heap of rice on Damodaran's leaf was a veritable hillock. He was very particular about each course being served in the right order. Took everything in large quantities but seemed to have a preference for the sour, peppery yellow *kalan*. Divakaran was apparently too fond of the *kadumanga*. He ate little rice, most of which he downed in the fiery chilly and mustard sauce, the tender mangoes were pickled in. He liked to talk and laugh as he ate. Mithran, Priya observed fondly, ate neatly and quietly. He had moderate amounts of everything, kept his leaf neat by finishing everything put on it. His favourite part of the meal was the penultimate course of rice eaten with fresh curd. The fourth man's portions were bird like. The only thing that he seemed to relish was the small ladleful of the sweet payasam.

It was a journey to Trissur that the visitors were breaking here in Pookottur, Damodaran mentioned at lunch. They had business in the Mangalodayam press. It concerned some pamphlets and journals and the young friend, whose appearance seemed a little familiar to Priya, was speaking at a meeting. Damodaran was all praise for his oratorical skills. Priya learnt that they were involved in some reform activities within the Namboothiri committee.

'Though that's not the only thing *he* does,' laughed Mithran Thampan's cousin nodding towards his friend. 'His world is a lot bigger.'

Their conversation was interesting and a change from the current situation with the Maplas in Malabar, which was all men wanted to talk of these days. Sethu's story still lingering in her mind, Priya found herself warming to the subject of Namboothiri reform. Their activities were apparently more centered on modern education. Damodaran mentioned the Namboothiri School in Thrissur and the funding for poor children.

Mithran Thampan showed little interest and merely grunted as his cousin talked but Divakaran was keen and asked many questions.

Lunch done, Mithran had settled down on his favourite arm chair and was already reaching for his pouch of Imperial tobacco while Damodaran was in the process of carefully applying lime paste on his betel leaf. Divakaran was on his own armchair, his eyes gently shut, humming 'Ajitha Hare'.

The friend whose name she had not found out as yet, was ambling beneath the tamarind tree in an attempt to get his meagre lunch digested. Just what Priya wanted. To get the writer alone. Ensuring with a quick glance that no one was around, she slipped into the yard, clutching the roll she had hidden in her clothes. She cleared her throat and the man's brows arched into his slightly receding hairline. She thrust the roll into his hands.

Sethu

'Is there any tea, Paru?' Sethu walked into the kitchens and asked one of the kitchen helpers.

'Tea? Of course I can make some. With plenty of fresh milk.' Paru looked delighted at the request yet surprised. 'But the Thampatti does not have tea at this time of the day.'

'It is not for me. Just send it round to the back veranda for Beeran the cart driver and his son's wife.'

The cook's help nodded. Clearly, she wasn't as enthusiastic to cater to the driver and his family.

'And if there's anything good to eat, bring that over too. Maybe some of that appam we had for tea yesterday.'

Curious, thought Sethu that she should feel nervous

about talking to the young Mapla girl. Not exactly nervous. But decidedly awkward. Unlike Priya, she was not too good at conversing with strangers. But she had wanted to meet Beeran's young daughter-in-law. It was but a fleeting glance she had had of the girl's sad and lovely face beneath the *thattam* but it had been etched in her mind ever since. She wanted to know the girl behind the face. She could sense the beginnings of a story there. As a rule, Sethu usually built her plots and fashioned her characters purely from imagination. During the first few days of her stay here in the manor, a story had begun to surface and the protagonist had the face of the sobbing girl they had bumped into in the village. She had been so busy putting in the final touches to Ittichiri and did not bother to jot down those thoughts. But with one story complete and only Priya's reading and a few changes here and there, the new one centered on a Muslim girl, began to loom large. She realised that she knew so little about a Mapla girl's life that she could not write it with any real authenticity. She had to talk to the girl and get a closer look into her mind. That was when she had asked Beeran to bring her to the manor on the pretext of the *mailanchi*. Beeran had to go to Nilambur just then but he would be back soon and promised to bring the girl then.

But during that week Sethu had lost her manuscript and her first priority was to rewrite it. Ittichiri was someone she had known for over a month and begun to care deeply for. She had become more important than the newcomer who was still a hazy figure in her mind.

That she had invited the girl here was all but forgotten when she turned up with Beeran, waiting timidly on the back porch.

The girl had placed a banana leaf with the balled up paste of herbs on the stone ledge and Sethu sniffed appreciatively. 'It is really fragrant,' she smiled as she settled down on the ledge. 'What is your name?' She asked after a moment's hesitation.

'Razia,' the girl was barely audible.

'Why don't you sit down there, Razia?' It was not a practice in the Kovilakam for Thampattis to ask the servants or their families to sit down when they came in to show their faces but Sethu wished to talk to the girl for some time and she could not do it while she was on her feet all the time. Beeran gasped in surprise and Razia stared wide eyed.

'Mmm,' Sethu urged. 'And Beeran if there is any work you have to attend to you may go and do it. Come back for Razia in an hour or so.'

'Then I will go,' said Beeran making a hasty retreat and Razia sat down on the topmost step a little away from Sethu's feet.

Sethu smiled kindly at the girl. 'My grandmother told me you have visited her at the Kovilakam soon after your marriage to Beeran's son.'

Razia nodded. 'The Baliya Thampatti is very kind,' she spoke softly, her Mapla accent emphasizing itself in the way the consonant B replaced the V. 'She gifted me a beautiful wooden box for my clothes and things. And the bed for the house. I have never seen such things in my life.'

It was a relief to Sethu that though Razia was a timid little thing, she needed no urging to talk.

'And he says he is alive in this duniya because of her.'

There is more to life than a bed and a wooden chest, thought Sethu, smiling to herself. Or maybe it was Beeran's employment at the Kovilakam she was talking about, the family's source of *kanji* when this girl's husband was growing up. But Razia continued talking and Sethu's eyes widened in surprise.

'She saved his life when he was so small.' She indicated the height of her hips.

This was news to Sethu.

'How?'

But Razia shook her head. 'That he did not say. Does not talk much, my Mapla.'

'Well, everyone at the Kovilakam knows she has a soft corner for Beeran's son.' Sethu cast aside her disappointment at not getting that story. She wondered how she could get it out of her grandmother.

She let Razia talk, quite fascinated with the new world that took shape in Sethu's mind as she spoke of her childhood and marriage and her Mapla's seriousness in contrast with the loving *kalbe* hidden within. Of an elderly woman in the village called Benazir Beewi and her kindness and the old gossip who sold Pathiris.

As the pair departed, her concern mounted and Sethu went upstairs in search of her cousin. She found her sitting on the west facing ledge of the first floor veranda, gazing at the rolling paddy fields beyond.

'What are you doing here all alone, my friend?' she teased. Dreaming of a time when you are Mithrettan's Kettilamma and the mistress of this manor?'

'I wish there were a nice, big swing here,' said Priya looking up at the strong wooden beams laid below the roofing tiles. 'Just the right place for a swing. One could rock to one's heart's content, looking out at the fields and the hills beyond.'

'As a matter of fact a swing would be nice,' said Sethu frowning suspiciously. 'But I know this little Kettilamma is disturbed when she starts changing the subject in such a random fashion.'

Priya flushed. 'Sethu Thampatti…'

Sethu knew her friend well and what she heard in her voice now was a funny combination of contradictory emotions – pride and guilt.

'What is the matter?' Sethu was beginning to feel a little worried now. 'Was it something in that letter you had this morning? Was it from home? I hope everything is fine there.'

'It was not from home,' Priya answered in a low voice.

'Then?' This was getting serious. 'Who was it from?'

'Er… You remember that man who was here with Damodaran Namboothiri last week?'

'Yes.'

'Well, the letter was from him.'

'Why would he be writing to you?'

Why was he writing to Priya?

He was a young man yes. But had it been a proposal, he wouldn't be writing personally to her, the correspondence would have been between families.

'Sethu Thampatti,' there was caution and a hint of doubt in Priya's tone. 'You mustn't be angry with me. I am your closest friend aren't I?'

Sethu simply waited for her cousin to come to the point.

'I am afraid I took the liberty… no I do believe I had the right…'

Sethu began to doubt her own patience.

'For more than a year I have been your only reader, critic and advisor,' Priya assumed a dignified pose to hide her embarrassment. 'I thought it was time I did something about it. I saw the opportunity and grabbed it. Forgive me if I did wrong. It was I who took your Ittichiri story and gave it to that man.'

'G…gave it to him! But why?'

'He is a writer. With connections in lots of magazines. I overheard them talk at lunch. They were saying he was now working on a series of essays on reform among Namboothiris. Especially widow remarriage and women's education. I thought he was the right person to show your story to.'

Sethu felt her head swim.

'And?'

'He took it with him, promising to read it. I got a reply today saying that if the writer has no objections, it would appear in next month's issue of a magazine he edits.' Priya spoke so fast that she was out of breath by the time it was out. She panted and looked Sethu straight in the eye, her expression part nervous and part challenging.

Not trusting her legs, Sethu sat down on the stone ledge. Clutching Priya's wrist, she pulled her down beside her. She had never been one to express her thoughts in an animated fashion but the slight tremble of her hand and small, shy smile might have given her away and Priya squeezed back with a grin of delight.

After their evening wash and prayers, Priya produced the letter and handed it to Sethu.

'The letter is actually for you. There was just a covering note for me, as I was the instrument who brought it about,' now confident that Sethu was happy about it, she was all smiles.

Sethu's hand shivered as she shook the letter out of its envelope.

> *Dear writer,*
>
> *I have read your story 'Ittichiri' not once but several times since your friend saw fit to hand it over to me. There may be people who think that as an editor I should not be raving about a submission to the writer herself, but I do not think it beneath me to honestly appreciate a good piece of writing when I read one. Clearly your story is one of the best short fiction works I have seen. As it is in perfect synchrony with the theme of our next issue of 'Young Namboothiri', I wish to put your story*

in it, with your consent of course. (I happen to know that your friend gave me the story without your knowledge).
I also write for a few other publications which may be interested in printing your stories in the future. Please send me a written letter of consent. Please feel free to choose a pen name if you so wish.

The Editor
Young Namboothiri
PS
I was absolutely delighted with the way you ended your story. It was so unexpected and so refreshing that if I, as an editor had any doubts about printing it (which I did not), it would definitely have made up my mind for me.

'Well, I had Umedathi to thank for that last twist,' Sethu smiled at Priya.

'Yes, thank the snobbish Uma Devi Thampatti who is the bane of your life. Not me who went to these extents for you.'

Sethu laughed and smacked her with the rolled up letter.

'It is true. I would not have come up with such an ending but for her. I was at the stage in the story where after the sudden death of her husband, Ittichiri had one tormentor less. For ten years she lived in the dark kitchens of the *illam* doing all the menial tasks her senior co-wives set her. It was from there that her rescuer, the young man who wished to set an example to the entire community by marrying a widow, would take her away. It was to be the first widow remarriage in the history of Namboothiris. That was how my story had ended. Why, I couldn't say, but I hated it. It was a positive ending. A significant one. But it didn't seem right. I racked my brains over it for days but couldn't think of anything. I was so unhappy that I actually cast the whole thing aside. Ittichiri became a stranger to me, an embarrassing stranger. It was as if I didn't want a thing to do with her anymore. I had all but killed the story. One day as I didn't write anymore I had nothing else to do but sit around in the *nalukettu* listening to the cousins' banter. As usual they turned to their favourite pastime – Sethu baiting.'

Why didn't that last proposal work out?

Did I say no or did Ammamma?

No one good enough for the Matriarch's favourite princess.

Little Lakshmikutti at fourteen has already missed her monthly cycle.

Why, Sethu, what are your intentions? Do tell us. If you keep shooing away every man who comes your way, what do you intend to do with your life? This came from Umedathi.

For a moment I lost myself.

There is a lot I intend to with my life, I retorted sarcastically. Unlike some I do not think that marriage is a woman's ultimate goal. I plan to use my god given abilities for some purpose. So that the world can benefit from them. Marriage will come when the right man comes. Not till then.

That was when I realised that Ittichiri felt the same. I rushed to the chest where I had shoved the papers right beneath the mundus as I had had no desire to see Ittichiri for a long, long time. And then I crafted the end of the story wherein she politely refuses the heroic revolutionary's proposal and requests him to send her to school instead.

This was the day before we started for Pookkottur.

Back Home In Nilambur

Nilambur, Ernad
10 March
Mathu

There was no reason for the Matriarch to expect anything unusual when her late nephew's wife requested an audience. Though her *tharawad* was in a village in western Valluvanad, a few miles south of Manjeri, her husband had had a bungalow built just outside the Kovilakam premises where the family stayed on their frequent trips to Nilambur. Even after his passing, she and her children came often and it was not uncommon for her to drop in at Mathu's quarters to pay her respects.

'Entha Thankam?'

The Matriarch acknowledged her visitor and sat down on her favourite straight backed chair with ivory inlay. True to her name, Thankam was bedecked in pure gold from her earlobes with their large spherical studs to her fingers each gleaming with a sparkling ring or two. Mathu indicated a seat opposite her.

Thankam of course did not sit down. She stood before the Matriarch with her hands crossed over her chest in a most reverential posture. This was one of the richest women in Malabar but looking at her gushing subservience one would think she was one of the lowliest of maids in the whole retinue. She liked Thankam well enough but Mathu Thampatti was quite impatient with all this unnecessary servility and preferred the cheeky impertinence of this woman's daughter, the vivacious Priyamvada.

'Thampatti, it is about Priyamvada,' Thankam said as if on cue. The Matriarch nodded for her to go on.

'I really don't know what to do about her.'

'Why?'

'About finding a suitable groom…'

'I would have thought princes and Namboothiri landlords were falling over each other hoping to win her hand.'

'Er… actually there are a few proposals but… but it is the girl herself…'

When the Matriarch raised her brow. Thankam continued with some hesitation. 'I don't know how to say this, Mathu Thampatti, lest you may think my child to be quite brazen. But she seems to have set her heart on someone.'

The Matriarch was not surprised. Priyamvada had

always had a mind of her own. Just like Sethu.

'And who is this paragon, Thankam whom my nephew's lovely daughter desires?' she chuckled loudly.

'That…' Thankam faltered again and mustering up courage, it burst out of her. 'It is… it is Mithran Thampan.'

The laugh froze on the Matriarch's face and for once, she lost her footing.

'Mi…Mi…Mithran!'

'I tried to dissuade her, Thampatti. *Satyam*. But she is adamant. She is my only girl. I do want her to be happy. And the Sixth Tirumulpad *is* her father's nephew. There is nothing technically wrong…'

A flurry of thoughts crowded the Matriarch's mind. Mithran, inspite of all their recent differences was someone she held close to her heart. He was a fine looking man and from her own angle youngish, at thirty-six. But… she would never have dreamt that someone as youthful and vibrant as Priyamvada would see him in that light. The way he carried himself was not unlike Sriraman, the tusker. Being in charge of Pookkottur had given him that extra bit of mature, masculine confidence that would appeal to someone like Priya.

Then it dawned on her that this could indeed be a blessing. Exactly what she would have wanted for Mithran now. A lovely new wife. A distraction from the rapidly heaving Mapla issues. Something to keep him safe.

The Matriarch was not one to waste time once she had decided.

'I will write to him at once, Thankam. Mithran shall give cloth to your Priyamvada without further ado.'

Thankam had not expected this to be so easy.

'I wish to talk to your daughter. Send her over to me soon.'

'I will, Thampatti. And er… there is something else that puzzles me. It seems Priyamvada has been writing letters to her brothers and some other young men in our family, who she is quite friendly with, trying to find out whatever she can about a young writer. My sons haven't said anything to me, never do. But I do have ears. Their wives are talking and some cousins who visit often. Apparently this writer goes by the pen name 'The Outcaste'. Some of them who know nothing about Mithran Thampan, seem to think she is enamoured of this man. I know it is not the case. But who is he? What is my daughter's interest in him? I wonder…'

Sethu

Ever since her return from Pookkottur, Sethu had been increasingly uncomfortable. It wouldn't be long before Ammamma's elephant ears got wind of the new developments in her life and their little escapade. She did not fancy having to answer questions. The first few days had gone by fairly uneventfully. Then her time in the Dark Room had come. Yesterday she heard that her elderly cousin, Cheriyettan, the Second Tirumulpad was here. It wouldn't be long now, she knew. He would definitely give Ammamma a report of the episode in Manjeri and he was sure to have heard of the small, tentative step she had just taken into the world of literature from someone at Swami's place. So that would come out too.

Something told her Ammamma was not going to be displeased with her writing. She might even enjoy the stories. Sethu knew how much her grandmother liked being read to. But she surely would be shocked to hear that her granddaughter had been romping through the town and meeting strangers at the residence of a non-relative. But if she chose to admonish, Sethu would have to deal with it. There was no way to undo it all.

If she could undo it, would she choose to? No, no. Sethu mentally listed all her experiences of the month away from home one by one.

She had overcome the language barrier in her reading. Finished Ivanhoe and Jane Eyre and borrowed a couple by Dickens to bring home with her.

She had become a reasonably good hand at billiards.

Then she had completed Ittichiri quite satisfactorily and thanks to Priya realised the unlikely dream of seeing it in print.

Then… she felt the heat rise to her ears and felt a mild flutter in her chest.

She remembered the excitement she worked hard to hide as she opened that envelope which contained a copy of the issue containing her story. The elation on seeing it in print was still surging within her. She still couldn't stop smiling at the penname she had chosen in curved artistic letters beneath the title. *Indulekha.* The illustration was a sketch of a girl's profile, the torn earlobe dangling in the midst of wayward curls.

The envelope had contained a covering letter. It

thanked her for the story. Invited more. Included the address of another publication from Kozhikode, run by a woman, especially keen on stories and articles concerning women. The writer who simply signed off as the Editor and stated how timely the story had been as it perfectly complemented his own article on remarriage and education for widowed Antarjanams, which was the highlight of the issue. Sethu had read the article, found it interesting and enlightening not to mention surprised at how well it went with her story. It was the byline which set her heart thudding. *The Outcaste*. Priya who had been reading the letter over her shoulder gasped.

Another letter arrived in a few days. Several people were getting together at Rama Ayer's family homestead in Manjeri. Chinnamalu Amma, the lady who edited the magazine *Navayugam* would be there. She had read Ittichiri and was keen on meeting the writer.

After having spent a rather dreamy week leafing through the magazine, alternating between her own story and The Outcaste's article, Sethu had just shaken herself up. It was just as she was coming to terms with things that the new letter arrived. She had no intention of going of course. Granted it felt good to have her story recognised and appreciated but she knew her limitations as a Kovilakam girl. She was not about to let things go into her head.

But would Priya take 'no' for an answer? Not she. And Sethu had never been able to stand up to her cousin. Would she be here in Pookkottur, involved in all these unbelievable things if she had been able to stand her ground with Priya? Sethu gave in and was not ashamed to admit at least to herself that she was excited about it.

Then Priya had taken it all into her hands and begun organising in earnest. The outing had been interesting and obstacle free till the Second Tirumulpad's motor car one of the very few in South Malabar had come to majestic halt right in front of the cart as they were about to leave Swami's Madhom. He saw them as soon as he climbed out and stared unbelievingly for a second. Cheriyettan then looked Sethu up and down once again, taking in her unusual attire of a sari. His gaze then fixed on Priya and her brother Unni who was acting as their chaperone with a hint of a frown. Cheriyettan nodded towards the cart and said 'alright then'. Sethu wished the earth would open up and swallow her whole. Just as she did now at the thought of having to talk to her grandmother.

Mathu

Priyamvada wrung her palms together, embarrassment etched on her face in a most dramatic fashion as she waited anxiously for her to say something. Her own granddaughter's demeanour was quiet and dignified as usual. Only the slight trembling of her lips let on her discomfiture. The Matriarch knew the girls had been expecting her summons and dreading it. Now her piercing glare made them even more jittery.

'Just who do you girls think you are?' Her eyes narrowed into the smallest of slits.

'Forgotten that this is the Nilambur Kovilakam?' She turned her attention to Priyamvada. 'That it is not the practice here for young girls to pick their own grooms? I suppose you think you live in England!'

Priyamvada flushed at her sarcasm.

'You may be my nephew's daughter and one of the richest young women in Malabar, but remember you are nothing but a chit of a girl. And you think you will make the Sixth Tirumulpad a good wife?'

To the Matriarch's surprise the girl's answer was just as downright as her own question.

'Yes. I do.'

Involuntary she thought. But honest.

Mathu's eyes widened and her lips pursed in what she hoped seemed like silent ire but in reality was an attempt to suppress an amused burst of laughter. She gave the girl a contemptuous sneer and turned to Sethu.

'Ah. And our own little Thampatti,' she watched her granddaughter cringe. 'Romping around the countryside. That too in fancy-dress, alle?' Clad in a sari, the Second Tirumulpad had reported. What next, the Matriarch had wondered. Mathu had often looked at the chiffon garments teamed with blouses with ruffled sleeves that the new generation of Kovilakam women liked to don on special occasions. 'And visiting strange homes. Socialising with a cross section of the population. Evolved a lot during your stay away from home, eh?'

The two girls shivered slightly at the controlled sarcasm in her soft voice.

Though she was looking steadily at Sethu, the Matriarch from the corner of her eye saw the other girl make a face and mutter something under her breath. '*Anachevi Mathu*'. She heard quite distinctly and checked a smile in the nick of time.

'What was it at that Swami's residence that interested you, Sethu?'

Sethu crossed her palms across her chest in slow deliberation and though her head remained hung for a few seconds, she raised her chin and looked her grandmother straight in the eye.

'Ammamme,' she said quietly. 'I have no idea if you already know, but I like writing stories. I started just for fun. To kill time. I have been writing them for months now. The last one came out better than expected. It got published in the '*Young Namboothiri*.' She paused apparently for breath but the Matriarch guessed she was gauging her reaction. Well, she is not going to get that satisfaction. Mathu's look remained cold and stony. Neither encouraging nor admonishing. The child was forced to continue.

'Apparently, the editors and the readers liked it. Some such people were at Rama Ayer Swami's family home that day and I was invited to meet them. I was hesitant at first but I really wanted to go. It was a rare opportunity to meet some interesting people. Priya came with me and Unni was our chaperone. We were there for about three hours.'

The Matriarch suddenly felt a warmth engulf her

insides and after a minute or two recognised it as pride. Of course, none of what Sethu said was news to her. The Second Tirumulpad, whose grandmother had been one of her oldest female cousins of her own generation, was close to her and had told her everything he had heard from Rama Ayer and some others after Sethu and the other two had left. They were all really enthusiastic about her writing, he had learnt and wished she would write more stories. Several magazines were eager to publish them. He himself had made it a point to get hold of an issue of the *Young Namboothiri* and read it. Not bad. He had said. Coming from him, she knew it actually meant very good. The girl was talented. But it was more than that. She liked the forthright way she related the whole thing. Yes, she was slightly nervous, from the mild tremble in her voice, but there was no beating round the bush, no excuses, no lies. Yes she was proud of the person Sethu had become. She almost smiled but settled for a serious nod.

'And who were the interesting people you met?'

'There was Rama Ayer Swami, of course. Though he keeps dropping in here at the Kovilakam to meet some of the uncles, I've naturally not had the chance to talk to him. I have always been fascinated by the work of Mrs Besant in Madras. Swami is a devoted follower and so is his wife. They have a lot of friends who are her disciples. They talked a lot about the aborted Home Rule League and Mrs Besant's internment. Her educational activities and the Panchama free schools in Madras.'

Sethu, it appeared had become calmer and more confident. Suddenly she smiled a shade mischievously.

'And I listened. Listened hard with my ears pricked up. After all I am not your granddaughter for nothing.'

The Matriarch's laugh was quickly and conveniently converted into a cough.

'And the Madama of Pullangode Estate was there. She and her mother know Swami well. They are very good friends of Mrs Besant. I spoke to her. I needed an interpreter.'

'And you, Priyamvada?'

'Er…'

She caught the girl unawares by suddenly shifting her attention to her.

'Did you meet interesting people too?'

'Er… yes. I met the same people.'

'What about "The Outcaste?' Did you finally succeed in finding this man you seem so curious about?'

The two girls stared wide-eyed.

'And may I ask what it is about this writer that fascinates you so much? Don't tell me it is because you simply like his articles. If that had been the case you would have been satisfied with reading whatever paper he writes for. Why would you want to know his identity?'

Priya remained stubbornly silent. The Matriarch could read her mind. 'Where did the old lady learn these things?' She expected another mutter of *Anachevi Mathu.*

Mathu Thampatti was tiring. Keeping the sarcasm dripping was hard work. She raised an eyebrow. 'Am I to understand that in addition to the Sixth Tirumulpad you have lost your heart to this man as well? Prankish yes, wicked sometimes. But not fickle surely,' she taunted the girl. Her barbs were well aimed. Priyamvada seemed to be bursting with indignation and denial and when she thought the Matriarch wasn't looking, she gave her cousin a vicious glare. Sethu shrugged and turned away.

'I suppose you think I am blind not to notice all the Kathakali going on in front of my eyes. Well, if you do not wish to speak, I have my own ways of finding out.' She stroked her ears and Priya turned red. 'But if you do speak now, some time can be saved and I can get on with preparations for the Sixth Tirumulpad's upcoming wedding.' She pretended not to notice the smile breaking out on Priyamvada's face and locked gazes with Sethu.

'Did you girls decide to call on Rama Ayer at his house in the hope of meeting this writer?'

'Ammamme, you can let Priya off. It was I who was curious about this writer. She merely made enquiries of my behalf. And no we did not go there with the sole intention of meeting him. When I learnt that a lot of people had read my story and wished to see me, yes I was hesitant at first but my vanity got the better of me. Pardon me if did wrong Ammamme. I promise I will not repeat it.'

The Matriarch's heart melted.

'I will be happy if you abstain from such adventures in the future. But if you stop writing your stories on this pretext, I shall be very angry. You girls may leave now.'

Smiling, the two made for the inner chambers when Priyamvada stopped. 'I am thankful for being vindicated, Valiya Thampatti. In truth, I was merely playing Chitralekha.'

The Rise Of The Black Thangal

Ernad,
June '21

Halfway through the month of Edavam not only had the monsoons officially set in but the skies were nearly always dark and ominous and the cloudburst earnest. In strange accompaniment the emotional clime in all Ernad and the northern parts of Valluvanad had undergone an uncanny shift.

'Never ever venture out alone, *makkale*,' mothers warned their young children, their eyes large and fearful, their forefingers waggling. 'Never! Do you understand? The Black Brigands could strike anytime.'

'They will convert you into their faith. If you don't comply, one stab of the dagger and…' Nair boys shivered as their uncles mimed fiercely.

Rumours had it that they were everywhere, these

Black Brigands. Masked faces. Black waistcloths. Shaven heads. Mapla speech patterns. They moved in groups and pounced on likely victims at the most unexpected moments.

'*Pudikkeen*!'

'*Ketteen*!'

They would grab the hapless Hindu, bind him up at dagger point.

'*Kalla Kafire*!' They would hiss in insult if he protested.

The victims' families would never see them again. If their bodies in various stages of mutilation, usually with the necks severed, turned up somewhere it could be presumed that they had not unprotestingly submitted to having their heads shaven and their penises circumcised. That they had not obediently repeated verses read out to them. If they appeared to have simply vapourised, one could be sure that they had been too helpless to resist.

'But who are the Black Brigands?'

It was a question that niggled in the back of all their minds and when one fellow happened to voice it, the villagers gathered at the peepal tree platform outside the temple and looked at each other in a moment's silence.

'Self-proclaimed protectors of the faith,' one of them answered in muted tones. 'The lieutenants of the Black Thangal.'

'Who they are we do not know for they never show their faces. Their masks and black waistcloths are their badges.'

'Has anyone ever seen the Black Thangal?'

Someone claimed that he knew someone who was in turn acquainted with someone else who had. Or had there been yet another someone amidst?

'He wears a mask too. And flowing black robes. But I've heard he has a voice that is quiet and compassionate. Gentler than the silken breeze.'

The peepal tree group dispersed without lounging about much longer. These were not safe times. What with the Black Brigands and the suspicious police.

Palikkal Pokkar's third *beedar* rarely smiled these days. Her poor boy Kochappu. Where was he now? What was he doing? Was he missing his Umma?

'Shut the mushy nonsense, woman,' an impatient Pokkar would scold.

He had suddenly taken to donning white shirts, mundus and fancy turbans in place of his checkered lungis. Of late, the house was filled with the constant aroma of biryani wafting from the kitchen. Kochappu's umma could never bring herself to swallow more than a morsel of the fragrant rice.

'Not when you bartered our son in exchange for all this.' Love for her boy foddered a sudden bout of courage.

'Shut up, will you,' Pokkar rose menacingly.

'*Nte mone*, Kochappu,' she, dodged her husband's raised hand and moved into the safety of the inner rooms to lament in private. 'Will I ever see you again?' A flash of hope came to her in the form of a memory. A secret Beerankutti's umma had whispered in her ears the other evening.

A few months before her Kochappu, Beerankutti

from across the village had also gone missing one day. Rice, coconuts, meat and money began mysteriously streaming into their *pora* too. Unknown to their husbands, the two mothers often got together to pour their hearts out and sob on each other's shoulders. When they last met, Beerankutti's umma had appeared happier and Pokkar's beedar wondered why. Her friend looked around to make sure they were alone.

'I saw him,' the words were nearly lost beneath her thattam.

'Who? Beerankutti?' Pokkar's *beedar* stared. The other woman nodded in earnest.

'Yesterday. At the crack of dawn,' she spoke almost voicelessly. 'He came here. There was no one at home. Beerankutti's *bappa* and *uppuppa* had rushed down to the Nair *tharawad* before it was light. Someone came over to call them. You must have heard, there was a commotion there the previous night. The house was attacked around midnight and by morning all of them had vanished. It was that day and the men were down there making enquiries with the rest of the village. My mother in law was snoring away as usual. I had barely risen from the mat myself when a hushed call startled me.'

Umma!

Nte Rabbe! There he was standing half hidden behind the banana trees in our backyard. He was wearing a black lungi and a mask covered his face. But I will know my boy whatever disguise he assumes. He patted my shoulder and somewhat hesitantly peeled off his mask. 'I am alright, Umma. Don't worry about me,' he whispered. 'Your son is the Thangal's warrior and Padacchon will always protect him'.

'My Beerankutti sounded so different. So grown up'.

A sense of hope and joy washed over Pokkar's *beedar*. Maybe Kochappu would come to her one day too.

Beerankutti had not stayed long. It would have given his mother much pleasure to give him a drink of hot black tea and warm up some left over pathiris, but he seemed fearful to linger. 'These are the days of fighting, Umma. I am a warrior. We do not have permission to meet our families. The Thangal has the power to see everything with his inner eye. I have to go. I may be in trouble as it is.'

'When will I see you again, mone Beerane'?

'When the war is fought. When the kafirs are no more. When the true Empire reigns in Ernad. Then I will be free to see you whenever I wish.' With that he dashed into the flush of the new day.

As to what he truly meant, Kochappu's umma was totally clueless. Beerankutti's mother too wondered what her son was fighting for. An Empire? What did she care about all that? It was only her boy who mattered. When in the consequent days, the villagers began to talk about the men in masks and black waist cloths slaughtering the Thoppil Nairs, she had listened in silence.

It was as if the Nairs of Thoppil *tharawad* faded off the face of the earth. So many human beings vanishing into thin air? The people of the surrounding *amsams* quite naturally wondered.

'It was past midnight and I was roused by a full bladder.'

The pale youth who was a servant of the Thoppil Nairs' nearest neighbours shivered and his newly broken voice was hoarse as he reported. He had been half asleep and fumbling his way towards the thorny fence to relieve himself. What he saw out there in the dark night terrified the lad so much that his bladder had given away even before he reached the fence, though he did not include this detail in his account. A group of people, flaming torches aloft, were making their way towards Thoppil. Their frenzied Allahu Akbar cries rented the silent night. 'It was too dark for me to actually see the men but I am fairly sure they were wearing black clothes and masks,' the terrified fellow stammered when his master questioned him the next morning. The Thoppil *tharawad* had been found empty of residents. Anxious neighbours and curious villagers were turning up to make enquiries.

Two days later, news began to trickle in. The body of Thoppil's septuagenarian Karanavar was found tangled among the bushes on the banks of a stream more than a mile from the village. There was a clean slice at the back of the neck and the head fell forward when they turned him over. A few yards downstream, his great nephew, a young man in his prime, floated face down. The other nephew's severed left arm was subsequently discovered drifting in the waters. Of the other senior Nair, the consort of one of the Thoppil women, there was no information.

What happened to the women and children of the family was left to the imagination of the villagers.

The air in the inner chamber was thick with the heady scent of incense. Several black-clad young men sans their masks sat cross-legged on the mats laid out on the floor. It was only the Thangal himself who concealed his face and head within the camp. The youngest recruitees, boys not yet into adolescence, fidgeted nervously in the far corner. The lectures would begin soon and go on till noon prayer. One of the cell's operational leaders stepped up, his expression grim. His glinting eyes searched the rows of young fighters ever so slowly and eventually settled on one lad. The stare deepened and the chin flicked. Among the children, twelve-year old twins, Abu and Abdu held hands behind the back of a tall boy in the row before them. They watched the young man who got up and moved towards the centre of the room in answer to the leader's summons. They did not know him personally but had seen him around the camp. He was known to be one of the bravest fighters. His name? Wasn't it Beerankutti?

'Do you know who you are?' The captain's voice could be heard loud and clear. Beerankutti nodded. His eyes downcast.

'Who?'

'The Thangal's fighter.'

'Do you know that the Thangal can travel through space and time?'

'Yes.' Beerankutti was still looking at the floor.

'Do you believe he knows everything happening in

his fighters' lives without being physically present?'

'Yes.'

'When you failed him, didn't you realise he would know?'

Beerankutti did not reply.

The leader pulled out from his broad leather belt, a vicious looking cane.

By then the children in the twins' course were trembling. Their shaven heads glistened with sweat, noted Abu and Abdu in the midst of their own panic. Most of the boys felt their eyes involuntarily when the cane rose with a swoosh. They heard a quiet creak and felt an accompanying gush of damp air. The door opened.

'No, no, Kasim.'

All the tightly shut eyes shot open in a thrice. The cane dropped noiselessly to Kasim's side. Everyone's attention was fixed on the man who had silently stepped in. His turban that usually floated behind him like a raincloud was today dripping and his cloak of the same black clung to him for hc had crossed the courtyard unmindful of the steady rain. His face as always was concealed behind the mask.

When the Prophet conquered Mecca, he had donned a black turban too, Abu and Abdu remembered their scripture lessons.

'*Pavam... pavam...* you poor dear!'

The soft, compassionate voice was heard by the occupants of the chamber even more clearly than Kasim's bark.

The Thangal patted Beerankutti on the back.

'When a good man momentarily meanders from the path Allah has ordained for him, his repentance is punishment enough. Anyway, you and I Kasim who have never known an umma's love cannot be expected to understand what made him forget his mission temporarily. But it will not happen again. Will it son?'

Once again the watching recruits sensed a spine curling threat in the kind words that even Kasim's cane lacked.

'Tuck your cane back in your belt, Kasim. All is forgotten,' the Thangal's voice diffused warmth. He looked around the room, his gaze fixing for a moment on the newest inmates of the camp. 'This once,' he added in a feathery tone which was strangely audible to all. The boys were all duly warned.

With that the Black Thangal turned his attention to the row of fourteen and fifteen year olds behind whom the twins and their course mates sat. They were to be assigned their first mission. He instructed Kasim to explain in detail what was expected of the novices. The leader, with the cane back in his belt went on to outline the job.

Abu and Abdu rewound in their minds the account of the Thoppil mission in Nannambra, which was much hailed in the camp as a task successfully completed. Three of the men were ruthlessly killed by Beerankutti and the other fighters. In their first days at the camp, the twins had been somewhat baffled by the Thangal's self-contradictory ways. He would see to it that they ate the choicest dishes and made sure they were comfortable. He himself taught some of the classes. The twins still shudder when they relived those early practical sessions

'Grab the head. Pull it back. Cut the neck!

He would sound like the kindliest of uncles even as he coached them in the art of beheading.

First they practiced on dummies. Then on lambs.

The twins and their mates had quaked all over during their first attempts with the small, bleating animals. When they managed to somehow complete their gory tasks, the Thangal would say in a soft, smiling voice, '*Pavam... pavam*'. Whether he meant the boys or the lambs, they never knew.

Fighting for the cause is our life purpose, was the camp motto.

But killing was not. It was the last resort.

Their agenda was to make as many people as possible realise that it was time they cast off the cloak of darkness which enshrouded them and emerge into the light of the true path. In time the Thangal's fighters would cover the whole of Ernad, Valluvanad, the other regions of Malabar...

'There is no question of compulsion. You could not force belief and enlightenment on anyone. But at the same time, we do not want a single person here who does not share our faith. So if there is no way they will understand... it is our duty to purge the world of them.'

The twins had been told that Thangal Uppappa's

prime objective was to wipe out the white sayippes but none of the recruits had even seen a sayippe, let alone kill one.

'Did you know, the young Thoppil Nair and Beerankutti had played together as children?' Kochappu was from the same village and knew a bit of their histories. 'His *bappa* and *uppuppa* did odd jobs at the ill-fated *tharawad*.'

The twins and their mates had shuddered inwardly. Would there come a time when they would have to kill their childhood friends too?

The other old man had quivered in fear. He saw what happened to his brother in law the Thoppil Karanavar. He had slid to the floor in a spate of dizziness when his grandson's arm formed an arc in the air on its way from the edge of Beerankutti's sword to the flowing creek. He had emptied the remains of the previous night's rice and curry on the floor of the shack. When his turn came, he was in no condition to resist. Now the elderly consort of the Thoppil lady went around with a skull cap over his shaven head. His circumcision would not yet have healed. The women wore *thattams* and joined others of similar fate in special camps deep in the forests where the new converts were taught. The prettiest of the Thoppil girls, the sister of Beerankutti's playmate turned victim was to be given in nikah one of the operational leaders. There was talk of Beeran himself being offered the dimple cheeked ten year old he had less than a year ago watched screeching in delight on the courtyard swing, her emerald necklace glinting in the sun. Thangal

Uppappa liked to reward his fighters.

'Remember, fighters,' Kasim was still instructing the batch of tall boys seated in the front row. 'We are not looters. You are not to touch the valuables in the site assigned to you. When the villagers inspect the place after the mission has been completed there should be no cause for them to say the Black Thangal's fighters are nothing but thieves. We hear of certain other gangs who have been operating in these parts who rob and kill for no reason. They too, it seems, attack with the Taqbeer on their lips. The Thangal's fighters should be distinguished from them in their work. And...' Kasim paused to stare into the eyes of his listeners. 'You will not treat the women with disrespect.'

'Maybe as a reward for special services, you will get a chance to choose one of the lovelies, once they are properly into our fold of course, and make her your begum,' he said as a cheerful afterthought.

Kasim had by now forgotten his earlier anger and grinned at his prodigies.

The Thangal had left the room so silently that Abu and Abdu hadn't realised he was gone.

Letters

Ernad,
June '21
The Outcaste

'I hope you didn't mind that message I sent asking you to pay me a call when you are in the vicinity. If you are wondering, I have something to show you,' Shekharan Nair the Congress leader informed his visitor.

'Not at all. I have become something of a globe trotter of late. My people call me a Sarvavyapi who can be found just about anywhere in just about the company of anyone. No trouble at all, Shekharetta.'

'It is a letter I wanted you to see. For one, it refers to you. But more than that it is a really special letter which I think I will put away safely. If, a few months down the line, or even years for that matter, someone wishes for an actual picture of these trying times, they will have something authentic to go by.'

'Let me fetch it so that you can read it yourself.' Shekharan Nair bustled indoors, his starched white mundu crackling with each step.

As I awaited Madhavan Nair's letter, thoughts of certain others surfaced in my mind. One of them had been rather worrisome. Never had the jolly Miss Cranford sounded more cheerless than she had in her last letter to him. Admittedly the incident she related had left him with an uneasy feeling too.

> *Dear friend,* wrote Mrs Winifred Eaton of Kerala Estates.
>
> *Yesterday was ever so horrible.*
>
> *The nightmare kicked off in the wee hours of the morning and went on throughout the day and most of the night as well. As I had been nursing a granddaddy of all head colds I decided to skip my usual walk and lay in bed enjoying feeling sorry for myself. It was just about three quarters of an hour after Stanley Pat, sporting his hardy boots and stout stick, had left on his own, that I heard a kind of buzz that steadily rose to a deafening racket. I scrambled out of bed and dressed in a hurry. Downstairs, Mother who was enjoying her first-thing-in-the-morning smoke in our bright little breakfast room had rushed to the window in her dressing gown. I joined her there to see people running helter-skelter and my sparse Malayalam did not allow me to understand a word of their*

bellows and screeches. In the background, Bob, Barker and Bruno could be heard yelping their heads off.

Sometime later, Stanley Pat came back from his walk at something of a run. His face was even redder than it normally was and his breathing faster. But he was his usual self by the time we sat down to breakfast.

'What's all this about for God's sake,' I enquired.

Stanley Pat merely shrugged and bit into his toast.

'A fellow just kicked the bucket,' he said between mouthfuls.'

'Oh! Who?'

'No one really. Just a lazy scallywag who was always shirking work.'

'Oh!' I exclaimed again. 'How did he die?'

'The fellow had absented himself from work for two days. He was rude to Koya the overseer when questioned. Can't have such impertinence can we? Koya was instructed to award him a few with the whip. After just three or four lashes something happened. The blighter simply crumpled down.'

'Jesus! Stanley Pat, you don't mean to tell me that you ordered a man to be beaten to death!' I think I was shrieking for all I was worth.

'Nothing to get so worked up about, Win, my dear. People do die sometimes, you know,' he playfully tweaked my nose, red from the cold or belligerence, I do not know. 'It will settle down

in no time.'

'What about the poor man's family? Will it settle down for them so soon?'

Stanley Pat was wrong anyhow. If anything, they worsened as the day progressed.

Soon after breakfast my husband left for work. This time Jack Horner, I will not refrain from wearing my heart upon my sleeve. I am going to share with you the thoughts that have been surfacing time and again for the last two months. Why did I marry this man? Ours may seem the perfect match in the eyes of many. But our ideologies, it is becoming clearer each day, do not coincide. At that moment I realised I have no more doubts.

To have a fellow human being beaten to death and not care two hoots!

My chest was about to explode and to my horror I could feel the sobs rent me apart. Suddenly I felt the gentlest of touches on my knee. It was the Crocodile-girl. Remember the tribal lass I mentioned in one of my earlier letters? I always think of her as the Crocodile-girl as that is what they say her name means. For what reason I am yet to discover but till that day she had always seemed to avoid me. Of course she does a lot of work in the bungalow but she used to squirm away from any direct encounter with me. At first I had brushed it off as my imagination but I do know it is a true enough fact. So you can reckon how surprised I was to see her sit at my feet and offer comfort in the timidest of fashions. She never left my side till the whole thing was over. Incidentally, the Crocodile-girl is looking a little wan these days. Her brown skin is paler. Whenever she gets a bit of time, she huddles in some corner of the servants' veranda and drops off to sleep. The cook is not pleased. Once or twice I have seen her rush into the bushes clutching her stomach. I have my suspicions.

Stanley Pat didn't come home for lunch.

Sometime during the afternoon, a group of women, wives and mothers of the estate labourers crashed into our bungalow howling and beating their breasts. They were supporting in their midst the recent widow. I just stood there rooted to the spot, simply staring at them. Not a word of sympathy or condolence could I offer. The tears bubbling within me refused to flow and I remained dry eyed. I suppose I must have seemed to them the heartless wife of a murderer.

By about half-past four, the news came in. Stanley Pat had stepped out of the office intending to call it a day when a mob of fifty to sixty workers swarmed around him from all sides. Some of them carried daggers and clubs. They refused to let him move a step. The gherao was their way of protesting against the terrible misdeed of the morning.

When provoked badly, even the most harmless of earthworms can turn into poison spitting snakes. Remember the Malayalam proverb you once translated for me? How apt it seems now!

I know Stanley Pat deserved it but that did not stop me from being afraid for his safety.

I sent Mother up to bed early for she wasn't looking too well. The Crocodile-girl did not go home that day. Not a word did she say but she saw to it that I ate what the servants put before me. That I took my steam inhalations regularly. I had forgotten my head cold but she clearly hadn't. It takes a crisis to recognise a true friend, eh?

It was past midnight by the time the police who had arrived on the scene managed to disperse the furious crowd and Stanley Pat came home by about two, visibly shaken. He had missed his lunch, tea and supper. Small price to pay for brutal homicide!

The rain had begun to pelt down with a vengeance and I got up to drag my chair from the line of the stream. The scraping of feet, the opening and shutting of doors and gentle coughs could be heard from within the house where Shekharan Nair sifted among his papers. From what I'd heard about Eaton, I had for some time been a little anxious for my friend's safety. A couple of months ago, when we met at Rama Ayer's family house in Manjeri, I had even tried to hint that she leave Malabar for a while and spend some time in Madras.

'With father away in the Sundarbans, there is no reason to go home. Why leave all this rain and green and get yourself roasted to a crisp in the unbearable heat?' she had argued.

Winifred was keen on finding out as much as possible about the situation in Malabar and all that but that she herself might be in danger was the last thing on her mind. She had brushed it aside and with a mischievous grin and retorted that there were more interesting things she would rather discuss just then. And much to my embarrassment she had slyly enquired about the widow.

Ever since that day at Mithran Thampan's manor, that impish looking young lady had handed me that story without so much as an explanation, I had not been able to stall the sense of wonderment at the coincidence. Seated on a log beneath the tamarind tree, I had read it then and there. Unbelievable! The writer seemed to have dived right into my own mind to dig out the story from there. It definitely had a feminine touch to it and I had then believed that the girl who delivered the story had authored it. Before leaving the manor I hunted her out and learnt that it had in fact been her cousin, a Nilambur Kovilakam girl who had written it. I had already decided to get it into the next issue of The *Young Namboothiri* which carried my article on the need for the Namboothiri community to accept the remarriage of widows.

I had never believed in mere words. It was never enough to talk about a theory or preach to others.

I needed to act. It was on my return from Madras following Mrs Besant's internment that I began to notice with horror the dark sides of life among my own people. Especially the women. They never saw the outside of gloomy *nalukettus*. Met no one but their husbands and other women. Many of them were packed off with men older than their grandfathers who died in a couple of years and the girls lived the rest of their lives as widows. They needed to be given a leg up.

I saw no need to dawdle over the decision. 'Narayana, do you consider me worthy of my sister?' I asked a young friend. The proposal had been as simple as that. The widow's brother had been over the moon but would need to convince his people. Whoever heard of such a thing? Widow remarriage in our circles! I was in no hurry. Take your time, I told Narayanan. The first two in my Widow Remarriage series had created a stir and then Ittichiri had come along to provide the necessary punch to the final piece. Things were going well. Now when I actually set an example myself, it would make people sit up and think and in time they would act themselves.

Winifred seemed to have heard something from Mrs Rama Ayer. All this in such detail would have been beyond the English girl's comprehension but in answer to her question I had summarised it all for her.

Sethu
Written for the perusal of the honourable Sethu Thampatti, cousin and most beloved friend, from

the pen of her humble companion and wife of Mithran Unni Thampan, the Sixth Tirumulpad of Nilambur, Priyamvada Kettilamma.

Priya's feigned ceremoniousness made Sethu giggle as she read the first few lines.

Looking at it from the point of view of a new Kettilamma, it does not seem to me that the Pookottur manor is the same place we visited together some months ago. Before I launch into more significant matters, Sethu Thampatti, don't you remember when we were here we used to fervently wish for a swing? I will have you know that I have exercised my power as the mistress of the manor and had the men tie a nice, huge one on the western side of the upstairs veranda. I now spend my afternoons swinging to my heart's content, gazing out at the rolling greens and thinking of you.

We have to meet soon, there is so much that can't be said in letters. I wouldn't want to be in the line of the Matriarch's steely gaze when I request her to send you to me for a few days. So, I suppose I should arrange a Nilambur visit as soon as I can. After all as a mature, married woman, I have the freedom to plan my own itinerary. But it may not be for some time I fear. You know it is my mother's birthday soon and we always gather at the family homestead for the occasion.

Unfortunately my husband the Sixth Tirumulpad

is too busy to make the trip with me and does not wish me to travel alone. Risky, he says, considering all this trouble with the Maplas. He thinks one maid and the cart driver may not be good enough escorts. I suppose I will have to start wielding some of that newfound power of mine to get him to change his mind. So, much as it pains me, my friend, I will have to wait a bit longer to see your lotus face.

Remember how your cousin used to barely glance at me during our post-Pattu visit? Before that no doubt, he was unaware of my existence. When the Matriarch sent for him and put forth the proposal, I was sure he would brush it aside with one of his typical grunts but it appears he was as meek as that new little elephant calf that recently arrived in the Kovilakam stables. So I guess he wasn't as immune to my charms as we thought him to be. He doesn't actually say so, (your cousin has never been one for verbal communication, has he?) but he does have his own strange ways of… to understand what I say, Sethu Thampatti, you will have to sample the married life yourself. (Now this is matter I intend to delve into in detail later in this letter when I have finished raving about my husband).

Incidentally, my friend, though nowhere up to your standards, your little Priyamvada's game is improving, thanks to the coach's newly visible willingness. We spend several delicious hours in our wondrous Billiards room not all of which is accorded to practice. (Can you in your mind's eye see the blushes and cast down eyes?) And remember that rich, warm scent pervading the Billiard's room? During our visit I used to sniff away for all I was worth when I was in the room and take deep breaths to carry away as much as possible of it when I went away. You may not have paid heed yourself but my olfactory modality now recognises that it was the Sixth Tirumulpad who let off that aroma. After some serious investigation (and inhalation) I have come to the conclusion that it is the stuff he puts in those pipes of his. My husband becomes a lot more loquacious if you happen to talk about pipes. He has that circular contraption which you might have observed, specially crafted by his own carpenters after a design in an English magazine, which he uses to display his collection of pipes in the library. I will now share with you some of my newly acquired knowledge about pipes. Who knows if it mightn't come in useful when you write a story centered on the Kettilamma of a manor?

The British tobacco companies do something to our regular pokala to make it smell so heavenly. 'Blend', 'treat', 'cure' are some English words he used. Thus the somewhat disgusting pokala achieves these exotic flavor nuances. At night when my eyes are finally closed, he gets off the bed to settle down in an armchair and lights a pipe. Once the aroma tickled me into wakefulness and there he was sitting, smoking, thinking. Let me tell you my dearest Sethu Thampatti, a pensive, contemplative man with a gleaming pipe dangling from his lips is a sight to behold.

Billiards and pipes are not Mithran Thampan's only passions. There is yet another collection that he keeps out of sight of most people. A smallish, concealed safe in his library holds his (I whisper in your ears) guns! Scary but fascinating. I am not allowed to open it but he has shown them to me a few times and explained how they are used. Nothing to it, I thought at the time. Even I could handle some of them. Not that I want to, do not worry.

A longish, dark gun is called the East India Company Sea Pistol. And a curved one that looks as if you could blow at one end and produce a musical sound akin to that of a trumpet. I would have made an attempt had not the thing been snatched from my hands. One is small, black and rather dear. He calls it the Beretta 1915. And... there is another one in his collection called Browning 1910. Let me repeat to you a story he told me. Seven years ago, a young man called Franz Ferdinand, the heir apparent to the throne of two European countries, Austria and Hungary, and his wife were touring the city in an open car. They were shot dead by a rebel, thus sparking off what turned into the Great War. The assassin used a pistol exactly like my husband's Browning 1910. Enough about guns.

By the way, just yesterday, when Mithran Thampan was away on business, I had the shock of my life. I had just finished my morning chores and was heading upstairs for the swing when I noticed someone move in the veranda outside the library. To my horror it was that nasty cat-eyed Mapla, your grandmother favours so much. I chided myself a hundred times for not double checking the doors. I plucked up courage and asked him what he was doing inside the manor. He kept saying he had to see the Tirumulpad regarding some money matters. It was with much difficulty that the men managed to drag him off. He says the Sixth Tirumulpad owes him money. What a horrible fellow he is! Can't believe he is that gentle cart driver's son. But I can't understand what your grandmother sees in this Mammad. My husband once mentioned that she is unreasonably partial to him, for Vettekkaran knows what reason. How it makes his blood boil. The Matriarch certainly has strange preferences, if you will forgive me. Anyway, he has threatened to come again and again till he gets his money. I wonder what all that is about. Your cousin does not like discussing official matters with me.

Let me tell you of another visitor we had at the manor. Not an awful Mapla tramp this time but a snooty, big shot Sayippe. It was none other than the Superintendent of police, Mr Hitchcock. Your brother was there that day too. Divakaran Thampan. They received him in the library first and then went to the Billiards room. I positioned myself very cleverly and managed to catch a good look. If we go by what I could hear from outside the library door, I didn't like the way he spoke. You have a good imagination. Try combining in your mind the snap of an angry dog and the hiss of a vicious snake and you will get an idea what this important policeman sounded like…
At breakfast the next day, the Sixth Tirumulpad and your brother were discussing his visit and they repeated some of this words. Listen to what Hitchcock had to say about what the Congress-Khilafat people were doing in Malabar: It is pure mockery to deck the excitable Mapla in the garb of a soldier and then tell him he should attain his aims by spinning! Harsh but accurate, both your brother and cousin agreed. Nor did they miss the sarcastic jab at Gandhi. From what they were saying, the Sayippe was indeed a sharp man. His analysis of the current situation, I personally felt was both fascinating and alarming.

What makes one think the Mopla so dangerous,

Tirumulpad? *The Sayippe barks.*

My husband responds with a non-committal grunt.

A system of communication one can in no way infiltrate, *he answers his own question.* This is far more important than the entire network of Khilafat bastards. And you will permit me to point out, my dear Tirumulpads, here lies the major difference between the Hindoos and the Moplas. Remember, they congregate at least once a week for Friday prayers and often at other times. Where? In mosques of course. Here they are able to form and share opinions, however misconstrued. . The Hindoo and the European remain happily oblivious beware of mosques, Tirumulpad, beware.

It sounded like serious business, Sethu Thampatti. But you know your Kovilakam men. Neither seemed particularly concerned.

Sethu read the rest of Priya's thick letter and leaned back with a sigh.

They had been talking about the story of Ittichiri at Rama Iyer's place in Manjeri that day when his wife had laughingly mentioned that *The Outcaste* had an Ittichiri in his life too. He had proposed marriage to a widow. Their union would make history. It would be the first ever widow remarriage in the history of their community.

Setting the letter aside, she decided that she would read Ammamma the significant parts.

The Outcaste

As I sat on Shekharettan's veranda awaiting Madhavan Nair's letter, there was the memory of yet another one which came swimming into my mind. The events leading up to it made me wonder again and again at how prophetic the young Thampatti's story had turned out to be. Her story had ended with the heroine refusing a proposal stating that marriage was not what she wanted in life. There were other things she wished to do. She did not want someone to dedicate all his life to her out of pity. I had been greatly impressed by both Ittichiri and her creator.

So when an embarrassed Narayanan had gripped my arm in earnest and exhaled audibly, I realised now that I had actually been expecting it.

'How long can I keep it from you,' Narayanan had blurted nervously, 'I had better say it now. Oh! I am so ashamed.'

'What have you done that is so shameful?'

'I... it is not I. My oppol... she refuses to marry you.'

Pranamam

I hope you will not think me audacious, writing to a man.

It shames me to confess that I seem to have forgotten to write even the few Malayalam letters I learnt as a child. My reading is limited to that disgusting tale of Sheelavati which we women have all had thrust down our throats for generations. How I wish I could torch every available copy! In a way I suppose much blame falls on her for setting such a bad example for us, leading us to believe that we were born for our husbands to trample upon.

I apologise for getting side tracked. It is my new found freedom that is causing me to get carried off. I only meant to tell you that since I am unable to write myself, I am dictating this to one of the girls here.

There are seven other young women apart from me who are inmates here. Three of them, including Parvathi who is writing this for me have been here for nearly two years. They have earned their school certificates and help to tutor newcomers like me. Sometimes when I wake up in the mornings I find it difficult to believe that I am now here, hundreds of kadams away from the hell-like tharawad I married into. I take a deep breath of the fresh air and tell myself that a beautiful new life has begun and the old memories need no more haunt me.

And for this new life, I have you to thank.

When that day, Narayanan came to me with your proposal, I thought that years of torture had actually affected my hearing. Has anyone in his right mind ever done anything so outrageous as to propose marriage to a widow?

Later it all began to sink in. Our community is on the brink of change. What we consider shocking today will be the generally approved way of life tomorrow. Women will venture beyond their stifling nalukettus and inhale the clean, invigorating air of freedom. They will gain knowledge and skills.

They will stand on their own feet. These are some things I dream of. Men like you will open new doors and eligible youngsters will actually marry poor, tortured widows.
I am so grateful that you bear me no ill will. That you understand my need for more. For doing all this for me. Offering to arrange for me to live here among likeminded women and to get an education is I believe an even more magnanimous act than your proposal for marriage.
The only way I can repay you is with prayers.

The widow had not actually voiced her hopes in words when she first refused me, maybe she didn't know for sure herself. She only knew she wanted something more than marriage to another man, just as Ittichiri had. All I had done was arrange for her to receive all the benefits the young Thampatti's Ittichiri had coveted.

When Shekharettan placed Madhavan Nair's letter in his hands, I flipped through the pages for a moment, silently admiring the shapely, curvaceous Malayalam script that covered the sheets. As if much time and effort had been put into the writing. Madhavan Nair confessed to exactly that in the very first paragraph.

A man taking repose at the British government's expense has much time on his hands. I am using this enforced leisure to soak up the books I have always looked forward to reading and to write long, unhurried letters to my friends. Had I not believed that this is a time my land needs my services most, I would have thoroughly relished this holiday.

You and I, Shekhara, are sons of Ernad and few people know the Maplas as we do. Having grown up in their midst we realise better than most how loving their sturdy hearts are. I always laugh at the childhood memory of the fuss you used to kick up at home insisting that you would wear checkered waist cloths. How your mother hated it when you would play with Kadar, Aboobacker and Pareedkutti all the time!

Last August when Gandhiji and Shaukat Ali were here, remember we did meet with them and explain how for the Maplas of Ernad, a fight meant the boiling of blood and wielding of weapons. How they would never understand nonviolent protests. How the call for revolt would mean disaster. We had however allowed ourselves to be brought around to his way of thinking. What we feared then may be coming true, Shekhara.

When the idea of inviting Janab Yakub Hasan came from the side of the local Khilafat leaders, I did hope that the Maplas would listen to one of their own. In spite of our close associations with them we knew that somewhere inside their steadfast hearts we are but kafirs. Outsiders. Non-believers. They needed a Muslim leader to convince them that their beliefs are in no way being targeted. That is why, in spite of being aware of the possible consequences, Gopala Menon and I insisted on going ahead with the public meeting on the beach. The arrival of Deputy Superintendent Amu Sahib and Inspector Kidavu came as no surprise. You were there that day for the relocated Town Hall meeting. You saw that we somehow managed to ensure that no violence ensued at the place of arrest. There did we part. I will tell you something of what happened later.

When we were presented for questioning, Mr Thomas barely raised his head. He was occupied with scribbling away at some paper or the other. The busy look being but a mask donned by the Magistrate to hide his inner kerfuffle.

I must say this surprised me somewhat for I have always known Mr Thomas to be polite and decent. It bothered me at that time but later I have been able to put it down to anger and confusion on his part that caused him not just to forget basic manners but to shed his discrimination as well.

Well, we have already served half the term slapped on us and all this is water under the bridge. We should be back home in August. However I must admit how thwarting it has been, how discouraging, to have our hands tied behind our backs just when duty calls. Helpless as I am now, Shekhara, I can only appeal to dear friends like you for help and support. If you will not consider me didactic, there are a few things I hope you will do. You have fought several eviction cases for the Mapla tenants and farmers and have been instrumental in creating kudiyan sanghams. I wish you would now talk to these very same people and tell them how illogical it is to combine agrarian and religious issues along with non-cooperation and the freedom movement. They are all crucial by themselves but much is to be lost by confusing one with the other. Worse still, if you put all these ingredients in the same pot, place it on the lighted stove and stir, you are sure to produce extremely toxic fumes.

It is, pointless now to try and influence the masses. We have to work on a personal level. In Ernad I believe that with me behind bars, you are the best person to go about it. And I have a suggestion to make. That young man from Madras who I have met once in your company, I think can do wonders so it would be an idea to seek his help. I have come to understand that his tongue is as golden as his pen. My sources tell me he has already started working on these lines in his own village and the surrounding areas. So he is your man. Get him on your side. I trust you as I would my own brother.

I hope your family is well and prospering.

Madhavan Nair signed off thus.

Reflections

June '21
Raziya

Raziya had been staring at the flames for a while when she became aware of a faint hiss. The froth from the *kanji* pot was bubbling over, causing the fire to crackle.

Nte Rabbe! She hastily lifted the pot off the stove and blew on her fingers. Even as she stirred the gruel with a wooden ladle the thoughts that had been haunting her earlier flooded back into her mind. Should she share her worries with her husband? How could she, when it would mean adding to the burden that was already weighing his mind down? But then, was it right to keep it from him?

The aroma of the mutton curry from Benu Thatha's kitchen filled her own humbler one. She hoped Mammad would enjoy his dinner.

'Bannolee', she called softly as she straightened her

clothes, fanned her red fingers with the ends of her *thattam* and stepped into the only other room in the house. Two surprisingly uncharacteristic pieces of furniture dominated the small space. In one corner sat a teak chest with polished brass corners and an ornamental lock. It held her few sets of good clothes and one or two pieces of jewelry. Then there was the heavy bed on which Mammad now lay staring at the ceiling where a pregnant spider scuttled about with the fat white egg fused to her belly. Made of fine teak from the forests off Nilambur, the bed had beautifully carved headboards stained with vermillion dye.

Both the splendid articles were gifts from the Nilambur Matriarch and more valuable to Mammad than any other possession. They didn't have a mattress to go with the bed but he insisted on sleeping on the bare wood with just a grass mat spread on it. Raziya herself had never in her life slept on a bed. Even now she preferred her own mat on the floor but when she craved his nearness in the night, she propped her left leg on the Matriarch's bed and entwined her foot with his.

'Come,' she told him now. 'Have the *kanji* while it is hot.'

As Mammad patted the space beside him, his smile was watery but tender.

Raziya did not sit down. She simply frowned at the raw gashes on his chest. First when he started coming home with these angry red wounds on his upper body, she had been scared beyond imagination. He had been reluctant to explain.

'These were made by the blades of friends. Do not worry,' he had said simply.

It took Raziya days to figure things out. In the depths of Alijan Sahib's cashew and tamarind groves each day, able-bodied Pookottur Maplas and some others from the nearby villages got together to undergo rigorous training. They learnt the use of swords, lances, daggers and rapiers. They practiced on each other to fine-tune their skills. They discussed strategies of defence and attack. They were preparing for war against the Sayippes. They were the Khilafat-kar. Even naïve Raziya knew how dangerous these meetings could be with the police so vigilant.

'Come and eat,' she said again. This time Mammad rose with a groan.

If she told him of her bitter encounters how would he take it? No. Maybe after dinner when his stomach was full. He was not going to like it. In his present mood he might go berserk. No man takes it lightly when others make advances on his wife.

Mammad sat down on the scrubbed kitchen floor and Raziya ladled out the hot kanji into the chipped bowl. Benu Thatha's curry sat appetisingly on a banana leaf square beside it.

It was a lonely stretch and Raziya had been hurrying down the track. She was not far from the main entrance to Benazir Manzil but she was walking fast because she had a premonition of lurking danger. She thought she heard the crackle of dry leaves behind her and smelt stale sweat. The footsteps as they got closer and the mocking titters set her heart pounding. She quickened her pace. To her horror the stalkers fell almost in line with her. There were four of them. She didn't dare raise her eyes and to see if she recognised them.

'Don't be afraid, we are here to give you some company,' said one yob in a sickly sweet tone.

'Yes. Poor little *munjathi.* Always alone. The *puthumaran* has no time for her.' False pathos.

'How can he? Such a busy, important man.' Sarcasm.

'Yes. Yes. Big Khilafat man.' Agreement.

'Don't worry, little one. You can always turn to one of us if you are on the lookout for a new *maran.*'

'Went begging at Benu Thatha's again?' Mammad frowned at the mutton. 'Why can't we make do with what we have? A few crystals of rock salt and a fried chilly would do fine for me.' Her Mapla was a proud man. He hated accepting favours even from Benu Thatha who was like a mother and grandmother combined. He never let anyone know of their troubles. A little guiltily Raziya remembered how she had poured out her woes to that nice young Thampatti. Raziya had met her twice at the Pookottur manor and the lady had been so interested in talking to her. She had mentioned the poverty they lived in since her husband had been sacked but that was the lesser of her sorrows. She had blurted out about her worries for his safety too. The young lady had wished to do something to help but Raziya had panicked. 'No. No. If my Mapla finds out I have been telling you all this, he'll kill me.' The Thampatti had been so understanding that she had let it go.

'Benu Thatha sent it over with the Pathiri Umma. Actually I haven't gone over to her place for a few days,' Raziya fanned the steaming *kanji* in Mammad's bowl with her *thattam* ends. Mammad reluctantly went on with his meal. It was true she hadn't visited Benazir Manzil since that terrible day. She was even scared to venture out into the busy market for a few groceries. Raziya wondered how she had managed to keep walking that day with the goons on her trail. Her whole body had been so tense that it felt as if it were made of lead. She badly wanted to act tough and shoo them away but the words stuck in her throat.

'That Mammad is a fool. He doesn't deserve a gorgeous begum like you.'

'Yes. You are wasted on him.'

'How about saying talaq thrice?'

'The women can do that too?' This was someone not too familiar with such practices, she noted absently.

All this was said amidst hoots, catcalls and much malicious laughter.

'And if you think we are unworthy of you, there is always Ahmed Adhikari. He is a rich man and has but three wives so far.'

Raziya shivered and was relieved when she reached the entranceway to Benazir Manzil. Naturally the men did not follow her in, they simply stood a few feet away, hissing.

'And if you have no objection to foreskins, you could consider me or my friend here,' one of them called out at her disappearing figure.

'Again, if we are not good enough the Sixth Tirumulpad might…'

Mammad ate hungrily. For all his objections he had enjoyed the mutton. Belching softly he got up to wash his hands.

'Raziya, I will be late coming home tomorrow and probably a few more days. I should be here soon after midnight. Hope you are not afraid being left alone for a while.'

She shuddered. In a moment of anger she decided not to tell him about the goons after all.

Mammad

After lunch Mammad made a bee line for the Matriarch's elaborately carved bed. He rolled up the mat spread on it and lay down. He craved the feel of the smooth, hard wood on his bare skin. The texture of the teak tended to adapt its temperature in tune with his mood. He lay down, propped the threadbare pillow into a more comfortable position. The warm food in his belly made him feel better. However much he may claim that plain salted gruel with invisible rice grains was fine for him, however much he may have admonished his wife for accepting handouts, he couldn't deny that it had been a good meal.

He could hear Raziya busying herself in the kitchen, placing the leftovers on the stove where the half burnt out embers would keep them warm till dinner. He rarely ate dinner these days. Lunch was his only proper meal of the day. He usually left home in the evenings and was hardly ever back before midnight and by then he was ready to drop and didn't bother to eat. Raziya put aside a little left over rice in water in case he wanted a morning meal but he never woke up in time for it. If he did he had some business over in the village and would leave hurriedly. He knew it pained the poor girl but he had so much on his mind, food was way down on his priority list. Still the good lunch had relaxed him a bit.

To relax was something Mammad rarely did. He sometimes compared himself with other men his age. Alavikutti and Basheer for instance. Basheer was as calm as they come and had a cool head. That made him a good decision maker and valuable to Alijan Sahib as a Khilafat man. Alavikutti on the other hand was impulsive and hot headed. He thought with his heart rather than his head. But he was a good worker and loyal ally. He himself, thought Mammad was the most high strung of the lot. He took things very seriously and when he watched his friends and co-Khilafatkar sometimes joke and laugh among themselves, he wondered why he never seemed to have a lighter side. Did poor Raziya find life with him suffocating, he wondered. Guilt, like a sack of stones weighed down his already heavy heart.

They had been married for nearly a year and what had he been able to give the poor girl? A comfortable life? Or at least a full stomach? Time? A reason to smile? She still had the clothes she brought with her. Not a length of cloth nor a trinket had he bought for her.

Mammad touched the knot in his waistcloth under his belt. It still felt heavy with a few coins and soiled, sweat stained notes. A couple of months before he lost his job, he had begun putting aside money, miniscule amounts, with a purpose. He had meant to surprise her and every day when he changed his waist cloth, he would undo the knot and transfer it into his fresh one. And Raziya, the one who washed his clothes still had no clue. He had stopped adding to it some time ago but he still kept it safe.

The twenty second day of the Ramzan month had always been special to the Maplas of south central Ernad. On that very day, in the Hijra year of 1152, twelve brave men had laid down their lives to protect the Pullara Juma palli, one of the oldest mosques in the Ernad region. To commemorate their martyrdom, the Pullara Nercha was celebrated every year on that day.

Mammad had never been of a sentimental or romantic nature. But since his marriage, he had nursed a tiny ambition, more of a dream. At the next Nercha, he would buy Raziya some nice things. Gooey halwas, luscious dates, pretty glass bangles in the colours of her choice, maybe a length or two of shiny material for the tops she wore over her waist cloth and a sturdy kitchen utensil or two. And he had begun saving up. It had not been so difficult for he had what he had then believed to be a steady, decent job. The money he'd earned as the Tirumulpad's rent collector was no fortune but it kept the *kanji* coming in. Then came the gatehouse contract. The Sixth Tirumulpad had wanted the manor gatehouse demolished to make way for a more modern entryway for he had plans to buy one of those motor cars. Mammad had been pleased to secure the demolition project for Alavikutti and two other lads as the Mithran Thampan had fixed upon an apparently decent sum to get the work done. But the structure had turned out to be sturdier than expected. More time and manpower would be needed. When the first installment was paid, Mammad had intimated the Tirumulpad about the unpredicted turn of things and explained that more work was involved and more men required it would cost more. Mithran Thampan, already a little displeased with Mammad for his Khilafat activities were causing his work to suffer, had lost his temper. 'Not a single paisa more than the amount initially fixed,' he had been adamant. In hopes of getting him to change his mind, Mammad had asked his friends to continue working. The demolition was complete and the Sixth Tirumulpad still refused to pay more than he had promised. Pride stopped Mammad, Alavikutti and the rest from settling for the amount offered. So there had been no money at all. Seeing his friends struggle without the pay due to them, Mammad had begun to help them from his own modest salary for he felt responsible. Since then there had been no money for household expenses let alone enough to put aside for baubles.

For some reason however, Mammad had been hesitant to touch the money knotted into his checkered waistcloth and it remained with him, getting grubbier by the day, even on days when the rice tin had been empty.

And what had come of it?

The Yakub Hasan affair had hurt the Khilafatkar of Pookkottur and nearby areas and they had decided that there would be no festivities at Pullara this year.

It wouldn't have been so bad if the Khilafat had been able to enforce things. When he thought back to the Nercha day, he fumed inside. All their plans had been in vain. The decision had come from a no lesser man than Ali Musaliar and it enraged him that the great man's words would come to nothing.

They had known that Ahmed Adhikari and his sidekicks would not give in so easily. He had learnt from his sources that plans were being laid to make things as grand as ever. A lavish feast with coconut rice and meat were to be served. The lads practiced duff mutt in earnest. Fireworks, tom toming and *kolkali* dances were to grace the Varavu procession. All the preparations were on in full swing.

Whenever he passed the Adhikari's hideous goons in the village, their titters and smirks were worse than ever. When he was near enough to hear, they hinted loudly how well the arrangements for the Nercha were going. How enthusiastic the townspeople were. How cooperative the Sixth Tirumulpad was.

'We have all heard of the Nercha at Idiyangara a few years ago, when Shrambikkal Mohammed organised a Varavu with twenty elephants, a cartful of rice and another of vegetables and fifty baskets of Appams, not to mention the dancers,' one fellow described at the top of his voice. 'Ours this year will be just as good.'

'Well, our Adhikari is so close to the Sixth Tirumulpad, it wouldn't be difficult to procure the Kovilakam elephants for our Varavu,' his friend added importantly.

Hoots followed as Mammad and Basheer walked by. He had turned red in the face and Basheer had patted him quietly.

'They are all bark and no bite, Mammade. It's not going to happen. The townspeople are loyal to the Khilafat.'

But Basheer had been wrong. On the day of the Nercha, the festivities started with the Assar Namaskaram which was well attended. Mammad and the rest of the Khilafatkar kept a watch out but didn't protest as it was a part of the rituals and not the festivities.

Later, to their shock the Varavu had started with great pomp. There had been no elephants of course but they had indeed filled a cart with rice, huge banana bunches, coconuts and such. The dancers were ready to join the procession. A display of fireworks set the celebration rolling and the group of Khilafatkar could stand it no longer. They jumped into the midst of the revelers, brandishing sticks and sounding Taqbeer calls. What followed was no mere scuffle. A proper little riot it turned out to be with men on both sides getting hurt. Then the police had arrived. Ahmed Adhikari emerged from the sidelines where he had been lurking and greeted them.

'Just in time, saare. I am so relieved to see you,' he said in his usual oily voice. 'I knew the Sixth Tirumulpad could be counted on. He had promised me to get in touch with you if things got rough.'

The police were well equipped and the Khilafatkar were temporarily marched to the police station and held there for the duration of the Nercha.

The Adhikari and his men had won this battle and Mammad found another reason why he could never forgive Mithran Thampan.

All these thoughts surged in his chest like hot boiling oil as he lay on the Matriarch's bed absently watching the spider scuttle furtively round a corner of the room, its movement hindered by the weight of the egg.

Raziya had finished her chores and come into the room to sit at the foot of the bed. His mind was too preoccupied to pay attention to her.

Benazir

Benazir Beewi sat in the women's room off her kitchen, legs swinging to and fro in tune to some nameless tempo that beat within her. She had never got rid of this childish habit of daydreaming and when she did daydream it felt so natural to swing her legs.

Her thoughts drifted back to her childhood home where she would sit on the low stone bench in the porch adjoining the house. She would pump her legs with the gusto that was impossible now at her age. She would sip sweet tea from earthen cups and dream. In her *kinaaves* she would see her *bappa* who was but a vague memory as she had not seen him since she was three or four. She would dream of his flowing white beard and his soft voice as he read from his Arabi books and addressed her by her full name, Benazir. Bappa's choice, her name. Uncommon for Malabar girls. In her daydreams as her small, plump legs made tiny arches in the air, she would see Bappa back home.

Sometimes Umma's voice interrupted her little sojourns. 'Benu, I have told you never to go off like that without telling me,' her scolding had broken into Benu's thoughts one day which she remembered particularly well. 'Umma, I didn't go anyway. Just to Suhratha's house. Imbichi ran off. I had to get him.'

'Imbichi!' Umma had sniffed. 'That animal is the cause of all my troubles. Wait till he ends up in a biryani chembu, girl. You will not have to wait long either.'

'No one will dare eat my Imbichi,' Benu had raised her little nose in the air disdainfully. She drained her cup and swung her legs even more ferociously. 'Umma,' she said 'You know what happened today?'

But Umma had not been in a mood to listen. 'This is not the time for chit chat, girl. Go and wash.'

Benu and Imbichi had been playing by the rocks when Suhratha appeared suddenly and said in a grave voice, 'Asalam Aleikum, Hajiyare!' Benu had covered her mouth with the loose ends of her thattam and giggled.

'He's not a Hajiyar, Suhratha.'

'Oh! He looks so much like one he quite fooled me.' The dimples in Suhratha's cheeks deepened belying her mock serious tone.

Snorts escaped from under Benu's *thattam*. 'You

know he is only Imbichi, my lamb.' As if on cue, Imbichi butted his head against Suhra's legs, skipped away and waited at a distance, inviting her to chase him. She accepted his challenge laughingly and ran. Suhratha was quite fast for a grown woman of eighteen but she was no match for Imbichi. He scampered off, bleating in joy as the girls followed him all over the countryside, over rocky boulders, through thorny bushes and across narrow streams. The sun had just risen over their tiny village. After having rained all night the skies were now clear. It had been during a monsoon like the present one, sixty seven years ago. Benu had been nine.

'Nte Rabbe! He's gone into the firewood *pora.*' Suhra exclaimed between pants as they neared the backyard of her home. 'Benu you wait here. I'll get him.' She clambered into the ramshackle shed her brother used to store his firewood logs. 'Imbichi, come out. You'll get hurt.'

Suhratha had been in there a while. Benu waited outside the shed as she had been instructed. She was beginning to lose her patience. She could hear logs tumble down as the two scrambled about, Imbichi's bleats and Suhratha's gentle voice as she called him. Then she heard a gasp and a stifled screech. Benu put her ears to the rickety door.

'Who are you?' Suhratha's voice had been full of fear.

Benu was scared too. She opened the door and peeped inside. There was a man in there! A slim bare chested man, youngish and bearded. Clad in nothing but a checkered waist cloth and a broad belt.

'Shh. Quiet.' His voice was low and harsh and then Benu saw his face. The eyes were green and jewel like and imploring in spite of his angry tone.

'Are you a thief?' Suhratha asked.

The man shook his head.

Suhratha craned her head towards the door and Benu had stepped back hurriedly.

'Ikka! Ikka! Mammadka! There's a thief in the firewood shed,' the older girl had screamed for her brother.

Benu peeped in one last time and saw the man's green eyes melt as they stared at Suhratha.

Benazir Beewi had almost forgotten that day in her childhood till the events came back to her years later, here in Pookottur when old Beeran Mapla had walked into their house that day with his little son in tow and the boys green eyes had haunted her till it all came back.

Then she had made enquiries and it all fell into place over time. Beeran the Nilambur Kovilakam cart driver had married a Pookottur girl whose parents still lived here. Benazir learnt that Beeran's mother in law was called Suhra. She had lost no time in paying them a visit and the long lost friends had been reunited.

Little Benu's daydreams had not been in vain. Her *bappa* had come home. She had not known till a lot later that he had been in jail all that time. His arrival had been in the middle of the night and all hush hush.

Past midnight one day following Bappa's arrival, she

had heard voices. They had visitors at that odd hour. The thud of their footsteps as they climbed the wooden staircase to the attic where Bappa seemed to spend all his time had sounded in the silence. Umma was asleep, Benu knew from her regular breathing and the rhythmic rise and fall of her chest. Her childlike curiosity had demanded to know who it was in her *pora* at this time of the night. Slowly she crept out of bed and up the stairs, as quietly as she could. Balanced precariously on the top of the steep flight of stairs, she had peered into the attic room usually used for storing coconuts and sacks of rice. It appeared to have been cleaned up. There were three men in the room apart from her father. One of them was Mammadkka, Suhratha's brother from the teashop. Another was a tall stranger dressed in a posh white shirt and a sparkling, starched mundu. When the third man turned his face a bit she saw that he was none other than the thief from the firewood shed.

'The grace of Allah and the prayers of our beloved Thangal in Arabia have brought us together again, Kadare, Mujeebe,' Bappa drew the suave stranger and the scruffy thief into the circle of his arms as Mammadkka looked on gravely. Her father was a small man and the top of his turban reached but the middle of one man's chest and barely brushed the other's longish beard. 'And we cannot forget our friend here who has been a firm and steady rock,' he smiled at Suhratha's brother.

'Rahim Haji, we have little time to waste. We must set about our task as soon as possible,' the tall man whom

Bappa had called Kadar spoke in a cultured voice.

The other fellow, Mujeeb stroked something bright and shiny in his belt, his strange, green eyes gleaming.

Bappa nodded. 'Yes. We must now shape our proceedings with a proper view of the goal. We have to reach our target at the earliest. Connolly Sayippe has forced our Thangal away from us. He has stripped the followers of Islam of their weapons. The barber's blade, the carpenter's chisel. Yes even the tools of their trade have been taken from them. He has sided with kafir oppressors. Malabar will be well rid of him.' The two other men nodded in enthusiastic agreement and just then green eyes had turned towards the staircase and for a moment panicked when from between the wooden railings, they caught sight of her bobbing face. Bappa noticed his expression and turned around to see her. He had heaved a sigh, probably of relief and said, 'Benazir, go to bed. This is no time or place for little girls to loiter around.'

The next day however, he called her up to the attic. There was no sign of the men having been there. Her father mentioned nothing of the last night's episode either and she had wondered if it had been a dream. He spent the whole morning talking to her, holding her against his wheezing chest. And reading to her from the Naiful Battar. It said all kinds of things about fighting white men. Fighting till the very end. Benu had understood little but she listened gravely and clung to every word. She still did. They were her last memories of her father.

The period following that event was a complete blur

for Benu. Was it weeks? Or months? She still didn't know. Later in their new home, Umma refused to speak of it. It was a chapter conveniently slashed off the story.

Bappa had disappeared again.

The village was in a chaos.

People said an important white man had been murdered in faraway Kozhikode. Connolly Sayippe. Benu wondered where she had heard that name before.

Police and army boots stomped about their village.

They came to Benu's house too. She did remember a cop kicking Imbichi. She had rushed out from behind the door and butted the fellow in the crotch and sent him crumbling to the floor before someone had grabbed her and pulled her indoors.

She and Imbichi were not allowed out anymore and she couldn't visit Suhratha or play with her friend Alikutti from the Yatim Khana.

No one knew where Bappa was.

Villagers said there was a reward on his head and on the heads of two other men called Kadar and Mujeeb.

People were arrested. Mammadkka for one. People were killed. Down at the Yatim Khana. In the village. The firewood shed near Suhratha's house was burned down and two men were killed in the fire.

In the middle of one night she had suddenly woken up in the arms of her Mamu, Umma's brother, crying for Imbichi. They were by the riverside.

'Where's Imbichi? Oh find Imbichi! They will fry him in the *biryani chembu*,' she had begun to howl but was hushed up. They would leave by boat as soon as Bappa came.

But Bappa did not come. On his way to the river bank, a traitor had bludgeoned him to death hoping to get the money they had placed on his head.

Years later as a young bride just settled in Valluvanad, she had asked her new husband, 'Do you remember anything of those horrible days?' Alikutti, now Alijan was a few years older to her and he had been at the orphanage in the village then. 'Did my bappa murder the Collector Sayippe?'

'Yes. He did.' The quiet reply had come not from her husband but his brother. Jawadikka and Alijan were inseparable and had been since their Yatim khana days. Not long after the assassination and the consequent events, the boy Ali had accompanied Jawadikka to the north where he had gone for higher studies. And so had the half-witted Aimutti, their loyal friend. The threesome had stuck together through thick and thin. They had witnessed firsthand the mutiny in Meerut. Travelled all over the hot plains. Jawadikka had acquired knowledge and Ali money. Aimutti had flourished in their love and support. When Alijan decided to return to Malabar in search of Benu, his friends would not let him go alone. They had all lived together in the Valluvanad house.

'And he didn't do it alone.' There was something of a tremor in Jawadikka's voice. A kind of emptiness brought about by loss, together with a quiet kind of pride.

'It is one topic you had better not discuss in front

of Jawadikka,' Alijan had later told her in the privacy of their room. 'Remember the other two men involved. One of them, Kadarkka was a special friend of his.' Though nothing had seemed out of the way then, Benu had later begun to guess the unsaid in his words. Jawadikka was not like most men.

Though he was always soft and polite and extremely kind, Benu had never understood the man her husband considered a brother and emotionally she had always remained aloof from him. But not so her sons when they were born. They called him Balyuppa and followed him around like little puppies and Alijan would smile in such indulgent pride that Benu had not dared to voice the protest forming in her mind. Even as grown young men they had an understanding with their Balyuppa that went way beyond words and actions. When The dumb Aimutti had been beaten to death by the police and her sons were arrested along with Jawadikka and shipped across the Black waters. She had never seen her boys since, nor knew their whereabouts.

The Lost Beretta

Pookottur,
27 July'21
Mithran

'I hadn't realised that the Tirumulpad's memory was so poor!'

The sneer on the Mapla's face pushed Mithran to the end of his tether. The strain of trying to check himself caused his ears to redden into a deep vermillion. If there was something the Sixth Tirumulpad detested more than anything else, it was losing control.

'Get the hell out of here, you mangy, stray mongrel and take away that flea bitten cock of yours as far away from my house as possible!' It would have given him immense contentment to shower his former employee with such choice expletives. But never in his entire life had such language dropped off his tongue. He didn't reckon it would happen now. A foul pauper like this fellow was not going to get the better of him.

Mithran took a deep drag from his pipe and rose from his armchair in as leisurely a pace as he could manage. He put together an appropriately steely, slit eyed glare and arranged a practiced twist of mockery on his lips that outdid the Mapla's sneer by far.

His cousin Divakaran, reclining on the twin armchair put his feet up on the long arms and wriggled himself into a better position, all in readiness to watch the proceedings in comfort.

'First and foremost,' Mithran tested the way his words came out. He approved of the clipped, faux pleasant tone and continued, 'There is nothing wrong with my memory. In the month of *Vrischikam* when you were still in my employ, I instructed you to find a contractor to demolish my gatehouse. You seemed to think that you could take on the project with some of your rundown friends to help you. I did not care who did it as long as it was done to my satisfaction and I gave the nod. I hope my memory meets your approval, so far?'

Mammad's green eyes flashed in rage.

'Four hundred and fifty rupees was fixed as the contract money,' Mithran was pleased with himself for having succeeded in provoking the hotheaded fellow.

'That was initially when I thought…'

'You don't alter the clauses in a contract with each wavering idea that happens to swim into your head. Well, I should have thought twice before offering the contract to fellows with no professional ethics whatsoever.

'Just what was the logic in demanding eight hundred half way through the job? The amount first fixed is the amount that will be paid. Not a single paisa more, as I have been telling you for months. Take it or leave it.

'Secondly, my dear fellow, I wonder if it has crossed that deranged mind of yours that this is my house. The manor in which the Sixth Tirumulpad of Nilambur lives, not the market square where any villager can drop in when it takes his fancy. This is not the first time you have been found inside the manor without permission. Once you actually dared to storm into my Billiards room where only the most honoured guests enter. Last week, when I was away, my wife saw you hanging about in the library. This is the third time. There-will-not-be-a-fourth. So please remove yourself from here this very minute.'

The young Mapla was beside himself.

His bare chest glistening with sweat, he hitched his waist cloth up a trifle and marched out of the grandly furnished living room where the Sixth Tirumulpad received callers. A few feet down the corridor, past the threshold across the veranda, he stomped down the entrance steps to plant himself in the front yard.

Mithran followed him as far as the veranda and leaned his hip casually against the rounded pillar.

'That's better. From now on, whatever business you may have shall be conducted from there.'

As the son of a loyal Kovilakam employee, Mammad's upbringing did not permit him to speak rudely to the

Tirumulpad. But he was a proud man. He couldn't take any more of the deliberate belittling without reacting.

'Nor did I come here to take up permanent residence. I am perfectly happy living in my own little *pora*, thank you.'

'And where do you think that *pora* you speak so highly of came from? If not for your shameless sucking up to the Kovilakam Matriarch, you would be out on the streets without your job here.' Mithran would have dearly liked to counter in this fashion but charity was charity. One did not boast of what one's family gave away for free.

'My visits have a purpose. I will keep coming till I get what is my due. The Tirumulpad knew perfectly well that the gatehouse was unusually sturdy and would take more than a month to pull down. True, in my initial estimate I had expected to finish faster but once the job was underway, I became aware that it could not be done so easily. The minute I realised, I did come here to explain the delay and request a hike in the fixed amount as more men had to work and for a longer period. But the Tirumulpad wouldn't hear of it. I know that the greasy Adhikari of Valluvambram is doing the advising. Maybe it is in exchange for such malicious advice that you offered him and his goons, protection to conduct the Nercha festivities against the Khilafat's decision. Why the Tirumulpad listens to such people is beyond me. Good for the ego, I suppose.

'Not a single rupee was paid to me after the initial advance. I hoped that the Tirumulpad would see reason and complete the job as promised. Quite well too. Alavikutti and the others who toiled hard on the project have not been paid for their labour. The injustice of it all! We will not take it lying down. There is a limit to what a human being can stand. We Maplas may be poor but we still have hot, red blood in our veins. We are bound to protest one day. And that day has dawned! It is time the Sixth Tirumulpad realises this truth. Gone are the days when the poor Mapla could be laid in manor courtyard and trampled all over. Times have changed. Every dog has his day. We may be poor dogs but our day has come.'

'Hear! Hear! There talks the Secretary of the Ernad Khilafat Committee! Unfortunately, your policies and agenda do not interest me in the least.' Mithran allowed himself the pleasure of a sarcastic jibe.

'I am leaving for now,' said Mammad taking a few steps backward without actually turning around. He looked Mithran straight in the eye, something he had rarely done during his tenure as an employee. 'But I will be back. Tomorrow. The day after. And the next day if need be. The Tirumulpad shall pay up. I shall see to it that you do.'

Mithran gave one of his choicest grunts as he went back into the house. This time it said 'just you try'. Back in the sitting room he leaned back into his favourite seat and picked up his pipe from the side table. Divakaran was now reclining deeply in his own chair with a magazine lying spine up on his face.

'Fellow gone, Mithretta?'

Mithran replied with yet another grunt.

One hour before dinner, two days a week, he invariably spent on sprucing up his pipes. He didn't like it when old residue marred the flavor of his favourite tobacco. But it was more than that. He enjoyed the procedure itself, prolonging the steps, paying attention to detail. It calmed him and helped him think.

Today, the first thought that came to his mind as he sat down to it was about the vacuum that Priya's departure had created in his house and his heart. What with his confrontation with the Mapla knave earlier in the day, he would have thought that the fellow's effrontery would take precedence over everything else in his mind.

Mithran smiled to himself in the privacy of the library. After he had removed the remaining ash with the aid of a specially designed scoop, he blew softly into the mouth piece to expel persistent particles. That chit of a girl was now his wife! It still came as a surprise to him sometimes. Till her gatecrash into his life, he had seldom considered the pleasure that the love of a beautiful woman could bring.

When he tried to change her mind about embarking on a journey to her *tharawad*, he had had two reasons in mind. The first of course was her safety. One heard of crazy things goings on these days. Not that it was an exceptionally long trip, yet, was the risk worth taking? Also he had astonished himself when he realised how much he would miss her presence. Her cheerful, lively chatter. Her bossy management of the house. The redolent perfume of something compound and mysterious that wafted from her hair, which even with his knack for cataloguing subtle scents of high quality tobacco, he had been unable to identify. The flash of the slender gold chains that encircled her ankles and formed rhythmic curves in the air as she swung higher and higher on her newly tied swing on the upstairs veranda.

There was no way he could go with her, not with all the pressing matters he had to attend to. And she wished to be with her mother on her birthday. What Priya wanted, he simply had to comply with, he thought with a laugh as he ran the cleaner back and forth over the bowl of the pipe before dipping down into it.

He had sat in this very library with her on the night before her journey. It had been his pipe cleaning day, but Priya would have none of it. She had smiled, pouted and grumbled till he put his paraphernalia away with a sigh.

'One, two, three, four, five,' she had lifted the delicate fingers on her right hand one by one. 'No. Six and seven.' Two others on her left hand went up. 'Just seven days my Sixth Tirumulpad. I'll be back within a week.'

Mithran grunted.

'Is that a grievance I hear'?

Priyamvada had in this short time become an expert in reading the meaning of his various grunts. In fact she had made a research project of it.

'Maybe. And some amount of concern too. It worries me to have my lovely little wife on the roads for hours with these crackpots on the rampage.'

'Lovely, eh? Little eh?' Priya scampered up to his chair

and perched on its arm. Her tiny fingers found their way to his sides and tickled.

'Hey! Get off,' he squirmed and gave her a shove.

'Ha! My most effective weapon. Can bring the mighty Mithran Thampan to his knees,' Priya had giggled.

'Don't be anxious about the journey, dear husband. I will be perfectly safe. I have in my custody the most powerful safety device to protect me from any rogue.' She wiggled all ten fingers in the air mimicking an onslaught of tickles. Mithran sighed again, looked heavenward in helpless surrender. Can't be too bad, he thought. Priya's elder brother, one uncle, two cousins and a whole retinue of musclemen not to mention the maids would come to escort her home the next day. She wouldn't come to any harm surrounded by all these people. He shrugged away the uneasiness.

'Fine. You are right. If marauders obstruct your path, you could always tickle them to death.'

Mithran took special care to stuff a bit of newspaper into the bowl of the pipe. The extra cleaning fluid should not run. It would ruin the outside of the beautiful briar.

When he was absorbed in his pipes and his thoughts, time always flew. Only the rim of the last one to go. He was always careful about polishing the rims well. Sayippes rubbed them with spit. Disgusting. Mithran preferred a dollop of sesame seed oil to polish his pipes.

'Mithretta!'

Divakaran popped his head into the library. While Mithran went about his business with his pipes, his cousin had been occupying himself in the Billiards room, fine tuning his game. That was why Divakaran was one of his favourite houseguests. He didn't expect to be entertained. That reminded him. He would be entertaining today. Damodaran, his cousin on his father's side would be arriving with the same man he had dropped in with a few months ago. This time they had been invited with a specific purpose. When Divakaran arrived from Nilambur this time, he had a special message from the Matriarch. Find out as much as you can from Damodaran about that young writer who goes by the pseudonym 'The Outcaste'.

Cheriyammamma's commands were never ignored, Mithran had grunted affectionately at the time. His Pattu-time clash with her had been forgotten over the months and his warm feelings for his Little Grandmother had resurfaced. Her instructions came as a surprise though.

'It seems you have a rival,' he had teased Priya and chuckled at her expression. 'The Matriarch has developed an interest in 'The Outcaste' as well.' Priya tried to find out whatever she could about the man whenever Damodaran visited. Initially Mithran had felt a twinge of displeasure at her interest in another man, but of course the feeling hadn't lasted. He had asked her about it once or twice but she had been very mysterious in her usual theatrical manner and said she would tell him when the right time came. Not particularly curious by nature, he had let it go. Now Cheriyammamma wanted to know more about him. Mithran had dutifully obeyed and collected all the information she required.

He had gathered all this information from Damodaran and a few days before Priya had left for her *tharawad*, the Matriarch had sent word that he was to invite the young man to the manor and discuss a proposal for Sethu! Marriage proposals and the related formalities had never been his cup of tea but there was no question of refusing Cheriyammamma. Priya had been over the moon. This had been her secret apparently. She had wished to unite Sethu and this Outcaste.

Well, he and Damodaran were expected that day. He hoped Divakaran would do all the talking.

'Damodaran Namboothiri is here with The Outcaste,' Divakaran announced as if on cue.

Ah! The two men would live long. Mithran nodded at his cousin. A silly little saying, he had always thought. If someone turns up just as you were thinking or talking of them, they live to be a hundred. The kind of logic he couldn't understand, he thought with a chuckle. Anyway, he'd been impressed by The Outcaste. May things work out for Sethu.

'I'll be there in a minute,' he told Divakaran and began to pack up all the odds and ends he had lain out. His gaze fell for a second on the far corner of the room. Something was amiss. He couldn't place it and went back to finishing up. What was it he looked up again and this time scanned that part of the room more attentively. Oh yes, the small safe was ajar.

'Hey, Divakara, just a minute.' His cousin stepped

back into the room.

'What's up, Mithretta?'

'Look at that cabinet over there. The latch is unfastened.'

'That one? But you rarely open it.'

'No, I don't. And I haven't. Not for… at least two weeks,' Mithran tried to recall when he had last been to the cabinet.

Divakaran went over to the corner. The key, on its silver chain was dangling right there. He locked up smoothly and the two cousins left the library to receive their visitors.

The Outcaste

After the initial small talk, and tea, Divakaran Thampan seemed to be stumbling over his words. As if he was having difficulty introducing a topic.

'You know my sister, don't you?' He came straight to the point and addressed me.

'Of course he does. The Thampatti of *Ittichiri* fame,' Damodaran answered for me. 'You could say it was he who initiated her into the world of published writers,' he laughed.

'Well… er… my grandmother, the Kovilakam Matriarch wishes to propose an alliance.'

Mithran Thampan contributed a low gruff sound which I had come to recognise as his trademark response to most situations.

Fortunately, I was spared having to reply when

Damodaran roared in approval. 'A wonderful idea indeed!'

The two Thampans seemed to be scanning my face.

This was totally unexpected and I experienced a loss of words.

Inside me a sudden cool and gentle breeze seemed to blow. Akin to nothing I had felt before.

I had always prided myself on my generally steady ways. But when I had expressed to Narayanan my desire to marry his widowed sister, it had been a rash thing I did. Not to mention arrogant and egotistical. I had simply taken it for granted that marrying me was the best thing that the unfortunate widow could expect in life. After making the proposal, I had felt good about myself for a few days. There were too many young widows in his community and they should be given a new opportunity in life for the life of a widow was worse than death. Someone had to take the first step so that people would begin to think. I had always believed in leading from the front in matters that mattered and reveled in the firm conviction that I had done the right thing.

Then the story of Ittichiri had crossed my path, making me think again. A feeling of uncertainty began to develop. Why hadn't I stopped to consider the girl's own wishes?

Coincidence, or whatever one wished to call it, the way things developed, it appeared as if either Narayanan's sister had read Ittichiri and been influenced by it or the writer of the story had consulted the widow before drafting it. But neither was true, I knew from plain logic.

The widow had refused my proposal. When Narayanan brought the message, I had not felt a single negative emotion. I may not have realised it at the moment, but what I did feel was strangely like relief.

Why hadn't I stopped to consider that the girl may wish for something else in life? The embarrassing question lingered at the back of my mind in the days following the rejection. And yet another kept raising its head time and again. Had I even stopped to consider whether I myself may wish for something else in life? Was one's ideology a strong enough foundation on which a sound marriage could be built?

When these new questions surfaced, my subconscious mind conjured up the image of the writer but I hadn't understood the connection.

But it came to me now. It was this girl I wished to share the rest of my life with. Her brother's proposal helped me interpret my own feelings.

'I repeat, it is a great idea,' Damodaran was still talking. 'But our friend here has certain principles. I do wonder if such an alliance wouldn't contradict the theories he propounds. For instance, you Thampans know that among our people it is unheard of for the younger sons to marry within the community. We invariably settle on matches from Kovilakams or Nair Tharawads. This practice has a lot of harmful effects. Especially on the women. Polygamy and early widowhood to mention a couple. In truth this angle of things had never crossed our minds till he began mentioning it in his writings. Given this, would he consider a Kovilakam alliance? And this is just one point against this alliance, Thampan.'

Damodaran had been talking as if I were not even in the room. Divakaran Thampan seemed to be thinking on the same lines for he turned to me, 'My grandmother specifically instructed me to find out what you yourself thought of it. It is perfectly fine if it is a no. But she will want straight facts.'

'Well, given my previous experience, I must abstain from impulsive decisions concerning marriage.' I must have colored for I felt the heat. 'Damodarettan can tell you the whole embarrassing story. If I were to consider this proposal or any other for that matter, I would need time to think it over. And I would need to know what the girl feels about it. And Damodaretta, I have learnt that when it comes to a relationship like marriage, one does not insist on going by ones principles alone. It is a matter of the heart and the heart alone. So if you will give me time…'

The Thampans, Mithran and Divakaran left it at that.

Interesting conversation spiced up the evening meal. With plenty happening all around there was no dearth of topics. Lively opinions and various accounts were passed around with the basket of pappadams.

The Sixth Tirumulpad frowned a little at the small portions on my leaf.

'I hope you find the meal to your satisfaction.'

'Oh don't let it bother you, Mithran Thampan,' said Damodaran with a laugh. 'He eats like a sparrow. Quite the opposite of the caricature of the gluttonous Namboothiri. Often skips meals too. I always warn him that by the time he turns forty he is going to have painful ulcers all the way down to his…' Mithran cleared his throat. His cousin caught on and refrained from mentioning the part of anatomy he had been about to.

'It is just that I need little,' I explained.

'Well, you can put aside your poor eating habits while you are here. We can't have visitors leave the manor looking emaciated. Not good for the Nilambur Kovilakam's reputation,' retorted Divakaran. 'Appunni, a little rice for me please and the *kadumanga*.' The man in charge of serving their meal, rushed to the basket of rice.

'Anyway, you couldn't accuse Damodaran of eating like a bird. More like a horse as the Englishman would put it.' A characteristic twisted grin, appeared on Mithran's face as he teased his cousin who merely guffawed and asked, 'Talking of the English, what does your friend the Collector have to say of the current situation, Thampan?'

'Oh, he is ready to burst into tears at the smallest of prods.' It was Divakaran who answered, his own eyes beginning to water as the *kadumanga's* fiery sauce found its mark.

'Poor Mr Thomas. Keeps making mistake after mistake. Too proud to accept them, too inefficient to make amends. Yes, he is in a bad way,' said Mithran.

'It's Hitchcock one should watch out for. Dangerous

man. He had called here some time ago. Had a lot to say,' Divakaran raised his *kadumanga* stained fingers to mime a snake crawling in the air above his leaf.

I remembered Madhavan Nair's assessment of the two officers.

'Yes, Hitchcock appears to be an epitome of what the British are trying to do here,' I said. Damodaran shook his head to indicate he didn't quite follow.

Divakaran lifted a mildly puzzled eyebrow.

Mithran grunted.

'It is one thing for poor Maplas to protest against oppression, nothing personal, Thampan. And no reference to Pookottur affairs of course. What I meant was, if the Maplas feel they are getting a raw deal, they have every right to demand justice. But this turn towards violence, this communal swing,' he stopped for a moment and considered, 'it is going to have dire consequences. This is precisely what the British want. What they have been wanting, and getting for more than a century. And what we are doing here is playing right into their hands. Gandhi realizes this, but when it comes to certain people, he just can't say no. I only hope it won't turn out to be too much of a mess.'

Mithran and Divakaran listened in silence.

Damodaran mentioned my friendship with Shekharan Nair, the Congress leader.

'You are a Congress advocate then,' Divakaran's direct question was tinged with surprise.

'Tough to answer, Thampan,' I had to laugh. 'I am an

advocate of what I believe is good for the land. Whether it comes from the Congress or someone else.'

'He has even visited that Mapla who calls himself Alijan Sahib in his house,' added Damodaran.

'Ha. Nice company you like to keep,' commented Mithran.

'Well, Sarvavyapi, is one of our nicknames for him,' continued Damodaran jokingly. 'Omnipresent. You could find him anywhere. The Samoothiri's palace or a poor Mapla's shack, an impoverished Namboothiri's *illam* or the bungalow of an English planter. You never know whose side he is on.'

'On the right side, I hope.' I had long finished eating and was sitting with my fingers pressed on my empty leaf to ensure that I was served no more. I was merely waiting politely for the others to finish before I got up to wash my hands.

'Your views are interesting,' said Divakaran drying his hands on the starched thorth Appunni had left for the purpose. 'To tell you the truth, there is someone back home who will wring things out of me the minute I get back to the Kovilakam. My grandmother, the Nilambur Kovilakam Matriarch simply soaks up information. Anachevi Mathu, she is fondly known as.'

'Glad to be of service to Anachevi Mathu, I mean the Matriarch,' I grinned.

'And she will expect an answer to the other matter. Take your time but say something and let it be definite.'

Mithran

A round of rummy was proposed before bed. Mithran declined. As he filled his pipe for his bedtime smoke. He listened rather inattentively to further banter from Divakaran.

'Make it a point never ever to play cards with Mithrettan's wife, the wicked Priyamvada or for that matter my sister, Sethu,' he warned the other two as he shuffled out the pack. 'The biggest tricksters in the game.'

'Oh. Your sister cheats at cards, does she? Another point to think over before I decide on an answer, Thampan.' The Outcaste did not take his eyes off his cards but he sounded playful, Mithran noted rather distractedly. There had been something else on his mind all through dinner. It didn't come to him till he reached the bottom of the stairs on his way to bed. Changing his mind, he opened the library door instead and called for a lamp.

He fumbled with the latch on the cabinet in the corner. Realising that Divakaran had left the key on top of the tall cupboard, he reached for it. The boy came in with the light. Mithran pulled up a chair and peered into the open safe to survey his collection of pistols. The Allen and the Thurber single shot with the look of an inverted bugle sat right in front. The Browning. It was the 1900 model with a unique finish. The model with the Great War connection. The Browning. He looked more closely. Why was it knocked carelessly to the left hand corner? He would never have left it in that awkward position with so little regard.

Mithran was a meticulous collector. He valued all his possessions. His stamps, his pipes and their fixings, his Billiard equipment and his five small pistols, all these had a special place in his heart. His pipes and the Billiards things he used regularly, he spent a few hours every week on the stamps but the guns were different. Except for admiring them once in a while, seeing that they were clean and well maintained, he rarely looked at them. He hadn't ever considered using them but he knew their mechanics quite well from poring over the instruction manuals while cleaning. Getting the required formalities completed hadn't been easy. But when Mithran wanted something he persisted till he got it. The Indian Arms Act stated that no Indian could possess a gun of any description unless a British officer of some authority certified his loyalty to the British Empire. Loyalty or no loyalty, a certificate had been issued.

The Beretta! Something thumped violently in his chest. Mithran frowned and carefully replaced the Browning in its rightful place. A trifle frantic, he delved into the cabinet's depths and searched. The small black gun was nowhere to be seen. His Beretta semi-automatic was gone.

He panted uncharacteristically.

'Divakara!'

Yes the Beretta had been stolen. Who would have thought that scurvy Mapla cad would have had the nerve to make off with firearms from the manor!

This time Mithran flew off the handle altogether. And he couldn't think clearly enough to hate himself for losing control.

Mapla Mob At Mithran's Manor

Pookkottur, Ernad
29 July 1921
Mammad

Mammad chose to ignore the steps, vaulting over them instead onto the *palli's*. Wraparound veranda to slip into the last row of worshippers. His breath came in rapid unsteady puffs that seemed to echo embarrassingly in the akapalli. He had made it to the mosque at a run.

He had spent the whole night with his eyes wide open and fixed on the ceiling. It would have been some comfort to light a lamp and watch the spider.

Before it was light, he rose and slipped out. After washing himself at the well and hurriedly scrubbing *umikkari* over his teeth, he left the house, walking aimlessly to find himself outside the village and plodding over wet fields. He had intended to be back home for a light morning meal but lost track of time. As he walked along the edge of the gushing Valiyathode Canal, completely preoccupied with his thoughts, he heard the distant vanq call. It made but an absent impression. It had even slipped his mind that it was a Friday. Closer to the market place at Palakkal when the second call sounded, he had raced to the mosque. Worshippers were giving him curious stares as he tried to regain his breath. Alavikutti, a few rows ahead, turned around with his eyebrows raised. On his left, Basheer gently dropped his eyelids in a calming gesture. Alijan Sahib sent a sidelong glance from diagonally across the room and fidgeted with his neck rumal.

When the *niskaram* rituals finally concluded, Mammad hastily slunk out before anyone could catch up with inquisitive queries. Behind the broad trunk of the jack tree, away from the direct line of anybody's vision, he flopped down on the ground amidst the crackle of dry leaves..

Each futile, disgraceful trip to the manor made him feel as if his skin was peeling off in pain and shame. What choice did he have but to keep at it till the Tirumulpad paid up. If the loss had been just his, he may have let it go but Alavikutti and the others had put in a lot of work. Months had passed and they were yet to be paid. Mammad felt responsible and it pained him. None of his friends had complained but Mammad knew they could ill afford to lose wages.

It wasn't long before Alavikutti came jogging around

the jack tree to find Mammad punching his palm in frustration. Basheer followed at a more dignified pace.

'What's the matter, *changathi?* 'Need you ask?' Basheer answered for him. 'He is worried about the Tirumulpad situation. What else?'

'Listen Mammade,' said the good hearted Alavikutti.' You should forget about the whole thing. If he who hoards thousands of rupees and paras and paras of grain chooses to be so stingy… I hate to see you worry over this when there is so much to do. I would say let it go. But…'

'The 'but' *is* an important thing, Alavikutti. There is the matter of principle. If we let him off then our relentless work was pointless.' Mammad frowned.

'Yes. It is one of our main objectives. Fighting for our rights. Not allowing these oppressive landlords to treat us like dogs. When we think from that angle…' Basheer looked thoughtful.

'I will not lower my hood and make a silent retreat,' Mammad insisted. 'I will keep hissing and spitting venom.'

'I know.' Alavikutti threw an affectionate arm around him. 'It is just that we don't wish to see our changathi so unhappy. Alle, Basheere?'

'I can't think what has come over the Tirumulpad.' Said Mammad setting aside his anger for a minute and thinking fairly. 'I have known him for years. He may be arrogant and selfish but he has never before refused to pay his workers. When I was in Nilambur, the Baliya Thampatti asked a hundred questions about this matter.

She seemed quite baffled too. You know what, I think that sleazy Ahmed Adhikari is behind this. He doles out this kind of advice in return for the Sixth Tirumulpad's support in his underhand schemes. Especially since that supposed victory over the Nercha affair, he's been acting all the more self-important.'

'The Nercha! Ha! Don't remind me of it,' Alavikutti ground his teeth.

'That's right. We are all trying to put it behind us.'

Mammad had the Nercha episode tucked firmly away in the corner of his heart where the need for revenge had burnt a hole. Basheer knew his friend well and saw the vindictive fire in his eyes.

'This is not the time to dwell on past events, *changathi,*' he patted Mammad's arm. 'What can be done to make the landlord pay up? Once that issue is out of the way, we can concentrate wholeheartedly on our Khilafat work.'

We need a more active approach.' Alavikutti's view made Basheer nod thoughtfully. 'What would you suggest?'

'We need to intimidate him,' was the quick response.

'How?' Mammad sounded a trifle disheartened.

'We must play on our strengths,' said Basheer.

'We are braver than the Tirumulpad's men and our intentions are purer. But for practical purposes, we have an even greater strongpoint. Our numbers. I mean we have more manpower on our side.'

Mammad silently processed his friend's theory in his mind. Alavikutti however had no qualms.

'Yes! Yes *changathi*! We'll round up the lads and mob the manor.'

Slowly and hesitantly a grin broke out on Mammad's tired face. His green eyes gleamed. It might work after all.

Excited murmurs from the direction of the mosque stalled further plans. Two Hindu villagers were in the courtyard talking to Alijan Sahib. And people were crowded around them. Astonishment, indignation and a general air of tension could be sensed from where the three friends stood. Some people were looking around searchingly when one man pointed to the jack tree.

'There he is! Come on! He must be told immediately.' People were soon hastening in their direction. Unable to keep up with the sprinters, Alijan Sahib's pace however was visibly urgent as he too made his way towards them. His neck was rumal-less and his expression grim. Sure shot signs that the tidings were dark.

'Mammade!'

The first man to reach them was panting too hard to say anything more.

'*Pora*!'

'Raziya!'

'Search!'

'Police!'

Abrupt and incomplete but alarming nevertheless. Alijan Sahib stepped up and placed a hand on the small of Mammad's back.

'Don't panic Mammade. But this is serious business. The police were in your house. One-armed Pakkaran and his friend saw the whole thing. He came to me at once. They raided the *pora*. Poor Raziya. She had no idea what was happening. Frightened out of her wits, poor girl. My Benu is there with her now. Some women came for her and she rushed over.'

'Raid? At my house? B-but why?'

'What were they looking for, Sahib,' asked Basheer.

Alijan shook his head. 'Pakkaran does not know. Anyway, we'll soon find out. Come. Let's go.'

As if in a trance, Mammad allowed himself to be guided down the lanes he knew like the back of his hand without actually seeing anything. The outraged voices of the accompanying crowd sounded more like a distant wind. Basheer walked steadily by his side and Alavikutti bounded at the head of the pack, waving animatedly.

His house was so full of women that they overflowed into the lane outside and the nearby field. Some stood by with long, worried faces. A few had tears running down their cheeks. Kunhaishumma, the Pathiri woman, her basket of snacks forgotten by the wayside, was giving a non-stop coverage of the incident to each newcomer. Her voice was cracking in the strain. When Mammad and the others arrived, the house looked as if a *mayyath* had taken place there.

A mild shock registered in Mammad's hazy mind as he glanced around the two small rooms in his house and saw the chaos. Their few belongings were flung every which way. The wooden chest, Raziya's wedding gift from the Baliya Thampatti was open and her clothes lay in a heap nearby.

The small shelf on the wall was empty and the bottles of medicated oils that she used to apply on his wounds were smashed. Two pillows stripped off their faded covers were ripped open and the cotton spilling out of their bellies flew about the place. Raziya crouched in a corner with her head on her knees and her *thattam* askew. Alijan Sahib's beewi had her arm around her. Mammad wanted to rush over to his wife, hold her at a distance and look her over to ensure that she was safe, to crush her to his burning chest and hold her there. But he found himself unable to move.

'There has been a robbery at the manor,' explained an elderly neighbor who had spoken to the police. 'They are investigating.'

'Here? In Mammad's house?'

'Yes, Sahib. The Sixth Tirumulpad has accused Mammad of theft. It seems he went to police station first thing in the morning and filed a complaint.'

The crowd saw red.

'Mammad, a thief? How dare the Tirumulpad make such an allegation?'

'What exactly is he said to have stolen? Money? Gold?' Alijan Sahib was angry too.

'They said it was a gun, Sahib.'

Everyone was dumbstruck for a moment.

A gun?

Mammad slumped down on the broken step at the entrance and buried his head in his hands.

'The landlord has gone too far this time,' one young Mapla was proclaiming emotionally. 'Does he think he can take advantage of our poverty? What he fails to understand is that we may be poor but we will not be trifled with.'

'And because we are Islam.'

Each word, each opinion felt like a nail being driven into Mammad's head.

'Deputy Superintendent Narayana Menon, you knew he was recently promoted didn't you? He arrived himself while the constables were making the search. Seemed to be disappointed that the stolen article was not discovered here. He left with special instructions that Mammad present himself at the manor with immediate effect, taking the gun with him,' the neighbor was informing Alijan Sahib in a subdued voice. 'That poor girl is in no condition to convey the message. That's why I took it on myself...'

'Mammade, pull yourself together. This is not the time to lose heart,' said Alijan Sahib briskly.

'There is no need for Mammad to go groveling to the manor. He has done nothing wrong,' pronounced the steadfast Alavikutti.

'But not obeying police orders could get him into trouble,' one man who had not left with the rest was worried.

'What do you propose, Basheere?' Alijan Sahib asked the most level-headed of his lieutenants.

Basheer pondered for a moment.

'Mammad should go. But not alone.'

'Ah yes!' said Alavikutti. 'We should go with him. Not just the two of us. We'll gather as big a gang as possible.'

'Sahib, earlier at the *pallithodi* we were discussing the matter of the money the Tirumulpad owes Mammad and some others for the project of pulling down his gatehouse, and we eventually came to the decision that we should round up a large group to gherao the manor and coerce the Tirumulpad to pay up. I think now, we can kill two birds with one stone.'

'The plan appeals to me' approved Alijan Sahib in his slow, raspy manner. He carefully knotted the rumal about his neck. 'Alavikutti! Gather the forces.'

For about two hours there was relative silence in the town. Except for the light patter of messengers' feet as they flew from *pora* to *pora* and a general buzz as Basheer's strategy and Alijan Sahib's instructions were conveyed all over, not much was heard. By about half past three, drumbeats began to sound. From the various lanes and bylanes echoed furious taqbeer cries as armies bearing daggers and sticks snaked out of them to pullulate into the field behind the mosque. From across the Valiyathode canal, a few people from the neighbouring villages who got a wind of the plan joined them. Every able bodied Pookottur Mapla, leaving his special Friday lunch cooling at home, was united in the cause.

It was this menacing spate that flooded into Mithran's manor by four.

Narayana Menon

The Deputy Superintendent, Narayana Menon was getting increasingly impatient. Twisting his large, khaki clad contour this way and that, he sat impatiently on the straight backed wooden chair placed beneath the tamarind tree in the yard so that he could speak to that Mammad outside when he showed his face. More than four hours since he had left the fellow's nasty little shack but there was no sign of him yet. He took off his uniform turban, ran his fingers over his balding pate and let out a sharp breath. The Sixth Tirumulpad who sat in the veranda without a word, was lighting his third meditative pipe. The most relaxed member of the group gathered at the manor was the Tirumulpad's amiable cousin who lounged nearby with a faint hum emanating from his throat and fingers drumming on the arm of the chair.

It was when Divakaran Thampan stopped humming and drumming to sit up straight that the Deputy Super sensed something and perked up his ears.

Allahu Akbar!

The taqbeer, sounding strangely sinister, drew nearer. Narayana Menon sprung out of his chair and barked orders to his distracted subordinates. By then the Mapla mob had thrown open the gate and thronged the manor. The cat eyed thief was right in the front of what seemed to the Deputy Super an angry ocean on a stormy night.

'What the...'

Narayana Menon found himself thrown off his feet by one Mapla who was splaying his hands as he rushed ahead. Before he could even scramble back on his feet, the Sixth Tirumulpad was surrounded, pushed back into his chair with a dozen knives pointing at his person.

The Outcaste

It felt like yet another sneeze was coming on. Seated on an upended bucket in the back room of the tiny, grocery shop in Manjeri, amid sacks of grain and tins of oil, I found the rising dust and strong smells causing cutaneous sensations in my nostrils.

Hari Krishna!

I dug my hand into my shoulder bag for a thorth. 'Hari Krish…'

A Hari Krishna for every sneeze. A childhood habit instilled by my mother still came instinctively to me. I had long ago given up, quite consciously, the ritual prayers and pujas that the men in my circle went about performing in the most mundane and mindless fashion day after day, but such little things stuck. I wrapped the thorth around the lower half of my face and settled down more comfortably on the bucket.

Sarvavyapi, Damodarettan had called me. He should see me here now. Perched precariously on the makeshift seat in the store of a Mapla's grocery shop. But that was how I functioned. When I accepted the Tirumulpads' invitation to stay at the Pookottur manor for a couple of days, I had scheduled my itinerary in such a way that I could spend today with Hamsa in Manjeri. Through the half open door I watched the Mapla lad wrap chilies in a newspaper cone for his customer. Hamsa was the nephew of Aboobacker, Shekharan Nair's childhood friend. Hamsa had helped draw me into several Mapla circles and many of them had stopped being wary of me as a kafir and an outsider. A few had even begun to see me as a friend and well-wisher. I seemed to have acquired a new human identity and now in these villages there were at least a few who trusted me and valued my opinions. Within this small but steady group I had been able to build a degree of levelheadedness. Things had worked out extremely well and more and more Maplas were beginning to understand that nothing could be gained by thoughtless violence. Still, they had a long way to go. I had marked out for my next project a group of young men who had taken to looting and torching Hindu homes. Some of them had been spotted in the woods torturing two Thiyya boys in a mock conversion ritual. It was my immediate goal to get to these young men. If I could only effect a shift in their perspectives, if only I could channelise their energies differently, my village would be clean. This was what I wished to discuss with Hamsa today.

I did not wish to disturb Hamsa while he was working. The lad had to make a living after all.

I had left Mithran Thampan's manor that morning with plans to return before sunset. Damodarettan had business of his own as well. Something niggled at the back of my mind as I recalled the early hours of the day. I had woken up to some mild commotion and gathering my thorth and other paraphernalia, was making my way towards the bathroom wing connected to the back of the manor by a long corridor when I heard cartwheels screech. Peering around the corner, I saw that the cart had been drawn up to the front portico. The Sixth Tirumulpad, less regardful of his attire today, was striding purposefully out of the house. His cousin was at his heels trying to deter him.

'Mithretta, don't you think you should wait till…' Mithran dismissed Divakaran with a wave and climbed into the cart.

At breakfast I had refrained from interfering in the Thampans' internal affairs but Damodarettan had asked after his cousin. Divakaran sighed resignedly.

'He's gone down to the police station.'

Damodaran's eyes popped out of his head.

'At this time? What for?'

'A pistol is missing from his collection. A Beretta 1915. He thinks it has been stolen and went down to place an official complaint.' We had all gone our different ways after breakfast agreeing to be back in the evening.

What had become of the affair, I wondered in passing. It was half past two in the afternoon. If Hamsa returned to the back room soon, I could leave for Pookottur in an hour or so. Early tomorrow I was due to return home. I leaned back for a view of the store front. There were quite a few people out there. Brisk business for Hamsa. But… I angled my bucket further back. These people weren't really buying anything. Just talking animatedly, their eyes wide and shaven heads glistening.

Hamsa dipped his head into the backroom and beckoned to me.

'Pookottur is on the rampage,' he said as I stepped

out into the store. 'They are rounding up men and arms. It seems they are planning a gherao campaign to the manor. There are even rumours that they plan to… er… assassinate the Sixth Tirumulpad.'

'Hamsa, could you close up the store now? I want you to come with me.'

When Hamsa and I with his small band of handpicked Mapla moderates arrived at Pookottur, the pathways and narrow mud tracks were all deserted. When the cart Hamsa had arranged for our travel clopped by, an occasional thattam would peep out. The menfolk were all at the manor. At the gates, our party had trouble entering. Elderly Maplas lingered at the periphery of the crowd gathered around the Tirumulpad and the Deputy Super, too old to actually partake in the gherao but wishing to guarantee whole hearted support to the undertaking. The Hindus of Pookottur, Thiyyas, Nairs, a stray Namboothiri or two were too terrified to interfere but at the same time too curious to keep away, hovered at the back, pulling themselves up on their toes for a better view of the happenings in the courtyard.

I managed to elbow my way into the crowd with Hamsa and the others close behind. It was shocking to see Mithran not moving a muscle as he sat upright in the chair, his expression absolutely impassive. Four men, daggers in their hands and taqbeer on their lips stood menacingly round him. Someone had bound Divakaran to a pillar and a stocky Mapla stood guard. Deputy Superintendent Narayana Menon whom I had met once when he had been the Circle Inspector was not better off. Two shiny blades were poised dangerously close to his throat. Searching the crowd for a less aggressive face I found a tall slender Mapla who seemed reasonably in control of himself.

'Hamsa,' I whispered and looked pointedly at the man I had selected. Hamsa guessed at once and nodded. Retreating to a quieter corner of the courtyard, I watched him touch the fellow's arm and say something in his ear. In a minute the two men made their way towards me.

'This is Basheer'. Hamsa introduced the man.

'Basheere, may I talk to you for a moment? I am not from these parts but I am the Tirumulpad's house guest for a couple of days. I left the manor this morning on some business and got back a few minutes ago. Can you tell me what all this is about?'

'Are you his relative?'

'No. Just an acquaintance.'

'Then I suggest you go back to wherever you are from. Don't let this concern you.'

'Ikka, what has the landlord done to anger you all so?' Hamsa's tone was so sympathetic that Basheer automatically sensed a receptive ear.

'He had the audacity to call one among us a thief and file a case against him. The police are threatening to arrest our Mammad if the stolen gun is not produced immediately. Mark my words, the Deputy Super will not leave the place alive in order to make that arrest. The boys can do a neat job with their daggers. You can't accuse a whole town of murder, can you? We will all be in it.'

'Will you consider withdrawing for a while,' I asked as the thickset man watching over Divakaran left him to walk towards us.

'What's it, Basheere? Who is this?' He scowled at me.

'Listen, if you can call back your friends for a while, I am sure I can find a solution.'

The second man roared in malicious laughter. 'Oh! So a peacemaker has arrived eh.'?

Basheer looked scornful too.

'We'll find our own solutions thank you.'

'But if your man has nothing to do with the theft, why should you fear? The police cannot make an arrest without proper evidence.'

Basheer said nothing.

'Listen, an innocent man has nothing to fear. At the same time you are not going to gain anything from all this. It only creates the impression that the accused is actually guilty and you are all trying to shield him. When their rage has simmered down and they have had time to think it over, even your own men are going to believe that to be the truth.'

'You… you foul Kafir!'

'No! Alavikutti,' Basheer clutched his stocky friend's arm.

'Ikka.',Hamsa looked Basheer straight in the eye.

'I am not a Pookottur man myself. Just passing by. That enables me to keep a cool head. No one can deny that our people are brave and good hearted and that we stick by our friends whatever may come. But I can't help asking myself if we sometimes don't let this work to our disadvantage. All of you here are unwavering in your trust for this Mammad. But pause for a while, Ikka, and think. This crazy exhibition you are putting up here is going to make things worse for him.'

I looked at Hamsa in admiration. The Mapla called Alavikutti attempted to wriggle out of his friend's hold with a cry of 'traitor'. Basheer however maintained the firm clasp on his friend's elbow and pursed his lips.

Basheer was rethinking.

I wasted no time in adding my bit. 'The Tirumulpad, however rich and influential is a mere man. This gherao drama of yours may succeed in giving him a jolt. But you must remember that the police are a force. A government force. Today, there are but three or four of them here and you can intimidate them with your sheer numbers. But your victory will be momentary. There is an entire body of police personnel out there, not to mention the army. Call the insurgents back.'

I studied the crowd. A visibly softening crowd. Those closer to the gates and the lane outside were scattering. Further into the courtyard, many of them had tucked their weapons back in their belts and were giving each other dubious looks. Hamsa's friends were doing a good job. The Mapla lads circulated in the midst with a hint here, a suggestion there and general comments how this could backfire, thereby managing to create a sense of uncertainty in them. The fierceness of their purpose had begun to falter.

Basheer did not fail to notice this change and exchanged frowns with Alavikutti. He had clearly not expected this. At least not so soon. Not before their goal had been achieved.

'All right,' he said with some hesitation. 'I can ask them to stand back for a while. Can you guarantee that our demands will be met?'

'How can I guarantee anything? I am just an outsider. I don't know any of you. My acquaintance with the Tirumulpad is very recent. I am certainly not in a position to make promises. But I can talk to the Deputy Super and the Sixth Tirumulpad. If they are assured there will be no violence from your side, they may agree to a proper investigation without an immediate arrest. If your friend cooperates and if he is innocent, then I don't see why there should be a problem.'

Narayana Menon stood up and brushed his khakis with his knuckles in an attempt to regain some dignity. For the last couple of hours, I guessed that he had found himself in a most awkward position. Between the devil and the deep sea. Arrest the fellow on the spot and get stabbed in the neck. Refrain and get chewed by his superiors for neglecting duty.

Satisfied that there would be no arrest the crowd prepared to disperse.

The accused's stocky friend nudged him suddenly.

'What about the money? We cannot leave until the landlord pays up.' The Deputy Super glanced at the Tirumulpad. The wooden expression gave him no answers. He turned hopefully to me, as if hoping I had a few more tricks in my bundle. I could only shrug in answer.

I had to see this through, I sighed in exasperation and raised a pacifying arm towards the Maplas. Then grabbing Divakaran's arm which the Thampan, now free of his bonds was flexing to regain circulation. As for the Sixth Tirumulpad, I couldn't resist fixing him with a glare as I marched Divakaran indoors. Mithran followed in silence.

'Believe me,' I said once inside the manor, 'You Thampans need nursemaids running after you all the time to keep you out of mischief. Now, what is this about money? Been taking loans from the Maplas?'

Mithran glowered, looked half sullen, half grateful. Divakaran scratched his head with a weak grin and went on to tell the tale of the gatehouse contract gone bad.

'Pay up for God's sake and send the poor fellows on their way. This is not the time to cling to false pride.'

'Poor fellows!' Mithran started to shriek indignantly but contained himself. 'But they are demanding more than the initial deal. It is a rip off.'

'Ah yes,' I know I sounded caustic. 'Better a Mapla's dagger in your chest than a rip off. Really, Thampan, stop playing these mulish games. Four hundred and fifty or eight hundred. What does it matter? Write it down as Kovilakam expenses or charity or even consider that the extra money was let adrift in the Chaliyar. But give the fellow his money and save your noble skin.'

Mithran grunted. This time it translated into mortification. And humiliation.

But… Er… I Er…don't have the money.'

'What next! Reduced to destitution?'

'Er.no',. Divakaran answered. 'After Mithrettan went down to the police station this morning, I took everything to the bank in Manjeri. Didn't want to risk another theft'.

'Then I suppose I'll have to see to that too. Hamsa!'

When the manor courtyard was finally free of dagger bearing Maplas and khaki clad policemen, I turned to the two Thampans, 'The next thing to do is to decide on a safe house for the Sixth Tirumulpad.'

'No way!' Mithran muttered under his breath his eyes on the floor. By the time he was brought around, I found my salivary glands drying up with the day's efforts.

The Matriarch Muses Again

Nilambur, Ernad
August 9'21
Mathu

The mahout's eyes widened in astonishment when she entered the stables with Ammalu, the maid close at her heels. Never during his tenure here had he seen her make this trip.

'How is she, Billi?' The Matriarch asked. Her own voice sounded strangely gruff to her.

The mahout crossed his arms across his chest and bent forward respectfully.

'She is not eating. And always seems tired.'

'Mm. I will see her.'

Her purposeful stride and straight posture made her seem a lot younger than she was. The heaviness inside was well masked.

Mathu felt a strange twitch in her insides as she entered Eli's enclosure which was set apart from those of the tuskers. It had always been one of her favourite places to be but of late she hadn't felt up to the long walk to the stables and Eli used to come to her instead. Billi, the Paniyan lad who was her mahout brought her twice or thrice a week, usually on the way back from the river. But for the past ten days, she hadn't seen Eli. It was only yesterday that the mahout came with the news that she had been unwell.

'I thought it would pass. But she seems to getting worse,' he had informed her. An odd pain seared through Mathu. She had been enduring terrible nights for some time now but last night was the worst. Sleeplessness, she could have put up with. She would have paced the *naalukettu* like the old *valyamma* from her childhood. But last night Mathu kept dozing off only to enter the world of horrible nightmares. She would wake up with a jolt and in a few minutes fall back into sleep and the nightmares would pick up from where they left off. She remembered that as a child, if she woke up in the middle of an especially pleasant dream, she would keep her eyes shut and try to continue the sequence. They never would come back. But this series of horrifying images involving Mithran and Mammad and Eli and what not all mixed-up, random and defying logic, she had no trouble resuming.

Ignoring the protests of her nieces, she had summoned her maid and walked to the stables.

'Eli', she whispered so softly that no one but the elephant heard her. Fan-like, her ears flapped, but the movement, Mathu noticed was feeble.

'I want both of you to wait outside the stall,' she said and when the mahout hesitated, she fixed him with such a cold glare that he retreated in alarm. 'And Ammalu, leave the *sharkkara* here.' The maid dutifully placed the wicker basket of jaggery balls at the Matriarch's feet and silently withdrew.

Mathu knew the two were worried whether it was safe to leave a seventy-five year old lady alone in an elephant's stall. But she and Eli had known each other since they were little and her friend would go to any lengths to keep her safe.

'Eli,' she said again stroking the pillar-like leg and extended a small bit of the sweet treat towards the elephant. Contrary to wont, the elephant did not reach out her trunk for it. 'Come on. Eat. It is your favourite jaggery.'

Eli merely tilted her head weakly and let out a low rumble.

The Matriarch felt something sharp and painful twist in her chest. Just as it did a week ago when Beeran Mapla, shamefaced and panic stricken, had burst in with the news of the attack on the Pookottur manor. Just as it did when she feared for the lives of her dear ones.

'Eli,' she uttered the elephant's name again and this time it came out as a sob stuck halfway up her throat. She gulped, trying to swallow the lump and rested her cheek against Eli's thick leg. The Matriarch glanced around the stall. It was clean and dry. More so than usual. The palm leaves piled in front of her remained untouched. Usually Eli liked to play with her food before she ate it and flung the branches here and there before retrieving them and lifting them into her mouth. The usual musky smell was absent. Mathu knew what that meant. Eli hadn't been passing dung for some time. That could be dangerous if it was what she guessed it was. The specialist had to be called in.

The Matriarch did not know how long she stood there leaning against the pillar like leg. No amount of blinking would stop the hot tears that welled up in her eyes. She was ashamed. With a small whispered prayer of 'Vettekkara'. She pulled herself together. The ball of jaggery had begun to melt in her palm and make her fingers sticky. She patted Eli one last time, cleared her throat and prepared to exit the stall when she felt a soft wind against her back. She smiled in spite of herself. Eli was blowing gently on the nape of her neck. Slowly, the elephant extended her trunk, picked up the sticky jaggery in the Matriarch's hand and put it into her mouth. Later Billi told her it was the first bit of food she had eaten in four days.

What was it about old age that kept bringing in flashes of the past so often.

That day in the Devil tree's shade, when everyone had eyes only for the bull calves and the little cow had been totally ignored. A memorable day for the Kovilakam members in more ways than one.

Actually there were three little elephants not one!

The moment Muthasshi Amma realised they were all out there under the devil tree, she sent a maid out with instructions for the young ladies to get inside. Mathu being a child had not been ordered in, she stood there with her cousins, the vanaras and watched the goings on keenly.

Just then. There was some commotion. The Sub Collector from the upstairs veranda of the mansion he was put up in had noticed the crowd by the devil tree and asked to speak to Manammama, one of the senior uncles.

'What's happening out there Tirumulpad, some kind of celebrations?'

'Take the two bulls around to the stables,' Innimmama instructed the mahouts. Turning to Moideen Mapla he added, 'The cow shall be let loose in the forests.'

Mathu let out a sudden wail.

'No, Innimmame, no!' In her distress she quite forgot it was her great uncle she was yelling at. 'You cannot send her away. She is only a baby. She will get lost in the forests. Please let her live here in our stables. She won't be any trouble.'

It was not Innimmama's way to take any notice of children and their opinions mattered little to him. He nodded to Moideen to take the little animal away even as the mahouts led the other two in the opposite direction.

'She will miss her brothers,' sobbed Mathu.

'Someone take the child inside,' ordered Innimmama.

'Who's the girl? Why is she crying?' Sub Collector

Collet asked Manammama who looked embarrassed. 'My sister's youngest.' Turning to Mathu he nodded towards the mansion where the women were housed. 'Mathu, go inside.'

'Why are you crying, small princess?' Collet asked her this time. Mathu did not understand English so she remained silent and tried to quieten her sobs.

'Do not pay attention to her, Mr Collet,' said Manammama in an apologetic tone. 'She's just throwing a tantrum and will be punished for it. My uncle has ordered for the female calf to be released into the jungle while the little bulls join our stables. The child doesn't want the cow to go.'

The sub collector looked at Mathu and admired the pretty picture she made in her gold bordered mundu, an exquisite gold necklace with mango shaped emeralds covering half her chest and droplets glistening in her sparkling eyes. He squatted down so that he was on eyelevel with her. In his careful, stilted Malayalam he asked, 'You have so many elephants in your stables, I have heard. And you have just acquired two new calves. Why not let this little one go back to forests and roam free?'

In spite of her distress, Mathu wanted to laugh at the Sayippe's way of speaking. Stiff and tight-lipped. The nasal singsong lilt so characteristic of her language was missing.

'No. she will die of heartbreak because her brothers are not with her. She cannot find her family on her own. Even if she does they will not love her anymore because she has been touched by people. They can smell us on her. Wild elephants are like that. I have heard Innimmama himself say this once. If they let her stay here, I will love her.'

Collet looked impressed.

'I apologise for interfering in your affairs, Tirumulpad,' he said and then dug deep into a pocket hidden somewhere in those leggings he wore and drew out a heavy looking money purse.

'I wish to buy this elephant for the little princess. Let her wish be granted.'

'Oh no Mr Collet, we wouldn't dream of taking money from you. Let the cow stay. I'll get my uncle to agree,' Manammama protested.

The Sayippe grinned happily.

'What is your name, little princess?'

'Mahadevi,' answered Manammama helplessly.

'Ha! Princess Mer-ha-day-vee, this elephant is yours. She will not be sent to the forest,' he explained in Malayalam. Mathu clapped her hands in delight and ran to the little elephant and threw her arms around the animal.

'Princess, I am taking the liberty to name your elephant. She shall be Elizabeth. After a great Queen.'

'Eli…Eli…' Mathu could not pronounce the whole name. Eli blew a warm little gust of air on the nape of Mathu's neck.

Back in the *naalukettu* after her trip to the stables the first thing she did, even before consuming a halfhearted breakfast and settling down to her routine reading of the

Narayaneeyam, was to get Sethu to draft a letter to the Vaidyan who specialised in healing elephants.

The clock had barely struck eleven and she had put aside her books when one of the girls brought the message that the Second Tirumulpad was here and would like to meet her. She rose with a sigh and went out to the entrance portal. Her heart thumped a little as it always did nowadays when she had a visitor or a messenger.

'Any news of Mithran?' She did not waste time with greetings and small talk.

'No, Cheriyammamme. I was about to ask you if you had heard anything.'

Mathu's heart sank. This was the story of her life these days. She pounced on any visitor, servant or passer-by and enquired after Mithran. But nobody seemed to know anything. He had been missing since that horrendous day when the violent Maplas attacked his manor.

'Did you make enquiries?' Her tone was mildly accusatory.

'Of course. The only information I got was that he left the manor the night of the gherao.'

'Why do I get the feeling that people are hiding things from me?'

The Matriarch suddenly felt she could not get anything out of anyone now.

'I want you to pay a personal call to Narayana Menon and see if he knows anything about Mithran's whereabouts,' she told the Second Tirumulpad. 'In fact I am surprised you haven't done it already. Am I the only one who cares about what has happened to Mithran?

Or…' she gave him a suspicious frown, 'Am I the only one who doesn't know?'

The hoarseness in her voice did not go unnoticed by her nephew. 'Of course not, Cheriyammamme. I assure you, Mithran is fine. He has apparently gone into hiding and wishes to keep his whereabouts a secret,' he said in a soothing tone.

'Secrets? Why should he have secrets from me?'

'It is not just you. I don't think anybody knows where he is, except those who helped him get away and remain under cover. I myself have no clue.'

It was with a distracted ear that she listened to the Second Tirumulpad relate random incidents happening all over Malabar. Killings here, lootings there. The general fear that loomed over the whole of Ernad for a certain Black Thangal and his band of brigands, the prospective release of Madhavan Nair and the others from jail, all matters that on a normal day, she would soak up greedily. She had not been herself since the mobbing of Mithran's manor and his consequent disappearance. Now with Eli's illness she seemed to be losing it. No this would not do, she told herself. She was a Matriarch not an ordinary mother, she was responsible for more than her small brood of children. She must pull herself together.

Ever since the news of the mobbing the Matriarch had hated Mammad. If he had been here then she could have clawed him to shreds. Even now she found it difficult to contain her anger but managed to do so when she thought of poor helpless Beeran's hanging head. But now, when her nephew berated him, she was tempted to jump to the young Mapla's defence.

No one at the Kovilakam really approved of the soft corner she had always had for Beeran Mapla's boy. But the fact remained that she cared for him. She fretted about how he would make both ends meet when Mithran terminated his employment. She would have helped him in anyway but to his credit not a word of complaint had he uttered when she had summoned him for an explanation soon after Pattu.

She couldn't help thinking fondly of Mammad. After all it was a special relationship she shared with him. When you save a life, you establish a bond no less than the one you create when you actually give life.

Even after her nephew's departure, the thought stream refused to leave her. Leaning back in her chair, the Matriarch exhaled slowly and cast her mind to a rather wet day more than a quarter of a century ago. The fourth day of her monthly period. One of her last if she remembered right. She had been past fifty and quite irregular. Mathu had stepped out of the Dark Room and set off for the river at dawn with two maids in tow carrying freshly laundered clothes. She had to immerse herself in the cleansing waters of the Chaliyar before she could resume a normal routine. A newborn sun was fast gaining strength causing the sky to flush in maternal pride. The Ananga Para held its head high daring the world to uproot it. The riverscape always gave Mathu a feeling of security and belonging. As did the Devil tree and the temple of Vettekkaran. The Chaliyar had flowed this way from the beginning of time. The Ananga Para had always towered in the background and the Devil tree had stood guard over Vettekkaran's shrine forever.

At fifty, Mathu had been as agile as a girl. Arthritis did not plague her knees. She skipped down the steps so nimbly that she was already in the water before the maids with their bundles were even half way down the steps. She slid into the flow and stood there waist-deep and drank in the air. In a cove quite far away from their own a Muslim woman was rinsing out clothes. She sat on the steps in her ankle length waist cloth and long sleeved blouse, her hair covered by the ever present veil. Mathu's eyesight was sharp. She saw a naked little boy of two or three sit on a nearby rock watching his mother.

She dipped into the water and came out with her long hair undone and spread out around her like dark rays. She took a deep breath and went down again. This time when she came up there were screams all around.

'Ayyo! Help!'

'Will someone come running!'

'Vettekkara!'

Her maids were calling out frantically, pacing nervously on the edge of the water.

'Nte Rabbe!'

The young Ummachi was thrashing about in the water. The clothes she'd been washing floated about around her.

'What' the matter?' Mathu asked her maids.

'The child, Thampatti. He has fallen in.'

She saw the small figure carried by the current and in few purposeful strokes she reached the spot, grabbed him and before the next screech ensued, she was swimming strongly with the child under one arm. His mother stopped floundering in the water and climbed out. She made a dash for the boy as Mathu deposited him on the river's edge and wrung the water out of her hair. She took one look at the child, his chubby face was flushed in fear and his hair plastered to his scalp. His eyes were an unusual green, a shade lighter than the emeralds in her favourite palakka necklace.

She *swam* back to her own cove and took the final cleansing dip.

Before noon, Beeran, one of the newly appointed cart drivers showed his face at the Kovilakam's front yard unable to contain his gratitude. It was his boy she had saved from drowning.

August 12 '21

No authentic news about Mithran's safety. No signs of improvement in Eli's condition. Worry had become a constant state of mind.

If someone woke up in the middle of the night they would see the Matriarch drift around the quadrangle. If they got close enough they might have heard her mutter to herself and covering their mouths with their palms, diagnosed Chinnan.

It gave her some relief when the Namboothiripad of Avanaparambu was announced. The Second Tirumulpad had been true to his word and the healer prompt. She briefed him on Eli's symptoms and sent him down to the stables with one of the lads to guide him. After a thorough examination he came back with his report.

'Thampatti, I agree there are issues with digestion. It is bad but I can treat her.'

'Will she be well soon?'

'If things go well, yes. It could take a few months though and the grace of the Lord of course. But…'

'What is it, Namboothiripad?'

'Well, Thampatti, it seems to be more than a physical condition.'

'What do you mean?'

'It seems to me that she is grieving. I can see it in her eyes. I can feel it in her heartbeat.'

After writing out the required prescriptions and promising to be back in two weeks, the vaidyan took his leave and Mathu's morale hit an all-time low. She admonished herself for not having realised sooner. Elephants had always been a part of her life. She knew them almost as well as she knew people. She was well-versed in elephant lore. Moreover, this was about Eli who was her closest companion ever. Still it had taken a stranger, a professional yes, but still a stranger to help her understand what was going on in her large friend's heart.

Less than a month ago, Eli had lost her mate and she, Mathu had barely given it a thought. One of the tuskers in their stables had fallen. A loss yes. But it did happen time and again in the Kovilakam stables which housed more than sixty elephants. It meant little else to the family. But Eli was pining. She was lonely. The Matriarch wondered what she could do to ease her friend's pain.

The Cross-Eyed Raid

Pookkottur, Ernad
18 to 20 August '21
Raziya

Why didn't the wretched creature go away?

Raziya indulged in a grumpy soliloquy as she pushed herself further up on her toes and jabbed the long handled broom fiercely into the corner of the ceiling.

In the back of her mind she could see only too well that she was becoming obsessive about the spider and her cobwebs. As soon as she realised that the eight-legged beast had taken up residence in her house, Raziya had put together a nice, bushy broom and bound it firmly to a long pole. Just right for getting rid of the cobwebs. Ever since, she had brushed and dusted with a vengeance. Now, pulling out the tuck in her waist cloth and smoothing it down her hips, she looked at the ceiling with some satisfaction. Tired, she sat down on the Matriarch's teak bed with a sigh. An imposing headache was threatening to burst her head open.

It was no wonder. Raziya had woken up early that day. Come to think of it. Had she actually woken up? Not when she hadn't slept at all. It would be more appropriate to say that she had somehow seen the seemingly endless night through, her attempts to fall asleep completely abortive.

Her husband, she remembered, had left home early yesterday. The pang in her chest returned with the thought stream she had been trying to block out with the cleaning spree. He hadn't come home for lunch. She had worried all day and when he hadn't turned up for the evening meal either, she panicked. Bad things always seemed worse after dark and later when the rest of the world was in deep slumber, they assumed monstrous proportions and it felt to Raziya as if she were burning in Jahannam. She had tried propping her left leg on the bed, but when her toes unconsciously sought Mammad's sinewy ankles usually crossed at the foot of the bed, and found nothing instead, his absence seemed all the more real. All the more scary.

Deafening drumbeats began to sound in the stillness of the night.

The Tirumulpad's men had grabbed him and taken him away to an undisclosed den. They had tied him up. Their whips were swinging. The horrible illusion lasted for ever before it transformed into the prison cell where he huddled in a corner surrounded by khaki clad tormentors. The sea of khaki turned into roaring waters which, before she realised it, became a blazing fire. By dawn the images that melted into one another had solidified into a hard rock inside her head. When Raziya rose from the mat and began rolling it up, she saw the only other occupant of the house scuttle nimbly up the walls into the niche where she had, in the night, woven a fine gossamer web.

Hurrying through her morning chores, Raziya launched into a laborious battle against the spider and her sticky strands. She didn't pause for a moment's rest till the trace of every cobweb had been wiped off and the spider was nowhere in sight. Now her headache had dulled making way for a mild dizziness and quivering knees. The sun was overhead and she realised she hadn't eaten. The industry of cleaning had succeeded in pushing Mammad's absence to the periphery of her mind but now it came hurtling back. Had he eaten since he left the house?

Raziya could endure it no longer. She couldn't bear not knowing. The solitude of her house was too much for her.

When she stepped out, a bright sun was reflected in each raindrop. Raziya suddenly felt better. She loved sun showers. It meant the fox was getting married and there would be biryani all round, toothless ummummas would tell the children. She smiled. Allah! It felt good to smile. A lot more relaxed, she made her way towards Alavikutti's house. He might be at home. If not his mother or sister-in-law might know where he was and whether Mammad was with him. In the open air, things seemed much more hopeful. Stupid of her to have imagined a kidnap or an arrest. Would the town be so quiet if such a thing had happened? It felt as if the bright little sun shower were actually falling on her heart. The coolness soothed, the warmth comforted.

Once she crossed the canal here where it narrowed to bottleneck width, Alavikutti's house was but a bend away. Her heart lightened of the painful load, Raziya skipped spryly down the tree trunk laid across the flowing ribbon of water. If she skirted around that abandoned building yonder instead of taking the regular path, she would get there in a couple of minutes. The compound was as dilapidated as the building itself and she had to dodge the overgrown bushes to as she made her way around the house.

She stopped to disentangle a thorny twig that entwined in her thattam and at that moment she sensed that something was amiss. Somewhere in the sweet smelling air lingered a trace of stale sweat. Though undefined, the smell was alarmingly familiar. Half suppressed sniggers and snorts egressed from within the unfinished laterite walls. Warning signals shot through her brain and fear, serpent-like uncoiled in her newly brightened heart. The prickly spikelet still dangling off the end of her headdress, Raziya scurried away as fast as she could.

Suggestive whistles and hisses.

This time they did not come from inside. Leaning

against the well was a brawny fellow with a leer splitting his face. She was sure he was one of the scoundrels who had previously harassed her. The other time she had taken care not to look at their faces but she recognised the reek of medicated oil combined with sweat. She turned around desperately, hoping to make her escape by retracing her path to the tree trunk bridge.

'Ah! The Khilafat man's *munjathi* again, don't run away, my *ponne*...'

Another of them. A familiar beaked nose with hairy nostrils swam before her eyes and a new malodour, this time of garlic and decay hit her senses before she screamed.

She was not sure if the sound ensued.

When Raziya came to at Alavikutti's house, her last memory of the episode was a frantic craving for the proximity of her eight-legged housemate and the sense of security she suddenly stood for.

Mammad

He didn't hear the noises from within the smithy. Had the anvils stopped clanging that second, the hammers clenched in the smiths' calloused palms ceased to pound, had the whooshing bellows suddenly gone dumb, Mammad would not have noticed. He absent-mindedly swatted a mosquito on his arm but did not feel its sting. His mind was otherwise occupied.

For the past two days he had gone about with his arms training and Khilafat duties with extra vigour, hoping it would ease the burning. He hadn't succeeded as yet. Whatever he did, he found his heart was not in it. Tonight he had kept himself busy for as long as possible and it was close to midnight when he dropped in at the smithy. He did not go in. the foundry's insides were more crowded than usual for twice the number of blade smiths were on duty. Everyone knew it was a matter of days before the British army charged to Pookottur. Yes. It was all over Ernad. Forces were to be summoned from other parts of the state and the enemy would be formidable. They had to be prepared, Alijan Sahib had croaked in his raspy voice, twisting his neck rumal fiercely. Training in combat had intensified. Daggers and swords were being forged in batches of hundreds.

Trooping wearily into the smithy, Mammad chose to stretch out on the narrow bench outside to rest his aching limbs. He inhaled deeply and took in the coal smoke mixed with a waft of something ferrous. The strong odour went unnoticed. For a fleeting moment he longed for home and the comfort of the Thampatti's teak bed. But there was no reason to go home. Without Raziya there…A painful, loathsome something lurched within. Anger? Grief? Guilt? Whatever it was, it rose upward from the depths of his belly and stuck in his throat. He wanted to retch.

Anyway with Raziya safely set up in Benazir Manzil where she had been since the women in Alavikutti's house brought her over that day, and so much to do himself, he saw no reason to go home. If only thoughts of his wife and memories of her ordeal would stay away. But they insisted on filling his mental space, rolling about in turbulent waves. With the swell of each billow, he felt less of a man.

Raziya's limp form haunted him. In his mind he kept seeing her as she lay like a broken doll on the wooden ledge in the ladies' room off Benu *thatha's* kitchen that day. Neighbourhood women bustled about trying to fan her into recovery. The moment Alavikutti had dropped the bombshell on him late that afternoon he had torn across the cashew and tamarind groves and burst into the anteroom and found the gazes of the *ithathas* stabbing him accusingly. The sympathetic whispers they had been showering on Raziya transformed into one harsh buzz. He even had trouble breaking the protective circle they had made around her. Raziya determinedly kept her eyes shut till he withdrew. He had rained frantic questions on Benu thatha but she simply pursed her lips and narrowed her eyes into slits. The rejection was final. It was Alijan Sahib who had led him out and explained.

The inference was clear. Everyone thought the worst of him. He was the responsible party. Mammad cringed. How was it his fault? True he had been unable to go home that night but he knew quite a few men who hadn't. The days following their attack on the manor had been that crazy. Every local Mapla was busy getting ready for the attack. Except Ahmed Adhikari and his cronies.

From the defensive, he swung in the opposite direction like a pendulum. The Adhikari's men! If only he could get his hands on them. He was sure they were the ones.

Once Raziya had recovered from the initial shock, she had described her attackers to the sympathetic neighbourhood *ithathas* and over the next couple of days, verbal illustrations of the goons flew around town. Alavikutti had later told Mammad what he heard from his Umma and *ithatha*. The gaunt fellow with the hawk-nose. Clearly the Adhikari's accomplice. The beefy Hindu. Realization hit Mammad. He was the Tirumulpad's servant who often went around with the other man. They were in it together. The landlord and the ass-scratcher. But to have poor Raziya attacked! A month ago he wouldn't have thought the Tirumulpad would be involved but now he knew even the so called nobles could stoop low enough to lie and accuse and whatever else they wished to victimise people like him.

'I will get my revenge,' Mammad whispered fiercely to himself. 'See if I don't.'

Plans took shape in his mind and continued to do so even as he dropped off into a fitful doze, his mind lulled by fatigue and the monotony of the bellows.

Alijan

There were more men in there than the smithy could accommodate. Contrary to wont, anvils did not clang. Bellows sat mum. There were no hammers clenched in the thick, roughened palms of the smiths. Though the work shop was not functioning that afternoon, it was packed with the confused and indignant men of Pookottur and work had been stalled. Alijan Sahib sat on his stool trying to think out answers to a hundred different queries and weigh the various opinions. For the past fifteen hours or so, furphies had been gushing in unrestrained from the western regions.

Kizhakkeppalli, the famous mosque of Tirurangadi has been besieged by the police.

Not the police. The army.

It has been bombed.

Demolished.

Previously, the army had entered the mosque with their filthy boots on and defiled the sanctity of the shrine.

Ali Musaliar has been arrested.

They have killed him.

Don't be absurd. They wouldn't kill someone like him just like that.

Allah! Our leader is no more!

Hundreds of Muslims have been shot.

Revenge! Revenge!

Yes, we must avenge the death of our brothers.

March to Tirurangadi.

March!

No. we cannot leave Pookottur unguarded.

They are on their way here.

That's what we believed two days ago. Someone is passing around fake information.

The White Sarkar is having us on. It is their tactic.

You are wrong. They led us to believe that Pookottur

is in danger and we focused our attention here. Now look what's happened.

We must go. No, we must stay here.

For once, Alijan Sahib was confused.

And angry. The skies decided to reflect his mood.

Mammad

It all felt hazy to him. The howl of the demon wind, the harsh little slaps administered on his left cheek by the rain, all the action going on in Pookottur… Even the pain in his ankles from sitting too long on his haunches on the floor of the smithy veranda were he had taken up permenant residence these days. The only thing that seemed real was the burning sensation deep within. The smoke from that fire was easily recognisable as it spiraled its way up to his chest and rose higher still into his head. If someone had told him that this smoldering was a manifestation of the fear in his heart, he would have vehemently denied it.

But yes. That was the truth. He was afraid. Afraid of going to Tirurangadi with the boys. Afraid of getting killed. The fact jumped out at him in all reality and he flushed. Was he really so spineless? He cursed himself. Allah! Did death scare him so? It had never done before. Why now?

The thought of British bullets in Tirurangadi brought spasms of terror. No. he couldn't die now. He dug deeper through the multiple layers of his thoughts and stumbled upon a niggling block in the pit of his belly. Something felt incomplete. As if there was something remaining to be done. Then the Tirumulpad's haughty gait swam into his mind. Followed by the look on Raziya's face as she lay slumped against Benu thatha. The look that said 'you failed me'. The accusing glances of the Pookottur *ithathas* appeared next. Ahmed Adhikari's oily grin. His henchman duo rocking in ruthless merriment. And it came to Mammad that second. The root of his uncharacteristic cowardliness.

A desperate need for vengeance spurted like venom. The wound he would inflict on the Tirumulpad and the others would be deeper and more painful than the hurt they themselves had caused in him. That done, he would go to Tirurangadi and die a warrior's happy death.

He began to make fervent patterns on the floor of the veranda with his dagger.

'Here he is ,' Alavikutti, visibly drenched, bounded into the smithy. 'Mammade, we've been looking for you. Come on. We are getting ready to leave. Just waiting for the Sahib's final instructions. Should be anytime now. Maybe as soon as his visitors leave…'

He suddenly stepped back and stared at his friend.

'What's wrong with you'?

Basheer who had just come in knitted his brows at Mammad. There was something about their changathi that day. Something… malicious? Lethal? Well something written over his normally serious but pleasant features.

'Mammade,' he said hesitantly.

'I am not coming to Tirurangadi with you all,'

Mammad said softly. 'Something has come up. Maybe I will join you there once it is done.'

'What do you mean?'

'Basheere, Alavikutti, listen,' he whispered urgently. 'I must find the Sixth Tirumulpad. I can't let him off so easily. I need my revenge.'

'Allah! What are you saying? Have you no sense of priority? Something as important as the march to Tirurangadi is on and you want to get back at the landlord for unpaid wages? For a false accusation?' Even the normally impulsive Alavikutti could not see reason.

'Exactly. We are going to fight the British in the name of our land and our faith and you talk of such petty, personal matters?' Basheer was shocked.

'It is not that. You don't understand. I must punish them for harassing Raziya.' Mammad's tone got softer and more dangerous.

'What kind of talk is this, Mammade?' Basheer took hold of his shoulders and looked straight into his eyes. The pupils glinted an icy green in a backdrop of bloodshot red. He found himself withdrawing from the heat.

'What has the landlord got to do with all that?'

'It was he.' Mammad resumed the frantic patterns on the floor.' His men did it. With Ahmed Adhikari's help. To punish me.'

That was too much for Basheer. 'Stop this crazy business,' he said grabbing Mammad's dagger to stop his feverish doodling. 'The Sixth Tirumulpad may be capable of a lot of things. But not this.' His tone was firm. 'Forget it and do your duties to the Khilafat.'

'Soon. After I am done with this.'

Nothing his friends said could convince Mammad.

'I have to find out where the brute is hiding. He is evidently not in the manor. I have to start my search somewhere. I am going to Nilambur.'

'Basheere, we can't let him go alone. I will go too,' said Alavikutti.

'Then so will I,' decided Basheer. Mammad was not himself and Alavikutti's company might push him into further rashness.

Armed with knives and daggers, they set off in the north easterly direction. A whole ten minutes before Alijan Sahib showed his visitors out, the threesome had crossed the tamarind and guava groves, passed the gates of Benazir Manzil and turned the bend.

Alijan

The rain had subsided for the moment and the Maplas crowded around in the front yard waited anxiously as the two visitors swiftly climbed into their cart and drove away into the night. Alijan stood on the porch steps with his hands on his hips looking around for Basheer and Mammad. Not sighting them anywhere, he unknotted his rumal.

'Usman,' he summoned a tall man over to his side. 'There are some changes in plans. We are holding off the Tirurangadi march for now. Inform everyone and get Basheer and Mammad to come and see me.'

'But why, Sahib?'

'It is not off altogether. We will just wait another day till we have more news. I guess it does not pay to be hasty. We are still to be prepared and arms kept in readiness. Expect to make the move anytime.'

Within half an hour the message had been conveyed to half the Pookottor Maplas.

'Tirurangadi is off.'

'Oh! Did the Sahib say why?' Kunjikadar whose cart was packed and ready with arms from the smithy asked in wonder.

'He is waiting for more information, I understand', Mammali thoughtfully inserted a finger in his ear.

'What exactly is happening? Will someone explain clearly?' Asked Moidu plaintively. No one took notice.'

'It may be that he is having second thoughts.'

'Surely those kafirs who were here earlier had something to do with his change in mind.'

'Haven't I always said? It is no good to associate with these fellows. Congressmen or not kafirs will be kafirs,' said Aboobacker of staunch, conventional views

'And that glib tongued fellow is very clever at swaying things his way. It was him with that Congressman, Nair, wasn't it?'

'Why should we listen to them? I think we should go,' said the fiery Umar with a toss of his head. His friend Hasan seconded at once.

Alijan caught the general trend from the snippets that fell on his ears.

The Outcaste

It had ceased to rain but the demon wind still blew with gusto.

'It is time for a good night's sleep now,' said Shekharan Nair with some amount of relief as we jostled against each other in the moving cart.

'Hmm.. there is nothing else to be done at the moment anyway,' I nodded after a moment's hesitation. Nair was surprised. 'You sound doubtful. I thought the meeting with Alijan went well. We managed to convince him after all. Granted his wife did her bit but eventually he did agree not to go rushing off to Tirurangadi. So we have stalled the riots for now. By the way the Sahib's beewi did seem more astute and sensible than he himself is, don't you think?'

'Hmm. I am not sure you are right, Shekharetta. No. Not about the Sahib's wife. I mean can we be certain the riot will not happen?'

'You don't think so?'

'It is a mindless and cruel wind, Shekharetta. It is likely to disperse strange standpoints, self-contradictory perspectives from one part of Pookkottur to the other. I can't help wondering if the propagules of unrest and confusion will be detached from the yard of Benazir Manzil to hit ground and take root elsewhere.'

Shekharan Nair shivered as the chill spread down his spine. 'The picture is so dismal, but so vividly, almost poetically put. I can only hope you are wrong this time.'

'Let's go, Shekharetta. I hope you have a warm bed for me in a corner of your house. I can't get back home tonight.'

Mammad

The Mapla dispatched in search of Mammad and his friends was barely out of his teens and a swift runner. He and his companion caught up with them before they had covered a mile.

'Mammadka, Basheerka, the Sahib wants you,' he panted.

'What for?' asked Alavikutti.

'How would I know? Something about Tirurangadi, I suppose. By the way, where are you three going?'

'Nilambur,' answered Alavikutti quite thoughtlessly before Basheer could stop him with a pinch on the elbow. 'We have important business there.'

'Nilambur?' The messenger cried in surprise.

'Oh! Something to do with the Tirumulpad, eh? I heard he has gone into hiding. Has he been found, Mammadka?' Asked the companion.

By then a few other torch bearing men had arrived on the scene.

'What's it?' The newcomers wished to know

'They are going to Nilambur.'

'You are carrying a lot of arms. I thought you were off to Tirurangadi.'

'But nobody is going to Tirurangadi. They are saying Sahib stalled the whole thing.'

'No way!'

'The Tirumulpad is hiding in Nilambur. We are going there to teach him a lesson.'

'Is he there? The coward! He needs to be taught a lesson after what he did to our Mammad.'

'We are with you, Mammadka.'

'Yes we will come with you. These landlords are powerful. You need all the manpower possible.'

'Someone run for reinforcements! And pick up all the knives and daggers you can gather.'

Nilambur March

Nilambur, Ernad
21 August '21
Sethu

The abundant tresses which had always been her pride and joy, now felt like a nuisance. She had no interest in her haircare routine and went about it more out of habit than anything else. Maybe she wouldn't go to the river today, thought Sethu. Ammamma didn't go these days. She saved up all her energy for her daily visits to the elephant enclosure. The maid could easily heat up some water for her as well after Ammamma's cauldron was ready. At least that way, she could fend off her giggling cousins and their pointed hints.

Her mind strayed to Priya as it often did. How she missed her friend! Poor Priya. News of Mithrettan's disappearance must have shattered her. Or did she know where he was, Sethu wondered. She hadn't yet received a reply to her letter.

On second thoughts, she decided to give the hot water a miss. Cool well water would feel good. The maid could draw a few cauldrons.

'Ammalu, I won't be needing any hot water. I am going down to the river today,' declared the Matriarch stepping out of the inner rooms.

Sethu sighed. So much for her plans. She couldn't very well opt to bathe indoors when Ammamma was going out to the river.

It was barely light but bright enough to leave behind the lanterns. The air was clean from last night's heavy rains. The bathing party trekked in a long, irregular crocodile formation. The maids making up the tail with their bundles of laundered clothes and bowls of hibiscus shampoo. The Kovilakam ladies walked in twos and threes, chattering busily and cracking Gulikan jokes.

One young girl who had been the butt of the traditional wisecracks for a day or two remarked, 'Well if something untoward happens today, we know who is Gulikan's current pet,' the girl giggled at her own boldness in targeting none other than the Matriarch.

The others laughed too. 'Why she decided to come down today, I can't help wondering. She hasn't for nearly a month.' The girl turned around stealthily to see if her quip had reached the Matriarch's ears and that triggered further giggles.

Sethu felt the cool touch of Ammamma's wrinkled

palm as it close over hers. Her grandmother had never been one to express emotion through touch, except maybe with her elephant. Sethu sensed an insecurity in her and panicked for a moment. Ammamma had always been the rock in their lives. A veritable Anangapara, she thought, that never stirred whatever happened. If she was…

The moment the crocodile had descended the first flight of rough, stone steps leading to the river, turned north to approach the second one, there was a combined screech from the ladies at the head. The shocking news was passed backwards in a second.

The Anangapara had vanished.

The huge, round rock, a little peaked towards the top, rose out of the Chaliyar, not far away from their private cove and had been a part of Kovilakam life for forever and ever. Only the most accomplished swimmers could dive off it. Sethu had never had the courage to try but she had heard stories that Ammamma had done it all the time when she was young. In the minds of the Kovilakam people, the Anangapara was synonymous of unshakeable strength and the early morning bathers were rattled to the core to see it gone. It must have been last night's rain that did it though it seemed quite improbable as it had withstood much heavier monsoons and floods over the centuries. Nobody felt like lingering over their baths.

Sethu felt a little numb. The only sensation she had was the trembling of her legs as she made her way up the steps. There were no giggles or chatter on the return trip and a quirky stillness prevailed in the air. Ammamma hadn't said a word. This time it was Sethu who clutched her grandmother's hand. The Matriarch panted a little by the time they reached the top of the steps. The Devil tree was visible from round the corner and Sethu's eyes strayed towards it quite by wont as she reached that particular spot. As a child she used to entertain herself by imagining different shapes to the tree. Often it assumed the shape of a dear little baby elephant with a raised trunk and a rotund body. It was one of her favourites. There were times when it turned into the rear view of a woman with her long hair swinging past her hips. If on one day it was a lotus on another it resembled a star. Sethu rather enjoyed these fantasies but they were not always pretty shapes. Ogres with protruding canines and cobras with raised hoods were not uncommon. Today, however, she could conjure no image. All she could see was the tree with its trunk and branches, as it appeared to less imaginative people.

Mathu

In the shade of the Devil tree stood cart driver, Beeran and even at a distance Mathu saw that his stance conveyed anxiety. He shifted his weight from his right leg to the left and back, all the time rubbing his torso as if his heart hurt. Then he discerned the Matriarch and broke into a run halting abruptly in front of her, his chest heaving.

There was none of his usual respectful hovering in her presence.

'Go,' he half gulped and half shouted. 'All the Thampatties must go inside and have the doors shut. Every one of them.'

Mathu remained composed. She fixed a steady gaze on the old driver and waited patiently for his explanation. He managed to muster enough control to burst out in huffs. 'They have reached the marketplace.' In answer to the Matriarch's arched brow, he continued, 'The rioters. From Pookottur. The echoes of their Taqbeer calls can be heard from there,' he jerked his chin covered in white stubble towards the gateway that arched at a distance. 'They… they are looking for the Sixth Tirumulpad. They will be here in no time.'

'But… but Mithrettan… he is not…,' her granddaughter began to blurt but when she threw a piercing look that translated roughly into the message 'let not the tail wag in the presence of the head', the girl shut up halfway through the sentence.

'Will you explain Beeran? Start at the beginning and make sure you are slow and precise. My brain is getting woolly in my old age and I may have difficulty catching on.'

The driver inhaled deeply.

'Yesterday the White army marched into Tirurangadi. I don't know if the Baliya Thampatti has heard… They are saying that the Kizhakkepalli on this side of the river, it is a holy place for our people, has been razed to the ground. They are even saying that our Ali Musaliar has been arrested. We don't know how much of this is true but the whole of Ernad is livid. Kozhikode and Valluvanad too.

The information we got here last night was that our boys in Pookottur would march to Tirurangadi and fortify the town. But I don't know what happened. The first thing we heard this morning was that they had marched here to Nilambur instead. That they are determined to get hold of Mith…er…the Sixth Tirumulpad to revenge last month's happenings. They are raising hell in the angadi. I am afraid, Thampatti, that my boy….' Beeran Mapla hung his head in shame and despair.

'The police?'

The Matriarch's quiet query displayed none of the terror that gripped her from within.

'They stormed the police station and attacked Unnyan the inspector. They are now headed here, Thampatti. Please let's make sure everyone is safely inside. And the Sixth Tirumulpad must be given tight security.'

By then several of the Kovilakam men, on their way to the river had gathered at the Palachod, their brows raised in mild curiosity. What was it that excited the old Mapla so early in the morning? Some of them cast twisted grins and went their way and some others hung around for the fun offered by the minor upset.

'All right. Enough is enough. Now off with you, Beeran,' Bhaskaran flicked a corner of his mundu up quite irreverently.

'There is no need for any unnecessary worry, Beeran,' said Ravivarman a shade more kindly.

'Yes. The gatehouse sentinel are on duty not to mention the specially appointed man patrolling the village,' Marthandan's tone attempted to pacify.

'I have special regard for the abilities of Narayanan, the washerwoman's son who is in charge of the gatehouse security,' added Adityan.

Beeran hovered and swung from one foot to the other, still rubbing his chest. Neither did he want to contradict the Thampans nor did he wish to go away without ensuring safety.

'Beeran, I will see to things. Why don't you go to the gatehouse and make sure Narayanan and the other men are properly warned?' On the Matriarch's assurance, the driver shuffled away reluctantly.

A deep rumble sounded just then as if a bad thunderstorm was brewing further away and Mathu quickened her pace. She hustled the crocodile indoors, seeing that the Thampans seemed to have seen reality, left the outdoor matters to them. She was slightly relieved to hear them give orders for the gatehouse and then the temple to be shut with immediate effect.

Mammad

The arduous hike of fifty or so miles over field and stream, through the rough country roads to Nilambur via Wandoor had apparently not tired the men. On the contrary they seemed to be bursting with energy.

Bolo Taqbeer

Allahu Akbar

Their feisty battle cries rent the early morning silence. It felt good to have so many friends by his side.

The bounce in Alavikutti's step as his *changathi* strode purposefully in the front made him smile a little. Friends like him were hard to come by. They had met with little resistance from the locals as their travel was by night but when they reached the Edavanna police station, a sleepy constable on night duty had tried to stop them and find out what they were up to. They tried to shake him off but he was more determined than he looked. One brief flash of someone's dagger and he was left clutching his bleeding arm and blubbering. When you had the force of friendship and loyalty on your side, there was no stopping you. Mammad felt brighter and more hopeful than he had in weeks. Now to find the Tirumulpad…

The marketplace was just awakening and vendors taking their time unpacking their wares. They stared at the Taqbeer calling army from Pookottur n sheer astonishment.

'Poreen!'

'Come on! Join us,' cried the boys. 'Let's fight for our cause!'

'Did you know? The Kizhakkepalli has been demolished! Islam is under threat. Fight!'

'We are off to the Kovilakam. We'll raze it!'

'Yes. We'll dismantle it stone by stone and bludgeon the haughty Tirumulpads with those very stones!'

'Bolo Taqbeer Allahu Akbar!'

There was a general buzz as people some hesitantly and others eagerly joined their midst.

'Mammad? What is happening,' Basheer caught

up with him sounding bewildered and worried. 'This is going way off from our initial plans. Our boys are forgetting themselves. See how they speak so randomly and contradict themselves. We must rein them in.'

Mammad had just been experiencing the thrill of seeing their army swell in size. Hadn't Basheer himself once said, their strength lay in their numbers? Though at the back of his mind something reasoned with him that Basheer was right, he was in no mood to spoil things just as they were going so well.

Someone in the angadi had informed Inspector Unnyan who arrived on the scene. The policeman however did not succeed in holding them back. Soon, a grin appeared on Mammad's face to see him in their midst with his uniform turban off. Someone had planted a skullcap on his head and stuck a sword in his hand and the Inspector helplessly walked in their midst with a young man's dagger warningly pressed against his back.

They were unstoppable. Today they would win.

As they approached the arched gateway, Mammad felt his heart lurch. How many times he had used this entrance. As a child he had held on to his father's finger and walked in his eyes wide, taking in the grand sights. Today, the scene would be a lot grander thought Mammad holding his head high and walking ahead of the pack. He had kept a safe distance from Basheer. He didn't wish to be demotivated when he was so close to achieving what he wanted.

The gate was locked. So they have been warned. But

the plus point was that there were only three men on sentinel duty. The timing was right. The men were taking turns to go for their morning chores. One of the three looked familiar.

'Open up,' Mammad walked up to him.

'You are Beeran Mapla's son. Ask your men to fall back. Why are you here?'

'Thurakkeen!' Alavikutti roared. His hand went meaningfully to his broad leather belt that held his collection of daggers.

'What do you think we are here for? We are not dummies. Stand back,' said another gateway guard stepping up.

Pushes and pulls, punches and abuses ensued. Weapons were not yet drawn in spite of Alavikutti's threatening mime.

Basheer attempted to reason with them. 'We need to see the Tirumulpads and present our grievances. Let us in. We will not cause trouble.'

Some of the younger Maplas looked at each other with raised brows. Spineless, or what?

Present grievances? Not cause trouble?

Can't leave him at the head of things.

Two of them raced ahead and pointed their daggers at the watchman's throat. The others raised their weapons and advanced, ignoring Basheer's raised palms. More staff quickly came in. Word had been sent for reinforcements.

Mammad recognised the washer man Narayanan. Yes. He was on security duty now. And had received professional training. He was singlehandedly managing to keep over twelve Maplas at bay. Usman charged at one of the other guards. Paree the fleet footed youngster and his *changathi* held him down and Usman's dagger was embedded in the man's belly. There was a shower of warm blood. Narayanan saw his colleague slump down. He produced his pistol and pointed it at Usman's chest.

Mathu

All the inmates of the Kovilakam remained in the same building. The men had opted to wait it out in the massive mansion that housed the women with three levels, its four quadrangles and over sixty rooms. Sixteen of them paced the entrance portal with their hands behind their backs while behind the heavy doors the women remained indoors. Mathu sat on her favourite couch in the southern *nalukettu* after sending all the other ladies up the wooden staircase to the upper storey with strict instructions to go on to the topmost floor if things took a turn for the worse. Sethu had lingered a few minutes but the Matriarch had not given in an inch.

She was sure people were wondering how she remained unmoved. Not a trace of fear appeared on her face. Her pale hands did not quiver. Her voice remained soft and firm.

As a child, Mathu had never lacked guts, fearing little and outdoing the Vanaras in daredevil adventures but no one guessed that deep within she nursed a pet angst. No, it was more than that, a terror might be the more appropriate word to describe it.

She was eight years old. Cross-legged, wide eyed in this very same *nalukettu*... Barebreasted Muthasshi Amma rocking to the tempo of her horror stories.

Triprangot, Trichambaram, Tirunavaya, Tiruvannur, Tali....

There was a sudden clamour in the capacious entrance portal. The menfolk pacing the perpendicular arms of the space, seemed to hear someone outside and rushed there. It was one of the gateway guards. She could hear the buzz as the man gave his report but not the words. The message however was clear – bad news. The man left and Mathu watched the body language of the Kovilakam men. They were not known for the animated expression of emotions. Their walk inwards was however uncommonly lethargic. They scratched their heads, their faces registered traces of helplessness and frustration. If Mithran had been among them he would have grunted and given a twisted smile. For the first time since his flight, she was glad he was nowhere around.

'Divakara,' she called out to her grandson when he wandered near enough to the window.

'Ammamme,' the creases on his forehead revealed that he had no desire to give her a blow-by-blow briefing but knew there was no way out.

'It's bad Ammamme. There are hundreds of them. All armed. We have no more than forty men altogether. And ... sadly one of them has been stabbed. They fear he is... Narayanan is fighting like a tiger. He has shot a

Mapla. The men have been instructed to try not to kill anyone. Only in extreme situations. He used the gun just the once when the fellow stabbed one of our men. They cannot hold fort much longer.'

Sethu

In spite of the spaciousness of the mansion's upper storey, more than thirty of them up there in a state of excitement and panic was suffocating. It felt safer huddling together. The east-facing windows provided a view of the Devil tree. The Palachod was literally deserted. Old Beeran stood beneath the tree, faithfully and silently watching over the mansion. He had been there so long that he had begun to look like a new branch the pala had suddenly sprung. A while ago a perturbed looking gateway guard had entered the *padipura* of the mansion and in ten minutes or so he was seen hurrying back in the direction of the gateway. Through the windows on the southern side they could not see as far as the gateway itself but the Vettekaran temple and the path beyond were visible. A resonant buzz rolled in the air from that direction but nothing was visible. But it wouldn't be long. Sethu would have longed to know what the messenger had to say but Ammamma had been absolutely firm that not a single one of them should descend the stairs.

The others were eager for news too. The younger ones kept rushing to the windows time and again and someone even tried to press her ears to the floor and looked comical doing so. Sethu would have expected them to sit in their huddle giggling and discussing the necklaces and earpieces they planned to buy the next time the Chettiyar from Pattambi came around. Or cracking Gulikan jokes. But not a word on those frivolous lines did they utter and she had felt chagrined for judging them so.

Yet another messenger was seen darting past the Pala. Beeran, under the tree stiffened but didn't budge from his position. Suddenly, Umedathi stood up and dashed out of the room. She beckoned to the others and scurried down one of the darkest corridors. At the end of the unlit passage was a window that was hardly ever unbolted for it opened out into the entrance portal and would hinder the privacy of the occupants of the mansion.

Why hadn't she thought of it herself! Sethu looked admiringly at Umedathi as she struggled with the stiff wooden bolts that held it shut. She rushed to help her cousin and together they managed to slide the clasps open. The others followed and as many of them as the narrow space would allow, crowded around the window and sent silent glances at each other when the messenger panted into the porch. Their cousins looked up anxiously and the man came to a halt before the Second Tirumulpad.

'We did our best, Tirumulpad…' his breath came out in puffs and Sethu and the other Kovilakam ladies strained to hear. 'Five of our men have been killed and… and two jumped over the wall and sought refuge in the neighbouring *tharawad*. But… are these Maplas men or demons? They attacked the *tharawad* and killed sixteen people. Two women and two children included…'

'They are coming, Tirumulpad.... Listen...'

Umedathi clamped her hand over her mouth, eyes wide in shock. Sethu clutched her heart. Some others leaned back on the wall afraid their feet would give away.

The distant rumble got louder and louder till it sounded like a collective roar.

The girls keeping watch at the southern windows came tearing in. 'They are here. They are here. Come and look.' There was a frantic rush into the south facing rooms.

Vetekkara!

They had never seen so many people at the Palachod ever. Not even during the Pattu days when scores of tribals camped there. Shaven heads, long beards, bare chests, broad leather belts, checkered waist cloths.

Allahu Akbar!

Allahu Akbar!

Bolo taqbeer Allahu Akbar!

Like a river branching off, a group of them meandered towards the Vettekkaran shrine. They were brandishing big sticks and shiny swords. Because the Agrasala building blocked their view the Kovilakam women couldn't see what happened there. The other Maplas raced about as if they had gone rabid. They could hear thuds and crashes as they attacked the temple door. The heavy wooden door was about fifteen feet in height, Sethu knew for the tallest of their tuskers bearing the Lord's idol could barely enter it, and made of solid teak.

'There is no way they are going to break open that

door,' one of the aunts voiced Sethu's thoughts.

'Oh!' There was a screech as something caught the attention of one of the girls. Some of the Maplas who had rushed down the path that led to the river was dragging someone by the hair. God! It was one of the young maids who had been to the river and seeing the sea of rioters in the Palachod had pressed herself to the wall hoping to remain unseen. She clutched the hand of her little boy. But they had detected the poor woman and hauled her forcefully along.

If the Maplas were here to find Mithrettan and take revenge on him and the Kovilakam people, why would they attack the poor maid? But the rioters seemed to have lost all trace of reason. One of them pointed at the little boy's forehead with the tip of his dagger. The woman screamed. Another caught the child by the scruff of his neck and wiped his forehead with the end of his waistcloth.

'The Mapla is annoyed by the sandal paste on the boys forehead,' a cousin whispered in Sethu's ear.

The fellow produced a skull cap, jammed it down on the boys head and flung him against the wall. The poor mother screamed again. Another fellow had a stick in his hand which he twirled into the maid's upper cloth and pulled, causing the garment to come off on the tip of his stick leaving her bare breasted in front of the whole pack. They leered and pushed her into the midst of the crowd.

The Kovilakam ladies watching at the windows automatically grasped their own upper garments protectively.

Sethu pulled away from the window. It would not do

to remain mere spectators when such atrocities happened in the Palachod.

'Sethu,' Umedathi said in a firm voice, 'I am going up to the topmost floor.'

Why! Did Umedathi want to hide?

'We have to do something. They will be in here within minutes. We will be prepared.' She briskly made for the narrow staircase leading upstairs. 'We are not allowed downstairs. We will gather whatever weapon we can from what is stored up there.'

Had she really believed her cousin to be superficial and catty? God! Umedathi was brave and could think on her feet. Soon a whole lot of them were up in the attic rooms grabbing broad bladed *vettukathis*, sharp *paras* meant for dehusking coconuts, heavy mortars and pestles.

'Umedathi, look at this,' said Sethu suddenly pointing at the tall jars of coconut oil in a corner. 'Yes,' said Umedathi triumphantly moving towards the bundles of firewood stocked in readiness on another side.

'Girls, light a fire'.

The youngsters scrambled downstairs with bricks and firewood bundles and in no time set up a makeshift stove in one of the verandas. Sethu's heart swelled in pride to see them busily get things done. Little Lakshmikutti, all of fifteen and five months along knelt in front of the stove blowing with all her might till the spark caught on. Cauldrons were hoisted on to it and jars of oil poured in.

Sethu would never look down on her female relatives

again considering how they had risen to the occasion in a crisis.

Mammad

Never in the several times he had been in here to see the Baliya Thampatti, had he crossed this particular threshold. Now he stepped in as sedately as possible though his heart was palpitating like a drum. He kept close behind Alavikutti who seemed to have no qualms whatsoever as he vaulted over the doorstep with a loud taqbeer issuing from his throat. There was a minor stampede as the men pushed their way in in a me-first, me-first rush.

Things seemed to be swimming in Mammad's head. He looked around to see so many of his own men fill the large entrance portal. Most of them had maniacal expressions in their eyes. They were flourishing their weapons in gestures indicating that they would do just about anything. Blocking their way was a line of Tirumulpads, arms crossed across their chests and their snow white mundus doubled up at knee height. Some of them he knew by sight. But there was no sign of the Sixth Tirumulpad. Anger surged up once more. Was he hiding inside behind the women?

Basheer took a few steps forward, turned towards the crowd and raised both his hands demanding silence. It took them a couple of minutes but Mammad observed that the Maplas of Pookottur quietened down and watched cautiously. He himself was relieved that it was Basheer who assumed leadership. He didn't trust himself to do the right thing and others were on the verge of losing sanity.

Basheer turned to the row of noble men lined in front of them. There were Tirumulpads in there as well as some of the consort Namboothiris and a couple of young Nairs, sons of the Kovilakam men. Not a single one of them was armed with the exception of the washerman turned guard who hung back with his pistol in readiness. It wouldn't take his friends more than a few minutes to finish them off with the number of weapons they had brought with them.

'We do not wish to cause trouble,' began Basheer and some of the Tirumulpads smirked noiselessly.

'But we must see the Sixth Tirumulpad. We have more than one bone to pick with him. When we have had our say, we will leave.'

'And you will believe me if I say Mithran is not here?' The Second Tirumulpad asked.

'He is lying,' roared Usman's brother Moosa, still smarting from the loss of his brother.

'He takes us for fools.'

'Yes. Like their honey tongued *changathi* did at the Pookottur manor the other day. One moment's hesitation and the bastard took over,' Alavikutti was beside himself.

'But I speak the truth. Not a single one of us knows where Mithran is. If you are determined to see him, you will have to look elsewhere.'

'He is in there, I tell you. Somewhere in the innermost chambers of this cursed mansion.'

'Think we can't find him in the crazy network of

mazes and corridors?'

'Bloody snob! Coward! Kafir!'

'Scores of bitches in there for him to crawl behind. Must be having a good time.'

Allah! His friends were clueless about what they were saying, Mammad began to tense.

The Thampan called Bhaskaran lacked the Second Tirumulpad's self-control. He took a threatening step towards Hasan, the firebrand who had spoken disrespectfully of the women, 'You scurvy mongrel!'

'You filthy pig! How dare…' seethed his cousin by name Adityan.

'He calls us suvars!'

'He insults the followers of the prophet!'

'Kill the bastard!'

'Allahu Akbar!'

The name of God had never sounded so barbarous, so blood thirsty to Mammad's ears as it did on the lips of his friends that day. One of the largest, sturdiest residential buildings in the whole of Malabar shook to the foundation that moment. Alavikutti swung his sword wildly in all directions. A gaudy red pattern formed on Bhaskaran's sparkling white shirt. A long and gaping cut appeared on the bare ribs of one of the consorts and the thread lying across his upper body snapped in two. Another Thampan clutched his hand with a cry after someone's blind stab had missed its mark and the dagger embedded itself in his wrist. The gateway guard's pistol cracked deafeningly and Mammad spotted at least four of his friends crumple to the floor before a wooziness set in and he began to see things in double and triple.

And suddenly a granite pestle came flying from nowhere and crashed on Koyakka's shaven crown and he slid down in a faint, its companion mortar knocked another Mapla down. A *vettukathi* soared by nearly slicing the vein below somebody's ear. Soon burning logs whizzed through the air into their crowd, blinding them as the sparks hit their eyes and set their beards on fire.

Allah! What was that? For a moment it seemed as if it had begun to rain. Each drop a cauldronful. But instead of getting drenched they were being scalded. Totally baffled his friends began screaming in pain, they had no idea where this attack was coming from.

And suddenly the door to the inner nalukettu's opened. And the Baliya Thampatti stood there and surveyed the savage happenings in her entrance portal. Her tiny figure, Mammad felt seemed to tower over him and all the rest. She walked slowly and fearlessly into their midst and did not stop till her searching eyes found him in the crowd. She came to a halt right before him and silently looked him over head to toe. And slowly, deliberately and even gently she placed a small wrinkled palm on his bare shoulder. It felt scorching hot and scalded him worse than the burn caused by splash of hot oil that had come from nowhere and landed on his arm.

'Mammade,' she said, her soft voice clearly audible to him above all the din.

She looked pointedly at the dagger in his belt.

'You shall kill me. Here. Now. I command that you kill me before another human being here is hurt. Thampan or Mapla. You shall kill me. In the name of your Allah you shall.'

Whether it took him seconds or minutes or even hours, Mammad knew not.

Stop! Stop! Retreat!

Was that his own voice?

Stop in the name of Allah! We have done enough.

Hurt and tired out, most of the men were prepared to obey. Raised arms dropped one by one. Daggers clanged on the floor. The pistol in the background ceased to crack and the crazy weapons from nowhere eased in frequency. Even as the general commotion was beginning to die down, with the corner of his left eye he saw one final splash of boiling oil find its mark on Basheer's chest, letting out a hiss and the odour of frying human skin. His changathi's eyes rolled upwards before he fell back. At the same time his right eye took in the mad Umar, wishing to make the last statement, driving his dagger deep into the abdomen of an unsuspecting Divakaran Thampan, the Thampatti's dear grandson.

He, Mammad was accountable for the whole disaster and the loser in the bargain.

Afterwards

August 22- 24 '21
The Outcaste

When I expressed my doubts to Shekharan Nair that day, using the seed dispersal metaphor, I had my worries about the course of action the Maplas would take, but in no way had I conceived something on these lines.

I was at home when I got the news of the attack on the Nilambur Kovilakam.

Ever since I had brought the Sixth Tirumulpad here and set him up in one of our more comfortable outhouses, I had taken care to limit my travels to some extent. If any difficulties came up I didn't want my family having to deal with them. The only time I had left my village was to go to Pookottur on Shekharettan's request to try and talk sense to Alijan Sahib. It seemed to me now that that trip had been ages ago instead of just the day before.

Yesterday, soon after the evening meal, my brother Unni had climbed on to the shiny, black bicycle which was his most prized possession and merrily pedaled off into the semi-darkness, his newest composition on his lips. The lissome garland-girl at the neighbouring Variyam would be awaiting his arrival with a betel-leaf package in readiness. Unniettan being one of the younger sons, was not destined to marry from our own community. He was cheerful enough about it, as he was a lighthearted fellow and maintained relations not just in the Variyam but in the Ayiramnazhi Kovilakam as well. After Unniettan left for the night, I planned to sit down to a few hours of writing. At least the leisure of being housebound had had positive results in that direction, I thought as I bolted the side door after my brother. By about nine thirty, I would check up on the Sixth Tirumulpad before he retired. I settled down in the corner of the eastern veranda where I had set up my desk. No sooner had I picked up my pencil and begun jotting down the outline of a piece I was due to begin, I heard the urgent clanging of the bell and the screech of the bicycle wheels. In a minute the side door rattled urgently. Unni Ettan. What was up? There was someone with him, who, when the person moved towards the lantern, I recognised a scion of Ayiramnazhi who was Unni ettan's brother-in-law.

'Udaya Varma brings news.' The jolly Unni ettan was rarely this grave. 'Bad news.'

The young man looked noticeably agitated. His narration was fast and furious and his report of the attack on the Nilambur Kovilakam gushed out in such speed that I found it difficult to keep pace.

When Alijan Sahib had listened to them with reasonable patience and on his wife's urging he had agreed to put off the march to Tirurangadi till they knew more, Shekharan Nair had been pleased with the success of their mission, but somehow I felt suspicious. In fact it should have been the other way round. It was Shekharan Nair who knew the Maplas of Ernad like he did his own brothers. But he was trusting by nature and took Alijan for his word. However, in spite of my doubts I hadn't expected a turn in this particular direction. Dozens of lost lives on both sides. And Divakaran Thampan dead! I had grown to like the man a lot during my visits to the Pookottur manor and of late had begun looking forward to having him as a brother-in-law. Dead! Stabbed in the belly by a fanatic.

God! I suddenly remembered that I would have to break the news to the Sixth Tirumulpad. I made up my mind not to tell him that it was in search of him that the Maplas had reached the Kovilakam. I didn't want Mithran Thampan blaming himself on top of everything. The Sixth Tirumulpad was not an easy man to cope with. Getting him to stay undercover for a while had been a task in itself. When finally he had grunted half-heartedly, he had insisted on going to Nilambur. If I had given in then, things would have been worse. He would definitely not have remained indoors and let his family face the rioters. And if he had come out into their midst, the

Maplas would have turned even more violent. There would have been more deaths.

I cleared my throat in preparation and leaving Unni ettan to give his own brother-in-law a bed for the night, I set out towards the outhouse.

Benu

Raziya was crying relentlessly and there was nothing Benu could do to comfort her. Her words spilled out in woeful outbursts, her words punctuated with sobs and hiccups.

'What has come over him, Thatha?' She asked plaintively. 'I just cannot understand. We have been together for a year and I thought I knew the man I married. I still cannot bring myself to believe that he is not the good man I knew him to be. But I do realise now that he is not an ordinary, simple, hardworking Mapla as I had assumed for so long.'

How could he think of attacking the Nilambur Kovilakam so brutally? He has always held them in high regard, especially the Baliya Thampatti. After all he grew up on the rice they put on his plate. I have never heard him talk ill of the Kovilakam. Except… except of late of the Sixth Tirumulpad…'

As she paused to consider, Raziya was caressing her stomach in subconscious possessiveness, Benu noticed with some interest.

'The Tirumulpad *is* a haughty person,' hesitation caused her voice to drop. 'And he *was* unjust. Refusing to pay the money for the gatehouse job, sacking him for no reason and to rub salt on an already hurting wound, accusing him of theft and setting the police on him… in a way his anger is justified. But… Thatha, was this *anger*? I think not. It was something a lot more intense, cruel and wild. Gathering those people and launching such an onslaught. And see what came of it. So many people dead! Oh! I can't bear to hear of the laments of Usmanikka's wife and young Paree's umma. And the Thampatty's grandson! Allah! How will he look at her in the face again? Thatha, do you know that the bed he sleeps on every night was her wedding gift to us? Tell me, do you think he can ever have a peaceful night's sleep again, knowing what he has done? And his own *changathi*! They say poor Basheerkka's moans and the smell of his burns reach as far as the Plakkal canal. Will he live or will he die? In the condition he is in, *mayyath* would be better than life. What has he done, Thatha… what has my man done!' She wailed and rubbed her belly again.

The fear in her eyes mounted as she voiced the question and dreaded the answer.

'*Orukku piranthano, Thatha*? Is he mad?'

The violent tremor that broke out at the nape of Benu's neck, went painfully down to the base of her spine, causing her aging body to reel.

This was a question that had been asked of her by another woman at another time, her still lovely face pale, memories of a long ago lover haunting her as she shared with Benu the secrets she had kept hidden in her bosom for decades.

'*Orukku piranthayrnno, Benu*'? Her voice had been barely a whisper.

Raziya had been living at Benazir Manzil for days now. Long enough for Benu to guess that a little living being was blossoming in the girlish abdomen. Watching Mammad's young wife caress her stomach in a gentle circular motion even as she stared sorrowfully at Benu's face, she made the decision. She should tell Raziya, she thought. The girl had the right to know. As this was the heritage of the baby she was carrying.

'Raziya, mole, will you listen to a story'?

She nodded in answer, half alarmed and half fascinated.

Benu sat up straight on the wooden seating ledge in her anteroom, her eyes fixed vaguely on the wall opposite and her legs swinging back and forth as she went into a daydream mode. The thick collection of rings in her ears glittered in the semi darkness.

The pretty village where she had spent her childhood. The house she lived in with her Umma and her uncle. The constant absence of her *bappa*. Imbicchi, the lamb. Her closest friend, Suhratha, a girl atleast ten years older to her. Benu was a good story teller as her daydreams had fed her imagination. She painted a vivid picture of the time, the place and the people. Raziya was now truly drawn in and seemed to forget her worries for a while.

'Why didn't your *bappa* live with you, Thatha? Where was he?'

'In jail'.

Raziya gasped.

The incident Benu wanted to draw Raziya's attention to, happened just a day or two before Bappa's return. The incident involving, Imbichi, Suhratha and the thief in the firewood shed. The thief with green eyes who was not really a thief.

Green eyes. Raziya stiffened. That definitely drove home.

There had been a jail break. Three prisoners had escaped from the Town prison. One, Benu learnt later, had been Bappa. Another was a man called Kadar who lived undercover at the local Yatim Khana. The third was the green eyed Mujeeb who had hidden in the firewood shed and fallen in love with Suhratha on first sight. It was Suhratha's brother Mammad who helped the escaped prisoners to hide and make future plans.

Mammad. From the look in Raziya's eyes, she had realised this had more to do with her than she had thought.

It was just for a few days that the convicts remained underground in their village but a lot happened in Suhratha's life in that short time.

What happened next was too fast and eventful for nine year old Benu to keep up with. Apparently the Collector was assassinated in his bungalow. A most violent murder. The murderers escaped once more and found their separate ways to the same little hamlet where they had earlier found refuge. This time the Yatim Khana had housed all three. There had been a blanket of anxiety all over the village. A sea of boots trampled the narrow muddy lanes. A clatter of hoofs and an occasional gunshot were the only sounds heard. The villagers chose not to step out of their houses. The police were everywhere looking for the three Mapla assassins. Benu remembered little else of the times, except certain hazy images.

Weeks later, when they finally settled down in their new home in Valluvanad after days of clandestine travel, the whole of Malabar was full of the news. The police regiment under Captain Hailey had seized the three Maplas responsible for the heartless murder of Malabar Collector and Magistrate H V Connolly in a village in South Malabar. Mujeeb, 25, and Rahim Haji, 70, were killed by the police in separate encounters on the 20 of September. Abdul Kadar, 32 was court martialed and shot to death at Calicut on the 22. Sergeant Archibald Ross and Constable Kuttan Pilla lost their lives in the endeavour. The British believed justice had been done.

This was what the British records stated, what the media reported but the fact that there was a lot more that happened behind the scenes, earth shattering for the people involved, that nobody recorded, no newspaper printed.

Benu mentioned the birth and loss of her sons but offered no details, opting to go straight to the time when nearly twenty five years had passed since their marriage and Benu and Alijan were trying to pick up the pieces and build up a new life here in Pookottur. Alijan Sahib was like a cat in that when he fell he did it on four legs. Even when his world went crashing round his ears, he would shake his mane and rise out of the ruins to charge ahead. Soon things began to go well for them. Several bullock carts, the timber factory, money, social position all came one after the other. It wouldn't be long before Benazir Manzil was built.

Their acquaintance with the Kovilakam cart driver and his little green eyed boy led to a reunion with her long lost friend. The driver Beeran, who lived in Nilambur most of the time had married the eldest daughter of a retired policeman called Abu and his wife Suhra who turned out to be none other than her own dear, Suhratha.

The renewed friendship flourished with regular visits. Benu got to know Suhratha's husband, a dear loving man, ever so protective of his wife. Of all his children he loved his eldest daughter best and whenever the family came from Nilambur for a visit which was often, the green eyed boy's favourite playmate was his grandfather.

By nature thoughtful and analytical, Benu began to put together the puzzle. The different pieces fit together in some places but in others there were gaping holes.

Till Suhratha herself decided to fill in the missing chunks.

Small Mammad sometimes worried his grandmother. She was proud of his good looks, his eagerness to learn and his willingness to persevere. But he took things too seriously and possessed no lighter side.

'It is as if he forgets he is a child,' said Suhratha

thoughtfully. 'Tell me, little Benu, have you ever seen him laugh?' Suhratha still called her 'little Benu' as she did in the old days.

Come to think of it, she hadn't.

'He is alright, Suhratha,' Benu said comfortingly but Suhratha shook her head.

'There is more,' she said. 'He has a streak of something in him. Something which I can't point out. But it scares me. He is … I think a vengeful child, little Benu. He remembers every wrong done against him and waits for the right moment to strike back. In every other way, Mammad is a good boy, but this… this is not normal. There is this rather mischievous boy who lives nearby and Mammad sometimes plays with him when he visits us. One evening there was a quarrel and Seydu punched him in the face giving him a black eye. By the next morning Seydu had forgotten all about it and came along to play with Mammad, cheerful as ever. And what do you think our boy did? He went out with the child, quietly but I saw something in those eyes of his. A kind of malicious glint. He had hidden in his waist cloth a sharp metal rod which he had torn off his grandfather's big umbrella, once they were out and there were no adults nearby, he wacked the other boy with the rod till he was black and blue and poked him in the eye with it. Poor Seydu had no idea why he was being beaten up. There had been no quarrel that morning. Now they never send the boy to play with Mammad.'

'This is just one of many such incidents, little Benu.'

Benu had nothing to say, except that he would outgrow it and Suhratha should stop worrying.

'But what if he doesn't? He may not outgrow it. Not if it is in his blood.'

Benu's brows rose a trifle.

'His grandfather didn't.'

Suhratha flushed a deep scarlet.

'You can't mean Abukka!' She was shocked. Suhratha's old Mapla, the retired policeman was the gentlest man she had come across. A soft spoken giant to whom Suhratha meant the world. Abukka revengeful?

'I don't mean him,' replied Suhratha quietly.

Before Benu could ask if she meant Beeran's father, Suhratha spoke again.

'You were too young to understand things, little Benu.I wonder if the name Mujeeb means anything to you.'

Mujeeb… Benu frowned in concentration. It did sound familiar. But it wasn't an uncommon name. Once again an image flashed in her mind. One that often did when she looked at Mammad's small, solemn face. Before she could voice it, Suhratha said it herself.

'The man in the firewood *pora*.'

Benu held her breath.

'I first set eyes on him in there when I chased your lamb. I was so scared then to see him crouched behind the logs with the animal in his arms. His eyes burnt into me.'

Are you a thief, I asked.

He shook his head and said 'Shhh. Quiet.' His voice was low and harsh but his jewel like eyes were … pleading.

Then I learnt he was my brother's *changathi*. He was hiding from something or someone. And Ikka himself had stationed him in the firewood shed. In the days that followed I found myself going into the shed whenever I could. I enjoyed looking at his serious expression as I teased him and we grew close.

One evening, in the twilight sun I saw his silhouette slip out of the shed. I ran out of the house.

'Where are you going?'

'I have to go out. I will be back a little late in the night.'

'Don't go. Mammadkka said you should remain hidden.'

'I have to go,' he repeated. 'Your brother will be with me. Suhra,' he said suddenly, his green eyes boring into mine, come to shed at night. 'I shall make a torch out of a burning log and wave it when I am back.'

'I wasn't sure where he went then but I think it was to your house little Benu. To meet your father and the other man.'

It was late when the torch flashed in the shed and I crept out.

'It was the most memorable night in my life.'

Suhratha's voice was laced with a long forgotten emotion.

On the old mat that Ikka had provided for his use, we stretched out and enjoyed the togetherness which I didn't know then would be our last moments together. He talked. And as he did his emerald eyes lit up the shed. I could see myself in each of them.

He unleashed the fire smoldering in his chest. A fire that had been burning since he was fourteen. A fire ignited by loss and hatred… and the need for revenge that was born of them. Only killing would satisfy the hunger of those flames, though he didn't tell me that then.

Mujeeb's Umma had worked in the fields of a Namboothiri landlord ever since he could remember. He had no memories of his bappa. Her job was to load the cow dung into bullock carts. When he was too young to stay at home alone, Mujeeb would trail after her all day. During the day, Umma smelt bad. Of sweat, dirt and animal excreta. When he was out in the fields, the landlord, clad in rich robes, his mouth oozing red betel juice twisted in revulsion as he looked at Umma. But Umma was not ugly or dirty. In the evenings in their tiny hut, when she had had a bath in a faraway pond, for they were restricted from touching wells, she was beautiful. Her skin was fair and soft. Her hair, usually hidden under a soiled *thattam*, was long and silky. She smelt lovely as she fed him his *kanji*. The sneering expression on the landlord's face etched itself on Mujeeb's mind. He was not a villain, Umma assured him. It was he who saw to it that their *kanji* pot was full. Mujeeb tried to believe her.

Not long after he turned fourteen, he was walking past the bathhouse by the pond where the landlords of the Mana bathed. There was loud cackling laughter there and he peered through the bushes. On the bottommost step leading to the king-sized pond, stood the lofty villain, clad in no more than a loin cloth and the thread across his chest. He climbed out of the water dripping. There was a leer on his face. Two others clad in similar attire squatted on the steps.

'How could you, Mampilli? That disgusting creature. Did you hold your nose while you went about it?' One Namboothiri sniggered, looking as if a bad smell lurked under his nose.

'And a Mapla woman! How could you touch her? Or don't *shuddham* and *aitham* matter to you'? Another appeared shocked.

The villain of Mampilli began rubbing himself dry with his starched towel.

'Well, if I hadn't seen her once in the evening behind her grubby kudi, toweling her hair dry, I would have never thought these creatures bathed. And I am not exaggerating, my man… my mouth literally watered.'

'And she simply agreed when you asked?'

'You think I would waste my time talking to… to that thing? And why would she say no? Her Mapla has been dead for years. Maybe she was longing for it too.'

'I wouldn't say that,' his friend howled in laughter. 'I am sure she has been at it with some sayippe. Have you seen her boy's eyes? Green! Can you believe it?'

And then Mujeeb realised. He rushed home, guffaws ringing in his ears.

Umma fed him his evening *kanji* as usual and later he

tossed and turned on his mat for Allah knows how long before dozing off. He woke up some time in the night and saw that the adjacent mat was empty. It was only a one room kudi and Umma was not anywhere in there. Mujeeb crept out. The moon shone brightly to reveal a silhouette hanging from the branch of a nearby cashew tree.

He left his umma's *mayyath* dangling there and dashed into the night.

The heat was unbearable. It could be felt at a radius of atleast one square kilometer. Mujeeb reveled in the joy and the sense of self-worth enveloping him as he watched the orange tongues dart about licking the big house and finally devouring it as a whole. As he stood there taking in the scene with pleasure he saw someone peering at him in shock. His cat-eyes glowing in the firelight and the eerie maniacal grin scared the man as he realised the truth. Mujeeb rekindled his torch.

Early the next day, the police arrested the young Mapla fanatic for burning to death seventeen Hindus in one night, twelve at the Mana and five at the neighbouring house. And for years the White Sarkar's police tortured the young boy imprisoned in the town jail. Only old Rahim Haji was kind to him and the good looking, soft spoken Kadar.

'Only death and fire had had the potential to make me happy,' Mujeeb whispered in Suhratha's ears. 'But now there is a joyous laugh that can cool my burning breast like the waters of a bubbling brook.' 'As he held me in his arms, I didn't know whether to fear him or to love him,' said Benu's friend.

'I don't know when he slipped off but when I woke up he was gone.'

Suhratha only saw Mujeeb once after that, Benu told Raziya and she could almost hear the girl's heartbeat.

In the days following the Collector's assassination, the police had the Yatim Khana surrounded. Suhratha and her old mother locked themselves in their hut. Her brother hadn't come home for two days. And then they got the news that he had been arrested. They were watching Suhra's house too for her brother had aided the assassins. Suhra kept her windows tightly shut.

Late one night she heard a movement outside and shivered. Then someone knocked at the window and she heard her name whispered. In a familiar voice, both dreaded and beloved.

'Ngalo!' Suhra partially opened the window and whispered back through the gap.

'Go away. The police are here. Begam *pokkolee*.'

But Mujeeb lingered. Two waving torches in a distance told him the police men on watch had gone to empty their bladders and he wanted to make use of the precious time.

'Go,' Suhra hissed again when she saw the torches bob back. And reluctantly Mujeeb moved away. Instead of leaving he slipped into the firewood shed hoping for another chance to see Suhra.

But the constables were a vigilant pair. They noticed

the swinging door of the shed and went to investigate. One of them handed his torch to his colleague and stepped in, with plans to catch the intruder unawares. Suddenly the constable outside saw his companion come hurtling out of the *pora* and fall a few feet away from him. A silver dagger stood upright in the middle of his back, his uniform drenched in blood. With his colleague dead the policeman felt the compulsive need to stop this assassin from committing more murders. He threw his torch on to the thatched roof and the *pora*, firewood, Mujeeb and all was lapped up by the flames as Suhratha watched from the window, rubbing a protective palm over her belly.

When things settled down a bit, the prison guard Abu who had formed a friendship with Mammadkka while he was in jail began visiting her house with his news. He married Suhra before her condition became obvious and took her off to his hometown near here after her mother passed and Mammadkka died in jail. She would have only daughters and she chose to name her first grandson after her brother.

Raziya began to understand the way her husband's mind worked.

Priyamvada

A short letter from the Sixth Tirumulpad written in his own hand on Sunday, the 31 July, which though it offered no details or mentioned his current whereabouts, assured her that he was alive and well, was the only thread Priya could now hold on to. When her brothers brought the shocking news of what happened in Nilambur two days ago, it felt as if the whole earth had shattered to bits and she was left roaming around in the rubble knowing it was all her fault. If it hadn't been for that letter, she would well have used the little black gun on herself.

The Sixth Tirumulpad had been mobbed.

He was now on the run.

The Kovilakam was attacked.

Divakaran Thampan was dead.

Many others were injured. ...

The consequences of one reckless action.

Priya thought of the gun her husband had called the Beretta 1915 when he had shown it to her and explained how it worked. It now lay at the bottom of the trunk she had brought from the manor, beneath her clothes, a silent evidence of her stupidity, a constant reminder of the horrible events that followed.

When the manor had been mobbed, her mother and uncles had made no secret of their relief that she hadn't been there at the time. But Priya had no desire to remain safe. She had to go to the Kovilakam. Confess everything. They would hate her. Sethu Thampatti would never again wish to see her face if she knew the truth. Maybe the Sixth Tirumulpad wouldn't either...but she had to do it.

Impulsiveness had been like a sibling to her since the day she was born. Forever with her in childhood and youth, influencing her actions. Sethu, dear Sethu had always said that it was her recklessness that made her the bright and interesting person she was. Hadn't it been the very same foolhardiness that helped her win her man?

That day, when Mithran Thampan said that he didn't wish her to go to the *tharawad* for her mother's birthday, she had thought of all kinds of little ways to get him to come around. She was used to having things her way. But neither did she wish to fall prey to packs of marauders and brigands on the way. And the gun cabinet came to mind. When no one was around she had opened it and peered inside. Being the smallest, the black one had seemed the best choice. Grab it! Impulsiveness, that wretched sister had whispered urgently in her ear. And she made the most terrible decision in her life. Just as one small gun, the Browning 1910, Mithran Thampan had once told her, had been the immediate cause of the Great War, so had this little Beretta that she had thoughtlessly purloined, triggered off hurt and loss and turbulence in her own land.

There was no way she could make amends, but she had to make a clean breast of it. Whatever the consequence, she would accept it as her penance. She had to go to Nilambur. In the current scenario, there was no way her family would let her go. But she would find a way.

Her treacherous sibling gave her a nudge.

Babes Of The Boscage

The forest
22 – 23 August '21
Winifred

Poor Mother had blisters on her feet and her thick ankles were covered in angry rashes, probably from having brushed against some weeds. Winifred was not better off herself but she said nothing. When lives turn topsy-turvy, one doesn't grumble about minor itches and aches.

On Sunday Stanley Pat had come home after an evening in the club with further news on the situation with the Moplas. It was getting worse and drawing nearer.

'I have decided Win, my love. You shall leave for Ootacamund tomorrow. And you too naturally, Mrs Cranwill. I have made arrangements for you to travel with the Colebrooks. The ladies and the senior Mr Colebrook are making an early start tomorrow. They are planning on staying with relatives till the whole thing subsides. Uncle Charles and Aunt May will have you,' he had announced at dinner.

'What about you?'

'I shall follow too. As soon as I can. Colebrook and Brown are staying back another day or so too. We have business to tie up before we pack up and leave. I myself will be going to the Pullangode guest house to meet the manager. I hope to be back by the evening. Colebrook and Brown will settle things here. If all is well we should be able to follow you on Tuesday.'

'No, Stanley Pat. Another day won't matter. Mother and I will travel with you.'

Arguments followed which surprisingly, Winifred won. Stanley Pat was in no mood to prolong the debate. He went to bed early in preparation for the next day's ride to the guest house. The earlier he left the earlier he could get back.

Stanley Pat mounted his horse before it was light. Winifred watched him bark a few instructions at his Chokra who was to follow on foot with a few essential papers. Later she busied herself packing small cases for herself and Mother. How much should she take? She had no idea how long they would be in Ootacamund. Stanley Pat hadn't said. Aunt May and Uncle Charles entertained quite a bit. Would she need her party dresses? It was colder up in the hills and she would definitely take warm things and some extra for Mother, whose wheezing was worse these days. And would she cut down on her cigarettes? Not she, thought Winifred with mild irritation. Well

Uncle Charles was a physician. So something good might come of this after all. She would take her writing case of course. Would she have time to write a couple of letters today? To Jack Horner. And maybe one to Mrs Rama Ayer. She pulled out a few sheets of paper, some envelopes and a pen before shutting the case and tucking it into the trunk. The Chokras would accompany them surely, but she didn't wish the bags to be heavier than necessary. She ran her fingers over her writing desk, enjoying the feel of the warm, silky wood and stroked the bob tail of the tiny rabbit sitting in the cubby hole of her desk. It was the latest addition to her collection of animal figures. An anonymous gift like the others, this had appeared about a week ago on top of a half -finished letter. On a whim, she picked up the rabbit and dropped it into her trunk. Mother's case was almost done too. She would just pop in and ask her if there was anything else she specifically needed. The Crocodile girl was hovering in the doorway as Winifred stepped out into the corridor and headed for Mother's room. Her condition was becoming all the more obvious as the weeks passed. She must be nearly six months along now, thought Winifred smiling at the doe eyed tribal girl. A few months ago, Cheenkanni kept as far away from her mistress as possible. What brought about the change of heart, Winifred didn't know but she was glad all the same. Ever since the day the Mopla worker had died and there had been a gherao, Cheenkanni had followed her around like a shadow, saying nothing but always more than willing to help.

Doors and windows were slamming. Loud. Urgent. The pregnant girl nearly jumped out of her skin. Winifred went downstairs quickly. The staff were rushing into the hall from all directions. Seeing her descend the stairs, the housekeeper and a pair of maids hurried over.

'We have locked up all the exits, Madame. And shut the windows too.'

'What's up?' She had been almost afraid to ask.

'Mapla mobs from Kalikave and Pullangode are pouring in from all directions. Our own workers are joining them. They are all over the Estate. '

'The Chokra is back after delivering the Sayippe's papers at the guest house. I have sent him with a message to Brown Sayippe in the neighbouring bungalow,' the cook burst in from the kitchen.

The frightened staff all huddled indoors.

It was like a chain, they said. The riots. A mob from Pookottur set the Maplas of Nilambur off before they went back home this morning after attacking the noble house and inflaming the locals. Forest Officer M C Chandy had gone into hiding. Then the ones in Nilambur rose, instigating others in Kalikave and Pullangode. Now they were here. They were destroying property, looting and running about like crazy with their daggers and javelins raised.

'Couldn't we get Koya, the overseer to talk sense into them?'

'Koya!' The cook almost spat. 'He is heading the pack. Now he is running about with that mad, old Kunjali, smashing windows and stabbing people. In fact they killed Mr Nair, the supervisor and injured Mr Jones.'

Winifred was shocked. Koya! Stanley Pat's right hand had switched sides! Kunjali, the old Mapla was none other than the father of the man Koya had beaten to death a few months ago! To think the old man would work together with his son's killer!

The Chokra came racing in. Brown Sayippe was not there. The servants believed he and Colebrook Sayippe had escaped into the forests. Their families went away early this morning. The Maplas had dragged the Browns' furniture out of the bungalow and were setting fire to it.

It didn't occur to Winifred then to glance at the grandfather clock in the hall and she had no clue what time it was. It seemed hours since all of them, she, Mother and the household staff crowded together in that one room. It was certainly not pleasant. She had understood only part of what they were saying and felt helpless.

House slippers weren't the best foot wear for scrambling about through thorny bushes on uneven territory, thought Winifred as she made her way through the forest path. They were walking in single file with the Crocodile Girl, in spite of her condition, nimbly skipping ahead of them and stopping every now and then till they managed to catch up. Behind her went Mother. Winifred purposely slowed down her own pace so that she could keep an eye on her. Doing so now she noticed that she looked distinctly out of sorts. It wasn't mere fatigue. The swelling in her ankles had gone up and her face looked an unhealthy scarlet.

'Cheenkanni, stop!' Winifred called out and unmindful of her own aching feet and flimsy slippers hurried over to Mother's side. God! Was she going to faint? Cheenkanni quickly traced her way back and pulled out a small bottle of water from the bundle she was carrying. Together they led mother to a small rock and sat her down. Mother drank the water and breathed deeply. Cheenkanni knelt down on the ground and lifted Mother's feet on to her lap and removing her slippers began to gently massage them.

It must have felt good for Mother closed her eyes and whispered,

'Bless you.'

Bless the girl. She had been a wonder.

Things had begun to get worse at the estate and the household staff appeared more and more anxious than ever. Then came the terrible news. The watchmen at the bungalow gates had turned traitors too. They had opened the gates for the rioters and looked as if they were going to join them in mobbing it.

The Crocodile Girl, when she managed to get Winifred's attention in a room full of babbling people, beckoned frantically and nodded towards Mother as well. She hadn't understood what Cheenkanni meant but something told her to grab Mother's arm and together follow her. Cheenkanni had with her a makeshift bundle she seemed to have put together with some sheets she found in the laundry. Winifred didn't think of asking her about the contents of the sack. The tribal girl pressed her fingers on her lips, her eyes wide. Silently she commanded silence. She slipped out of one of the side doors turning around time and again to make sure the two Englishwomen were keeping up. She seemed to have a clear idea where she was going. Soon they were on a descending path behind the bungalow and before they lost sight of it, Winifred turned back to see that the mob had it surrounded and were smashing in the windows with their javelins.

Before it even sank in that they had escaped by the skin of their teeth, they were well into the woods.

'Bless you,' Mother had said when it eventually dawned on her.

'Bless you,' she said when the girl, ignoring the awkwardness of her protruding belly, gave her a foot massage.

'Bless you,' she said when after silently urging them to walk a little further, they reached a kind of rock settlement deep in the forests and Cheenkanni had them set up in a little cave and even found a thrcc legged wooden contraption for Mother to properly sit down on.

Winifred herself stretched her feet out as she sat on a grass mat, apparently handwoven, and wondered at Cheenkanni's loyalty. If it hadn't been for her timely action, God knows what would have become of them.

Cheenkanni walked into the cave just then armed with bunches of bananas, berries and an earthen jar containing a hot drink smoking on the top. Mutely as ever she laid out the food on little leaves and poured out the fiery smelling concoction in cups made of palm leaf. Winifred and more so Mother, had looked suspiciously at the drink but Cheenkanni would not take no for an answer. She smiled, looked at one Englishwoman to the other and her doe eyes melted with an unconditional love that brought a sting to Winifred's own eyes. The drink had actually tasted good, if a little spicy and surprisingly their fatigue was gone in minutes and a comfortable warmth set in.

'Bless you,' said Mother.

The sun was going down but it made little difference in the tiny settlement among trees so tall that the sky was barely visible and it was dark throughout. Winifred understood that this was Cheenkanni's village and they were to spend the night here.

Curious about Cheenkanni, she had once read up on the tribes of the Nilambur valley. Cholanaikars, they were called and were a primitive race. Though they spoke Malayalam when they communicated with others, they had a dialect of their own which, the book said was a compound of Tamil, Kannada and Malayalam. Feeling better, Winifred wondered if she could walk around and got up a little hesitantly. Cheenkanni was helping Mother lie down on a fresh mat of her own. The girl pulled out a light blanket from the bundle she had carried on the trip and covered her feet with it. God! She had thought of everything. When she opened the small sack, Winifred saw that there were a couple of changes of clothes for her and Mother, all hurriedly pulled out of the half open trunks she had been packing for Ootacamund, there were towels, a couple of sheets, combs, face-creams and everything she felt they might need. From under a fluffy towel Winifred glimpsed something that looked like the bobtail of her wooden rabbit. The girl had packed that in the bundle too. She smiled encouragingly and got up, giving Winifred an inviting nod. They stepped out of the cave. Curious, she looked around and the few tribals she saw around the settlement looked even more curious than she had imagined. But they said nothing as Cheenkanni had already filled them in.

They were short in stature, all of them and had dusky complexions like Cheenkanni's. A bubbling brook gurgled past the settlement and a group of women was at the stream filling earthen pots. One look at her and the women scurried away like frightened deer and one of them, bolder than the rest said something to Cheenkanni in their nasal, singsong tongue.

There were five or six similar cave houses set around and an open space in the centre where a cheerful log fire burnt and it was probably dinner that was cooking in a huge pot over it. Alai, ah yes! Winifred remembered that the book had referred to the cave houses of the Cholanaikars by that name. They stopped outside one such Alai from which a rather bad cough could be heard.

This was Cheenkanni's home, Winifred realised. The middle aged forest dweller who sat on his haunches tying together bits of twig was her father. She discerned that he was actually making repairs to a kind of leaf shelter erected with reed poles and thatched with leaves and twigs. Winifred stared in awe. The scenes fascinated her. At the entrance to the cave appeared a small boy wearing no more than a skimpy loincloth, the clearly visible ribs straining against his thin chest with each violent cough. He held in his hand a strange looking knife and a small block of wood which he dropped on the ground and latched onto Cheenkanni's hand. She stroked his head and the smile on her face was almost maternal. Winifred had heard the maids say that Cheenkanni had a sick brother to provide for. So this was the boy. The little fellow gave her a shy yet dazzling grin, even as he hung on to his sister's forearm.

They left the settlement to go deeper into the forests the next morning.

Last night, when Winifred entered the cave allotted to them after a refreshing splash in the stream, she was astonished to see Mother fast asleep on the mat laid out on the hard floor, filling the cave with snores. She herself hadn't slept much for she kept wondering at what hour Stanley Pat had returned from the guest house. How had he managed the Mopla situation? Would he have guessed that they had made an escape? Would he leave for Ootacamund in the morning without them? Though sleep evaded her, she did get some rest and felt most relieved that Mother had had a good night. She had no idea what Cheenkanni had in store for them the next day.

Come morning and they were off.

They really had no idea how long they had travelled.

They walked, stopped for rest, ate some of the fruits Cheenkanni had brought with her and then walked again. They were fairly deep in the forest when voices caught her attention. For the first time since they set off yesterday, she gave the forest girl instructions in her limited Malayalam which she understood immediately.

'Let's go in that direction. I must see who's there. Don't let's show ourselves.'

Silently they moved towards the voices and when in a small clearing by a relatively large stream, they saw a camp. Shelters were created here and there with poles and cloth tops. The smell of cooking rose in the air and small groups of women sat around talking to each other in quiet tones. This certainly wasn't a tribal settlement. The women looked well born and though Winifred could not really hear what they said, their tones indicated that they were speaking a cultured Malayalam and not the tribal dialect.

Cheenkanni had withdrawn behind Winifred and even Mother. She was like a little forest creature that feared strangers and took time to get used to people.

Winifred looked around the camp again. On the periphery were a few armed men. One of them had a gun and the others held swords. They looked like security personnel from their body language and attire. No ordinary people these. Then her attention was drawn to one particular face. A familiar face and a lovely one at that.

She had seen this girl at Mr Rama Ayer's a few months ago. She was the one Jack Horner referred to as the Story Girl.

Sethu

If someone had told her that she could become good friends with a woman she had met but once and very briefly, in a matter of hours, she would never have believed it possible. She had spoken a little with the English woman when they had met at Swami's place. But the circumstances they were in now certainly made things different.

They were both deep in the forests living a life neither of them would have seen themselves living even in the most outlandish of nightmares. They had both recently witnessed terror as they had never known before.

Sethu had had a couple of days for Divakarettan's death to sink in. Not that that made it any less painful. But Sethu had been there. Seen his still form rest on the floor in their entrance porch and watched silently as they bore him off to the cremation ground in the southern most corner of the Kovilakam premises before they had hurriedly set off. She knew he was no more. But this woman was in something of a shock.

No more than five or six hours ago, Sethu had been sitting on the ground idly crushing the dried leaves under her palm and absentmindedly listening to their crackle and staring at her grandmother sit on the one chair Beeran Mapla had managed to get into the barge amidst their other things that night. And then she saw people emerge from behind a clump of trees. Two English women! Certainly not the sort of company one would expect in the middle of the forest. And she recognized them. There hadn't been too many occasions for her to socialise with White women and these ladies were the only ones she had actually spoken to. But in times such as these, one forgets all these barriers. She had rushed over and greeted the two ladies warmly into their midst. The maids were preparing a simple meal with the limited supplies they had brought with them. The idea of economizing occurred for the first time in the brains of the Kovilakam women. Umedathi was after the maids to use as little as possible of all the ingredients. They didn't know when the next barge would be able to bring in more rice, coconut and vegetables. Anyway, the English women were invited to share the meal.

Mrs Eaton, the younger of the two, kept turning around as if searching for someone.

'The tribal girl who brought us here... haven't seen her for a while. Where could she have disappeared?' Before and after the meal, Mrs Eaton walked around the camp calling what sounded like 'Cheenkanni!' In her funny British accent. Sethu had earlier seen the girl hanging back a distance away when Mrs Eaton and her mother joined them. She seemed to have vanished.

'Oh God! Where could she be,' Mrs Eaton fretted. 'You know she is in the family way. What if something happens to her? She is the reason we are alive and well today. You'll never see anyone as faithful as the dear little thing.' She went on to tell Sethu of the happenings at their estate in Pullangode. Their own staff had turned against them! 'Well we were fortunate in that, said Sethu. 'It was our cart driver, a Mapla himself who helped us come away in the barge. We are so many of us, women and children. It was not easy. He had to make all arrangements by night. He had with him another Mapla whom he trusted. And here we are. Thank goodness you had this girl.'

'Bless her,' said Mrs Eaton's mother softly.

'Don't worry. She is a tribal girl. She knows the forest like the back of her hand. She will be safe,' Sethu consoled her and went on to tell them the tale of their Lord Vettekkaran who was said to have grown up in these forests with the tribals.

'That was what my grandmother said when we got here. This is Vettekkaran's real home. His presence here is much stronger than it ever was in the Kovilakam or the temple.'

She took them over to meet Ammamma who quietly gave orders that the two of them were to stay at the camp till some safe arrangement was made.

It was about four hours later that the tribal girl appeared among the trees. She was as white as a sheet and her lips were trembling.

'Cheenkanni,' Mrs Eaton pounced upon her. 'Where have you been?'

The girl turned back and a young fellow walked out from where he had been concealed by the trees, his steps hesitant.

'It's Stanley Pat's Chokra!' cried the Madama.

Chokra meant some kind of servant boy, Sethu guessed. The chap was blubbering and panting.

'Madame,' he burst out and what he said next was said so fast and hysterically that nobody understood anything. Mrs Eaton shrugged helplessly, 'Would you please ask him what happened?' She requested of Sethu.

Sethu wished now that she hadn't been the one to translate the terrible reports the Chokra gave.

This had happened yesterday. The planter, Eaton Sayippe had gone to the guesthouse on business, said the boy. The Chokra himself had made two trips to the guest house. First with the Sayippe to deliver his papers. He had then returned by midmorning to find that the rioters were everywhere. The cook then sent him to the neighbouring bungalow with a message for the Sayippe there. He couldn't deliver it for the Sayippes had escaped into the forest. Then the rioters attacked their bungalow and the Madamas were nowhere to be seen. Everyone was scared stiff. The Chokra then thought it his duty to warn Eaton Sayippe at the guesthouse and made his way there once again.

Sethu was finding it difficult to grasp what he was saying as his voice cracking with the strain and at the same time interpreting his words in her own broken English.

The Sayippe was furious, said the Chokra. He would teach these Mapla scoundrels a lesson, he raged as he mounted his horse to make his way back. He rode through the woody path and the Chokra walked. The Sayippe was almost home when suddenly a mob of armed Maplas charged into the woods and when Eaton Sayippe saw them coming he dismounted and hid in the bushes.

At least he was sensible enough to do that, said Mrs Eaton in her stilted Malayalam and the Chokra wailed.

He had caught up with the Sayippe and seeing what was happening clambered up a tree.

The Maplas had seen the horse without the rider and guessed that the Sayippe was somewhere around. They searched and searched but he was too well hidden. They were about to turn back, said the Chokra, when the Sayippe's dogs in the Bungalow who had been craving for their master's presence all day had sniffed him. All three of them bounded into the woods and accurately sniffed out the bush he was hidden behind. The Maplas saw him too. The Chokra, saw everything from his perch.

They pounced on him with the same cries the rioters at the Kovilakam had on their lips. And what he said next, Sethu could not bring herself to repeat to her new friend.

The boy was now beating his breast and howling.

Mrs Eaton insisted. 'What is he saying? Tell me! Come on,' she urged.

Sethu bent her head and said nothing.

'Is he dead? Tell me at once. Is Stanley Pat dead?'

Sethu still hung her head and nodded ever so slightly.

What she didn't tell them then was that it had been a horrible death. The blood thirsty rioters had not stopped at merely killing him. His own overseer had beheaded the corpse while the dogs howled pitifully in the background. Later the head was found in the middle of a public road.

And the acephalous body floated in the stream on its way to meet the Chaliyar.

The older Madama had swooned and some of Sethu's cousins, helped by the maids were trying to revive her when Mrs Eaton whispered 'Why? Oh God! Why? Why my Stanley Pat?'

Now as she sat by Sethu in a quiet corner away from the others, the Madama, who seemed calm and controlled, said in a quiet voice, 'He brought it upon himself I guess. In more ways than one.'

This time nothing would drive the tribal girl away. She had put aside her apprehension of strangers, ignored Sethu's presence and sat at the Madama's feet, saying nothing.

Venturing

24 August '21
Alijan

Things are changing. The British government is crumbling to bits. Alijan couldn't help chuckling. Not a policeman in sight. Now we have a free hand. We, the Maplas to whom Malabar belongs. It will not be long before the whole kingdom is in our hands. It is a good beginning we see here in Ernad. The power of Allah will be established all over.

Alijan couldn't suppress the delight bubbling within him.

This was exactly what he had secretly thirsted for. What he had in mind when he had instigated the Yakub Hasan affair months ago. Morally bound by his word to Ali Musaliar, he had felt as if his hands were unfairly tied behind his back. But the way things were going, he only had to sit back and let the tide take over. Yes Alijan was happy.

The Maplas of Pookottur were running haywire. It was passion not reason that ruled them as they roamed the country in bands, showing off their new found power. There would be just the one faith in Malabar, they had decided. They were on a mission. They would make sure everyone in Pookottur, Manjeri, Malappuram and all the surrounding villages were absorbed into the fold. To achieve this, they were prepared to do just about anything. They coaxed people, propositioned them. Threatened them and when they did not comply, attacked and burgled their homes. Sometimes they tortured and killed when the need arose but by and large their intention was not to harm people, thought Alijan.

He himself had remained in the background and surveyed the way things were working out to his satisfaction.

The men however did not hesitate to use his name when it suited them. Alijan chortled again and straightened his rumal.

One of them even had gone to the extent of accosting Madhavan Nair who got back just a week ago after serving his time in prison, in his home and announcing that Alijan himself had sent him.

'Your friend, Gopala Menon has already embraced Islam. Alijan Sahib has sent me to find out what your plans are,' the impetuous ass had blabbered. As if Madhavan Nair would be foolish enough to believe him.

But Alijan had to admire the fellow's spunk.

Thinking about Madhavan Nair led his thoughts to what happened in Tirurangadi.

The Congress-Khilafat leaders were released from prison after a six month internment a week ago. An event in the whole of Malabar. On the 17 when they were to arrive in Kozhikode, the city, they said had been in a festive mood bringing back memories of Gandhi's arrival last year. So much for Mr Thomas's hopes of nipping the Congress-Khilafat nexus in the bud. Alijan leaned back in his chair and rocked on two legs, something Benu always warned him not to do. The pleasure brought on by the mental image he formed of Mr Thomas's disappointed countenance had induced him to try the stunt.

Mr Thomas! He thought contemptuously. Was the man cock-eyed or what? Concept in one direction, action in the other. He could understand the Magistrate's anger as he stood on the top floor veranda of his office in the Huzoor Kecheri as the festive procession passed by. He sympathized with the Englishman's need to get back at everyone involved in flushing his plans down the drain. He must have set about in earnest, readying the necessary warrants, strengthening his forces with the special troops he ordered out from Malappuram for the purpose and setting off on the night of the 19. But Tirurangadi! What must the man have been thinking of!

If Mr Thomas had set his sights on Pookottur where the Maplas were generally agitated, he would not have been so astonished. In fact, he had been expecting it in one way or the other. For that matter, so had most of the Pookottur Maplas. But to rush like a blind man to Tirurangadi where things had been relatively peaceful for a while! To have the Kizhakkepalli surrounded and searched! That was what created this sudden upsurge in all the taluks. The terrible scenes the Khilafat leaders had conjured in the minds of the Maplas the fate of Turki and how the British demolished the holy sites and rage drove them mad. They didn't really know who to take out their anger on. A total mess up of misunderstandings and thoughtless decisions all round. But yes. It was all working to Alijan's advantage.

Sultan Alijan. Lord of his own kingdom. No. he wouldn't have to wait long.

Ali from the Yatim Khana had been good at achieving his goals, however insignificant. But it was a few years down the line that ambition began to take shape in Alijan's mind. During those years in the hot northern plains in the company of Jawadikka and poor Aimu, he had used his instincts and street smart ways to become a rich man by the time he was twenty. That had not been enough for him. He had never forgotten his boyhood dream of marrying the lovely Benu and he had achieved the next to impossible feat of finding her in spite of the lack of clues about her whereabouts. He craved power. This fruit was rather high up on the tree but during his post marriage days in Mannarkkad, he had felt his fingertips brush the branch on which it hung. He had had money and loyal manpower on his side. He knew that if he wanted power, he had to thwart the British and the Hindu landlords who were the biggest obstacles in his path. This he was able to do to a large extent. With Jawadikka as his mentor and his young sons as his right and left hands. Then suddenly all he had built up had come crashing down. The Mannarkkad rebellion had been crushed by the British. Jawadikka and the boys were taken across the Black seas…

Their days in North India, the rebellion of the sipahis, his education under the greatest masters and more importantly the impact of those last days in the Yatim Khana, had made Jawadikka a different man too. By the time their North Indian sojourn came to an end, the gentle orphan boy who had left Malabar so many years ago had hardened into a man whose hatred for the British ruled him. One murder of a British officer committed all those years ago in the orphanage compound had wiped away all abhorrence of bloodshed…

Jawadikka. What Alijan knew about him could shock the world…

Raziya

The story Benu Thatha had narrated loomed large in Raziya's mind. She replayed it several times over and formed her own impressions. She found herself seeing things as they might have happened and using those images and logic to fill any gap. She saw herself in her husband's late grandmother and identified with her mixed feelings for Mujeeb.

She shivered, as for a second she became Suhra, standing at her window in the dead of the night, caressing her unborn baby, watching fierce orange flames reduce her father to dust. At that moment, Raziya feared for her own baby. And its father. Would this tendency for nurturing revenge in his heart, which Mammad had inherited from his real grandfather, be his downfall? She shivered a little at the thought and spotted the subject of her fears walk up the backyard of Benazir Manzil.

Mammad got back from his misadventure in Nilambur more than twenty-four hours and Alijan Sahib had sent for him immediately. But he hadn't shown up till now. Was he worried that Sahib would give him a piece of his mind? Mammad made his way around the big house to the front veranda where Sahib sat on his usual chair. Raziya crept up to the Window where Benu Thatha liked to sit when she wished to eavesdrop on conversations with visitors.

'Ha Mammade! And about time too,' Alijan Sahib's gravelly voice greeted him.

Mammad said nothing. To his credit, he held his head high and looked boldly into the Sahib's eyes.

Alijan Sahib remained silent for a while too. But seeing that Mammad was not going to break the ice, he enquired after Basheer. The fiery red of Mammad's flush clashed with the green of his eyes.

'Bad.'

It was not as if Sahib didn't already know that. He had paid a visit to poor Basheerka's home the day before and arranged for the best physicians to treat him.

'And I hope the consequences of your rashness have been a lesson.'

'My stupidity was in letting the others come with me. I had planned to go alone. But things got out of hand.'

'A simple explanation. One which anyone can blurt out after making the worst mistakes. I would have thought what happened to the other men like Usman and young Paree and the worse fate of your *changathi* would have put you off this kind of foolishness. But do I see remorse in you, Mammad? No.'

'I can't tell you how much it hurts me. What happened to Basheer and the others. Nor did I want that Divakaran Thampan to die. He has personally done me no harm. But the Sixth Tirumulpad… when I get my next chance to get my own back it is going to be bad for him. I'll get him in the worst way possible. I am not going to let him go scot free. Only this time I will not involve the Pookottur boys.'

Raziya shivered again. It was Mujeeb she saw in her husband's eyes.

Priyamvada

She would have preferred to do it at night but that wasn't an option. She couldn't travel in the dark. It would have to be in the afternoon. When everyone would be enjoying an after lunch nap. Even the maids would stretch out in the back veranda before they began their evening round of cooking and cleaning. Between two and three. She had it all planned. It would not be a problem to reach

Nilambur before sunset. She had made this journey hundreds of times before. She knew the route well. That this time there would be no chaperones or a driver, was a mere technicality. The cart was her own. Nobody would miss it in a hurry. And she was sure she could drive as well as any man. She did not plan to take anything with her. She had plenty of clothes in their house there just outside the Kovilakam premises. But a woman driving a cart down the country lanes was sure to draw attention. She would need a disguise.

She crept into her younger brother's room when there was nobody about and raided his chest of mundus and most importantly a shirt. Unni was just seventeen and slight for a man. But his shirt was sure to float around her own tiny frame. But that couldn't be helped. It was the best she could manage. The other men in the family were larger in build.

After lunch, she would creep upstairs to her room and don her disguise in peace. And then when things were quiet she would make her start.

It was a good plan.

Normally Priya would have felt the thrill of excitement at the thought of such an adventure but today her heart was still wallowing in the lowest of spirits. It was unlikely to ever rise up, she thought. She would never be the old Priya again. How could she? When she had caused a tragedy that the Kovilakam would never forget. She didn't deserve to be happy again. At least she had the satisfaction of having given things a thought this time and outlined her plan well. She had not let impulse, her masterful twin take the lead this time.

But once she had owned up about her role she would feel better. More honest about herself. Even if it meant a rift with her dear ones.

Sad but determined, she went downstairs to lunch.

The men were at their meal. Her uncle, her brothers and two of her cousins. Just as it had been this morning and the whole of yesterday, the Kovilakam incident was the topic of conversation.

'It was the Sixth Tirumulpad's former tax collector who was behind the whole thing they say,' a cousin was saying as she approached the dining hall.

'And to think our girl was in the manor all along with this dangerous fellow wandering in and out,' her favourite uncle shuddered.

'How fortunate that our Priyamvada was safe with us while all this…' the speaker cut himself short as he saw Priya enter the room.

To spare her feelings, the unsaid yet unanimous decision was to leave her out of it.

'Think of the poor Matriarch and her daughter.'

This was even worse, thought Priya.

'What with the death of the Thampan and having to flee as soon as the funeral rites were done with,' said her uncle with another shudder.

Flee! Priya felt as if someone had bludgeoned her on the head.

'What do you mean, Ammama? Are they not at the Kovilakam then?'

'No, Kutti,' his tone was affectionate and indulgent as

it always was when he spoke to his only niece. 'It was not safe for them to remain there. They have been moved.'

Priya felt her heart plummeting to the vicinity of her feet. So much for her well laid plans.

'But where are they?'

'It has to be a secret. Very few people know.'

'Yes. Best not to discuss it, Kutti. You know, even the walls have ears. You can rest assure that they are safe for now.'

But she had to know, thought Priya desperately.

When the men had finished their meal and filed out of the dining hall, Priya followed and caught up with Unni, her younger brother. She grabbed him by the elbow and dragged him into a corridor.

'Unni, tell me. Do you know?'

'What?' The boy blinked.

'Where are they?'

'Who? Oh the Kovilakam people! We are not to discuss it, Edathi.'

'You can whisper in my ear so that the walls don't hear. Come on. Tell me.'

Unni had never been capable of saying no to his sister. He looked around cautiously and lowered his voice. 'Nobody actually told me anything. But I heard Ettan talking to the uncles. The driver, Beeran and another Mapla arranged it for them. They crossed the river in a barge went past Amarambalam and descended into the woods at Pullangode. I believe they have set up a camp there. When things settle down a bit they will be moved to a safe house.'

She ate a nominal lunch so that no questions were asked, and returned to her room in a daze. What would she do now? Things wouldn't work out as planned. But if she didn't do it now, she never would. The trip had to happen. Only she would be travelling in a different direction. She would not stop to worry about that now. If she had to leave while the others were napping, she had to get going now.

Priya quickly changed into her brother's clothes. Before she put on the shirt, she bound up her chest tightly to underplay the curves and topped it all off with a turban hiding her abundant hair. It helped that she didn't have to carry any baggage. As an afterthought, she walked to her trunk she had brought from Pookottur and fished out the Beretta wrapped in its musty smelling silk pouch. She lifted the too large shirt and tucked the pouch carefully into the waist band of the mundu and tightened it.

Slipping off had been easier than expected. At least there had been no hurdles on that front, she said aloud to herself as the cart passed out of the large compound of the *tharawad* smoothly enough. But she had spoken too soon. There was someone blocking the path. It was Unni.

Her meticulous disguise had not been enough to fool him.

'Edathi, whatever are you up to?' His eyes were flashing in anger. He might think the world of his sister but he was not pleased with her now.

'Unni, go away?'

'Tell me what you think you are doing. Do you really think, I will let you go out all alone in fancy dress like this? Tell me where you are going.'

'I can't, move out of the way, Unni. Or you will attract attention. I need to get away, I tell you.'

'Then I will come with you.' He clambered into the cart.

Footsteps could be heard round the corner and Priya had no option but to drive away as fast as she could.

In a way it was a relief to have Unni with her. It felt good to share her plans with someone. He had a better sense of direction than she did. He may be young but he was a man. It didn't rouse suspicions when he stopped in one or two places and asked directions. After about an hour and a half of travel, they crossed Pookottur and Priya felt an intense yearning for her old life. She thought longingly of the manor but the Sixth Tirumulpad wasn't there. What was home without her husband? They travelled further in the north-eastern direction and passed through deserted land where they hadn't seen a single human being for the last three or four miles. As they approached a tiny hamlet, the name of which she did not know, it was a terrible cacophony that greeted them. There was no way the cart could pass. Ear splitting shrieks, roars of Allahu Akbar, cries for mercy and then the spitting and hissing of a fire. A few black clad figures could be seen flashing swords and eight to ten people were huddled together. The women were quaking in fear. One man was groveling on the floor, with the tip of a sword pointed at him. A whole house burnt in the background.

The Black Thangal's men! The whole of Ernad had been talking about them for months. You never know when and where they would appear. And when they did…

'Spare us! Spare us!'

This was the sort of thing they heard everyday but never had Priya imagined that she would see such an incident in front of her eyes.

Though mild mannered by nature, Unni had never been able to bear injustice. And he was her brother. Recklessness was his sibling too. He leapt off the cart armed with the driving whip and charged towards the man who held the poor fellow at sword point. With one swish of the whip he sent the weapon flying. The men in black were taken unawares and Unni had time to grab the fallen sword from where it lay on the ground. It was the first time he was holding such a weapon in his hands he had no clue how to use it. He clutched it tentatively for a second and began to swing it around wildly.

'Let them go, I tell you. What have the poor people ever done to you?'

The man on the ground had found his feet by then.

Though the entire Black Brigade was taken aback at the newcomer's fearlessness for a while, one man burst out laughing.

'What do we have here? A brave young soldier? Just the sort of person we want on our side, eh?'

The others cackled too.

Unni was fuming. He swished the sword again and that made the men stand back.

'Yes. He shall accept the faith and become one of us,' another leered. He ducked the sword and another had Unni by the waist.

Priya could bear it no longer. She forgot everything, even the fact that she was a woman inside her masculine attire, and tore into the crowd. One of the villains looked smaller than the rest. She ran straight at him and in a thrice, he was on the ground and his sword in her grip.

The Black brigade was used to protests and occasional fight backs but they were trained to handle each situation. Those who cooperated would join the fold. Those who didn't would be finished off. Women would not be hurt. But they were not used to surprise attacks.

'Allah! There's another of them,' cried one of them.

'These young fellows may be small but they are fiery,' observed another.

Unni and Priya succeeded in giving the Black Brigade a jolt but there was no way they could get the better of the Thangal's men who functioned smoothly. Soon their weapons were wrested off them and together with the other men they were bound up.

'Put the women in there', commanded one man who seemed to be a leader of sorts, pointing his chin in a particular direction.

There were three women. Two old and one very young.

'Noooo. Don't take them,' one man cried trying to break his bonds.

'Amme! Radhe!' The youngster next to Unni screamed.

His cries fell on deaf ears and the women and the men assigned to accompany them were soon out of sight.

What remained of the Black Brigade turned towards the group they had bound up.

'Now for you. Will you take the faith?' The senior brigand asked in a kinder voice

'Noooo. Never,' the other four yelled for all they were worth. . Unni and Priya said nothing.

'No? We'll take you one by one.' He walked over to one man who seemed to be in his thirties and fairly strong and fit.

'Will you take the faith of Allah?'

'NO.'

'No?'

'No.'

The tip of a dagger scored a long line across the man's bare chest and blood oozed.

'No?'

'No,' persisted the man though in a lot of pain.

Suddenly they all heard thuds and a slight vibration and a palanquin borne by four men in black came into sight. Two warrior like men, also black clad and face covered strode beside the *manjal.* There was a respectful hush as the tormentors paused in their business. Slowly the *manjal* was set down and a person folded out. Just like the rest of the brigade, he too was clothed completely in black but there was something strange about him. Something surreal as if he were from another planet. He walked noiselessly. Almost floated. Was this the notorious Black Thangal? Priya shivered.

He glided over to where they stood, the two lieutenants who had flanked the *manjal,* close at his heels. His eyes, almost invisible behind the black scarf covering his face seemed to examine the red line on the man's chest.

In the softest, gentlest of tones, he whispered, 'Paavam, paavam! You poor man.'

It was the cruelest thing Priya had heard in her life. She saw the captured men cringe from him.

'Will you take the faith?' The tormentor asked once more, invigorated by the presence of his Chief.

The victim must have been brave for though he couldn't find his voice, he shook his head.

'Bloody Kafir,' with that the dagger plunged into his stomach and a fountain in red spurted out.

'Allahu Akbar,' cried the murderer.

'Paavam,' said the Thangal, compassion and tenderness oozing out of his voice inducing a weird sense of terror in everyone, even in his own men. 'Paavam. Blood. How I hate the sight of it. But my own feelings are mere trifles. May Allah's will be.' He surveyed the remaining prisoners one by one, clicking his tongue in sympathy. Priya felt he lingered an extra moment in front of her, before moving towards the palanquin, beckoning to his body guards.

'Allahu Akbar,' said the tormentor wielding the sword and turned towards his next prey.

'Vettekkara,' thought Priya in silent prayer and suddenly the thought occurred to her. Allahu was the name of God just as Vettekkaran was. How could they take the name of God while committing such hideous sins?

The next victim was no older than Unni. He could only blubber in answer to the question. The sight of the corpse at his feet and the bloody dagger pointing at his chest gave him little choice. He nodded feebly.

'Good boy. Allah be with you.' As a part of the Black Brigade there was a specially appointed barber with his own sharp blade in readiness. The young man's head was swiftly shaven and a skull cap jammed on his head even as tears flowed from his eyes.

'This will do for now,' said the man with the bloody dagger looking pointedly at the boy's crotch. 'The rest can be done later.' The victim let out a weak moan and fell down in a faint.

The two people between Unni and the lad who had just been converted were no cowards. Priya preferred to keep her eyes shut as their staunch nos were answered with daggers.

'And now for our brave young man…'

'Yes. I agree,' said Unni quickly even before the question was asked.

There was a roar of appreciative laughter as the symbolic rituals were completed. They had not expected it to be so easy. As they went about their work, Unni squeezed Priya's hand trying to convey something.

'Finally you, little kundan?'

She would have liked to say, 'Go to hell you Rakshasa,' but the words wouldn't come out. She didn't trust herself to speak.

'His silence is his consent.'

'Off with the turban, little kundan. You are one of us now'. A flick of his sword and the turban she had tied so meticulously that afternoon came off with it. The dark, lustrous tresses that adorned the Sixth Tirumulpad's snow white pillows, came tumbling and hung down to her hips.

There was a collective gasp.

'Allah!'

'Rabbe!'

'This is no kundan!'

The men put away their weapons.

'She can be put in there with the other women,' said one of the leaders when he'd recovered from the shock. The speaker kicked the bodies of the murdered men and muttered a curse, 'Bloody kafirs!' Two of the smallest men one of whom Priya had earlier attacked, dragged the corpses to the side of a bush and dumped them there. And they marched off into the wilderness.

Priya was separated from Unni and taken away. A few metres down the path and into the trees till they reached a rustic looking shack built of planks. 'Put her in there, lock up and you, young Kochappu, keep watch outside. Don't forget to tie her up to a pole first just as we have done the others. Keep her mouth bound up too. She is a feisty one. 'the senior brigand instructed.

He turned to Priya and the other women and spoke politely. 'You shall remain in here till the Thangal can come over. He always makes plans for the women himself. Don't worry, no harm shall come to you. In the meanwhile, you shall be sent some appropriate clothes so that you look like our women.'

Priya found herself in the rather stuffy hut with the other women. Her mouth being gagged, even breathing wasn't easy. Having completed his job, the younger of the brigands locked up.

Inside, gagged and bound, Priya finally had the time to admonish herself. Once more she had given in to her impulses and landed herself and poor Unni in this mess. Why couldn't she have waited and cleared her head before setting off on this foolhardy business. Why hadn't she listened to Unni?

Now she couldn't think of a single way out. Fortunately for her, thoughts of the future did not drift into her mind which seemed to fill with darkness and even the dim light in the shack seemed blinding and she shut her eyes.

She thought of the Beretta she had tucked into her waist band and felt somewhat comforted.

Visitors To The Forest Camp

24 August '21
Mithran

Considering that it had been nearly a month since his enforced isolation, he would have expected himself to be enjoying the freedom of cross country travel. In light of the tragedy that befell his family, of the death of Divakaran his favourite cousin, he ought to have been deep in mourning. But all Mithran felt was a numbness. As if he were living in a vacuum bubble watching everything happening around him but feeling nothing. It was as if it was all happening to someone else.

In a way this odd sense of apathy had begun to set in after his initial protest against having himself moved from the manor. Once it had all been fixed and that very night he had been moved to a secret refuge, he had begun to function mechanically. He would have preferred to go to

Nilambur but others seemed to be making his decisions for him now. If the Maplas were to go looking for him, the first place other than the manor of course would be Nilambur. He was that predictable a man. Then Damodaran's *illam* was suggested and vetoed. It would be better to put him up with a total strangers. He lived completely at his host's mercy with none of his own relatives or servants around. A weird stupor began to engulf Mithran. The recent events had begun to seem like a blur. Not unlike a story someone had mentioned in passing and he had tucked away into a corner of his subconscious mind as something not really concerning him.

After that time in the library when Priya had occupied his thoughts he hadn't given her much thought either. On his first day at his hiding place he had to be reminded to write a short letter to her and another to his cousin the Second Tirumulpad, to let them know he was safe. He had been instructed not to mention his whereabouts to either of them. Mithran had done as he was asked to without an opinion of his own. There were moments now when he thought Priya and his months with her had been nothing but the fantasy of a middle-aged widower's warped mind.

That night, the news of the Kovilakam attack and Divakaran's murder had been conveyed by that young man from… what was it Mankada? Ayiramnazhi? Mithran had listened in absolute silence. No shocked cry had escaped him. There had been no tremor in his voice when he asked one or two questions about the whole affair.

Mithran wasn't really paying attention to the route they were taking or where they actually were. He barely peeped out of the canvas covered cart.

'Thampan, we'll take a small detour here if you don't mind.'

Mind? Why would he mind? He grunted in assent.

'I would like to drop in at the Kerala Estate and enquire after the people there. The planter's wife is an old acquaintance of mine. It won't take long. I just wish to make sure they are safe. I've been hearing things about some sort of riots in the Estates.'

Mithran grunted again.

Cheenkanni

She had never felt as strong as she did in the past two days. Physically, after the initial month of mild nausea she had been perfectly all right. That was the way tribal women were made. Their bodies were like those of the other forest creatures. Something as natural as pregnancy or childbirth never weighed them down. She was active as ever. But that was not what she had meant when she had been thinking of how strong she felt. She felt strong in the mind. The happenings at the Estate did not scare her. Even when the rioters were closing in on the bungalow that day, her only thought had been of the Madama and her mother. No matter what, she would not let anything happen to them.

Over the past few months, the Madama had begun to hold such a special place in Cheenkanni's simple, steadfast heart that she was second to none but Muthu in her affections. There had been a time when nervousness and guilt had kept her from even looking at the Madama in her face. Cheenkanni knew she was kind and just, unlike the Sayippe. But the fact that she had been weak enough to give in to the Sayippe whenever he demanded it made it difficult for her to face his wife. Whenever the Madama looked at her, she felt shame, hot, demeaning shame wash over her. It wasn't a pleasant feeling and she had avoided her whenever she could. But deep inside, she had begun to care for her. She wished to give vent to that emotion but didn't know how.

That last day in the bungalow, she understood that they were to go away. The Sayippe had announced it and there was talk in the kitchen. And she saw the Madama pack her things. She hoped they would be back soon for Cheenkanni's life here would be empty if she could not see her adored Madama. Then she noticed that the little rabbit, which had been Muthu's latest work on top of the suitcase, she had been so proud to see her gift was treasured enough to take away on a journey.

That was why when things had turned for the worse she had packed the rabbit figurine in the bundle she had tied up with the basic necessities she thought the Madama and her mother would need.

That first day, she knew they would be alright for some time in the forest camp where those posh ladies lived. Cheenkanni did not understand their presence in the forest but guessed that they might be refugees too like the Madamas. So she left them in the hope of running back to Pullangode and getting them some things which she thought they would need. But that was the day she learnt of the Sayippe's murder. It didn't make her sad that the Eaton Sayippe was dead. It never crossed her mind that the child she was carrying in her belly would be born fatherless. Nor had it ever crossed her mind that he would have a father. This was a child of sin. Those in her own settlement had initially been angered and wished to have her ostracised. It had only been because she was a favourite with the Moopan that she still had a home among them. That Eaton Sayippe was no more didn't mean anything to her, except maybe relief at not having to succumb to him anymore. But she cared that the Madama had lost her man. She had been so hesitant to come and break the news herself and had dragged that Chokra along. Two days had passed and yesterday she had once more returned to the estate and grabbed some things and dropped them into a sack. Those long outfits with ties at the waist that they liked to wear when they were relaxing in the evenings, some comfortable footwear and generally whatever little thing she could think of that might make their life in the forest comfortable. Her trip had yet another purpose. She had to check on the situation there regularly. She could not take them back till she was sure it was absolutely safe. Once they were able to get back, she was only too aware that they wouldn't stay long. Not with the Sayippe dead. But they couldn't live in the jungle forever either. So it was her job to make regular surveys. So far, the estate was still in a state of turmoil. Most of the servants had escaped to their own homes. The rioters still roamed around with those war cries on their lips. They looted and plundered and destroyed, though the intensity had subsided a little. Koya, that sleazy overseer who had done all the Sahib's dirty work for him had caught a glimpse of her yesterday as she escaped into the woods. She hated the man. It was he who had whacked the Sayippe's body into two and left the head on a public road. It was as if he took pleasure in violence. Be it towards the poor workers or the mighty Sayippe. He never missed an opportunity to cause pain.

Eaton Sayippe's Madama dragged her over and said in her broken Malayalam.

'Listen Cheenkanni. You can't go running off without a word like this. It scares me. And I think it is time you started talking to me now. I know you are not dumb. The servants say you can yell at the top of your voice when you fancy it. So why won't you talk to me?'

Cheenkanni got an overall picture of what the Madama was trying to say, though the words were quite unintelligible. Her mistress wanted her to talk to her. Tell her when she went off.

But all Cheenkanni could do was to look at her like an adoring puppy.

The Madama sighed and went off to talk to her new friend. These people were nobles from the Kovilakam in Nilambur, she had gathered from the conversation of the two maids they had brought with them.

At least she knew that when she went away for a few hours, her Madama and her mother were in capable hands.

The Outcaste

I would have to make it quick, if we were to reach the forest camp by noon and return home before it was too dark.

The Sixth Tirumulpad was the most wanted person among the Maplas of Pookottur and it wasn't safe to wander around the whole of Ernad with him in tow. Especially as the emotional climate in the area was worsening day by day. I would have preferred not to move Mithran Thampan till things were safer but his attitude had been a little alarming. I wouldn't have been as concerned if he had expressed his sorrow or shock. I knew he was not a heartless man. And though he rarely exhibited it, he did care for his people. But this was a little extreme. Unniettan had suggested that the Sixth Tirumulpad was probably in denial. Maybe he had not really accepted what had happened at the Kovilakam with his heart though his brain understood things well enough. This was not good for his emotional health. He needed to be in the midst of his family and see for himself. And hence this trip was essential.

And yes, there is no point denying it. I did want to see how the Story Girl and her grandmother were faring and offer my condolences. I had even chosen some reading material I thought she would enjoy.

As we approached the Kerala Estates, I began to sense that things weren't right. At the entry post, I leaned out of the cart and informed the man on duty that I would like to go to the Estate Bungalow.

The sentry seemed surprised.

'To the Bungalow? But why? Who are you?'

'The planter and his family are known to me. I am here to see them.'

'The planter? Eaton Sayippe?' His voice was a coarse whisper and he looked around as if he were afraid someone would overhear. 'But… Eaton Sayippe… is dead.'

'What!'

'Yes. Slaughtered by the rioters.'

'And his family?' The thought of Miss. Cranford, no Winifred Eaton in danger was so terrible.

'No one knows. They say the Madama and her old mother descended into the jungle.'

I felt my heart beat fast.

'Is there anyone here who knows where they went?'

'I don't think so,' the sentry shook his head. 'Except maybe… the Sayippe's Chokra. I am not sure, but he is the only likely person.'

'Where can I find him?'

'Wait a bit. I'll see if I can find out. You had better move your cart into a less visible spot. This might take a while.' He pointed out a place amidst some very tall trees where it would not be obvious from the road. He went into the Estate with a slight nod at his colleague at the post who nodded back.

It was better to maintain silence in case we were spotted, so I said nothing to Mithran Thampan. Anyway in his present state, he was not likely to do more than grunt. We remained concealed in the cart's canvas enclosure, the Sixth Tirumulpad staring at one spot, his expression blank. I peeped out once in a while to see if the man was back.

Then a bit of a hullaballoo was heard at a distance and I leaned out a little further to see. Further down about a quarter of a mile away was a narrow track leading down from another part of the Estate into the woods. There were people moving about there. Nothing was clearly visible but the sticks they carried told me they were not your regular villagers. There was a cruel urgency in their movements. They seemed to be dragging something behind them and moving closer. They were the rioters for sure. Had the Sixth Tirumulpad not been with me, I would not have remained hidden in this fashion.

As the stick brandishing Maplas got nearer, I jumped in shock. It was a corpse they were dragging. The corpse of a girl! Even Mithran Thampan in his present state of mind could not help reacting to the horrible scene. His grunt sounded pained as he turned his face away.

I could not bear to stay hidden any longer.

'Make sure you stay inside,' I told Mithran and rushed to the scene. There were other people crowding in to see what had happened. I joined them and immediately wished I hadn't.

They had dragged the girl's body to the middle of the

road leading to the Estate's main entrance. It was a dusky beauty attired in the tribal fashion, her shapely eyes were wide open and the fear she had experienced in her last moments were imprinted on her face. The lower part of the girl's abdomen had been ripped open and hanging out by the umbilical cord was something small and pink that resembled a bird with a large head. As they dragged the girl along the bumpy track, the foetus bounced against her side, as if refusing to leave its mother.

All the onlookers looked green.

One of them, a Mapla who seemed to know the gang of murderers addressed the short mustachioed man in some kind of uniform, 'Padachone! It is the tribal lass who works at the Bungalow. How could you do this to her, Koya!'

Winifred's Crocodile girl?

The man called Koya laughed uproariously.

'We are putting an end to the white race. And that filthy creature hanging out of the whore's belly is the Sayippe's child. I should know. There is no end to the number of times I have set it up for them.'

His companion rioters joined in the laughter while the others looked horrified. I had never felt so helpless in my life. My line of expertise lay in the use of words, written or spoken and turning people around to my way of thinking. It had worked to a large extent with the turbulent Maplas in my own village and in many parts of Ernad. It had worked with the mob in the Pookottur manor. It had worked more than once with Alijan Sahib, their leader. But of what use was it to the poor girl and her baby?

I had no choice but to slip to the periphery and remain silent. When the rioters like a pack of rabid canines made their way in another direction, in search of another prey, the sentry who had gone in search of the Sayippe's servant boy approached me as I moved silently to the clump of trees where the cart was parked. His face was as white and stiff as my thorth and mundu when it arrived from laundry.

'The Sayippe's Chokra… he cannot tell us anything.'

'Why? Doesn't he know where Mrs Eaton is?'

'I think he does. But… they have …' he gulped, 'they have ripped his tongue off. But he kept pointing to the forests in that direction,' the sentry indicated the track down which they had dragged the poor girl's body.

That was the route we were going take anyway as directed by Beeran the Kovilakam cart driver. Hopefully on the way to the Kovilakam forest camp, we would find Winifred Eaton and her mother as well.

Mathu

When she woke up in the mornings, the first thing that occurred to her was the ache in her bones from sleeping on a mat on the hard and bumpy floor of the tent. As a child she had slept in the southern *nalukettu* on a row of mattresses lined up by the maids soon after the lamps were lit. That was the experience closest to this but even then the mattresses had been of soft cotton, patted by the maids till they were nice and fluffy. But the aches and pains and the rough life was a blessing, thought the Matriarch. The new surroundings and new life experiences kept Divakaran and Mithran off the surface of her mind.

The two maids they had brought along prepared frugal meals in the makeshift kitchen with whatever supplies Beeran was able to get to them. He was here today with sacks of rice, coconut and bunches of bananas which they would have to make do with for the next few days for he couldn't say when he would be able to come next. That young tribal girl who was the English woman's shadow often brought them little baskets of odd vegetables when she returned from her sojourns. Like the tiny finger sized gourds that grew on creepers that, back in Nilambur, even the goats belonging to some of the maids refused to eat when they grazed in the Palachod. Today, they, the Kovilakam people, not the goats, were grateful for the break from thin coconut gravies and rationed portions of raw banana cooked with hardly any oil. Even the small children were settling down to forest life after the first couple of days when they had howled their heads off for their milk and sweet bananas roasted in clarified butter.

The women of the family had adapted in their own way too. In a way, the Matriarch was proud of them for the way they had risen to the occasion that terrible day. The bravery and innovativeness they had shown in dealing with a crisis. Now they were getting accustomed to their new surroundings and had gone back to gossiping about frivolous matters and cracking endless Gulikan jokes. Sethu had fallen into an odd friendship with the young Madama. She was glad to have the English women join their camp. It stopped her from wallowing in self-pity and gave her mind a hold on to reality. Tragedy was not the prerogative of their family. On the barge as they made their escape that day, she hurt as if there were a hundred pus-filled boils inside her hot and full waiting to burst. Why? The question rose within. Why me and my family? Why my Divakaran? Why Mithran?

When she heard about what happened to the Madama's husband, she knew they were not the only ones.

Only two or three of the Kovilakam men lived in the forest camp. A new batch had arrived with Beeran when he came the other day and the first set and returned to the Kovilakam. Now the first three had come back with Beeran today, bearing the news that Bhaskaran's wound was getting better and Sridevi's Namboothiri who had been slashed across the chest was recovering too. But things outside were still bad. Beeran's son and his pack had returned to Pookottur, reported Marthandan, but on their way out they had destroyed a lot of property. A couple of the Thampans and their *karyasthans* were in the process of accounting the loss. The rough estimate now was over fifty thousand rupees worth of furniture and brassware and grain were either set fire to or stolen. The Records room had been plundered and a lot of papers burnt down. They were still trying to find out what was lost and what had been saved. The Gopuram door of the Vettekkaran temple, strong and solid, had not buckled under the Mapla weapons, though deep scratches had been made in the wood. Marks that would forever bear evidence of the blackest day in Kovilakam history.

Though the Pookottur Maplas had retreated they had stirred the beehive in all the neighbouring villages and Maplas were running helter-skelter damaging life and property for no reason whatsoever. It would take a few days for things to calm down a bit and they would be able to leave the forest.

The Matriarch's thoughts went back to Mithran and thanked Vettekkaran that at least his young wife was safe in her family home and had escaped the mobbing of the manor and the consequent events. What was that? She cocked her head. The cling clang of the bells round a bullock's neck?

Sethu

Everyone at the forest camp heard the bells and glanced anxiously at each other. A cart in the forest? It was only Beeran who ever came here in one and he had already arrived a couple of hours ago and was getting ready to leave as he had to reach Pookottur on some business after dropping her cousins at the river to take the barge back to the Kovilakam cove.

So who was this?

Her heart thrilled in joy for a moment when she saw

the slender figure in white stepping into the clearing through the thick clump of trees.

The Outcaste! Here!

But her mind had no leisure to dwell on the pleasant surprise for behind him came the familiar form of none other than Mithrettan.

Gasps and oohs and aahs echoed all over the camp.

'Vettekkara!' Ammamma said hoarsely in thanks for a prayer answered. The men, Marthandan and Ravi Varman arched their brows in mild surprise as if it was a matter of mere passing interest.

Then there was a little screech as Winifred the younger Madama threw herself on The Outcaste with a cry of 'is it really you' and clung on to him with all her might.

That distracted the Kovilakam campers from Mithran for a second. They had never seen such an exhibition in their lives.

The Outcaste patted her back in a gentle but embarrassed way and held her away from himself.

'I made a stop at the Estates on my way and that was when I heard... my heartfelt condolences, Mrs Eaton,' and he moved towards Ammamma, 'And to your entire family, Valiya Thampatti, on the loss of Divakaran Thampan. But you will be glad to see the Sixth Tirumulpad safe and sound.'

Mithrettan stood in front of Ammamma, just as he always did at the Kovilakam. His arms crossed at his chest and his head slightly bowed.

'Mithra,' the Matriarch's voice an unusual croak.

As the cousins swarmed around for a glimpse at Mithrettan, The Outcaste left the family to themselves and moved towards Winifred Eaton and her mother for a quiet chat. He promised to make arrangements for them to be moved as soon as he got back into town.

'Stanley Pat had planned for us to go to Uncle Charles and Aunt May in Ootacamund.'

'Then Ootacamund it shall be. There wouldn't be room in the cart or I would have taken you back with me now.'

'I couldn't leave without saying goodbye to Cheenkanni. She has slipped off without a word again. I know she slept outside our tent but she's been missing since early morning.' The Madama sounded exasperated to Sethu.

'Miss Cranford, er... I mean Mrs Eaton... I am afraid your Cheenkanni has left without saying good bye to *you*.'

Satisfied that Mithrettan was safe, Sethu saw no reason to hang around him. Even the edathies and the younger girls had retreated to their own corners after they got a good look at him. The men asked him questions which he answered in grunts and monosyllables. Sethu turned her attention back to the English women and their friend.

'What do you mean?', Mrs Eaton looked puzzled. 'How could you possibly know where she is?'

'I hate to be the bearer of bad news. But the girl is

no more Mrs Eaton. They killed her. Mercilessly. And her unborn baby. I witnessed it first-hand. Not the murder but what happened afterwards. The worst, most grotesque thing I have ever seen. I do not wish to go into the details.'

The older Madama's whisper was almost inaudible, 'Bless you, girl, bless you,' and Mrs Eaton who had not shed tears for her husband broke down into sobs.

The Outcaste

One look at the Sixth Tirumulpad and the difference was obvious. He was still quiet and communicated mostly in his usual snorts and murmurs but he seemed visibly relaxed. The family's presence was doing him good. I had never cared for blind pursuit of rituals just because one's people had done it for generations but now I realised why it had been a practice for families to gather together in the *pula* period after someone died.

I felt some amount of satisfaction for having done the right thing in bringing him here. And there had been the extra incentive of having found Winifred and her mother. It had altogether been a horrible day but halfway through it, I was actually considering myself fortunate for the oddest things.

I wasn't surprised when Mithran announced that he would rather not return with me. Then the Matriarch wished it too. 'We are all in some degree of danger. We will face it together. He can stay here with us and shuttle to Nilambur and back with Beeran like the other men.

He can't hide forever.'

'If that is your wish, Valiya Thampatti and the Sixth Tirumulpad's. Anyway it is time I took my leave. Since there is room in the cart, the English ladies can return with me. I can see that they get away to wherever they think they will be safe. Ootacamund, Madras or even the Sundarbans where Mr Cranford is.'

'Of course if that is what the ladies desire. My granddaughter tells me you have known each other for long.'

When after fond farewells and promises to write as soon as they had both settled down somewhere, Winifred and her mother were ready to leave, I allowed myself a moment with the Story Girl and handed her the bundle I had brought.

'I don't know if your present mindset is conducive to reading. But I took the liberty to bring you some material I thought you might enjoy. And when all this is over, can I hope to read the tale of a refugee princess in a forest camp?'

Unforseen Aid

Pookottur, Ernad
24 August '21
Raziya

The sight of Kunhaishumma shuffling across the backyard of Benazir Manzil struck her as odd. Her inevitable basket of snacks that seemed to Raziya as almost a part of the old woman's anatomy, was absent from her hip today. The urgency of her gait reddened her face.

'Benazir beewi! Benazir beewi! Begam bareen,' she dropped down on the steps of the kitchen side veranda. Benu Thatha was sitting in the anteroom rubbing medicated oil on her knees.

'We can always depend on Kunhaishumma to bring the Pookottur households their supply of goodies even in the worst of times,' Benu Thatha smiled. 'Raziya, mole, go and check her wares. I will be there in a minute after I wash my hands.'

'But Thatha, I don't think she has brought any Pathiris today. It appears she has left her basket behind.'

'What! Kunhaishumma minus her basket? I have to see this with my own eyes to believe it,' she dried her hands quickly. 'Come Raziya. Let us find out what this is about.'

'Benazir beewi,' the Pathiri woman was beginning to holler again when the two of them stepped out.

'Alright, alright. I am here. There is no need to flip the house upside down,' Benu Thatha settled down on the lone chair on the back porch and Raziya sat on the steps opposite the visibly excited old woman.

'Where is your basket? Have you no pathiris for us today?'

'I left it on the ledge by Koyakka's shop when I heard the news. I wanted to get down here as soon as I could. I didn't want the weight slowing me down.'

The past few days being highly eventful, the Pathiri Umma had taken to visiting Benazir Manzil at least twice a day bearing news. She was adept at keeping the townspeople up to date with the happenings in different parts of Ernad and sometimes beyond. Raziya was a little wary of her but Benu Thatha seemed to appreciate not just her succulent snacks but the information she brought with her. She liked the objective, unbiased fashion in which Kunhaishumma presented the news, her own opinions on the matter rarely coming in. She didn't fabricate news. She was just clever at sniffing out the relevant events, gathering details and passing it all on.

She even cited her sources accurately. And that was why Benu Thatha found it beneficial to listen to her.

Recently she had told them of the Amsom official in Melmuri whom Mapla rioters had cornered outside his own residence and demanded that he take the Prophet's faith. 'When every other Hindu has done it, so will I.' Kunhaishumma stuck out her chest and held her head high in imitation of the man's show of dignity. They imprisoned him in the house of someone called Moideenkutti whom both Thatha and the Pathiri Umma seemed to know, but he'd managed to give them the slip and escape into the hills.

Raziya and Benu Thatha had listened in shock as she told them that more than seventy five people in Pookottur had been forcefully converted to Islam in the last couple of days alone. Most of them belonged to lower castes but at least thirty, said Kunhaishumma, were members of one well-known Nair family in the locality.

'Ponnunikkattu?' Thatha had gasped. 'Isn't that the residence of that retired Assistant Salt Commissioner Koman Menon?' Even Raziya had heard of the elderly gentleman who loved and trusted the Maplas and was revered in return.

'Allah! Will those fiends leave no one alone?' Benu Thatha had exclaimed. Can't they even discriminate between friend and foe?'

Thatha was a devout Muslim and well versed in the teachings of the kithab but above all she was a lover of humanity. That was the difference between Thatha and

Alijan Sahib. Sahib was clever and his sense of justice accurate when he conducted those hearings in his front yard. He was a good leader and the Maplas of Pookottur looked up to him no end. But to Raziya he always seemed crude while Thatha was refined. Hard while she was tender. Thatha resented the contempt with which the rich landlords treated Mapla *kudiyans* and when the Khilafat took shape in Ernad and *kudiyan* issues became one of their prime concerns, she had wholeheartedly supported the cause. But this ruthless turn hurt and puzzled her. That the followers of the Prophet would indulge in burglaries and killings and forced conversions made her heart ache.

'It is the Black Brigade,' the Pathiri woman now burst out.

'Allah!' Benu Thatha responded in a moan. She resented the Black Thangal's men more than any of the other rioters. There was something too calculated and intentional about their cruelty.

'This time they have got the Sixth Tirumulpad's lady and her brother.' Kunjaishumma's voice was a bare whisper but Raziya and Benu Thatha were sent reeling.

As the old woman reported what she had heard at the angadi, Raziya felt her insides turn into a molten mass.

Two local Maplas, Kunjuveeran and Ahmed kutti were returning from an errand in Tuvvur and had taken a shortcut through the orchard on the other side of the Plakkal canal when they came upon a scene. Two young men were bound to a tree and three corpses lay on the ground among the dry leaves. Considering the times, there was nothing strange about such a scene but the young men, new converts with shaven heads and skull caps called to them.

'Get help if you can.' They must have been desperate to appeal to Maplas. Ahmed kutti and Kunjuveeran and were about to shrug and leave when what the prisoners said next grabbed their attention.

'Forget us. We are prepared to die. But save the ladies,' said one of them.

'Yes,' continued the other. 'They are locked up somewhere there,' he cocked his chin in the direction behind him. The two Pookottur Maplas were decent men and would have untied the prisoners quickly but it was what the young man said next that stopped them. 'My grandmother is in there. My Radha and her mother. And his sister too.' The other youngster had begun to nudge him in an attempt to silence him but he didn't take the hint. 'She is the wife of none other than the Sixth Tirumulpad of Nilambur.'

The Sixth Tirumulpad. There was not a Mapla in Pookottur who did not hate the Sixth Tirumulpad. Kunjuveeran and Ahmed kutti were no different. They had been part of the crowd that had mobbed the manor the day Mammad was accused of theft. The fellow had hoped that dropping the important name might persuade them to do something but in fact it had the opposite effect as the Tirumulpad's brother-in-law had known it would. Ahmed kutti took one step back and another and then turned away. Kunjuveeran followed suit. They took a short detour behind the trees in the direction the youngster had indicated and saw a shack guarded by two brigands in black. This was where the lady was being held. They had hastened home with the news and flashed it at the angadi.

Kunhaishumma had heard everything first hand.

Raziya began to feel dizzy. She had met the lady at the manor a few months ago when she had been there with the *mailanchi* paste for the young Thampatti. They had not been married then, she remembered. Raziya had liked the pretty girl of approximately her own age and now she felt her heart sink low into the vicinity of her feet as she thought of her plight.

Then a sharp flash of pain stabbed her heart and slid into the cavity of her stomach and even grazed her womb. Allah! It couldn't be? Or could it? In all likelihood it could, logic told her as she remembered Mammad's hatred for the Sixth Tirumulpad.

'Has the Sahib heard of this,' wondered Kunhaishumma aloud.

At that Benu Thatha rose purposefully and straightened her clothes. 'You shall tell him yourself.' The Pathiri woman was a little hesitant as she had never spoken to the Sahib face to face. But she hobbled off in Benu Thatha's wake. Raziya did not follow. She was too weary, body and soul. But the need to act was urgent and indispensable. She had to do something to make up for Mammad's wrongs. She had to do it for his sake and her child's.

Alijan

'Ah Benu, my ponne! Who is this you have brought to me? What choice treats do you have for us today, Kunhaishumma?'

But Benu did not appear to be in a mood for his jokes just then. 'She brings serious tidings. Come tell him Aishumma,' his beewi urged. When it came to news mongering the Pathiri woman needed no encouragement.

Alijan bobbed his head gently and rearranged his rumal several times as he listened to the old lady's report. This was news indeed! The Sixth Tirumulpad's lady in the clutches of the Black Thangal's men. Even when she had finished her tale. he kept on nodding as if he had forgotten to stop.

'Allah!' Benu exclaimed. 'You hear what happened and sit there jouncing your head like a dimwit? Get up you old Mapla, and do something about it.'

Ente Padachone! Dear Benu was in a dangerous mood. She had called him a dimwit and an old Mapla in front of this hag! She had to be handled carefully.

'You expect me to interfere in the Black Thangal's business, my ponne?'

'I expect you to do what is right. You have been meting out justice in the town for years. You can very well do so now.'

'But these are turbulent times. Benu, my dear, you must see that the idea of justice differs in peace and in war. Anyway, there are disturbing things happening all over Ernad every day. How do you think I can find solutions for all those problems? I am just plain Ali, not Allah.'

'But this is the wife of the Sixth Tirumulpad who is being held by the Black Thangal and his men. Allah knows what they will do to her.'

'Benu,' said Alijan, his tone slow and distinctive. 'Bad things are happening to many women across the land these days. The acts of certain antisocial elements. I cannot protect them all. The Sixth Tirumulpad's wife is just another woman. Let us pray to Allah that she is safe. Anyway, if you understand the way the Black Thangal works, you will realise that his men never ever harm women. He is very fastidious about that. When they attack the locals all they want to do is to get them to believe in Allah. It is the White Sarkar and its allies that the Black Thangal actually hates.' Alijan hadn't noticed the trace of reverence that crept into his speech till he saw Benu's eyebrows arch in surprise.

'Faith in Allah has to come from the heart. If someone is made a Muslim at the point of a dagger, is he a Muslim at all? Imagine that happening to the Tirumulpad's lady! And how do you know so much about that brute's strategies?'

He wished he could tell her. Maybe sometime after all this was done with, he would.

Now he had to pacify her somehow. He didn't want this conversation to stretch out. Especially with the Pathiri Woman hanging around with her ears wide open.

'Alright, my Ponne. I will see if I can send someone over to the grove to find out what is happening.'

Mammad

He had been squatting all by himself on the ledge outside the teashop when the messenger found him. The sun had been down for more than half an hour and the generally crowded village square was empty. The shops were closed and the people seemed to have gone their respective ways. With Raziya in Benazir Manzil, Mammad was in a way homeless. Today he didn't even feel like going back to the smithy.

As he was making his way through the backyard of Benazir Manzil that morning after his conversation with Alijan Sahib, Benu Thatha had beckoned him over and whispered something in his ear. She couldn't be sure yet but she thought he ought to know. Her words had had an effect not unlike a sip of cool, sweet sherbet after having eaten one mouthful after another of unusually spicy food. He whispered another silent prayer that the world become a better place by the time his son was born. His child would lack nothing. He would be the best father in the world. But the Matriarch. His actions had filled her heart with sorrow. If the hurt he had caused rebounded… he deserved to suffer, but his son? He wished he could make amends for what he had done. It would give the Baliya Thampatti some peace and protect his child and Raziya from harm.

News of the next in the never-ending line of shocking occurrences had come a couple of hours ago when people gathered in Koyakka's shop for tea, refreshments and gossip, all hot. The two witnesses themselves were in the teashop describing what they had seen in the grove across the canal. At first it hadn't seemed worth particular attention. The Black Thangal's men who had been making steady inroads for the past few months seemed to have been on a rampage of late. Nobody really understood their aims and goals. Not the Maplas of Pookottur and the nearby amsoms. Not the Khilafat officials or the Maulavis and other men of religion. The Black Thangal remained a mystery and they all watched wonderstruck at the way he and his brigade worked. So when Ahmed Kutti excitedly relayed what he had seen with Kunjiveerankka adding interesting tidbits in between, Mammad hadn't paid much heed.

'The men we found, tied up to the tree were young. At first we mistook them for one among us because of their shaven heads. But their speech patterns gave them away,' explained Kunjiveerankka.

'They were begging us to get help. We were sorry for the poor boys. It was not their own safety they were worried about,' said Ahmed Kutti. 'Brave lads they were. They wanted to protect their women. The Black brigands were holding them captive somewhere nearby. One of the boys had a sister out there. The other had been so distraught because they had taken away his old grandmother and a girl who was obviously special to him. They went on to explain how they guessed the fellow had feelings for the captive girl. They held back the most shocking part till the end. The other boy's sister was none other than the Sixth Tirumulpad's wife! There were gasps all round and widened eyes. The Pathiri woman rocking on her haunches, let out a coarse cry of 'Allah'!

Mammad had never for a moment imagined that there would come a time when he would feel anger on behalf of the conceited landlord and sympathise with him. However haughty and unjust Mithran Thampan may be, it was obvious he cared for his young wife. He could clearly envisage his horror when he heard. He, Mammad could understand only too well. How upset he himself had been when a couple of eve teasers had targeted his wife! This was so much worse. Quite suddenly the hatred that filled his heart was pushed down to make way for a rush of sympathy. The pressing need for revenge gave way for the desire to do something. And he made up his mind to hurry over to the grove and if there was something he could do to save the lady from the Black Thangal's clutches, he would do it. He first considered asking Alavi kutti and some others for help. But then remembering the Nilambur fiasco, thought it better to do it himself. When Mammad resolved to do something, he didn't dawdle. He would have liked to make a quick trip to the smithy for some weapons but decided against it as he didn't wish to waste time. He did have his dagger with him. He would have to make do with that. Choosing to skip dinner, he set off into the darkness. Soon he had left the village behind and stepped on the road that lay between Manjeri and Mongam. That was when he heard the grating of cartwheels. His father in the Kovilakam cart! It struck him that instant that a cart would be useful on a rescue mission.

He stretched out his hand to stop the cart.

'Bappa!'

'Mammade eeyyo,!' The old man looked tired. As if he had been driving the whole day. He had a suspicious expression on his face as he peered at his son in the darkness. 'Where are you going at this time of the night? Need I ask! Some bad business as usual, I am sure. When are you going to learn, my son?' Old Beeran sighed sadly.

'It is nothing like that Bappa. There is something important I have to do. Could I have the cart for a couple of hours, it is really urgent.'

'The cart! Allah! What next? Have you lost your senses? One day you attack the Kovilakam, destroy property, injure people and kill a young Thampan and the next you wish to borrow their cart for your dirty work?'

'It isn't what you think, Bappa. It's… er… someone is in danger. I have to do something about it. It would be much easier with a cart.'

'You wish to rescue someone in danger? Who is it? One of your Khilafat goons?'

'How am I going to explain to you?' Mammad heaved a sigh of frustration. 'I suppose I will have to tell you. Bappa, it is the Sixth Tirumulpad's lady. The Black Thangal's men have her.' 'Mammade, you lie,' Beeran barked. 'This is no joke. I won't have it, I tell you.'

'I must get there as soon as possible if I wish to do something. There is no time for small talk. Please do let me have the cart, if you will. Or else I will walk.' He glanced at his father's suspicious face for a moment and choosing not to wait, turned around.

'Mammade,' Beeran called after him. 'Do you speak the truth? How can I believe you? Why would you want to save the lady when you hate Mithran Thampan so?'

'Listen Bappa, this is no time for unnecessary chatter. I am going.' 'All right. I will come with you. Get in.' Not wishing to waste time arguing, Mammad climbed in without a word. 'I will drive. You look tired.' Beeran frowned but Mammad took the reins from him.

He drove fast, opting to take the path east of the big fields that would enable them to go straight into the grove without having to stop at the canal and go the rest of the way by foot. Once inside the grove they couldn't travel as fast for the cart had to be maneuvered through the coconut trees. As he slowed down to squeeze his way in through a narrow gap, a shadow moved a few yards away. It was late and this was not the sort of place people casually frequented at this time of the night.

'Did you see that?' he whispered. Bappa had. 'Yes I am certain I saw someone pass. I may be mistaken, but I did catch a glimpse of a *thattam*.'

'Mm. We will ignore it. If a woman wants to conduct her trade here, it is none of our business,' he murmured and proceeded towards the clearing Ahmed Kutti and Kunjuveerankka mentioned.

Priyamvada

To Priya it seemed as if she had been bound to the post in the middle of the shack forever. The sun had been down for quite some time now, so she guessed it was past seven thirty. She had listened to the terrified conversation of her co prisoners to while away the time but now they seemed to be drained out. The old lady was called Panki Amma, the middle aged one, Janu and the girl, barely sixteen was Radha. They had wailed and sobbed on each other's shoulders and worried about what happened to their men folk. They had not seen the three men murdered for they had been moved here before that. Priya had opened her mouth to tell them what had happened but not wishing to add to their misery, decided to keep silent. The girl Radha was Janu's daughter and old Panki Amma, their neighbor. She gathered from their laments that Radha was betrothed to Panki Amma's grandson Kuttan and guessed he was the frightened young man who had saved his skin by agreeing to wear the cap. Well Unni had done the same. Clearly with her safety in mind. Where was Unni? She knew her brother had no intention of living the rest of his life as a Muslim but what would happen to him now? What would happen to her once the Thangal and his men got back?

It seemed pointless to ponder.

If some unexpected means of escape didn't materialise… Priya thought of the little Beretta tucked in her waistband.

In the meanwhile she had allowed her mind to occupy itself with the other women's talk. The welcome distraction had however stopped now as they fell into exhausted silence. She thought she heard a crackle of dried leaves behind the shack. One of the guards relieving himself among the bushes, she thought. Ever since she had been brought in here, she had heard their soft exchanges among themselves on and off but they seemed to have been quiet for a while. It did appear as if they were taking a break. If only she could loosen one of the knots she might be able to find a way out. There was yet another faint noise outside. A snap of a twig as someone stepped on it. This time on the front side of the shack. So they were back. There was a small creak and the rough wooden door slowly began to swing open. The movement was measured and even a little hesitant. It brought with it a slight breeze and the tiny lamp they had left in the shack flickered. So the men were coming in here. The door groaned again. Someone quickly slipped inside and shut it. To her surprise it was a woman. A young Muslim woman! The other prisoners gasped, fear and doubt writ on their faces, obvious even in the dim light. The woman picked up the lamp and held it up in an attempt to see clearly.

Priya squinted at the face framed by the coloured veil. She was young. And familiar. She flinched a little as the girl drew nearer.

'Don't fear,' she whispered, 'I am Raziya. I have come to save ... you.'

Raziya? Priya repeated thoughtfully. And then it struck her. This was that Mapla's wife. That irritating employee whom Mithran Thampan, unaware of the fact that it was she who had pinched the Beretta, had accused of its theft. Priya had seen the girl months ago when Sethu Thampatti had wanted to write her story and had her summoned to the manor on the pretext of delivering *mailanchi* paste.

'Let me undo your bonds,' the girl whispered. 'We have to be quick and do it before they come back. I have been hiding in the bushes for a while now, waiting for them to leave their watch.' Swiftly she slid behind Priya and loosened the rope that fastened her wrists against the pole.

Priya couldn't believe she was actually free. She shook her hands to regain circulation and undid the cloth that bound her mouth. Raziya moved towards Radha when a rhythmic heaving was heard outside, moving closer to the shack. She knew the sound. The heavy breathing of the Black Thangal's palanquin bearers. He was here. There was no time to think. There was a scuttling on the other side of the door. The guards had apparently heard the grunts too and were hurrying back to their posts. She nodded towards the darkest corner in the shack and Raziya moved over there to crouch in the semi- darkness hidden behind Janu's ample form. Priya retied her gag, patted her stomach to confirm the presence of the Beretta and positioned herself back at the pole with her hands behind her back. In a matter of minutes, the crude door swung open again and the Black Thangal glided in, flanked by his lieutenants. In spite of the extra lamp held up by one of the guards, she could not make out what the men looked like. They were clad completely in black, masks, headdresses and what not.

There was a noise like the chirp of a lizard. The Black Thangal clicked his tongue sympathetically.

'Paavam, paavam! Oh you poor ladies, I hate to see you like this. *Alle makkale*?' He turned towards one lieutenant to the other. Apparently they were close.

'But do not fear my dear ladies. You will be comfortable soon. You will live well. Eat the choicest biryanis. Wear the prettiest silks. You girls, he indicated Priya and Radha will marry the bravest of our kundans and live happily ever after.'

Never had Priya imagined how cruel such amiable, courteous words could be. The way he said paavam, paavam in that gentle, kindly tone sent creeps down her spine.

'You will be safe forever as you will learn to trust in Allah.'

The henchmen nodded vigorously.

The girl, Radha suddenly screeched, 'I don't want biryanis or silk clothes! I don't want to marry any Maplas. I don't want to become a Muslim! I only want my Kuttettan! Where is he?'

There was the lizard noise again. 'Paavam, paavam. Loosen the child's bonds and lead her to the cart.'

As if on cue, a cart came to a halt outside.

Priya had no intention of getting into their vehicle and going away with them. She tried to think calmly. What could she do? True her bonds were loose but with so many brigands here that wouldn't do her any good. Raziya could do nothing in their presence either. The only option would be to move fast and whisk out the gun. But she trembled at the thought. Would she be able to use it? She was sure her hands would shake. To shoot a human being, to kill him… even if it was in self defence. Could she bring herself to do that? One of the henchmen moved towards Radha.

'Mone, Suleimane,' the Thangal spoke to his other lieutenant, his voice dripping with affection for a favourite son or grandson. 'This little *munjathi* here,' he said even as the man led poor Radha out, 'is different from the rest.' His eyes glinting between his mask and headgear were trained on Priya. 'The disguise makes her even more beautiful. Look at her eyes sparkle. She will suit you well. She will be my gift to you, my son,' the indulgent smile was evident in his voice and Priya was suddenly nauseous. 'She shall not be taken to the camp with the others. We will perform the necessary rituals soon and you shall make her yours.'

Priya wanted to screech like young Radha had done. That she was the wife of the Sixth Tirumulpad and was certainly not going to be gifted to the Mapla, but she held her tongue. Voices could be heard. More men with the cart, she presumed. There was no way out. There were too many of them in and around the shack for her to make an escape. Only one idea came to her. The Beretta.

Thoughts of her husband, her mother and the others in the *tharawad*, poor Unni, wherever he was, of Sethu Thampatti began to fill her mind but she flooded them out. She could not be sentimental. Not if she was going to put her plans into action.

'You filthy, Mapla,' she said. Her voice muffled under the gag.

The Black Thangal clicked his tongue again. The lizard click mildly admonishing this time.

'You do not speak to the Thangal like that my *munjathi*. My Suleiman's woman is my own child, my dear...' his gentle voice was interrupted by further noises from outside. There seemed as if there were several men out there. And the clip clop of another cart began to echo in the night. That roused the Black Thangal's suspicions. For a moment his black clad form stiffened and he turned his attention from her to the rickety door and then dismissed it as probably nothing. 'Mone, you may now lead your lovely lady out,' he invited the fellow called Suleiman in that silken-sinister voice, 'and ask one of the kundans on guard to take the other ladies to the cart too.'

'As you wish Thangal Uppappa,' Suleiman made for her and in one swift movement, Priya pulled her right hand from behind her back and drew the Beretta from her waistband.

The Outcaste

The two ladies had been looking tired out for a while. It had been a tedious journey from the depths of the forest for our driver had taken a wrong path and we'd had to retrace the route. This had taken us an extra hour. Now we were nearing Pookottur, the man, now sure of the way had opted to take a shortcut through the coconut grove which would take us straight to the Manjeri road and we would have a mere five miles to go. I didn't wish to spring the unexpected houseguests on Shekharan Nair at this late hour but at least Mrs Cranford and Winifred would be safe there till further arrangements could be made for their travel.

'We should soon be out on the main road. And then it isn't far.' I glanced at Mrs Cranford swollen ankles worriedly.

Hushed whispers sounded in the dark.

But we were late as it was and I had no intention of stopping to satisfy my curiosities and certainly would not have had I not seen the Nilambur Kovilakam cart. I would recognize it anywhere from the Kovilakam emblem. It was in this cart that I had, all those months ago seen Sethu and her cousin outside Alijan Sahib's compound. It was in this cart that old Beeran had left the forest camp today a couple of hours before we ourselves had started. It was from behind the cart that the whispers came.

Now I couldn't ignore the scene and go away. I got out and walked round the two vehicles to find Beeran and another young Mapla untying the bonds of two people tied up to a tree.

'Beeran, what is going on?'

'Master, it is you? We have come on an urgent mission…'

The younger man turned out to be none other than the Tirumulpad's employee in whose name the Maplas had mobbed the manor. I remembered he was Beeran's son.

'Who is it Bappa?' His eyebrows rose as he recognised me. 'Mammade, he can help us,' said Beeran.

'Master, the Sixth Tirumulpad's lady is being held by the Black Thangal's men. This is her brother.' Beeran pointed to one of the young men they had just freed.

It was then that the gunshot rang in the air.

'Stay in the cart and don't move,' I instructed the English women. 'Beeran, you stay here and keep watch.' I sped in the direction of the shot, Mammad and the two other men at my heels. Beeran's son had a lamp from the cart and in its feeble light they saw a man coming out of the shack leading a very young girl out, temporarily paralyzed by the shot. There were others in black standing guard at the entrance. At the sight of the girl one of the free captives yelled, 'Radhe!' And her answering cry rent the air. That young man, Kuttan pounced on the girl's captor who seemed momentarily confused by all that was happening and had him on the ground. A scuffle that followed. We heard the girl scream.

Mammad, the only one among us who was armed, swung his dagger in a vicious arc slicing through the arms of the men doing security on either side of the door. I entered the wooden hut with Mammad and the other boy.

The first thing we saw was a man covered in black from head to toe. He was clicking his tongue and whispering 'Paavam...paavam'.

The Black Thangal.

The sight of the mysterious and notorious man

responsible for so many atrocities in the area had us all stunned for a moment and he floated out of the door the sympathetic words still on his lips.

Mammad held up his lamp. There were gasps and surprised yelps all round. Inside, there was a slight figure in a man's shirt and mundu but the waist length hair indicated that this was a woman. She was crumpled on the floor and bleeding. A young Muslim woman crouched at her side, trying to stem the flow of blood.

She looked up, saw Mammad.

'Ingalo!'

'Raziya! You here! Allah! The Tirumulpad's lady? Who shot her?'

'That Thangal… he said she was to be given in Nikah to him,' she pointed at the last of the Thangal's men left in the hut. 'He was going to take her away. The lady shot herself.'

The Thangal's man who had watched stunned all this while sprung to action.

'Out of the way all of you. I will take her away. She will be fine.' The other young man growled and pounced on the brigand, 'You shall not touch my sister!' So this was her brother.

Mammad was quick and his dagger well aimed. It plunged straight into the brigand's middle and he crumpled with a cry.

'Unni,' the injured girl moaned.

I was no man of medicine but I had to act fast. The lady's wound needed to be checked. It was obvious she was alive from the way she was groaning and writhing. 'Turn her over and move the cloth aside. Let me see if I can do something for her.' The Muslim girl was hesitant at first. Probably worried about the other woman's modesty. I knelt down on the floor.

The wound was on her side a few inches below her left armpit. It was difficult to see in the dim lamp light. The girl called Raziya was holding up the lamp while the other two women noticing that the door was unguarded took the opportunity to slip out, calling out Radhe! Radhe!

'The bullet hasn't actually penetrated deep, I think. Not more than a couple of inches from the look of the wound,' I observed. 'Can you see it,' asked Unni, bending to get a proper look.

'I am not sure. Not in this light. But even if we could there is no way we could remove it without proper instruments. All we can do is to bind it well and get a doctor to look at it as soon as possible.'

'My elder brother is one. And he is in the *tharawad* now. Back from England a month ago.'

'That is indeed fortunate. We will try to be quick. Beeran can take her in the Kovilakam cart.'

Mammad's wife took off her thattam and it was bound tightly round the injured girl. That must have given her some comfort for she moaned and smiled weakly. She looked around a little frantically till her eyes fixed on Mammad. She beckoned feebly. Surprised, he went closer, a trifle hesitantly.

She raised her right hand which still held the gun.

'Take it,' she said between gasps. 'Give it to the Sixth Tirumulpad when you see him. He must know you are no thief.'

The Battle Of Pookottur

Pookottur, Ernad
26 August '21
Alijan

He spent half the night tossing and turning and finally decided that a trek to the smithy might be better than continuing in this fashion. It felt odd. Alijan was used to sleepless nights but they were seldom caused by worry. As if something bad was about to happen. Emotion had little place in Alijan's mind, generally preoccupied by ambition and plans of action, that is why this feeling for apparently no reason felt strange. No point lying around in bed if he couldn't sleep.

As usual, he found his shawl in the dark and slipped out into the night, Benu's little snores sounding gently in his ears. Was it the upcoming battle, yes, the battle was inevitable now, that brought this on? Not likely, thought

Alijan. The thought of fighting the British created waves of excitement in him. Not a premonition that something unpleasant was in store.

Earnest preparations had been going on for a couple of days now. The Pookottur men were raring to go. They had it from reliable sources that the authorities had, soon after the siege of Kizhakkeppalli, begun attempts to organize sufficient forces to aid the Malappuram Divisional Officer, Austin Sayippe. These troops, they said, were to be headed by a certain Captain McEnroy. As soon as this information had reached them, his men, quick as a flash, had blasted all the bridges and culverts on the way, thus winning them more time to get ready. McEnroy and party, delayed by the necessary repair work, were now almost here. It would take no more than a few hours, Alijan calculated. Buses and lorries, countless men on foot, machine guns and what not, the Maplas of Pookottur were prepared to take them on. By nature fearless, the lads had been rendered expert fighters through months of training. That one of their best men was down with burn injuries and another distracted by a host of personal monsters, could prove to be a disadvantage of sorts, but it can't hurt too much, thought Alijan. Mammad was still available and however preoccupied, was the sincerest and most skilled man he had. Yes they would make mincemeat of the White Army. The Pookottur Maplas would make history. The world would know this battle as they knew the one in Meerut all those years ago. It wouldn't be long before an Islamic Raj would rein in Malabar and he would be known as Sultan Alijan…

The smithy was full of people. Their excitement reflected Alijan's own hopes. Weapons were being polished, varieties of possible strategies discussed and some of them were practicing sword and dagger moves. There was a moment's silence as Alijan walked into their midst and settled down on his three-legged stool. He glanced around. Mammad was nowhere to be seen. Surprising. Even on normal nights he preferred sleeping here. Where was he today on the eve of the battle when the whole town had assembled together?

Ah! There he was. Alijan smiled as the young man's slender form could be seen in the shadows, whispering to someone, probably Alavikutti from the silhouette's stocky build. Alijan cocked his head to one side and slid the rumal in a circular motion around his neck. There seemed to be an urgency in their body language. Now Mammad was pulling out something from his broad belt, something small and lumpy, and handing it to Alavikutti with a quick pat on the shoulder as if to say, 'off you go, hurry'. And sending his friend on whatever errand it was, Mammad joined the group now gathered around Alijan.

'It is a matter of hours now my men,' Alijan croaked, pulling off the neck rumal and pausing to retie it rather meticulously as the Maplas held their breath in anticipation. 'The White Army is on our doorstep. Our chance is finally here. I know, my brave lads, that you have several strategies swarming in your brains. But we need to have a single plan by which we can go. We cannot afford to slip. I see that most of you are here now and it is the ideal time to fix something effective. You shall all go through this in your minds over and over again so that you know exactly what to do when the time comes. What do you say, my brave fighters of Pookottur?'

'Bolo Taqbeer, Allahu Akbar,' the collective reply was feverish.

'When it comes to courage, and skill, you my men, are equal to any number of British soldiers. In purity of aim, we are far superior,' he continued, watching their bare chests swell in pride at his words, their shaven heads glisten and their lips twitch into smiles beneath their luxuriant beards. 'But remember, in one aspect, they are one up on us.' 'Machine guns,' the whisper echoed among the listeners. They were not unaware. 'Never let such things set you back. Not even a thousand machine guns can prove a match to the most important weapons we possess – bravery and unity. If we all stick to one plan we shall function like a machine more efficient than their guns.'

'Bolo Taqbeer… Allahu Akbar!'

'Alijan Sahib… Zindabad!'

'Listen carefully, my men. The twenty six-mile point on the Kozhikode-Malappuram road. That is where the action is going to be. We shall decide what will be to our advantage. Remember our Valiyathode at Plakkal. The canal will be our very own moat. Some of our men shall take position in the canal and the others shall remain out of sight in the background. I know it is gushing with water this monsoon but when has a little dampness held us back? In absolute silence, our men shall keep watch. When the army, the entire army, buses, trucks, men, all, repeat all pass, we shall attack from behind. That will take them by surprise and we shall be one up. They will have no time to set up their machine guns. Those hidden in the background shall close in and… and my brave men, we shall tear into them and finish them in no time.'

Enthusiastic cheers and taqbeer calls ensued and Alijan smiled.

'Your ardour pleases me,' he chuckled and on a more serious note issued the warning. 'But we don't want a single mistake. Remember the machine guns. There is no way we can take them on face to face.'

Mithran

Deep in the jungle off Pullangode, the Kovilakam camp had retired. Stretched out on a mat, gazing at the starlit sky through the gaps in the makeshift shelter's roof, Mithran felt a peace which had eluded him since the mob was at his manor. The numbness that had set in after the Kovilakam attack and Divakaran's murder eased a trifle. There was a strange comfort in the companionship of the family which he would not have believed possible a day or two ago. Cheriyammamma had said little but her presence assured him he had something to hold on to. She was relieved he was safe. She did not hold him responsible for what happened to Divakaran. The others, determined to put the worst behind them moved on cheerfully and their ability to laugh at Gulikan jokes at this time served as a kind of assurance that the world hadn't turned topsy turvy. Mithran had never been one to pay much heed to the children but their antics before they had finally retired to their mats relaxed him. His eldest sister's grandchildren, little Cherunni and what was her name… ah yes Rukmini, who had never dared to come close to him had actually approached him with cheeky grins. Life and his own view of it was different in the forest from that in the Kovilakam or the manor at Pookottur.

Priya. All this softness around him brought on an urgent need to see her. When he had gone into hiding he had written her a halfhearted letter at his host's insistence and her reply had come in a day or two. It hadn't sounded like his little wife. Her little note had been short and subdued and he had even sensed vaguely an unusual emotion. Was it fear? Guilt? At the time his senses hadn't been functioning properly but now in his newly relaxed state, he understood. Something was troubling her. Something more than worry about his welfare.

Whether he had slept for hours or merely a few minutes, Mithran was not sure when he was jerked awake by something grating in his ears. Wooden cartwheels on pebbles. At this time of the night? He sat up, wide awake now and his cousin, young Adithyan next to him was stirring too. 'What's it, Mithretta?' His cousin's voice was thick with sleep. He too had heard. So had most of the camp as was apparent from the sudden movements and hushed whispers emanating from the various shelters.

'Narayana,' the Matriarch's voice sounded in the dark, addressing the brave washer man turned security guard who was on duty at the camp that day. Narayanan was one step ahead. He had his gun out and was moving in the direction of the noise. Mithran's move to step out of the shelter was stopped by Adithyan's hand on his shoulder. 'No Mithretta. Stay put. We don't want your presence here known to an outsider.'

There was an astonished gasp from washerman Narayanan. 'What's up?' Adithyan enquired, marching out of the shelter with his mundu doubled up.

'Is there any bad news? What brings you here at this time of the night?' Anxiety and some amount of suspicion laced Narayanan's voice.

'Beeran! You just left a few hours ago? Is anything the matter?' Asked Adithyan.

Beeran! Mithran moved to the entryway but still remained in the shadows.

'Beeran, is that you,' Cheriyammamma was up now and out of the shelter with young Sethu at her heels, her silver hair slightly askew. One by one the Kovilakam men and women and the servants became aware of the commotion and were trickling into the clearing. All eyes on old Beeran Mapla.

'If I could see the Sixth Tirumulpad, there is something...'

'What do you want with the Sixth Tirumulpad at this time of the night?'

Narayanan was clearly hostile. It was a fact that he

did not trust Maplas and Beeran, however loyal he had proved to be, was still one.

'What is it Beeran?' It was Cheriyammamma. 'Mithran Thampan has had a tiring day and is resting. You can tell me.'

'Baliya Thampatti, I…' before Beeran could finish, there was a shuffling noise behind him and someone climbed down from the cart and slowly stepped out of the shadows into the clearing where he was visible in the light of the torches held aloft by two of the man servants.

Vettekkara!

Mithran was not sure if the exclamation was made by himself or by one of the others. Maybe it was a chorus. It was the heavyset Mapla who ran around with that scoundrel Mammad. The fellow who was involved in the gate construction business. It was he who had bound Divakaran to the pillar that day at the manor and stood guard over him.

Vettekkara! Guruvayurappa! The Kovilakam refugees appealed to their favourite deities.

Such deceit! Such a breach of trust! Who would have thought it of Beeran?

Mathu

Something akin to the percussionist, Thrithala's *chenda* echoed in her ears and Mathu realised it was her own heart. As her gaze, surprisingly steady, fixed on the cart driver's wizened features, for a moment Mathu feared that like the fire emanating from Shiva's third eye reduced anything or anyone in the line of vision to mere ashes, so would the pain in her heart metamorphose into the flame that would shoot out of her eyes and engulf the traitor. She pursed her lips and slowly, ever so slowly shook her head at him and he cringed.

A mild breeze stroked the torches and the flames flickered for a second sending sparks all over. She looked at the other Mapla. Yes, she recognised him. The fellow who had waved his dagger wildly that terrible day, injuring Bhaskaran and the young consort Namboodiri. The man's eyes glinted fiercely in the torchlight. Suddenly Mathu's primary emotion as the Matriarch of the clan took over and the mother hen in her feared for the lives of her brood. A blinding terror that made her forget everything else. For a moment she went back to her girlhood when she believed, the little-boy-Krishna at Guruvayur would have answers to all her questions, solutions to all her problems. Her eyes were still firmly fixed on Beeran, her slight frame motionless and only Mathu herself heard the sob within.

'Krishna! Guruvayurappa!'

Beeran looked as if he were about to burst into tears while the other fellow slowly moved his palms over his bare chest and suddenly slid them into the leather belt that held his checkered waist cloth up and produced something. Something small and black. There was a series of sharp intakes of breath as the onlookers realised what it was.

A gun.

'You sick traitor! You filthy old Mapla!' Washerman Narayanan had pushed Beeran on the ground and planted his foot on the old man's middle. Adityan had the other rogue's arms twisted behind his back and was wresting his gun away from him.

There was nothing to worry after all. Mathu's family was safe. Guruvayurappan had saved them all.

'Baliya Thampatti,' Beeran was sobbing. 'Spare me. Spare me.'

'Spare you?'

It was Mithran who growled striding formidably into the middle of the scene.

'Mithretta, step back,' warned Marthandan who was now assisting his cousin to hold down the writhing Mapla.

Mithran paid no heed.

'Spare you? You who cosied up to a vulnerable old lady to win her trust? You who took advantage of it? You who brought this filthy fellow here?'

'Oh Sixth Tirumulpad, forgive me. Maybe I shouldn't have. But which father does not wish to clear his son's name? This man, this Alavi Kutti brings you your lost gun.'

'What!'

'It is your Beretta, Mithretta.' Adithyan had now wrenched the weapon from the Mapla's grasp.

'Where did you get it?' Mithran was astounded as he took it from his cousin and examined it.

'My son wished it delivered to the Tirumulpad. It was not he who took it. And when it came into his hands, he asked this man to bring it. I told him I would do it myself as he had no idea where you were. But… but my son did not trust me enough,' Beeran hung his head sadly. 'He insisted that Alavikutti here do it. I had no desire to bring this man here. But I had no choice. I had to clear Mammad's name before… before… there is soon to be a battle. What if he… what if he lost his life before this blemish on his character was erased?' With that the old man broke down into uncontrollable sobs.

'Forgive me Baliya Thampatti… but I had to do it for my son.'

The entire audience was left gaping

The Matriarch could not bear the sight of the broken man. Before she could say anything, her granddaughter sprang into action.

'Kittunni,' Sethu addressed one of the men. 'Help Beeran Mapla up and give him some water.

'Beeran, if what you say is true…' Mithran was a little flushed. 'But where did Mammad find the pistol? I can't understand who else had access to it if it wasn't he who took it.'

Beeran hung his head and said nothing.

'Beeran Ikka, it is time we went. I have no time to waste,' the Mapla called Alavikutti fidgeted. Still silent, Beeran drained his water rose to leave.

'Beeran, answer me, first,' Mithran urged.

'I don't think Beeran Ikka is going to open his

mouth. I will answer your question, er…' The fellow was obviously not inclined to address Mithran by his respectful title. 'Apparently it was none other than your own lady. You landlords are… what can I say… unbelievable. To think you had been accusing our Mammad all the time! Anyway, she must have felt some remorse, for she decided to shoot herself,' the Mapla shrugged and scrambled into the Nilambur Kovilakam cart as if it were his own, motioning for Beeran to join him.

The Matriarch felt the ground slipping away from under her. It was the image of little Everest with a lotus aloft that gave her the strength hold herself steady long enough to order Beeran not to leave till he had reported the entire incident.

And learn that Priyamvada would recover.

Mammad

Again and again the Maplas of Pookottur went over Alijan Sahib's strategy till they were word perfect. They enacted the scene in their minds till they were satisfied that they would make no mistake. Then when it was nearly two in the morning, they finally dispersed. Some of them went back to their own homes for a few hours of rest before it all began. Others, scattered themselves on the smithy floor to catch a few winks. Mammad escorted Sahib back to the house. Just as he turned the corner of the house on his way back to the smithy, he heard hasty footsteps somewhere behind him. Someone was running towards the front porch of Benazir Manzil. It was too dark to see anything. Sahib had probably heard too. There was a lantern on the porch and Mammad, retracing his steps could see him halt at the door before entering the house and frown in the direction of the sound.

'Sahibe,' a whisper was heard, hushed and urgent. Alijan began walking towards the person and was soon hustled into the guava grove. Mammad was mildly curious but wouldn't have considered pursuing the matter if he hadn't heard Alijan Sahib cry out sharply. What if Sahib had come to harm? He walked cautiously into the guava grove. His eyes widened in astonishment. In the light of a flickering lamp someone was holding up, he saw a *manjal* parked beneath the trees. With both hands on Sahib's shoulder stood none other than the Black Thangal. Mammad would have jumped to his rescue had the Sahib not for a second leaned his head on one of those hands. The Thangal patted Alijan comfortingly. 'Paavam...paavam... our Suleiman.'

'How?' The Sahib croaked falteringly.

'It is a long story, Ali. But it was your man. That cat eyed lad who did it.'

Mammad panicked and fled.

With sunrise came the news from those on watch duty. The white army would reach Plakkal in no time. The forces were to gather. When Mammad stepped out of the smithy, he had already side-lined the Sahib's night-time encounter with the Black Thangal in his mind as something not concerning him. The business of the gun cleared and the fact that he was able to save the

Tirumulpad's lady from harm had lifted off the burden that had weighed his heart down for months. He felt like a new man. Ready to take on his soldierly duties. But he needed to see Raziya first.

He hardly ever used such endearments to address his wife in more than a year of marriage. But today, on Benu Thatha's back porch it felt right to do so. 'My ponne, you should go back to the house. It is a happy day. When the battle is won, there will be a new world for us to live in. For our little one to be born in. We shall celebrate, my Raziya.' He reached into his belt and pulled out the grubby cloth purse that contained the money he had planned to spend on Raziya at the Pullara Nercha. . 'There is enough money in here to buy rice, meat and coconuts. We shall serve it to our friends and neighbours. I want you to make your *thenga choru* with chicken in roasted coconut gravy and start distributing it to all our friends by lunch time. We shall enjoy the food together when I get back.' Giving her a final smile, he skipped back towards the smithy where the men were gathering.

Alijan

Life for him had never been smooth sailing, right from the time he was an orphan Alikutti in the Yatim Khana. Whatever success he had achieved had been built upon a solid foundation of tragedy and tough times. But now, he wondered if the whole minar would come down in a crash, just as the golden dome was about to be put up on the top. He supposed it was old age that was making him feeble of heart but he wished he could share his sorrow with Benu. He would. But not now. When all this was over. The battle was for the benefit of the whole land. Suleiman's mayyath was but a personal loss. Even as he steeled himself and rose for the final pep talk, his eyes had refused to focus on Mammad in the front row.

Things were going per plan. Their chief men were positioned at various points in Valiyathode, the canal at Plakkal. The rest were hidden among the surrounding trees and in the many houses in the vicinity. Old as he was, he didn't trust himself in the front line so he found a spot where he had a clear view of things and he was among the first to glimpse the first truck as it rolled down the road, followed by more such vehicles. There were soldiers on foot and on bicycles, all blissfully unaware of the Mapla fighters carefully positioned in the canal's muddy waters. Alijan watched as the White army drew closer. Soon they would cross the bridge over Valiyathode. That was the moment the Pookottur men were lying in wait for. The minute the last vehicle and the last man had crossed the bridge and reached the open field the attack would come from all sides. The houses on the south. The orchards beyond. The hill on the west of the houses and from the canal itself. The truck at the head of the procession rolled on to the bridge and Alijan held his breath.

Suddenly gunshots sounded and from behind a rather large mound of earth a few yards from where he stood, someone jumped out and began firing for all he was worth.

Who was the idiot?

Allah! It was that hot headed Alavikutti. He had not been there when the strategy was being discussed last night. Alijan remembered him taking something from Mammad and slipping off.

Kazhutha! Alijan muttered.

It was too late. The White Army was on its guard. Initially they had seemed nonplussed, unable to decipher the source of the bullets but they soon spied the fellow shooting away like a maniac. There was no choice and some of the others had to come out of their hiding places too. Soon bullets were being fired from left and right, orchard and canal, hill and house. Alijan guessed that his men were confused. They probably thought this was a change of strategy. But by then the enemy had caught on. The Mapla fighters were suddenly blinded. Smoke bombs. And by the time the air cleared, Alijan found himself burying his face in his hands, they had set up their sophisticated machine guns. And the thunderous shots that followed! Alijan was sure they could be heard as far as Manjeri in the north and Malappuram in the south. He had to hand it to the lads. They were foolish but brave. Seeing that their own guns were ineffective, they leapt out with their daggers and swords severing several enemy heads.

Raziya

As soon as it was light enough she set off home lugging the bags of provisions. Benu Thatha would not hear of her wandering in the market place on a dangerous day like this. She did not approve of Raziya going home today either but couldn't say no as it had been Mammad's wish. So she had had a man kill a cock and pick out a few of the choicest coconuts and dehusk them. It was with these and a whole bag of rice that Raziya made her way home after so many days.

She smiled to herself, she was so glad of the way last night's adventure had turned out. It had been in a totally flummoxed, worried state that she had crept out into the orchard last night. What could she, all alone in the dark do to rescue the lady from someone like the Black Thangal? The question had loomed large in her mind but she knew she had to do something. Suspicion like a serpent had raised its head and she had truly begun to believe that Mammad had had something to do with the lady's capture. That he was actually a part of the Black Brigade that the whole of Ernad feared. She had simply had to try and make amends.

But now, it felt so good to know that she had been wrong. Not only had Mammad not had anything to do with the act but had been good hearted enough not to let his hatred for the Tirumulpad stand in his way. It was a relief to know that they had been able to save her in the nick of time. The thought of the Tirumulpad's lady shooting herself sent shivers down Raziya's spine. What happened to the other ladies she did not know. The Thangal's men had killed one of the young captives and the other, the lady's brother had been with them in the shack, but had suddenly disappeared. Mammad and the man who came out of nowhere had searched and searched when it was time to get into the cart. But he seemed to have vanished into thin air. They feared the brigands had got him.

Putting herself in Priyamvada's place, she supposed she would have done the same thing. What an ordeal the lady had suffered! Imagine being offered to someone as a prize! Raziya had never in her life heard anything as sinister as the Black Thangal's kind voice saying '*Paavam, paavam*'.

It was reassuring to know that the lady would be alright. The gentleman who had arrived in the middle of it all had bound the wound with Raziya's thattam and claimed the injury wasn't as deep as feared. She smiled to think that last night, for the first time in her life she had been without her *thattam*, outdoors and in the company of strange men. She would never have thought it possible but how trivial such things seemed in matters of life and death.

Raziya hadn't entered her house for weeks and when she turned the corner in the lane, it was the spider who came to mind. And sure enough as she opened the door and stepped into her home, a garland of cobwebs greeted her and the creature came scuttling out, another white egg fused to her belly. Raziya realised how much she had missed her. She talked to her friend to friend as she went about cleaning the kitchen and lighting the stove.

'We are two pregnant ladies here together aren't we?' She grinned conspiratorially as she squeezed the rich creamy milk out of the mounds of coconut she had shredded on to the large banana leaf. The fragrant rice was already boiling merrily in a pot she'd had to borrow from Cheeru next door for she hadn't one big enough to cook for so many people.

The cloves, cardamom and cinnamon that Benu Thatha's maid had bound up in a little pouch began to let off an aroma that not only filled the house but wafted out into the neighborhood as she roasted them and the neighborhood women began to drop in for a chat. Raziya talked and worked feeling truly happy for the first time in months.

Gunshots began to sound deafeningly. She and her friends put their fingers in their ears and smiled at each other, proud that their men were fighting bravely for the land. The walls began to shake and bits of lime plastering began to dust the floor. The spider dashed off into a crevice.

By the time the chicken bubbled in its roasted coconut gravy, the cacophony had nearly died down.

'It is almost over,' said one of the women.

'Our Maplas should be home soon,' said another.

Raziya sent them all to their homes to bring back pots. 'The thenga chor and the kootan are just about ready. I will pack it up for all of you. Then I'll have a bath and eat when he gets home.'

Mammad

The battle was lost.

Mammad surveyed the field with a sigh. The Taqbeer calls of his co fighters, now fallen, still rang in his ears. When Alijan Sahib called it off, it was a mere formality. From the corner of his eye he could see the enemy soldiers piling the corpses of some of his changathis into a truck. Others were kicked over irreverently.

The minute Alavikutti had made the mistake, Mammad had known it to be a lost cause. But he did not stop to think about the debacle. Nor did he pause to even blink at the sight of his *changathis* drop down by the dozen, falling prey to the monstrous machine guns. When a series of bullets pelted poor Alavikutti's chest, his own reacted with a piercing pain but he didn't turn his head in his friend's direction. He used the small pistol allotted to him to injure several and maybe kill some. When he ran out of bullets, he drew his dagger out. The fact that he knew it was pointless, did not stop him. The only time he was distracted from fighting was when the hordes of black clad fighters swarmed in from the depths of the orchard beyond. Those Pookottur Maplas left on the battle field had been perplexed. They did not know what to make of this. Were the Black Brigands friends or foes? Even as he fought, he kept an eye on their moves. It appeared to him that they were tearing into the White Army.

Now when the enemy was pulling back there were several dead brigands on the field too. They had fought well. When their cruelty was directed at laymen, it was terrifying but on the battle field fighting the enemy they were brave warriors too. Mammad himself had fought alongside one of them who had actually given him a gun seeing he had none. It was with this weapon that he had shot down the important White officer and jittered the enemy for a while.

Now he saw Alijan Sahib walk up to him slowly. His shoulders hunched and his neck rumalless. He was accompanied by the Thangal and the masked fellow who had given Mammad the gun.

Sahib patted Mammad on the back.

'Allah be with you my lad.' Mammad's response was a helpless nod and a feeble taqbeer.

'I hear your Raziya is keeping the thenga chor and kozhi curry warm for your lunch.'

'Thenga chor!' Mammad spat. 'Not a morsel shall I be able to swallow.'

'That my Mammad, is the truth. You shall eat no thenga chor today.' Alijan shook his head sadly.

'*Paavam, paavam*', whispered the Black Thangal in a voice as light as a feather. 'Mone, Sulfi,' he turned towards his lieutenant who had fought so bravely. 'Isn't it time to avenge your brother's mayyath?'

Before Mammad had the time to wonder what he meant, the man drew out his dagger and plunged it deep into his belly.

'Yes, Thangal uppappa.'

Mammad heard him agree softly as the unbearable pain gripped him for a second. Alijan Sahib's steely eyes fixed on his green ones as they fluttered shut.

What Followed

Ernad
26 to 29 August '21
The Black Thangal

Desperate times call for drastic actions.

A lesson learnt long, long ago when a gentle young man with an aesthetic soul grabbed a gun and shot a British officer with several people looking on. Not just one shot. Two, three, four, maybe more. He hadn't counted. When they bore the white suvar away, the fellow's back resembled a sieve. *Paavam, paavam.* He had pitied his victim for a moment but there was no stopping the young man after that.

But never more than eight decades of his life had the urgency in his kalbe been as pronounced as it was at the moment. As if time were running out and he had to do as much as he could as fast as he could. The pressing nature of his thoughts was translating into frantic strokes with the bit of charcoal which had turned his fingers as black as his robes. The walls of this room had once been white. As white as the young man's heart had been. Those on the north, east and west were almost completely covered in sketches and now he had started on the southern wall. If the Black Thangal's mind were a flat surface, this was what it would have looked like. The life he had lived, the world he had seen, the people he had known, the dreams he had dreamt, the ambitions he had nurtured, everything was depicted. No one in the camp knew that this was what the Thangal did in his spare time. Only Sulfi and Suleiman ever came in here.

As if on cue, Sulfi entered the room.

'Balyuppa!'

Though in public the boys called him Thangal uppappa like everyone else in the camp, when they were alone with him he was still their Balyuppa.

Sulfi's sudden appearance reminded him that Suleiman was gone. He glanced at one of the other walls where he had once made the silhouette of a man seen from the back. Two little boys sat on either shoulder leaning towards him and playing with his flapping turban. They were all faceless. His heart swelled with a near-paternal emotion that only Sulfi and Suleiman had ever triggered in him.

Sulfi knew that when the Thangal was doodling, he wouldn't talk. The lad retreated in silence and the Black Thangal's left hand in which he held the bit of charcoal began to move feverishly over the wall. In spite of his advanced years his brain had always remained as sharp as ever. This camp he had set up here was proof of that. The lads he trained were further evidence. A few years ago, he had masterminded an unbelievable escape from the prison across the sea. He knew that in the island and in Madras, the police were still looking for him and the boys. The camp had been a perfect camouflage and their identities remained unknown. No one ever suspected that the Black Thangal was a nonagenarian Mapla arrested and taken away by the police long ago in Mannarkad and imprisoned for years beyond the Black waters. This unit, he had engineered himself and dear Ali had kept the money flowing.

The Thangal was involved in every assignment he set for the senior fighters and even the progress of the novices did not go unnoticed. All this needed clear rational thinking. Even now as he doodled in a frenzy, the Thangal knew he was in full possession of his mental faculties. Why else would he realise the danger and fear it? If he were not sane enough, how would he be able to chart out such detailed plans of action for the coming days? It did not matter that the pictures flowing out of the fast diminishing piece of coal in his hands were beginning to look muddled. The serene bearded face his pencils had avoided for so many decades suddenly appeared on the wall now, floating on the churning waters of the Black seas. An Indian sepoy on horseback bearing a fierce expression on his mustachioed face was rushing at Sayippe who was holding up his hands helplessly. Only, the scene was set on the little bridge over the Plakkal canal. A dumb boy, drooling from the corner of his mouth was beheading a chicken…

If he could observe and note the disarray of his thoughts, there was no doubting his own lucidity…

When he had scribbled his heart out the results on the wall actually terrified the artist himself. He had to get away from these walls for a while.

Plans for the coming days had to be formulated and communicated. Now Suleiman's murder had been avenged, they would turn completely to their primary aim. Destroy the British. And anyone who helps or supports them. There would be no restraints this time. Man or woman, Hindu or Muslim, Government employee or common man. They would show no mercy. The Black Thangal would pump his fighters into every nook and corner of Ernad. There would be no limiting themselves to the night time. No rule against harming women. The lads would be let lose to wreak havoc as never before.

The British army had begun a slow retreat, savouring every moment. Taking pleasure out of destroying Mapla homes, killing the men, dishonouring the women. The Thangal's men would begin a parallel attack. Wiping out the whites and all those who backed them.

There was nothing left of the charcoal save the dust on his fingers. The Thangal stepped out of the room and sought Sulfi.

Benazir

She wished to visit the mourning families and offer her condolences. 'But Benazir Beewi,' said Kunhaishumma, 'that will be a hundred houses. You cannot do them all today.' She was right. Every other Muslim family in Pookottur had lost a loved one. Mothers were beating their breasts, shock had rendered widows too numb to cry and little children played on the muddy streets blissfully unaware that they would no more see their fathers and older brothers.

'But Raziya. I have to go to her. Will you accompany me, Aishumma?'

Alijan was lying back on his canvas backed easy chair. His face was drawn into a tight mask and there was no rumal around his neck. He hadn't had one on when he had come back a few hours ago and still hadn't bothered with another one. She was about to tell him that she was off to see young Raziya but decided against it. He had no desire for conversation. So she left with a little nod.

Raziya was not alone. Beeran was already there, sitting on the entrance steps. He glanced up as Benu and Kunhaishumma walked up to the house, immediately casting his eyes down as if he did not wish her to see his pain. His wife's sisters, Suhratha's younger daughters were inside with Raziya. Tears streamed freely down their cheeks but the young widow was dry eyed as Benu had somehow expected. The rich aroma of rice, coconut, chicken and spices pervaded the little house. Allah! Benu swallowed the lump in her throat remembering the joy on Raziya's face as she left Benazir Manzil this morning and sat down beside the girl on the innately carved teak bed.

'Benazir Beewi', Beeran came in. 'As you are here now, I shall go out for a while. I... I need to see to... to the,' his voice cracked a little, 'the mayyath,' he added under his breath as if he didn't wish Raziya to hear. 'H... his Umma... will be here soon. Someone has gone for her. Her sisters will look after her when she comes. But I am glad you came now. I am worried about this girl. Not a drop has she shed...' Mammad's old father shuffled out before he broke down.

For some reason the look on the bereaved old man's face reminded her of Alijan as he leaned back against the canvass backed chair as she got ready to leave the house. She did not understand the connection but the stream of thought was broken as Raziya clutched her hand. But it was the Pathiri woman the girl addressed,

'Umma, do me a favor please. There is plenty of thenga chor and kozhi curry in the kitchen. Please see that it does not go waste. Let it feed as many hungry bellies as possible now that he cannot eat it. I don't want it here when he comes... when they bring him in... will they bring him here, Thatha? Or will he be taken straight to the...?'

Kunhaishumma glanced Benu's way, as if to see if she approved and hobbled away. Benu patted Raziya's back. She had no answer to this question. News had it that most bodies were not even being retrieved from the battle field. They said the enemy soldiers carted them away to be dumped irreverently somewhere. She had no idea if Mammad would be found. She should have spoken to Alijan about it. He had been there. He ought to know where the boy had fallen.

The Pathiri woman was away for more than an hour. In the meanwhile some people had come in to offer their condolences. Not too many, for most neighborhood families had their own tragedies to deal with. Mammad's Umma had arrived and there was a fresh bout of tears as her sisters rushed to her side. They had drawn Raziya into their huddle when Benu looked out of the window and saw Kunhaishumma outside. She was back with a couple of men and was leading them to the kitchen. Benu decided to step out for a few minutes to give the family some private grieving time. A few feet away, Mammad's elderly Hindu neighbor was conferring with one-armed Pakkaran and a relatively young Mapla who had sustained injuries on his limbs. One of the survivors, Benu guessed.

'Poor Mammad, to fall prey to the white man's bullet,' the old neighbor mourned.

'And his wife with child,' said Pakkaran.

'But it was not the white man's bullet that killed Mammadkka,' exclaimed the young Mapla.

Pakkaran and the old man stared wide eyed. 'Then?'

'I saw the whole thing. I had just dragged the mayyaths of Mammali and Alavikutti behind a mound of sand. So that they wouldn't take them away in the lorry, I saw it happen with my very eyes. It was no sayippe but the Black Thangal's man. He plunged his dagger into Mammadkka's belly. The Thangal was there too, egging him on. '*Paavam, paavam*', he said very softly but I could hear him clearly enough, 'Mone Sulfi, isn't it time to avenge your brother's mayyath'? And yes. Our Sahib was there too. That was what I couldn't figure out. He said something about thenga chor and kozhi curry to Mammadkka before the fellow killed him. Now that's exactly what I smell here, in the house.' His expression was puzzled as he sniffed the air.

Mathu

Their forest days were drawing to a close. Now that the Maplas were weakened by the battle, it was considered safe to venture out. As soon as it could be arranged, maybe tomorrow, they would leave for Thangam's *tharawud* where a whole mansion was being prepared for their use. The best decision considering that Priya was recuperating there. Mithran would want to be with her of course and she, the Matriarch, would not let him out of her sight for a while. Priya's recovery was sure to be quicker with Sethu there. So all in all they would stick together for a while. Some of the men would return to Nilambur of course. Later on, if possible, they would move away from Malabar for a while. She had to admit the family had adapted well but there was no denying they had been through much and they needed a change. Trishur may be. She thought of the exodus of Muthasshi Amma's childhood when Tipu had driven them from home. They had spent months in the State of Kochi. It must have been worse then, the acts of savagery. But, truly speaking, things were more complicated now, thought Mathu. Tipu was nothing but an offender in their minds, an outsider whom it was easy to hate. That was hardly the case today. The local Maplas were a part of their lives. Mathu for one could not cast them as clear cut villains. They were human too with human emotions and human problems and the human tendency to do wrong. What was happening now was horrendous. But the Matriarch, when she was not blinded by her love for her own, knew well that the Maplas of Malabar were a true-hearted ilk. There were people taking advantage of them. Stray individuals from their own midst and the national leaders with their own aims. A typical case of prodding the baby monkey to scratch about in a plate of rice and mess it up so that it gets all the blame and those who actually encouraged it come out clean. The Maplas were as much the victims as they were villains.

The Matriarch ached secretly when the image of Mammad lying dead on the battle field came to mind. Of course she did not share her grief with anyone for they would be shocked. The Kovilakam camp was silently celebrating the death of the traitor who had brought the pack of wolves to the Kovilakam, killed Divakaran, hurt the others and turned their lives upside down. If they knew she mourned him, they would think her unbalanced in her old age. It was only dear Eli who would have understood. Mathu craved the company of her friend.

Then this morning they had received a detailed letter from The Outcaste, describing what he had seen that night on his way back with the English women in tow. Some of them still suspected Beeran but the letter had reconfirmed what the old driver had told them. It was indeed Priya who had rescued her from that fiend they called the Black Thangal and killed his main lieutenant. It was a big risk he had taken for the Black Thangal was clearly not one to take such blows lightly.

She prayed that Mithran had put aside his abhorrence of the poor boy and seen him in a redeeming light.

As for the English women from the estate who had spent a few days with them in the forest camp were safely on their way to their people in the Nilgiris. The Outcaste had enclosed a letter from the younger Madama to Sethu.

All for the best, sighed Mathu and rose from her chair set under the big tree to get rid of the bunch of silver strands that came away one by one as she finger combed her hair and loosened the knots.

She dropped the little twist of hair behind a bush. She would make her way to the shelter and go about her evening prayers. She looked around for someone to carry her chair in and gave a small gasp of pain as something pricked her foot. A thorn. The Matriarch had to smile again. Vettekkaran was teasing her by doling out yet another taste of forest rigours.

The Black Thangal

He glanced at his fingers, the only part of his anatomy

other than his eyes, not covered in black. He examined the gap between them. Things seemed to be slipping through them.

The British army had receded. The lads had succeeded in killing several of the soldiers and policemen. Some white but most them ass licking back stabbing locals. But in turn they were falling into the hands of the police themselves. The license to loosen the discipline had made the lads reckless. The young recruit called Beerankutti who had been progressing so well was nabbed after setting fire to a police station. Kasim, one of his senior men and a whole lot of young tyros were taken away after marching into a Hindu temple, killing the priest and anointing the piece of stone they called God with his blood. A group of the younger trainees, Abdullakutti, Kochappu and some others, given a free hand for the first time had gone about molesting the women in two households in the same neighborhood. They had been so rough that one of the women died. For the first time in his life the Black Thangal did not frown upon such deeds. There was no place for scruples anymore.

But the police, hundred percent vigilant now, waiting to pounce upon Muslims at the slightest provocation had nabbed Abdullakutti and his mates as well. Some of these policemen were Muslims themselves, traitors to the faith who couldn't see that what the boys were doing was for the good of the land.

It was not just his men. Other sons of Islam all over the land were being arrested. Even those who had done nothing for the cause.

Paavam, paavam…

The Thangal peered at his fingers again and again.

It wouldn't be long before they got him. He was nearly ninety. Death was anyway round the corner. But he didn't wish to die at the hands of the filthy sayippes and their Hindu side kicks. He refused to. At the same time he couldn't afford to waste a minute. He would kill the whole lot before dying himself. The white men were out of the area by now. But he would go for all those who stood by them… that would mean all the Hindus he could get his hands on. Even the Muslims who had turned traitors… he would make them confess to their crimes and then punish them. They would each die a deserving death.

Paavam, Paavam.

He inspected his fingers once more, twisting them this way and that… no one would slip out of his hands…

'Mone, Sulfi!'

It was time to organise things.

Where was Sulfi? Wasn't he back yet? He had been gone the whole day and half the previous night. Out on a mission. But now it was nearly sundown. Where was he?

'Sulfi!'

'Balyuppa?'

'You are back? Allah! Praise be with you.'

On a barren hillside between Thuvvur and Karuvaramkund, not far from the Black Thangal's lair was a well. He stood under a solitary tree, surveying the line of people who cowered before him. Their hands were tied behind their backs.

One by one, they stepped forward. One of his trainees stood by reciting the charge against the fellow.

'Do you confess?'

'No… spare me… I did none of that.'

'Didn't you?' The Thangal's voice was as light as a soft breeze.

The man shivered and screamed as a whip landed on his back. Again and again.

'I confess. I confess.'

'Good. You shall be punished for your crime. Bend over.' Another one of the Thangal's men held him down. The Executioner took a step forward. The accused didn't see the long blade swing. It sliced into the back of his neck.

'Well done, Sulfi my boy.'

In one swift move the dead man was dumped into the well. His body went in first. The head was tossed in carelessly later.

'*Paavam, paavam.*' The Black Thangal condoled even as the next man was pushed forward.

This man was the first of many.

He had reached up to sixty-three before he had stopped… counting.

The well, hewn out of solid rock, had no wall around it or it could have held more of these traitors.

The Petition

Ernad,
31 August -1 September '21
The Outcaste

Shekharan Nair had never seemed so out of sorts. 'Was he ill?' It was two days after the Pookottur battle. I had gone over to see Mrs Eaton and her mother off to Ootacamund. It had taken him an extra day to arrange their transport because of the general tension in the area. The roads were not in a condition to be used considering the number of trees the rioters had felled across it and the broken bridges. They had had to wait a couple of days. Then a car and an armed policeman to escort them had been arranged. It was only after the ladies were on their way with a policeman specially appointed to escort them, that I noticed Shekharan Nair looking a bit wan.

He invited me to have lunch with him and had his wife set a plateful of avil laced with coconut and jaggery shavings in front of me as Nair himself picked on his own meal as if his heart wasn't in it. I wondered how Shekharettan came to know that this was my staple food. At home I had it for breakfast and even lunch and dinner whenever I managed to escape the watchful eyes of my mother and step mother. Sometimes I added a banana.

'Is something the matter, Shekharetta? You do seem a little under the weather.'

'I am glad you asked,' he said and paused as if organising his thoughts. 'I am tired, my friend. Tired of all this that's going on.' 'We all are, Shekharetta, but we have to bear it while it lasts.' 'But... but I feel responsible,' his voice was almost inaudible. 'When the Congress joined hands with the Khilafat... when after Bapu and the Ali brothers came to Manjeri last year and called for unity... I never thought it would amount to all that. I should have known better. Trying to rope the local Mapla lads... I am beginning to think it was a big, big mistake. No one in the Congress knows them as I do. I grew up among them. I ought to have expected this... I could have prevented it...'

'No you couldn't. The tide would have swept you off. Your intentions were good. Leave it at that.'

But Shekharan Nair refused to be consoled. He was determined to try and make amends in some way and kept racking his brains.

Mathu

Had she grown so accustomed to the ways of the jungle that civilised life felt alien? The upholstered chair felt strange. Thangam's *tharawad* with its huge compound, numerous houses and modern amenities, was far plusher than the Kovilakam. Her doctor son, an image of his father, Mathu's nephew, even went around in one of those new-fangled motor cars.

They were magnificent hosts, genuinely honored to have the Kovilakam people to stay. They ought to have come sooner, Thangam said. Wouldn't agree when the Matriarch replied that at the time, the forest was the safest place. She felt that her daughter might have thought twice before embarking on her crazy adventure if Sethu Thampatti had been there. That, Mathu had to concur with. She would have liked to see the reckless lass. But she would have to wait till she was well enough to come to her. It wouldn't do for the Matriarch to go into their personal quarters and visit the girl in her room upstairs. Well, she was going to be alright, and that was one thing less to worry about, sighed Mathu, absently rubbing the sole of her sore foot.

Since her arrival here there had been several callers to see her.

Beeran had come. A ghost of his old self. Mathu found herself lacking the right words to say to him.

'Baliya Thampatti, he has hurt you all badly. But he is gone now. I beg you not to think ill of him. Not to curse his memory.'

She found it difficult to breathe let alone reply. But in her sharp exhalation, Beeran read the ache she felt.

'I don't mean to cause you more pain, Thampatti, but the girl worries so. She is with child you know.'

'Her child shall have all my blessings if that is any comfort. Beeran, I wish to see her. Would you bring her to me while I am here?;

A brief visit, sad and quiet.

The local Congress leaders also came. It was not often that the Kovilakam Matriarch met with strangers. But they had specifically requested. Mithran, more at ease now, had brought them to the sitting room she now used. She had been trying to examine her tender foot as she was doing now when he came in and announced that Shekharan Nair and his colleagues were here and wished to pay their respects. She had seen no reason to refuse. And indeed she had to admit she was curious about the information they would bring. Staying at an influential Nair tharawad had its benefits. Lots of people dropped in. People who had been around and the old Anachevi Mathu with her thirst for news rejoiced. Mithran, Bhaskaran, now fully recovered from the dagger wound, and Thankam's middle son, Vijayan Menon came in with them. Along with Shekharan Nair and his two junior colleagues was Narayana Menon, the senior police officer who had been there when the Maplas gheraoed Mithran in his manor. Madhavan Nair, who was the Congress Secretary was to have come too, Shekharan Nair said but he had been called to Kozhikode on an urgent business.

After the initial exchanges, enquiries about the safety of the second Tirumulpad who was a well-known personage in the parts and a Congress supporter, the men began speaking among themselves. She wondered with a silent chuckle, if they had forgotten her presence as men often did with women, however senior or respected they happened to bc. Mathu did not mind. She widened her ears and absorbed all the tidbits they threw around. Not pleasant conversation topics. Especially when they went into detail. Another reason for the Matriarch to think that they had forgotten a woman was in their midst. But she wanted to hear. She needed to. This was what the whole land was experiencing, she did not wish to be protected from the knowledge.

The policeman, Narayana Menon said he had been lying low for a while after a gang of Mapla marauders appeared one day, threatening to burn his house down and he had escaped by the skin of his teeth. The others warned him not to get too complacent. The police were the rioters' biggest foes.

Countless people had been forced to convert. Mathu shuddered as Muthasshi Amma's stories about slicing off unmentionables rang in her ears. These poor people had had their heads shaven and forced to wear those caps. Even the women had to don the costumes of the Ummachis. If they resisted the rebels thought nothing of chopping off their heads instead of their hair. Several who feared for their lives had surrendered meekly.

It was apparently not just the poorer and weaker

sections of society they targeted.

At some stage the conversation moved on to brutality against women and though Mathu cringed she inwardly, she didn't show it.

There was this lady in a Nair tharawad in Melattur. A family many of them seemed to know.

'God! Imagine their plight!' One of the men said with his eyes shut. 'The attackers stripped her and took turns at having their way with her. And would you believe it! The men in the family were there while all this was happening and tied up as they were, helpless. All her brothers and even her husband.' 'Krishnan Menon, one of her brothers who escaped their clutches did come and meet me to try and register a complaint,' said Narayana Menon, the police officer. 'But what do you think I can do in a time like this?'

'A race who is believed to respect women! They have apparently put aside those principles for a while.'

'There is this incident which I believe happened in the Pullangode Estates. A pregnant tribal girl was killed on a public road and… and… her stomach was torn open. Witnesses say she was found on the deserted road with the foetus hanging out. Looked like a skinned chicken, it seems.'

There was silence for a few minutes as the men fought nausea.

It was Mathu who shut her eyes now. Pullangode Estates. Pregnant tribal girl. There had been one such girl with the English ladies. Sethu said it was she who had brought them safely to the forest. Mathu remembered her well enough. She came to Kovilakam camp on and off to spend time with her mistresses. Then she suddenly stopped coming. They said she had died a tragic death. To think this was what happened to her.

Then the conversation turned to the most recent and most horrendous act of all. This was the first the Matriarch had heard of it. It happened a couple of nights ago in the village of Tuvvur that she knew lay somewhere between Pookottur and Nilambur. Nearly a hundred houses in the village and the neighboring ones, were surrounded by the fiends in black. The attackers marched into the homes and dragged people out, tied up their hands and feet. The houses were set ablaze. Scores of people were marched to the well.

'The Well of Death, it will come to be known in the years to come,' said one of the men in starched white.

'Where exactly is this,' Bhaskaran wished to know.

'It is not far from Pangod. Midway between Tuvvur and Karuvaramkund. There is a bare stretch of land called Palurkuzhiparambu. The well is situated there beneath a small hill.'

This was where the prisoners were taken. The leader of these black clad demons sat under a tree and acted Master of ceremonies. By him stood two assistants and an Executioner. This was information gathered from the few who managed to flee the scene.

'I saw the well once when I passed that way,' said Shekharan Nair. 'It is not a well in the proper sense. The sides are cut in hard laterite. There are no walls or steps leading down. Neither a well nor a pool. It was in this hole that they were thrown. Dead and half dead. One on top of the other. Scores of them.'

Mithran's face had gone white at the mention of this black clad villain. It was Bhaskaran who asked, 'Who exactly is this man?'

'Well, the truth is that no one knows,' replied Narayana Menon. 'They call him the Black Thangal. There are lots of speculations on this. People keep saying this and that but his identity is still a mystery.'

'I have heard that it is the Thangal of Chambrasseri,' said Vijayan Menon. 'The man who they say actually skinned someone alive. Any truth in that?'

That is Kunhikoya Thangal,' the policeman said. 'But the story about the flaying, that is not true, I know that much. I did make enquiries at the time.'

'Some say it is not this man but his cousin. An Imbichikoya Thangal,' said another man.

Mathu found all this discussion about the villain's identity going over her head.

A sense of dejection settled like a dark cloud over her thoughts. After all she was the Matriarch of one of the largest and most influential families of Malabar. Was there no way she could put an end to all this, instead of sitting here listening to the men talk endlessly?

'If the Senior Thampatti agrees, it might have some good result', Shekharan Nair's words brought her back to the conversation though she had lost the thread.

'Thampatti,' repeated Nair noting her blank expression. 'As I was saying, we Congress workers here, like the rest of Malabar are so full of sorrow. We wish to do something from our side.' Mathu nodded. That, she could relate to.

'We have had a meeting about this and we all felt that it needs to be brought to the attention of the highest level of authority in the country. And today, that, whether we like it or not, is the Viceroy. Though some papers outside India have been reporting the incidents, we don't know how seriously they have taken it up there. The Viceroy has the executive and legislative council under him. If he can't put a stop to it, who can? It is time he got an accurate picture and the information has to be first hand. It has to come from us and in detail.'

Mathu leaned back in her chair. She had been sitting upright for a long time.

Vijayan, Thangam's son guessed the man was taking too long. Not wishing to tire his elderly relative, he took over.

'Thampatti,' like everyone in his family, he addressed his father's aunt by her title. 'This letter, everyone thinks that it will strike a chord if it is from you. From you on behalf of all the ladies in Malabar. If it is addressed to the Viceroy's wife. Woman to woman. The majority opinion is that it would be more likely to have the desired effect if it is done that way.' He waited for her to say something.

The men had obviously spent some time over this for a letter had already been drafted. They read it out to her. Vijayan read the original English and for her own benefit, carefully translated every sentence to Malayalam. It was addressed to *Her Gracious Excellency, the Countess of Reading*. Mathu knew no English but she had a feel for the way it sounded on a person's tongue. She didn't understand a word till they interpreted it but she did sense that Thangam's son, having spent a couple of years in the land of the sayippes, had learnt to speak their language just as he did his own. *It was a humble memorial,* he read, *from the bereaved and sorrow stricken women of Malabar.*

Mathu listened in silence. She had to admit the letter was well written, if slightly groveling in certain parts. As it was meant for an English lady who had never set foot in Malabar, it explained the history of the Mapla's tendency for agitation and violence. For over one hundred years this has been going on, indicated the letter. Yes, Mathu knew the outbreaks kept recurring every few years. Sometimes it assumed horrible proportions. She had seen it with her own eyes as a child during the aborted Guruvayoor trip. She shuddered inwardly as she remembered their cries of *Benam, benam mayyathe*. She glanced at Mithran as she remembered her debate with him during Pattu. The massive eighty percent rent hike. Denying the poor tenants and landless laborers, most of them Maplas of their already meagre income. This kind of thing in some form or the other had been going on for a century too. Maybe more. Her attention was drawn back to the Vijayan's voice explaining the petition.

They had not minced words in explaining the present

situation. *Wells and tanks filled up with mutilated and half dead people. Corpses of pregnant women left on roadsides and in jungles with unborn babies protruding out of their bellies, feeding babies, torn from their mothers' breasts and slaughtered mercilessly.* This Lady Reading was told of it all. And of *husbands, fathers, brothers and sons, tortured, flayed, burnt alive…*

The combined voices of the women of Malabar rang in her ears and she was one of them as they lamented their *sisters taken away forcibly from their families and subjected to every shame and outrage possible* like the fate that Priyamvada had so narrowly escaped. Homesteads looted and reduced to cinder-mounds. And the sacrilege in places of worship. Idols broken to bits, stomped on or else their flower garlands replaced with the entrails of slaughtered cows…

The Malabar women did not seek vengeance but compassion. The Matriarch liked that.

'You know that we write the truth, Thampatti,' said the congressman Nair. 'We request you to sign this letter, on behalf of all the women..'

Sethu

At first Priya wouldn't even talk to her. When the Kovilakam party first reached here, Sethu had rushed to see her friend as soon as she could but the other girl had turned towards the wall and stayed that way till Sethu had no choice but to leave the room.

Guilt and shame were eating at her, worse than the

pain from her self-inflicted gunshot wound. On seeing Sethu, the feelings had sharpened. She knew Priya and could clearly see what was going on in her mind. Though she left quietly enough that first day, she persisted on visiting Priya in her room and bringing her around. Though pale from loss of blood, she was beginning to look better and her brother, the doctor had permitted her to leave her bed and sit up on a chair in her room sometimes. Sethu made an unsaid pact with her not to ask her any questions. Instead she kept the conversation light and casual as if nothing had changed. This, Sethu noticed was a technique the Kovilakam people all employed.

Beeran brought Raziya in to see Ammamma. The poor girl, she had lost so much too. Sethu remembered her story about a Muslim girl modelled on Raziya. She would write a sequel to it someday. And it would be rich in detail for unlike the Kovilakam relatives Raziya had no reservations. She was grieving but she allowed herself the comfort of talking. She came to terms with her loss that way. Sethu had spent some time with her and the girl would not stop talking about her Mammad. Sethu learned from her everything that happened the night before he died. Of how she had suspected him and set off to rescue Priya. How Priya had shot herself. Of how unnatural and sinister the Black Thangal had seemed. Sethu found herself recoiling inwardly when she thought of her cousin in the midst of all that.

Sethu had let Priya know that Raziya was there. She

knew her cousin felt a deep bond with her after that night. But there was no way her brother would allow her to tackle the stairs and come down to meet the cart driver's daughter in law. Priya indicated the wooden chest in the corner and Sethu opened it for her. Inside was a jewel box which she handed to her cousin. Priya pulled out fistfuls of necklaces and bangles.

'Tell her this is not in any way an attempt to recompense what she and her husband did for me. It is the only way I can apologise for the sufferings I caused them.'

Raziya accepted the gift after a glance at Beeran for permission. Ammamma gave her more gold and money and made her promise to bring Mammad's baby to her after it was born.

'We have all suffered, Kutti,' Ammamma told her, a burst of warmth making her forget that it wasn't appropriate to address the Muslim girl in such familiar terms. 'And we have all caused suffering. Now we put it behind us and move on.' Tears flowed freely from Beeran's eyes into his straggly beard.

The contents of the petition had been discussed in the house and Sethu knew what it was about. The men seemed to think it was extremely well worded and gave an accurate picture of the outrage, and was sure to melt the heart of the Viceroy's wife. To think of other women experiencing so much of agony for no fault of theirs, was sure to arouse compassionate feelings in her. They expected her to use her influence on the Viceroy and motivate him to do something quick and definite to put an end to it. Good ploy. But the Viceroy and his wife were miles and miles away, the distance being not just physical. Could they get to the bottom of the trouble? Sethu thought of Amma's foot and the thorn that had been lodged in foot, causing her to limp, how she had carefully removed it with the help of another thorn. Would they be able to identify the particular thorn lodged in the flesh of Malabar? To extract it quickly and gently with minimum bloodshed and damage in the surrounding areas. Meaning, thought Sethu coming back to reality and casting aside the metaphors, the atrocities that the renegades were committing should be stopped as soon as possible. Much harm had already been done, the land could not bear the burden of more. The Hindus of Malabar should be left alone to live peacefully and slowly recover from their losses. At the same time, as the petition reportedly said, revenge or punishment was not the aim. The Maplas had been through a lot over the years, the innocent among them should come to no harm either. Too much to hope for, considering all, but it had to be achieved to the largest extent possible. Could a petition to the Viceroy's wife alone do that? The Maplas, from what she had begun to understand of them, had kind hearts underneath all this hot blooded passion and anger. Shouldn't we be appealing to that kindness within them?

Approaching the Maplas directly, appealing to them… it all sounded fine. But it was not one or two or even a small group of them. Their population, she remembered Mithrettan mention once was a lot more than that of the Hindus. If there was one person who could be approached, who would that be?

The prospect of actually doing something excited her. There was no way, her grandmother could. Not at her age when it was difficult to ignore the pressures of society and the norms she was used to. No, certainly, Ammamma couldn't walk up to some Mapla kingpin whoever he was and appeal for peace.

But she, Sethu could.

If possible, woman to woman…

She felt exhilarated. She would do it? But not without help. She wondered whom she could trust enough to open up about this. Sethu racked her brains even as her young cousins created a din chasing each other up and down the long veranda and some of the older ones clung to the railings watching the front courtyard which was always a busy place with visitors to the *tharawad* coming and going, making remarks about the people they saw. A fresh burst of giggles and whispers from the adolescent girls made Sethu turn absently and the glance at the courtyard below. The Outcaste had just walked in.

A Surrender And A Dream Realised

Pookottur, Ernad
5– 6 September '21
Alijan

Alijan Sahib was an unhappy man. This duniya was a bleak and miserable place. For one, the battle was lost. It wasn't in the least pleasant having to surrender before that man McEnroy, but they were left with little choice. Those cursed Lewis guns! That blasted ass Alavikutti! Besides, Suleiman was dead. For so many years, he had not seen his sons. It was just over a year ago that they managed to escape the colonial prison and make their way back across the sea. Even during that one year, Ikka and the boys lived a clandestine life. Alijan and Benu could not acknowledge their sons or enjoy their company. Poor Benu knew nothing of what had happened after they were taken away years ago by that hateful policeman. But at least she had accepted their loss long ago. Suleiman's mayyath would not hurt her now. But it was different for him, thought Alijan. Now Ikka had cast aside all secrecy and thrown caution to the winds. What would become of him? Of Sulfi? Alijan Sahib had never allowed personal grief or anxiety to hold him down, but today, he was a broken man. A man who was losing everything he cared for, one after the other. His ambitions of a kingdom where all governance would be his to control, no longer seemed possible. It did not feel good to be suppressed by the white swine and the local traitors. The kingdom he had erected in his dreams had crumbled. The army he had assembled and trained, the army he had invested everything in had disintegrated with all the Pookottur Maplas having either died or surrendered. He could not fight alone. The way Ikka was acting now.

Benu... at least he still had her. Her love and support was his biggest strength. The power he banked on. While she was there for him, Alijan would never give in.

He set off for the Black Thangal's lair. He knew where the camp was located but never had he set foot in there. When the secret, camouflaged unit was set up deep in the woods, the understanding had been that never would Alijan's connection with the mysterious Black Brigade be known. But today he was breaking that pact. When he tackled the Thangal, he wanted to be one up and take him by surprise. So, the minute his cart was out of the premises of Benazir Manzil, he pulled on a Black cloak and mask of his own. Pakkaran, his faithful one-armed driver turned back to ask him something and shock registered in his eyes when he saw Alijan thus attired.

'Say, not a word, Pakkara,' his own voice sounded different. Unlike his own raspy croak, what came out of his lips was the light, silky tones, so typical of the Black Thangal. Pakkaran looked ready to scream. 'Shut that mouth and keep driving'.

Once inside the Thangal's camp he climbed out of the cart, unwound a length of rope from his waist and bound Pakkaran tightly to the spokes of the cart's wheel. He didn't want the fellow fleeing in fear and confusion. He needed the ride back. Pakkaran lay crumpled on the ground by the cart, whimpering, 'Sahibe…Sahibe', as Alijan walked away. For the first time, he surveyed the project he had sponsored. He sensed something shaky in the air. Things, he knew were not functioning as before. Many of the Thangal's fighters had fallen into the hands of the authorities and those who remained were out running wild. The camp looked deserted. Only the very young recruits could be seen walking about. He caught sight of an identical pair of youngsters practicing sword moves behind a tree. He made a hissing noise and when they looked up he crooked a finger. Because of his black cloak and mask, they didn't realise he was an outsider.

'Where can I find the Thangal'? He asked as they approached. Now they were on their guard. No inmate of the camp would ask such a question. Everyone here knew that a pair of young tyros wouldn't be expected to know where Thangaluppappa was. Only the most senior fighters were supposed to know where the chief's quarters were.

'Who are you'? One of the boys asked with a wary frown and his twin gripped the hilt of his sword to attack if the need arose. Alijan was well aware that only a select inner circle were privy to information about the Thangal's whereabouts. But boys, curious by nature, were bound to snoop around. These little fellows were unlikely to be completely clueless.

Silently, he reached inside his cloak, drew out the pistol and proceeded to caress it gently.

'Er… we may be able to show you. But we can't be sure, of course,' he chuckled as they lead him through the grounds to a small, isolated building, pointed their chins in its direction and fled.

The Black Thangal had his back to door and did not see Alijan push it open. He was adding subtle strokes to the picture on the wall, his head tilted to one side to view his work from another angle. Alijan too peered at the drawing in progrcss and it took him a while to understand what was depicted. It appeared to be a long javelin, held aloft by silhouette figures. On its sharp end was propped a head. The features looked familiar. He recognized the face of their arch nemesis, the Inspector, from their Mannarkkad days, now retired.

He must have reacted audibly for the Black Thangal turned around.

'Alikutti! Eeyyo?'

'Yes, Ikka. It is Ali.'

'I certainly didn't expect you here,' the Thangal sighed. 'But policies have gone to the dogs. There is no reason why you should be expected to adhere to them.'

'And where does that leave us in the end, Ikka?'

'The end…' the Black Thangal turned away from Alijan to focus on his sketch again. ' I prefer to talk about the beginning…'

Of the Yatim Khana. Of Uppuppa, the warden, the other boys… Of how as a boisterous toddler of two, you were brought to the orphanage after your whole family had fallen to British brutality. Just as mine had, mused the Thangal. It was a story Alijan knew well enough considering he had heard it from Uppuppa as a child and later from Ikka himself as they lay on their coir cots under the open skies in Meerut and Muzaffarpur and later Aligarh, with poor Aimutti snoring next to them.

'Ikka…

The Black Thangal held his hand up without turning his attention from the wall, adding yet another light stroke to the creases around the wicked policeman's eyes, improving the likeness. 'Don't try to stop me, Alikutti. Allow an old man this pleasure. I was but ten then and they entrusted you to my care. Aimutti came a few months later. Poor, dumb bastard. From the day he arrived he followed you about all day and cried if he wasn't allowed to sleep on your mat at night. And I ended up caring for him as well. In those days, I knew the meaning of love for its own sake. Of brotherhood… I knew how to feel every emotion deeply. That was how I learnt to draw.'

'Then one day, Kadarkka turned up. I did not understand why but I felt as if I was swimming in an ocean of pure happiness. You boys at the Yatim Khana had always been my world. But that changed. What I felt for Kadarkka was so different, so all consuming… he would pour his heart out to me. Tell me of his youth when certain distinct ideas had begun to take shape in his mind. He used to talk to small crowds of people about the need to be free of white supremacy. He started nursing dreams of making this possible. He told me about those dreams, Alikutti. The hopes he'd had for a future. A future with a boy called Mohammed by his side. Mohammed. I remember how I myself began to feel about this stranger. I loved him with the same passion that Kadarkka did. I also hated him for fear that Kadarkka loved him more than he did me… till he told me about what happened to Mohammed. It was a public yogam in Ponnani . Kadarkka was addressing a sparse crowd and Mohammed was with him. He had actually succeeded in stirring something in the minds of his scanty audience when the British police rode in and began to arrest the speakers. There was a Namboodiri among them and a Nair. They opened fire and Mohammed flung himself in front of Kadarkka, shielding him from the shower of bullets, taking them all himself. Numb and hand cuffed, Kadarkka had had to step over that beloved, blood soaked form as the police dragged him away. That was how Kadarkka went to jail and spent years there till he escaped and came to the Yatim khana where he would be safe from the police. When he left, I thought he would never be back. But he was. There were rumours about the murder of the Collector. But I didn't care that Kadarkka was involved.'

'But, Alikutti, Mohammed was a better man than I was and... Allah! His love for Kadarkka must have been greater than mine. For when my turn came, I was unable to save him from the white bastards. Instead he gave himself up to protect me...'

The Black Thangal let his charcoal pencil drop on the floor and slumped down.

'Ikka. Stop it. I don't know why you are doing this to yourself now.'

'I must do it, Alikutti. I must,' he attempted to rise but failed. 'Though ineffective, the first constructive thing I did was to shoot that swine, Ross. Two years later, in Muzaffarpur, while you were already busy earning money, I got together with Waris Ali and the rest in inducing the Danapur Sepoys to rebel against the Whites...'

Alijan could do nothing to stop him. He went on and on about everything he had done against the British. He still sat on the floor in an awkward crouching posture and his eyes were blank. He panted as he spoke but wouldn't pause for breath.

'And when you decided that you wanted to come back to Malabar and look for your Munjathi, I chose to come with you. All my education in North India, all the men I had met there could not hold me back. You and

Aimutti were my family. I couldn't live without you. I know your Benu loved Aimutti like a brother but she did not care for me. Especially when she saw Suleiman and Sulfi getting attached to me. She is a clever girl. She knew right from the start that I was not like all men. She saw me as unnatural and I think she feared me…'

'Alikutti…' he turned to the drawing. The vacant expression in his eyes turned maniacal as the pupils darted from one corner of the eye to another. 'I want that head on a spear. Just like that. That traitor… that licker of the white suvar's dirty boots… the bastard who murdered poor Aimutti and took us away, ruining the boys' lives.' The Thangal's breath was fast as he frantically looked around the room he pointed to something long and thin in a corner. 'That's my harpoon. Bring it here, mone.' Alijan had to obey. 'I want the bastard's head at the end of my harpoon. Just like that.' He glanced at the wall again. 'Will you do it for me?'

'I will do it Ikka. I shall bring you the head. It will not take me long. Just enough time to get to Anakayam and back.'

Ikka shook his head slowly. 'I won't be here when you get back. You know, it is time the Black Thangal surrendered.'

'Ikka! Surrender to the British? After all you have done?'

'No. Never to the suvars. I shall surrender to you. You, Alijan, shall render the blow that finishes the Black Thangal once and for all so that they can never get at him. And no one shall know my whereabouts. The Black Thangal shall remain a mystery forever. A hundred years later people shall still talk about the enigmatic Thangal who fought the white swine and their local sidekicks, the kafirs who would not stay loyal to the followers of Allah. But they will not know who he was. Yes, mone, the Black Thangal chooses to die at your hands.' He slid to floor and lay there curled up in fetal posture, muttering '*Paavam, paavam*'.

By the time Alijan got back to Benazir Manzil it was late and he had committed five murders with his own hands, all in a day. First he had laid his beloved Jawad Ikka to rest. Then came the twin boys at the camp. He had needed assistance making the Black Thangal's remains disappear forever and they had been too scared to refuse. He could not let them live to tell the tale. Then one armed Pakkaran, untied from the wheel, still blubbering in fear was made to drive him to Anakkayam where the retired police inspector's head was soon left in the empty market square, propped up on Ikka's harpoon, for everyone to find when the sun rose the next day. A few yards away from the compound of Benazir Manzil, Alijan ordered Pakkaran to stop. And with the rope he had earlier used to bind him to the wheel, he hung the disabled fellow by the neck on a nearby branch.

He was so tired that all he wanted to do was go to sleep with Benu's comforting form by his side.

Benu

The sun was barely up when Benu rose, careful not to wake Alijan. When he got home in the night, she was not sure. She had pretended to be asleep, not wanting to start a conversation. After so many years of togetherness, he felt like a different man. He even smelt like a different man, Benu had thought as he settled down on his side of the bed with a sigh of 'Allah!'

The woman who came in early to cook their meals would not be here for at least an hour. So, as a treat to herself, she made a glass of suleimani tea with all the fixings. She took her time brewing it, crushing the cardamom and cinnamon sticks in the mortar and letting the spices infuse in boiling water along with the black tea leaves. She didn't even leave out the saffron which normally went in only during the perunal or other festivities. And a final twist of lemon.

Carefully straining it into a silver tumbler, she took it to the ante room off the kitchen and sat down on the wooden seat. As the hot, sweet and sour brew seeped in, her legs began to swing and a new day dream spread out its wings. She was so engrossed in it that she didn't notice that the sun now shone through the wooden bars of the window. Nor did she hear the clatter of pots and pans as the cook proceeded with her preparations for the first meal of the day.

'Ah my Benu!'

She nearly jumped.

'Did I scare you, my Ponne? Allah! Is that a suleimani I smell? Hope you have saved some for your old Mapla?'

'Pathu', she called out. 'Suleimani for the Sahib.'

'Pathu? I was hoping you would make it for me with your own hands and share your precious early morning kinaaves with me.'

Benu said nothing for a while. The suleimani arrived and he slurped noisily.

'I was thinking of Sulfi. I saw him in my mind. Here in this very anteroom.'

It was Alijan's turn to jump but he hid his shock quickly.

'It has been more than twenty years. A mother's heart can't help craving for a glimpse of her son.'

Alijan's sparse, grey eyebrows arched and he fiddled with the rumal which was back on his neck.

'In my kinaave, it was just Sulfi. Suleiman was dead.' Her eyes met Alijan's and bore into them. 'You were leading Sulfi in here and saying 'Benu, look at your son, he is no more the boy whom the police took away that day.' My heart was beating fast as I stroked him, on his cheek… that was the only part of him I could actually touch. The rest was covered in black.'

Her eyes crinkled as she observed Alijan's reaction. Though he was trying to keep a straight face, something flickered in his eyes and a hiss escaped from between his pursed lips. She didn't tell him about the remaining part of her daydream.

'Benu,' he said cautiously.

'You have been telling me for years, 'Benu, my Ponne, I shall one day make your dreams come true'. But you are all talk. When are you going to keep your word?'

'But... but... I have done so much... haven't I picked up from nothing after Mannarkkad and made all this for you? This beautiful house. Acres of orchards, fifty carts and a hundred bullocks...'

'But those were your kinaaves, not mine. Even that kingdom you have claimed you would win for me, the throne you kept promising to seat me on... they were what you wanted. I wanted a life with a good man...'

'Benu!'

'And my boys.'

'Have I not been a good husband? A good man?'

'Have you?'

'My Ponne, the people in the entire locality love and respect me. I have done so much for them. Given them jobs when they needed to earn a living. Justice when they were in trouble. Protection when they were in danger. They think the world of me. I thought you did too.'

Benu did not wish to talk too much and have him reading her mind. She decided to hold her tongue.

'Perhaps I do. But will you help me realise this daydream of mine. One moment here, in this house with my husband and my surviving son. That is all I ask. Will you do it for me?'

'But... but how... how did you... about Suleiman, I mean...'

'It doesn't matter. Will my dream of being a family again for a short time come true? If it does, I shall be happy all my life. I shall feel I have been a good mother...

a good wife… and a good woman. Will we be together for a few moments again? Will you bring Sulfi to me, just as I saw you doing in my dream?'

Alijan drained his glass of suleimani and jumped up sharply.

'I shall, my ponne. I shall. We will have our morning meal together. I will be back with Sulfi. Ask Pathu to prepare something special.'

When Alijan retied his rumal, jammed his cap on his head and departed with determined strides, his slippers squeaking louder than ever. Mixed feelings of joy and sorrow, excitement and a sense of purpose enveloped Benu. She had no more leisure for daydreams. Not now.

Pathu was given instructions on the menu. Kunjaishumma, the Pathiri woman was sent for and choicest pathiris selected from her basket. *Kannan* pathiri, shaped like an eye which Sulfi had loved as a boy, *adukku* pathiri made with layers of rice and egg which Alijan especially liked, and the delicious coconut pathiris.

'What is the occasion, Benazir Beewi?'

'Nothing, Aishumma. Just a craving,' Benu smiled and the Pathiri woman settled down on the back porch.

'Did you hear? Our one-armed Pakkaran was found hanging dead from a tree not far from here!' Kunhaishumma as usual was the one who brought news to her. Allah! Poor Pakkaran! She thought of his little boy Velu who came here for guavas every other day. The snack vendor then told of various other killings in the area. That of the Inspector in Anakkayam shocked her a man she would never forget. But now there was no time to dwell on these tragedies. There were things to be done. By then the old Pathiri woman had moved on to a new subject. There was an eagerness in her manner, thought Benu. Sure enough, the question popped out as if she had been suppressing it for a while and couldn't bear the suspense any longer. Her eyes were wide and there was a hush in her voice.

'I saw the Kovilakam cart come in here yesterday. What was it about?'

Benu gave a nonchalant shrug. 'Can't say I noticed. Probably old Beeran to see the Sahib.'

'No, no. That is unlikely. The cart was still here when I came back half an hour later after my pathiris were all sold out. And I happen to know the Sahib was away all day. Do tell, Benazir Beewi.'

'I do not know, Aishumma. I really don't. Anyway, there is something very urgent I want you to do for me.'

Just as she had hoped the old woman, delighted at being entrusted with a task, forgot about the Kovilakam cart. She nodded briskly as Benu told her what she wanted done.

'I'll tell everything about it later,' she said hastily before further questions were asked. 'Go Aishumma and do it fast.' All eagerness, the Pathiri Umma had started hobbling away, leaving her basket behind. 'Do not breathe a word to anyone, please,' Benu called out after her.

What a relief it was that she had been able to

stall Kunhaishumma's inquisitive questions about the Kovilakam cart. She never felt good about telling lies but at times it was necessary. She couldn't tell the town's biggest gossip that the young Thampatti from the Nilambur Kovilakam had actually come here. To see her, Benu.

Since the day after the battle, Benu had not been herself. Small wonder, considering that there was death all round. But when at Mammad's place, she had overheard the dead man's neighbors talk, their conversation had brought her more grief than she had ever felt. Even when the boys were taken away and Alijan had to go away on exile. But it had also been enlightening. She realised what a naïve fool she had been. Her husband was keeping things from her. Her sons had not been in prison as she had thought for so many years nor dead. Suleiman had died but only a day ago. Here in their own village. Their talk had given her clues as to who the so-called Black Thangal was. The horrendous shaitan who killed and tortured and made forcible conversions, setting a bad example for the ordinary Muslims of the area, giving them ideas. The Devil whom Hindus and Muslims feared alike. The man she had never trusted, the man who had taken away from their mothers, so many young boys and introduced them to the path of evil, just as he had done to her own. From what the men were saying to each other, she had learnt that Alijan had actually stood by as Zulfi murdered poor Mammad who had been like a son to him…

It was the Kovilakam girl's arrival and her words

that drew Benu out from the well of grief she had been immersed in and given her a new purpose in life.

The girl had been escorted by the silver tongued young man. The one with a receding hairline and a longish dimple, who had come here a few times with the congress leader, Shekharan Nair. When the girl had followed him out of the cart, Benu could not believe her eyes. A malaikha descended from firdaus, was the first thought that entered her head. But as she walked towards the house, Benu saw an ordinary girl with an extraordinary glow on her lovely face. She looked slightly nervous but determined.

Benu informed them that Alijan Sahib was out.

'But it is you, we are here to see. This is Sethu Thampatti from the Nilambur Kovilakam,' said the girl's companion. His tone gave the impression that they were glad the Sahib was away. The Thampatti joined her hands respectfully, her manner quiet and dignified.

'Allah! What brings you here?' Benu offered them the two porch chairs but the girl chose to perch on the edge of the stone ledge that lined the veranda and the man stood by leaning against the pillar.

'I have a message for you, er…' she paused for a moment, probably trying to decide how to address Benu. 'Er… Benazir Beewi,' she added carefully.

'A message? From whom?'

'From my grandmother, the Kovilakam Matriarch, who would have liked to come herself. Also from each and every woman in Malabar. I do not wish to talk in riddles. I hear your husband is considered a wise and influential man and that your people listen to him. I may not be married myself, but I do know that only a wife has the power to sway her man. I request you to use your power over your husband and make him see the need to put a stop to all this. I don't need to tell you that people are dying horrible deaths, their honor, their pride, their faith, their homes, everything is being taken away. No human being should be doing this to another.'

'My own brother was killed brutally when our Kovilakam was attacked. My cousin was humiliated and barely escaped a fate worse than death. Her brother was taken away and we haven't seen him for days. But I am not here to complain about my own sufferings. Most people are going through ordeals much worse.'

I think your own people are not much better off. The authorities naturally consider it their duty to punish such crimes. Muslims are killed in battle and arrested. Your women are being dishonored brutally. The land cannot bear it much longer. I entreat you to call a halt to this brutality. I may not have seen much of the world, Umma, but I am not naïve enough to think that you alone can stop all the violence in the land. But you can help bring it down in these parts and there is the hope that others will take the cue.'

Please make your Sahib see reason.'

The girl joined her palms together again. She had spoken clearly, confidently and humbly but once she had finished speaking she looked nervous again. It had slipped out quite inadvertently but the young Thampatti had called her Umma.

Benu had nodded gravely.

'I shall do my utmost. And Insha Allah, I shall succeed.'

And she had made careful plans.

Sulfi came. Just as he had in her kinaave. Benu stood on the veranda and watched as Alijan lead him through the guava grove and towards the house. He had cast off his black robes, probably to avoid suspicious glances. In the middle aged Mapla walking towards her, Benu saw the teenager who had been handcuffed before her eyes and taken away by the police. Her heart swelled with love.

He hesitated at the porch steps. Benazir Manzil had never been his home. The elderly woman who stood before him was a stranger.

'Let us not linger on the steps, Mone. It is not safe,' Alijan led his son inside.

Benu got a close look at Sulfi's face. A face toughened by hardships and hardened by evil. The love ebbed and she too looked at him warily.

'Benu, my ponne, Sulfi, my boy… after all this time, you stare at each other like strangers!' Benu could not bring herself to stroke his cheek as she had done in her kinaave.

Instead she said quietly, 'Come in my son. Your Umma shall serve you a feast today.'

Sulfi relaxed over the meal. His eyes softened as he

looked at his mother. When he spoke of Suleiman she sensed his sorrow.

'Umma', his voice was quiet and grave. 'Balyuppa is no more.'

Benu's heart rejoiced. Jawad Ikka was dead. The Black Thangal could do no more harm.

'But we will not let his efforts be wasted. Suleiman's mayyath shall not be in vain either. Bappa and I shall continue the work. Our land shall be purged of Whites and kafir traitors…' He sat up, the muscles in his face tightening for a second.

'Mone, have another pathiri, it is delicious,' Alijan was serving his son a succulent coconut filled snack when footsteps sounded. First in the porch, then in the house and soon right in the kitchen where they sat. Deputy Superintendent, Narayana Menon and his men stomped in.

'I believe these are the men you are looking for,' Benu told the police. 'The Black Thangal's closest associates. The men responsible for many recent killings, including that of the Khilafat secretary Mammad, and the retired Inspector in Anakkayam. Take them, saare.'

Handcuffs were clamped, police boots thudded and Benu followed them to the veranda and watched them steadily till they were out of sight. Then she seated herself on the ledge and began to swing her legs to the tempo of her new kinaave.

Yet Another Pattu

Nilambur, Ernad
7 January'22
Mathu

The southern *naalukettu* was not where she ought to be right now. Not with Vettekkaran on Sriraman's majestic back inching closer to the devil tree and Thrithala's percussion in full swing. When every Kovilakam member, decked in his or her best would be out in the frosty cold enjoying the festivities and offering heartfelt prayers. Here she was, curled quietly on the couch, all alone in the mansion, but for an occasional maid who looked in.

For quite some time now, to be precise, since their return home nearly two months ago, Mathu noticed in herself a sense of gradual disengagement. She was getting slowly but firmly detached. She didn't feel like the Matriarch anymore. The Mother hen in her seemed to have vanished without a trace. No more did she feel responsible for others. She had little interest in anything happening outside her own mind. Anachevi Mathu did not prick up her ears for little tidbits of information about the happenings around the world. Over the weeks she had been carefully analysing the change in herself from a third person's perspective. It was as if her mind was acting deliberately.

Mathu remembered a short and sudden twinge piercing her heart at the mention of Sethu moving away to set up a home in faraway Madras soon after Pattu, but the feeling had passed soon enough. Her granddaughter could take care of herself and what more she now had a proper husband to stand by her which was more than what Kovilakam girls could hope for.

While they were away, Mathu's one desire had been to come back to Nilambur. When they finally arrived, surprisingly no nostalgia had struck. Memories of the attack, of Divakaran, of their leaving in the middle of the night, bundled together in barges manned by Beeran Mapla's trustworthy accomplices did not come hurtling back to her as would have been natural when their carts entered the arched gateway leading to the Kovilakam premises. It all remained at the back of her mind like a long forgotten story. The memory was clear enough. It was just the emotion that had dulled. On reaching the Palachod, she had halted the vehicle and got off to bow before the Hunter Lord. As she did so her mind was blank and weightless. Strangely, the long journey had apparently had little effect on her. There were no aches in her body, no fatigue or need to rest. In spite of protests from all, she had made her way to the stables.

Billi, the mahout had come running at the sight of her, paused and held his usual reverential pose before bursting into tears.

'Eli?'

Her voice had sounded so neutral, so matter-of-fact that the mahout was momentarily nonplussed.. He, on the other hand had not been able to check his own feelings. A bout of tears followed in between which he informed her that Eli had not stood up for days, had nothing except an occasional gulp of water if he poured it into her mouth.

As Mathu already knew from the physician's own letters, Billi reported that the Vaidyan Anapparambu had visited quite a few times in the months they had been away. He Billi, the mahout had sobbed, had followed the specialist's instructions word for word. He had never left his charge even to go home when tragedy struck his own family and one of his uncles had been killed by a rampant Mapla gang and the other taken away, never to be seen again. But Billi's devotion had apparently been in vain. The old girl was sinking.

Eli was lying on her side when Mathu entered the stall, intermittent groans ensuing from her throat. The elephant's eyes were closed. As Eli in lateral position filled up the space, there was no room for the mahout to go in with her. He hovered around the doorway gulping.

'Eli...'

'Doesn't she open her eyes?' Mathu asked the mahout.

'Hardly ever. Only when Everest comes.'

'Everest?' Mathu was surprised. Tuskers were never brought to Eli's stall. Even when a decade and a half ago, Eli in her middle age had shyly yet staunchly chosen a mate, he wasn't brought in here. Mathu remembered the present Anaparambu's father had suggested that a special open air enclosure be created and the couple given privacy. Not even Everest, the son born of that gentle union usually came to his mother's quarters.

'Yes. The Vaidyan insisted that he be brought every day', said the mahout. 'He said she was pining. First for her mate. Then for you, Valiya Thampatti. She needed to feel close to those she loved.' This was something Anapparambu had neglected to mention in his regular reports on his visits and the treatment methods he had decided on. 'It is really wonderful how she opens her eyes only for Everest,' the mahout was saying.

'Eli...' Mathu had whispered again. The elephant's eyes had opened slowly and fixed plaintively on her before fluttering shut again.

In the naalukettu's semi-darkness Mathu recognised the increased tempo in the Palachod percussion. The Pandi concert was approaching a feverish culmination. Soon there would be a shift in the roll of the drummers' wrists and the Adantha would begin. Sriraman, bearing the festival idol would sink just a little on his mighty legs as he entered the temple. Mathu could see everything in her mind's eye. Yet the urge to rush over and join the festivities was missing.

It felt good to recline quietly on the couch with nobody around. Of late she craved little more than her own company. But these were Pattu days. All day visitors poured in. Everyone connected to the Kovilakam by blood or marriage would be here at the time. Today, being the festival's most important day, had been especially busy.

The first visitor of the morning had been the Senior Tirumulpad. At times, Mathu still thought of him as the Second Tirumulpad. While they were in Trissur, the oldest male had passed on and the Kovilakam, unable to transport his mortal remains to Nilambur had eventually bought land for the funeral pyre. No Kovilakam member, especially a Senior Tirumulpad, could be cremated on another's land.

The new senior had offered his condolences on Eli's passing, a little tentatively for he was worried about how she was taking it. For quite some time now, whenever they met the conversation would mostly concern Mithran. So it was not surprising that he mentioned his younger cousin.

'It is a relief that he is fine. He was the one we were all worried about. Well he has settled back to his life in Pookottur with relative ease. And the girl seems to have recovered from her misadventure too', the Senior Tirumulpad, his mouth twisting a trifle in amusement. 'It seems so long ago since he kept trying to evade a meeting and you smartly cornered him and coerced us all into sitting on him. You will remember it was a year ago. Almost to date. Well, at one glance, he appears to be much the same. Smoking pipes, playing Billiards, managing Pookottur affairs with the same commitment. He told me his new motor car is soon to arrive.'

'But the changes in him are subtle. He hasn't made a big thing of it but he seems a lot more easygoing in tenant affairs now. And believe it or not rents are down! I wouldn't have thought it of him. I believe he has given the tax collector's job to that fellow who sustained burns and is incapable of physical labour. And I have it from some of the new papers in the Records room that a decent pension is being paid to the wife of that Mapla... his nemesis you know... And they say that slimy Adhikari of Valluambram is not allowed within a mile of the manor...'

Mathu smiled to herself. It was funny how little morsels of news found their way so easily to her now when she never really sought them, when they had begun to matter so little to her. Mithran had settled down again in the Pookottur manor weeks before they themselves had returned from Trissur. Not once had she enquired about how he was getting on. She had no desire to poke her nose into his business concerns. Mithran, like everyone else she had till recently been so protective of, whose affairs she had always found herself involved in, could handle things on his own. If he made a mistake, he would soon learn from them. Like he appeared to have already done, if you went by the Second...no Senior

Tirumulpad's reports.

The Senior, if he had appeared a bit puzzled at her lack of response to his news of Mithran, looked visibly relieved when she said,

'I am glad you came to see me today.'

He smiled and Mathu continued,

'There is something I would like you to do. It concerns Eli's calf.'

'Everest?' The Senior Tirumulpad laughed fondly. Though the men in the family had secretly scorned Eli, her son was everyone's darling. 'He is fast growing out of the calf-stage. Going to be one mighty tusker, the little fellow.'

'He must go. As soon as you can make the arrangements.'

'Go?'

The plan had been so firmly implanted in Mathu's mind that she actually forgot she hadn't discussed it with anyone yet.

'I have decided that Everest shall go to Guruvayoor. And spend the rest of his life as the Lord's own elephant.'

'You mean offer him to the temple?'

'To the Lord.'

The Senior Tirumulpad cleared his throat. 'I am all for offering an elephant to Guruvayurappan. But can't it be another tusker? We have so many. Everest is our very own. The only one to be born in the Kovilakam. He is special to us while all the animals will be the same to the Lord.'

'It has to be Everest. When you make an offering to the Lord you give up what is most special to you. That is the point.'

He had tried logic in different forms but Mathu did not budge.

'All right,' he had agreed resignedly. 'I'll do what is necessary.'

When the news that Everest was to go spread, there would be an uproar in the Kovilakam. But Mathu didn't care. The women would cry. 'Matriarch or not, women shouldn't be allowed to take decisions regarding the elephants. It was fine with that cow of hers. But this… the men would growl.' But the minute Mathu had had the vision in the forest… Everest offering lotus flowers at the Lord's feet… her mind had been made up and the only thing that had kept her making the final decision was Eli. She thought it her duty to tell her friend herself and seek her permission.

The Fifth Tirumulpad had called on her that morning without her having to chase him. His vivacious wife, having cheerfully cast aside her nightmarish experiences was enjoying life with her usual gusto. Her mother however had been teary eyed and made generous offerings to the temple in hopes of finding her missing younger son. A few months ago, Mathu's heart would have been heavy at the thought of Unni but life had finally taught the Matriarch to unload all the burdens she had taken on her shoulders. Thankam would deal with her grief in her own way and accept whatever fate had in store for her. So would her son, wherever he was.

Another visitor who had called on the Matriarch that day waited outside the door and Mathu had gone to her. It was Beeran Mapla's wife come to bid farewell. She was leaving Nilambur for good. With Beeran gone, she was all alone here and her sisters in Pookottur had been insisting that she move in with one of them. The pension that the Matriarch had sanctioned guaranteed a comfortable life in her old age. Mathu did not enquire after Mammad's young wife but information was volunteered anyway. It wouldn't be long before the baby was here. Another reason why she wished to move to Pookottur. The girl Raziya now lived in the home of that Mapla kingpin who was to be court-martialed in less than a month, the man whose wife had turned him and her son in. Raziya was a companion to the old woman.

'The girl was in seventh heaven to meet the young Thampatti and the Sixth Tirumulpad's lady when they visited Benazir beewi,' said Mammad's mother. Apparently, the woman knew nothing of Mithran's promotion up the order. So Sethu had visited a Mapla residence. Mathu was a little surprised but it didn't rile her as it would have a few months ago. Why would Sethu wish to call on the wife of a Mapla magnate who had been one of leaders of the outrage? Mathu found herself unable to answer the question but surprisingly, she had no real desire to know. Sethu's social circle would soon grow larger and more diverse but her grandmother was not going to be around to pry into her affairs. The Matriarch smiled.

As the events of the day rewound in her mind the multidimensional acoustics of the Panchari sounded in her ears. Even without paying conscious attention she noticed the different stages of its progression. Before the Oracle moved on to the expunging of the kalam there was to be the ritual of *pantheerayiram*. A special offering to the Lord, following the previous year's mishaps. A grand ceremony with the Karayil Panicker cracking open twelve thousand coconuts. Seated on a mount of coconuts himself, he would begin at a slow pace, gently spinning one in the air, deftly catching it only to smash it into a hundred flying pieces. The rhythm, not unlike Poduval's percussion, would build in tempo till both his hands would operate nonstop to make short work of the twelve thousand. The spiritually charged occasion was definitely one that demanded the Matriarch's presence.

But Mathu was not going.

To the little boy of Guruvayur, she had made an offering of a playmate in young Everest. To the Hunter Lord she had surrendered all. Her worldly attachments, her emotional ties and all such, bundled together in her burden-sack, she had already discarded for Vettekkaran to manage as he pleased. Being present at rituals mattered little now.

The ceremony of the twelve thousand coconuts would take about three hours and in the small hours of the morning, the Oracle would proceed to make his kalpana. This year it would be neutral and mundane enough to suit the Kovilakam. Vazhunnoramma's tears paid for, life here would be blissfully uneventful once more. All the rituals of the penultimate day of the Pattu fest would be carried out smoothly. Tomorrow, there would be a minor hassle. Kovilakam members would not be able to attend the final day's ceremony, for no one was allowed in holy premises of the temple while the pula period was being observed following a demise in the family.

If the Devil tree could talk, the tale would be retold a hundred years from now.

Glossary

A Grim Portent

Dhanu: A month in the Malayalam calendar (mid December to mid January approximately)
Makaram: A month following Dhanu
Pala: An evergreen tropical tree (Alstonia Scholaris or Devil tree)
Pattu: A religious festival
Chenda: A cylindrical percussion instrument that originated in Kerala
Kovilakam: Traditional family homesteads of royals
Paniyan: An ethnic group constituting the single largest scheduled tribe in Kerala
Shashtipoorthi: Sixtieth birthday
Kathakali: A major form of classical dance drama that originated in Kerala
Vazhunnor: Literally translates to 'one who rules'. A title given to a person in charge of vast landed property
Vazhunnoramma: Vazhunnor's mother
Thampan: Title given to men of Kshatriya/Samantha families
Thampatti: Title given to women of Kshatriya/Samantha families

Ezhuthupalli: A school for traditional education
Bhagawatham: One of the eighteen Puranas attributed to Veda Vyasa
Akkara: Opposite bank
Aanachevi: Elephant ears
Matanga Leela: Treatise in Sanskrit on life and behaviour of Elephants
Palakka: A traditional piece of jewelry that gets its name from the Pala tree whose leaves the design resembles
Melam: A performance involving several percussion instruments
Panchari: A major form of chenda melam popular in temples
Kalam: Drawing
Kalpana: Prediction
Valiya: Big
Tirumulpad: Title given to male members of some Kshatriya/Samantha families
Naalukettu: Quadrangular building with open central courtyard, a style common in Kerala architecture
Gulikan: Son of Saturn or Lord Shani. According to astrology the bringer of bad luck

Pookottur Abuzz

Maplas: A Muslim community living along the Malabar coast
Amsom: A partition of land for administrative purposes. A taluk comprises of several amsoms
Sayippe: A Malayalam version of Sahib. Used to refer to white people
Adhikari: Officer in charge of an amsom

Mundu: A length of white cloth generally worn around the waist
Khilafatkar: People involved in Khilafat activities
Rumal: Handkerchief
Jenmi: Landlord
Thiyya: A Hindu community of North Kerala
Patthiri: A snack made of rice flour popular in North Kerala
Pora: House/building
Yogam: Meeting
Pallithodi: Mosque premises
Thattam: Head dress worn by Muslim women
Umma: Mother/ elderly woman (Mapla dialect)

The Sixth Tirumulpad

Cheriya: Small
Para: Unit of measurement about 13 liters/ a cylindrical container used to measure grain
Irikku: Please sit
Ettan: Elder brother
Kanakkar: (or Kanakudiyan) Tenant who is given land with an agreement that a predetermined share of produce would be given to the landlord)
Verumpattakaran: Subtenant
Kudiyan: Same as Kanakkar
Paniyathi: Woman belonging to Paniyan tribe
Narayaneeyam: A medieval- era Sanskrit text. A summary study in poetic form of the Srimad Bhagavatham composed By Melpathur Narayana Bhattathiri
Muthasshi Amma: Grandmother/great mother/ very old woman

Benazir Manzil

Kuthirikkeen: Please sit (Mapla dialect)
Changathi: Friend.
Purayidam: Compound around a house
Payar: Long beans
Vaidyan: Traditional man of medicine
Kanji: Rice gruel
Kinaave: Dream
Biryani: A dish made of rice, meat and spices

Merry maids

Eeyyo?: You? (Mapla dialect)
Namboothiri: A man belonging Kerala Brahmin community
Indulekha: First major Malayalam novel. Author of Chandu Menon. Published in 1889
Tharawad: Homestead of traditional families usually Nairs
Marthanda Varma: A historical romance novel by C V Raman Pillai. Published in 1891. Recounts the history of King Marthanda Varma of Travancore
Dharmaraja: Sequel to Marthanda Varma
Kundalatha: The first Malayalam novel. Author Appu Nedungadi (1887)
Vidyavinodini: Magazine/periodical
Bhashaposhini: Magazine/periodical
Kerala Pathrika: Magazine/periodical
Sanchari: Magazine/periodical
Chettiyar: A man of a trading community from Tamil Nadu
Sheema Kuripukal: Notes from England

The Flaming Forge

Jahannam: Hell

Mullakhah: A person learned in Islamic theology and ancient law

Yatim Khana: Orphanage

Ikka: Elder brother (Mapla dialect)

Nikah: Marriage

Uppuppa: Grandfather/elderly man (Mapla dialect)

Paavam: Literally means poor. Generally used to express sympathy

Balyuppa: Uncle (father's elder brother)

Arabi Malayalam: Traditional language of Maplas (writing is in Malayalam using Arabic script)

Kafir: Non believer

The Matriarch's Musings

Chinnan: An indicator of death. Refers to changes in breathingas death draws near. Some times refers to various stages of dementia in old people

Satyam: Promise/swear

Ananga Para: Immovable rock

Pathakkam: Pendant

Kodakadukkan: Ear ornament resembling jhumki

Padayottam: Huge, organised attack

Maya: Magic

Manjal: Palanquin

Benam: We want

Mayyathe: Death/corpse (Mapla dialect)

Nayinte makkade: (Of) the sons of a bitch (Mapla dialect)

Friday Flashes

Mukri: An employee in a mosque usually a prayer leader
Salat Al jumah: Congregational prayer in a mosque held on Friday afternoons
Banq: Call for prayer in a mosque
Khutbah: Public preaching in a mosque before prayers commence
Niskaram: (Namaskaram) Prayers or Namaz
Madirashi: Madras
Akapalli: Inner sanctorum in a mosque
Purappalli: Area outside the Akapalli
Theevandi: Train
Kambi: Telegram
Kalli mundu: Checkered waistcloth (lungi)
Pattakkar: Tenants
Nercha: Annual feast and carnival in a mosque
Muttumviliyum: Traditional orchestra popular among Maplas
Kundan: Lad

In the Pullamkode Valley

Ayyo: Exclamation of pain/surprise/fear
Madama: Corruption of the word Madam refers to white women
Penne: Girl
Chelai: Sari
Alai: Cave home of tribal communities

The Woes And Jos Of A Stroyteller

Illam: Home of Namboothiri community

Kaikottikali: Traditional group dance involving clap ping of hands. Usually performed by women for personal enjoyment

Thondi: A sweet and sour fruit bright red in colour

Chetthi: A common flowering shrub. The red flowers are used in Pujas and other religious rituals

Arpoo: A vocal sound made by groups of men on auspicious occasions like marriages

Mailanchi: The leaves of the plant Lawsonia Inermis (henna) used to prepare a reddish dye to adorn hands and feet

Kadumanga: Pickled baby mangoes in a very hot chilli-mustard sauce

Ajitha Hare: The opening words of a popular Kathakali song

Appam: Sweet snack made of rice, ghee and jaggery

Baliya: Big (Mapla dialect)

Kalbe: Heart

Kettilamma: Nair wife of an important Kshatriya man

Back home in Nilambur

Entha: What's it?

Antharjanam: Womenfolk of the Namboothiri community

Rise of the Black Thangal

Edavam: A month in the Malayalam calendar (mid May to mid June approx)

Makkale: Children

Pudikkeen: Catch! (Mapla dialect)

Ketteen: Tie up! (Mapla dialect)

Kalla Kafire: Thieving non believer!

Beedar: Wife (Mapla dialect)

Nte Mone: My son!
Nte Rabbe: My God!
Padachon: Creator (God)
Karanavar: Male head of the family

Letters

Sarvavyapi: An omnipresent person
Pokala: Tobacco
Sheelavathi: A story about a chaste woman who groveled in her husband's presence
Sangham: group

Reflections

Thatha/Ithatha: Elder sister (Mapla dialect)
Bannolee: Common (Mapla dialect)
Munjathi: Pretty girl
Maran: Bridegroom/beau
Kolkali: A group dance with sticks
Varavu: Festive procession
Assar Namaskaram: Third of the mandatory Islamic prayers
Saare: Sir
Hajiyar: One who has been on a pilgrimage to Mecca
Saiful Battar: Literally means A strong Word. A pamphlet asking Muslims to disobey British authorities and unjust landlords

Mapla Mob At Mithran's Manor

Thorth: Course cotton towel

The Matriarch Muses Again

Valyamma: Aunt (elder sister of parent)
Sharkkara: Jaggery
Ummachi: Same as Umma

The Cross-Eyed Raid

Ponne: An enderment. Literally means gold.

Nilambur March

Poreen: Common (Mapla dialect)
Thurakkeen: Open (Mapla dialect)
Padipura: Gatehouse
Vettukathi: Big knife
Para: (first vowel sound long) big shap device used to dehusk coconuts
Suvar: Pig

Afterwards

Variyam: Residence of a person belonging to Variyar community
Orukku piranthano: Is he mad?
Orukku piranthayrnno: Was he mad?
Shuddham and aitham: Related to untouchability. Literally means purity
Kudi: Hut
Mana: Namboothiri residence
Ngalo: You (Mapla dialect)
Begam pokkolee: Go away soon (Mapla dialect)

Babes Of The Boscage

Chokra: Servant boy (Hindi)

Venturing

Huzoor Kecheri: A major administrative centre. Literally means office

Moopan: Headman of a tribal village

Karyasthan: Manager

Gopuram: Temple entranceway

Pula: Period of mourning after death. Duration varies community to community

Unforseen Aid

Begam bareen: Come soon (Mapla dialect)

Kithab: The holy Koran

Ente Padachone: My God!

Alle Makkale: Isn't that so, children?

The Battle of Pookottur

Kazhutha: Ass

Thenga choru: Coconut rice

Kootan: Side dish/ Curry

Kozhi: Chicken

The Petition

Malaikha: Angel

Firdaus: Paradise

A Surrender And A Dream Realised

Perunal Id: Literally means main festival

Yet Another Pattu

Adantha: A form of Chenda Melam

Pantheerayiram: A religious ritual involving cracking open a 12,000 coconuts

Acknowledgements

I owe this book and whatever success it may enjoy

To my late mother, Rema Varma for whom it would have been the realisation of a dream long believed to be lost.

To the rest of my family for pushing and prodding when it went to the back burner and remained there for months on end.

To Rajendra Varma for all the valuable input on the history of the Nilambur Kovilakam. To Dr Yasser Arafat for helping me understand the Maplas and for recommending interesting reading material. To Anoop Varma for helping me procure the books.

To Jayakumar Raja. Had he not browbeaten me into doing a particular show for an annual family meet, I would not have done the research and come across the Petition sent to Lady Reading by the Rani of Nilambur on behalf of the women of Malabar, which actually triggered off the story.

To Masters of the Kodungallur Kalari for their blessings and the gene that may have been transmitted down the generations.

To Renu Kaul Verma and the Vitasta team for agreeing to bring it out and ensuring that the process was stress free and comfortable.

To Soumitro Das for being such an understanding and accommodating editor.

To Balram Parappil (cover) and Mahesh Raja (map) for their artistic input and bearing with my constant badgering amidst their busy schedules.

And not necessarily in that order.